Praise for Jo Beverley's Malloren Novels

"Beverley beautifully captures the flavor of Georgian England. . . . Her fast-paced, violent, and exquisitely sensual story is one that readers won't soon forget."
—*Library Journal*

"Jo Beverley has truly brought to life a fascinating, glittering, and sometimes dangerous world."
—*New York Times* bestselling author Mary Jo Putney

"Delightfully spicy . . . skillfully plotted and fast-paced . . . captivating." —*Booklist*

"Delicious. . . . a sensual delight."
—*New York Times* bestselling author Teresa Medeiros

"A fast-paced adventure with strong, vividly portrayed characters . . . wickedly, wonderfully sensual and gloriously romantic."
—*New York Times* bestselling author Mary Balogh

"Romance at its best." —*Publishers Weekly*

continued . . .

Winter Fire

Jo Beverley

A SIGNET BOOK

SIGNET
Published by New American Library, a division of
Penguin Group (USA) Inc., 375 Hudson Street,
New York, New York 10014, USA
Penguin Group (Canada), 90 Eglinton Avenue East, Suite 700, Toronto,
Ontario M4P 2Y3, Canada (a division of Pearson Penguin Canada Inc.)
Penguin Books Ltd., 80 Strand, London WC2R 0RL, England
Penguin Ireland, 25 St. Stephen's Green, Dublin 2,
Ireland (a division of Penguin Books Ltd.)
Penguin Group (Australia), 250 Camberwell Road, Camberwell, Victoria 3124,
Australia (a division of Pearson Australia Group Pty. Ltd.)
Penguin Books India Pvt. Ltd., 11 Community Centre, Panchsheel Park,
New Delhi - 110 017, India
Penguin Group (NZ), 67 Apollo Drive, Rosedale, North Shore 0632,
New Zealand (a division of Pearson New Zealand Ltd.)
Penguin Books (South Africa) (Pty.) Ltd., 24 Sturdee Avenue,
Rosebank, Johannesburg 2196, South Africa

Penguin Books Ltd, Registered Offices:
80 Strand, London WC2R 0RL, England

First published by Signet, an imprint of New American Library,
a division of Penguin Group (USA) Inc.

First Printing, November 2003
First Printing ($4.99 Edition), November 2007
10 9 8 7 6 5 4 3 2 1

 REGISTERED TRADEMARK—MARCA REGISTRADA

Printed in the United States of America

PUBLISHER'S NOTE
This is a work of fiction. Names, characters, places, and incidents either are
the product of the author's imagination or are used fictitiously, and any resemblance to actual persons, living or dead, business establishments, events, or
locales is entirely coincidental.

The publisher does not have any control over and does not assume any
responsibility for author or third-party Web sites or their content.

If you purchased this book without a cover you should be aware that this
book is stolen property. It was reported as "unsold and destroyed" to the
publisher and neither the author nor the publisher has received any payment
for this "stripped book."

Winter Fire

Chapter One

December 1763, in Surrey, en route to Rothgar Abbey

"*M*any people pray for tedium," Genova Smith's mother had often said to her as a girl if she complained that she was bored. It had not convinced her then, and didn't now. Two long days in a slow-moving coach, no matter how luxurious, had tested her tolerance to the breaking point.

Her companions were not dull. The elderly Trayce ladies could be excellent company. Fat Lady Calliope Trayce was gruffly insightful. Thin Lady Thalia was charmingly eccentric. They could play three-handed whist forever.

However, being eighty-four and seventy-seven, they slipped into a doze now and then, as now. Tilted against the sides of the coach, they looked like mismatched bookends, one snorting, one whistling.

Genova's books had worn out their appeal, and she couldn't do needlework in the swaying, jolting coach. Though she'd never say so, even cards had become tedious. *Dear Lord, send a diversion. Even a highwayman!*

The coach stopped.

Genova looked out with alarm. Surely prayers like that weren't answered. Heart beating faster, she slipped her pistol out of her carriage bag. She had to admit that her rapid heart was caused by excitement rather than fear.

Action, at last.

She'd checked and cocked the gun before she real-

ized that highwaymen would make some sound. Didn't
they shout, "Stand and deliver!" or some such?

Besides, no sane highwayman would attempt to stop
an entourage of three carriages and four armed outriders, not even if tempted by the gilded ostentation of
this vehicle. The Trayce ladies were ensconced in the
personal traveling chariot of their great-nephew, the
Marquess of Ashart.

Genova had a low opinion of the marquess from a
portrait of him that hung on his great-aunts' wall in
Tunbridge Wells, showing a vapid, powdered, and
primped creature. This coach had confirmed her opinion. No true man needed deep padding, silk-lined
walls, and ornate, gilded candle sconces—not to mention paintings of nubile nymphs on the ceiling.

The coach was still stationary. Genova was sitting
with her back to the horses, so she couldn't see the
cause. She leaned forward and craned.

Ah. A coach was in the ditch, and the stranded
traveler, a lady, was talking to Hockney, the chief outrider. The sky was low and trees whipped in a sharp
wind. With the icy temperature out there, the poor
lady must be freezing. They would have to take her
up to the next inn.

Genova glanced at the Trayce ladies, wondering if it
was within her powers to decide that. They'd asked her
to come on this journey as their lady companion—"For
you've had such adventures!" Thalia had exclaimed—
but her precise duties had never been specified.

Anyway, Genova knew her "employment" had been
an act of charity as much as necessity. The ladies had
known she was uncomfortable in her stepmother's
house, and offered escape. She wanted to reward them
with good care, however, so what should she do here?

Her neck was protesting the angle, so she straightened. Perhaps Hockney, too, wasn't sure he had the
authority. She shrugged and gathered her cloak from
the seat beside her. She despised ditherers, and what
choice was there?

She opened the door and climbed out, gasping as

the icy air bit. She shut the door quickly before too much of the warmth escaped, then swung her cloak around herself, pulled up the hood, and fastened it.

The thick blue cloak was a gift from the Trayce ladies, and the most luxurious Genova had ever owned. It was even lined with fur. Rabbit, to be sure, but fur, and in this situation, she appreciated that. She wished only that she'd remembered the matching muff.

Tucking her hands under her cloak, she hurried over, feeling the cold already nibbling through her thin-soled shoes.

The woman turned, showing a pretty but sharp face framed in rich, dark fur. She looked Genova up and down. "Who are you?"

Well! No wonder Hockney was hesitating. There was a saying about not looking a gift horse in the mouth. Of course, the sable-trimmed woman probably knew rabbit fur when she saw it.

"This is Miss Smith, ma'am," Hockney said in a flat tone. His long face was chapped with cold, and an icicle was forming on the end of his nose. "Companion to Lady Thalia and Lady Calliope Trayce. Miss Smith, this is Mrs. Dash, whose coach has come to grief."

"Trayce!" Mrs. Dash exclaimed, transformed. "How kind of the ladies to stop! I am quite overwhelmed by the honor."

Perdition. A toadeater, and just the sort to presume on this encounter.

"Oh, would you possibly, could you possibly . . ."

How in the stars could she say no?

". . . take my baby on to warmth?"

Genova gaped. *"Baby?"*

Shining smile was replaced by piteous pleading.

"The dear one is in the coach with the maid. It's so cold. If you could . . ." Mrs. Dash brought gloved hands out of her muff to clasp them in prayer. "I'm to meet my husband at the Lion and Unicorn in Hockham. He will take charge of everything, I assure you. I will not mind waiting here if only my poor infant is safe and warm."

There could be no question now. "Of course, Mrs. Dash. Please, I'm sure we will be glad to help."

Mrs. Dash hurried over to the tilted carriage and shouted at someone inside. A bundle was tossed out, then another passed with care. The baby.

Then, Mrs. Dash's coachman virtually hoisted out a bulky maid. The mother thrust her baby back into the maid's arms and urged her over toward Genova. It took some urging. The maid's round face expressed sullen anxiety.

The poor creature was probably freezing. She wore a hooded cloak, but it wasn't fur-lined, and Genova doubted that Mrs. Dash's coach was kept as warm as the Marquess of Ashart's, which had regularly refreshed hot bricks. The baby, at least, was so bundled up it was scarcely visible.

"Go with this lady!" Mrs. Dash yelled, pointing, then added in a normal voice, "She doesn't speak much English."

"Then what does she speak?"

"Irish. What they call Gaelic. Please, Miss Smith, get my poor baby into shelter!"

Genova stiffened at the shrill command, but the woman was right. That was the most important thing. Genova picked up the bundle and steered the maid toward the gilded coach. It was easy as dragging an ox, almost as if the woman didn't want to go.

She must be afraid. She was in a strange country among people who didn't speak her language. She'd been tossed around in an accident, possibly hurt, and now was being handed off to strangers.

Genova began to explain to her in a gentle, soothing voice. She herself had spent most of her life traveling with her mother and her naval-captain father, often in places where she didn't know the language. She'd learned that even when people didn't understand words, they could often understand tone.

Perhaps it worked. The maid turned her round freckled face up to Genova, then quickened her steps.

Another outrider had dismounted and stood ready

to open the door. Genova passed him the maid's bundle, which gave off a sour smell. "I don't suppose
anyone here speaks Gaelic, do they?"

"Not that I know, Miss Smith."

"Pity. Ask anyway."

He opened the door and Genova hefted the maid
into the warmth, then scrambled after so the door
could be shut again.

Thalia stirred, then her eyes opened brightly. "What
have we here, then?"

Despite her years, Lady Thalia Trayce could be
called pretty, with her fluffy white hair and big blue
eyes. It was unfortunate that she insisted on dressing
in a very youthful style, but she was invariably kind.
She and Genova had become good friends, which was
why Genova was on this journey.

"A traveler requiring succor," Genova said, realizing that not all the smell had been from the maid's
bundle. "Or two, really. Maid and baby. Maid only
speaks Gaelic."

"My, my!" Despite the stale, cheesy smell, Thalia
looked as if she'd been given a treat. With the tedium
of traveling, that was probably true.

The coach jerked into movement, and Genova
looked out at Mrs. Dash, intending to wave or give
some gesture that all would be well. She should have
said that they would send help. It was obvious, but
she should have said it.

However, the woman's expression stilled her.

The bright smile could be relief that her child was
in good hands, but it did not look like that at all. It
almost looked gleeful.

Was that because Mrs. Dash now thought that she
had the entrée to the grand Trayce family? Genova's
instincts said no—that it was something else, and that
she might regret this act of charity.

Three hours later, she knew her instincts, as usual,
had been correct.

Chapter Two

*I*t had not taken long to reach the Lion and Unicorn Inn at Hockham, but there'd been no sign of Mr. Dash.

It was a simple establishment, not at all like the grand ones carefully planned on their itinerary, but the early winter dark had been settling as they arrived, and the temperature plunging, and the place had rooms. Thalia had insisted that they stop for the night.

"I know you," Genova said. "You want to see the end of this story."

"Well, why not, dear? Oh, brandied tea. How very nice!"

The crafty innkeeper had done his best to tempt the rich guests, and Genova had not tried to interfere. She worried about the Dashes presuming on the acquaintance, but she worried more about the tired old ladies, and it would be cruel to force the outriders to spend more time in the bitter cold.

Mr. Lynchbold showed them two good sets of rooms, but on different floors. Lady Calliope took the ground floor because she couldn't climb stairs, and in fact could hardly walk. Her menservants carried her there in her sturdy chair, her personal maid following.

Genova went with Thalia and Thalia's maid, Regeanne, up to the next floor to find a good-sized bedchamber with adjoining parlor. The fires were already lit and the rooms tolerably warm, so it would do once the Trayce servants had hauled in all the old ladies' comforts.

Genova would sleep with Thalia in the big bed, and Regeanne would use the trundle bed that slid out from underneath.

Supper was promised within the hour and Thalia went back down to her sister's room. Genova felt obliged to stay and keep an eye on the nursemaid and baby, even though the maid had nodded off under the influence of brandied tea. At least she'd put the bundled baby on the floor first.

On the short journey, they'd managed to coax names out of the Irishwoman. She was Sheena O'Leary and the baby was something like Sharleen. They had decided to call him Charlie.

Charlie Dash. He sounded like trouble and was making a good start. The sooner this pair was back with the parents, the better.

Genova put a hand to her head, which was fuzzy with brandy, and tried to think what to do.

As soon as they'd arrived, she'd told the tale, and Lynchbold had promised to send help. Had he forgotten in the excitement of titled guests? Even so, where was Mr. Dash?

Suspicions were forming like dark clouds on the horizon, and Genova was not one to twiddle her thumbs while a storm rose. She wrapped her warm shawl around herself and headed off to sort things out. She was almost at the head of the stairs when an icy waft of air told her someone had just arrived.

"Ho, there! Innkeeper!"

Cold air blended with the pure energy of that authoritative male voice. It reminded her so much of her father issuing orders from the bridge of one of his ships that she halted for a moment in wistful memory. Then she walked onto the landing to look down.

Could this be Mr. Dash at last? It was not the sort of voice she'd expected.

Below, in the darkly wainscoted hall, a tall man stood with his back to her in front of the blazing fire. He wore a long cloak, no hat, and tousled dark hair simply tied back. She hummed to herself with approval. She did love a vigorous, virile man, and it rose off him like the steam from his cloak.

He'd stripped off his gloves and as he turned long hands in the warmth, green light flashed from a ring. Genova's brows rose. An emerald of absurd size? It must be. This man would not wear glass.

A vigorous, virile lord, then. Where was his entourage?

Servants burst into the hall and flocked toward him, eager to make up for any lack. No wonder. Inn servants made most of their money from the vails of rich guests, and this one looked good for guineas.

Still facing the fire, he unfastened his cloak and pushed it back with remarkable faith that someone would be there to take it. A manservant rushed to gather it in, staggering slightly under the weight.

It looked like leather lined with fur. Thick gray fur. Wolf?

What decent Englishman used wolf fur to line a cloak?

One thing was certain. This was not plain Mr. Dash.

Another was that he was gorgeous.

Genova hadn't seen his face yet, and the clothes beneath the cloak were ordinary—leather breeches, plain brown jacket, and high riding boots. All the same, everything about him, from cloak to ornaments to bearing, spoke of a truly splendid specimen of manhood.

Genova had never been reluctant to enjoy a show of masculine delights, so she leaned on the railing and watched, pleasantly aware of faster heartbeats and deeper breathing.

Turn around, she thought at him. *I need to see your face.*

It would be a disappointment. There was always a flaw in the package.

He turned to the right, speaking to a maid, and she saw a flash of gold. An earring! Better and better. She knew a single earring was fashionable among the wilder set of young gentlemen.

He turned a bit more, revealing a promising profile and jewels catching fire in the lace at his throat. Lud, had the man been riding around in the dark loaded with treasure? He was either magnificent or a fool.

Feeling as if she watched a play, Genova saw Lynchbold appear from stage right, bowing. "Sir! Welcome to the Lion and Unicorn."

The man inclined his head the slightest degree. "I'm here to meet Mrs. Dash. Lead me to her."

Genova straightened. Impossible!

Many of the elite were plain Mr. and Mrs., being a generation or two removed from their titled ancestors, but this man was not a suitable mate for Mrs. Dash. She, though finely turned out, was a common vixen. He was a king of wolves.

In Genova's fanciful imagination, anyway. Ah, well, the moment had been pleasant while it lasted. Her king of wolves was just another spoiled lordling, title or not, and she had better deal with him.

Before she could move, Lynchbold said, "I wish I could, sir. As soon as the ladies told me of your wife's accident, I sent help. But my man found no coach."

What?

"Accident?" Mr. Dash inquired. "Ladies?"

A note of hostility sent a shiver down Genova's spine. She couldn't allow this . . . this *wolf* near the Trayce ladies. She had to get rid of him and the baby immediately.

She gathered her skirts and headed down the stairs. "I can tell you about that, sir."

She realized too late that it was an overly dramatic entrance, and that it forced her to continue down the stairs under the lordly gentleman's inspection. Face forward, his lean features and heavy-lidded eyes did not disappoint, and here she was in her most ordinary gown with her hair still disordered from the wind.

He watched in eerie stillness, dark eyes steady, but

when she reached the bottom, he moved into a bow
worthy of court. "Ma'am!"

The sweep of his hand from chest to elegant extension caught her eye, or perhaps it was flashing emerald
flame. She fixed on that. Mr. Dash was clearly a
wealthy man and it was shameful that his child and
nurse be abandoned to strangers.

Genova gave him a moderate, chilly curtsy. "I was
in the party that assisted your wife, Mr. Dash, and I
can give you a full account. If your wife's coach has
been pulled out of the ditch, I can't imagine why she's
not here, but please don't distress yourself about your
child. We have little Charles and his wet nurse safe in
our rooms."

"Charles?" he said, in a strange tone. His eyes
might have widened, but lids shielded them too
quickly for her to be sure. "She brought the precious
darling with her?"

Perhaps he was a better father than Genova had
hoped. "Unwise in this weather," she agreed, "but the
infant seems healthy."

"Then take me to him, Miss . . . ?"

"Smith," Genova said.

She led the way upstairs, wishing, not for the first
time, that she had a more interesting name. In the
presence of this hawk of fine plumage, *Miss Smith*
made her feel like a house sparrow, which she most
certainly was not. She hoped he was noticing that her
figure was excellent and her hair thick and blond, even
if straggling somewhat from its pins.

She felt a ridiculous temptation to tell him that
she'd fought Barbary pirates, and won. She couldn't
remember a man ever putting her so on edge, and
she'd met many interesting ones.

She led him into the parlor to find the maid and
the baby both still asleep. Because she'd been away
from the room, the smell of soiled baby and grubby
nurse hit her nose afresh, but that, of course, was the
Dashes' fault, not hers.

Mr. Dash strolled forward, remarkably quietly for a

man in boots and spurs, to look down at the infant. "Dear, sweet Charles. You said he's well?"

Genova joined him. "As best I can tell, sir. The maid speaks no English."

His brows rose. "What, then, does she speak?"

"Irish Gaelic, I gather. You are not Irish, sir?"

"No, but Mrs. Dash is." He contemplated the sleeping baby, making no move to pick him up. That was hardly surprising. Many men thought babies none of their business. Genova just wished she didn't feel that she should protest if he did.

"She has a terrible time keeping servants and must often take what she can get. She also has a terrible sense of direction. She's doubtless set off back east. I'd better ride after her."

He walked toward the door.

After a startled moment, Genova realized he was leaving. She rushed past and put herself in his way. "Surely her coachman would know better?"

"He drinks, which is doubtless how he came to leave the road."

"Then I'm surprised you haven't dismissed him."

"He's her coachman, not mine. Mrs. Dash, as you doubtless noticed, is accustomed to having her own way." Those heavy-lidded eyes held hers. "So, I might mention, am I."

His expression could be described as tranquil, but Genova's every instinct screamed to get out of his way.

He made no aggressive move, but his intent beat against her. She knew this ability men had to give off danger, but it had never been directed at her so forcibly before. She was astonished by how hard it was not to slide away and be safe.

She stiffened her spine. "You must make arrangements for the child before you leave, sir."

"Must?" The word seemed to astonish him. "The arrangements seem satisfactory. I will, of course, pay you to continue your hospitality for a few more hours."

"I do not want *pay*!"

He inclined his head. "Then I thank you for your charity." He took a small, significant step closer. "Are we going to fight for the right of way?"

She made herself hold her ground. "Why should you wish to?"

"An inveterate requirement that I have my own way."

"Your marriage must be interesting, then."

"A bloody battlefield—which does give me useful skills." He put fingers on her shoulder and traced a line toward her neck. Even through the cloth of her winter gown, the invasion sent shivers through her.

"Sir!" She seized his wrist, but he broke her hold with ease and cradled her neck. Not tightly, but her throat constricted and she felt she could hardly breathe. Even so, she would not move away from the door. She would not. He could hardly throttle her, here in a public inn.

"Remove your hand, sir, or I will scream."

He pushed her back against the door, captured her head in both hands, and kissed her.

Genova had never been assaulted with a kiss before, and shock held her captive for a moment as his mouth sealed hers. When he pressed closer, pressed his body against her, she came to her wits and gripped his wrists to pull his hands away.

Hopeless.

She kicked at him, but her skirts and his boots made the effort pathetic. She couldn't twist her head, and when she tried to scream, his tongue invaded. Oh, for a knife or a pistol!

Then something had an effect. He freed her lips, eased the pressure of his body. . . .

She pushed him away with all her strength and scrambled out of reach, gathering breath to cry for help if he came near her again.

With an ironic, victorious bow he opened the door and escaped.

"Perish it!" She ran after, but the damnable man

must have slipped the key from this side and locked the door on the other.

It took only moments to run through the bedroom and leave by that door, but by that time he was down the stairs. She arrived at the landing to hear the door slam, and reached the hall at the same time as the bewildered innkeeper.

"He's left his cloak and things! He'll freeze."

"Not him," said Genova grimly. "The devil looks after his own."

Chapter Three

The Marquess of Ashart left the inn and flinched in the blast of cold air. Damn the harridan who'd forced this on him, but he wasn't being stuck with that child.

He raced around to the stable where he'd left the horses and his groom, Bullen. A door showed light around it. He opened it and entered blessed warmth heavy with the tang of burning wood, tobacco, and spiced ale. Five men sat at a rough table, smoking pipes and drinking, and Bullen was one of them. They all rose. This must be a kind of grooms' parlor—a place for them to take their ease between service.

Ash addressed Bullen. "Get the horses. We're leaving."

The middle-aged man didn't move. "Your cloak, sir? You won't want to travel without it."

Ash didn't, but wasn't going back for it.

"No matter. Let's be off."

"By your leave, sir," Bullen said in a tone of patient martyrdom, "you may wish to know that Lady Thalia and Lady Calliope Trayce are staying at this establishment."

"The great-aunts? In December? You must be mistaken."

"No mistake, sir," said one of the other men, his age and dignity suggesting that he was in charge of the stables. "An unplanned stop, sir, possibly because of the cold. And begging your pardon, sir, but your man's right. You'll court death if you ride off into this night in your jacket."

Plague take it, the men were right, and there was

the mystery of his great-aunts. If they truly were here, he'd better find out why. Great-aunt Calliope in particular had no business traveling in this weather.

It was also occurring to him that the intriguing Miss Smith might have information he wanted. She was clearly part of Molly Carew's schemes.

He addressed the head of the stables. "Do you know the Trayce ladies' destination?"

"No, sir."

"How many people do they have with them?"

"Three coachmen and grooms, sir, and four outriders, as well as a bunch of maids and footmen. Quite a turn up here, for we're not an inn that normally serves the nobility, though I hope we can do our part."

It was said with pride, so Ashart said, "I'm sure you can."

"By your leave, sir," said Bullen, with rather heavy-handed patience, "you might remember that the ladies requested your assistance with a journey, and you ordered your coach and servants be put at their disposal?"

"I might," said Ash with an edge, but recollection was stirring. A letter from the great-aunts, which he'd tossed to his secretary to deal with. He'd assumed a short trip, however, and here they were days from Tunbridge Wells in blood-freezing weather, their travel arrangements obviously in chaos. If this was due to mismanagement by his people, heads would roll.

"We stay the night here," Ash said. "We may have to escort them on tomorrow." He turned to the head groom. "What do you make of tomorrow's weather?"

"Milder than today, sir, but that's not saying much. I hope your relatives don't have far to go."

"So do I. Perhaps they've gone batty. Could be said to run in the family."

The grooms shared an uneasy look.

"Don't worry," Ash said. "It only strikes at the full moon."

"It *is* the full moon, sir," the head groom said, but he was clearly too sensible to take nonsense seriously.

"That probably explains everything." Ash looked at the disapproving Bullen. "Where's Fitz?"

"Said he'd wait in the tap, sir."

Ash tossed a coin on the table and thanked the men, then headed back out into the cold. Gads, but it was perishing out.

A lit door at the back of the inn beckoned. He headed for it and found it opened straight into the tap room, another place fugged with smoke and smelling of ale. It was warm, however, which was a blessing.

Most of those drinking looked like local men, but Ash spotted his friend Octavius Fitzroger alone at a table across the room, a flagon and a plate in front of him. Trust Fitz to get right to the serious business of food and drink.

Ash was aware of silence and of people watching him as he crossed the room. They would be recognizing that he was a stranger, not just to the inn, but to their lives. He realized he was still wearing jewels, which he wouldn't normally do in circumstances like this. He'd put them on only before arrival, hoping to remind Molly whom she dealt with.

Too late to correct that now, and he couldn't pass himself off as an ordinary man if he tried. Being a marquess from the age of eight left its marks.

The locals settled back to their talk and drink as Ash slid onto the bench opposite Fitz.

"Well?" Fitz asked. He was tall, blond, and slender, but it was the slenderness of a rapier. Though only two years older than Ash, Fitz had been an adventurer and a soldier and matched Ash's temperament well. A recent friendship had rapidly become close.

"Not well. Molly's not here."

"That sounds excellent to me."

"I need to deal with her. This can't go on. Apparently her coach went into a ditch a few miles east of here, but some other travelers came across her and took up her baby and nurse."

Fitz straightened. "The baby's here?"

"Guarded by an adventuress by the unlikely name

of Miss Smith, who did her best to stick me with it. I was planning to leave, but now I find the great-aunts are here."

Fitz stared at him. "The Tunbridge Wells great-aunts? What have you been drinking?"

"Unless the whole staff of grooms is lunatic, it's true."

A blowsy barmaid sauntered over, prepared to fetch Ash a drink. He shook his head. "I do remember providing the traveling chariot and some servants, but I assumed a short trip. I need to take care of them, and I want to discover what this Miss Smith knows. I'm quite looking forward to that."

"Poor woman."

"She'll deserve everything she gets."

Fitz drank from his tankard. "What's Molly up to now? How can abandoning her baby here help her cause? Does she think to touch your tender heart?"

Ash swore at him, but without heat. "I intend to find out. Perhaps she heard about the king's decree."

"That you marry a suitable woman before appearing at court again? He didn't specify whom."

"Thank Jupiter. It would be like Molly to seize on that, though, with reason. Since she's the cause for royal disapproval, any other bride will only cause a slight thaw."

"If the king had wanted you to marry her, he'd have said so."

"He doesn't approve of her, but he approves of my supposed callousness less." Ash muttered something treasonous.

"Never mind," said Fitz. "Miss Myddleton awaits."

When Ash swore again, Fitz added, "She's clever, of tolerable looks, and extremely rich. Other men would snap up such a prize."

"I don't like having my hand forced."

"The Dowager Lady Ashart can be forgiven for pushing you toward an heiress."

"Desist. Yes, I'll doubtless marry the chit, but at the moment, I need to sort out Molly. That's the only

way to truly vindicate myself. Rothgar has to be behind this. It's too devious for Molly alone."

Fitz tilted his chair back against the wall. "If your
cousin is behind this peculiar incident, perhaps you
should let me take care of it."

Ash looked at Fitz. He hadn't told him about a
recent development. "I might have something to force
Rothgar to reveal the truth."

Fitz whistled. "Watch your back. What?"

Ash found that he didn't want to tell even Fitz yet.
The incriminating papers felt like a smoldering keg of
gunpowder. "Safer for you not to know. I only men-
tioned it so you would cease fretting. I have the whip
hand now."

Fitz straightened his chair with a thump. "Over
Rothgar? Ash, this enmity has to end before it wrecks
the Trayces and the Mallorens both."

Ash looked away, scanning the room full of people
with simple problems. "Ending it would be pleasant,"
he said, then looked back at Fitz. "But when two
swordsmen stand with points at each other's throat,
who lowers his blade first?"

"That demands an impartial intermediary."

Ash laughed. "Whom Rothgar and I would both
trust? Enough of this," he said, returning to practicali-
ties. "Someone must pursue Molly, and I have to escort the great-aunts."

He saw the sudden tension of resistance. "For
Zeus's sake! It's as if you fear to let me out of your
sight. You're neither my guardian angel nor my
conscience."

"Perhaps I simply enjoy your company," Fitz said
in his usual light manner. "Life with you is certainly
never dull."

"Life chasing Molly Carew won't be dull either."
Ash wondered if he'd imagined that expression, but
he didn't think so. That sort of thing had happened
before. Perhaps Fitz really did see himself as his
guardian against folly and sin.

Perhaps, Ash thought, he needed one. Fitz had been

part of the shift in his life over the past six months or so.

He rose and clapped his friend on the arm. "I don't suppose she's gone far, but if you don't find her soon, don't persist. Rack up for the night somewhere. Molly's not worth your death of cold."

"I'm not one of the pampered great." Fitz drained his flagon and stood, picking up his cloak and gloves. "If she eludes me, I'll catch up with you."

"We'd probably miss each other on the road. Go on to Garretson's and I'll join you there. I go no farther tomorrow than my cousin's door."

"I'll return to the London house."

Ash remembered that Fitz had no high opinion of Nigel Garretson, who was hosting a bachelor Christmas party near Kent. Strangely, he had no great enthusiasm for the gathering himself.

"What do I do if I find Molly?" Fitz asked.

"Drag her to London by the hair and keep her there. Good hunting!"

Ash watched Fitz leave, then asked the barmaid the way to the entrance hall of the inn. It was reached by a narrow corridor that ended with a door. He opened it, then stepped back.

People were arriving. He had no desire to be recognized and have to play social games. When he glimpsed the Brokesbys, he congratulated himself. They were casual acquaintances he'd made through Molly, but just the sort to presume upon it.

Then questions stirred. Were they, too, here as part of Molly's plan? Of Rothgar's plan?

Perhaps he should have taken Fitz's advice. He was feeling ensnared—an unpleasantly familiar sensation since the night last January when he'd left a masquerade with Lady Booth Carew, widow. In April she'd claimed to be carrying his child. When he'd denied it, she'd wailed all over London about his promises and cruel abandonment.

When that hadn't moved him, she'd fled to Ireland, but kept up the barrage from there in letters to friends at court. Letters full of revolting details about swellings and aches.

Ash had expected the absurdity to die, but it had become an issue with the king. How clever of Rothgar to use King George's desire for propriety to strike such a blow. Of course, Rothgar, plague take him, had the king's ear.

The Brokesbys were going upstairs with a maid now, leaving the innkeeper alone. Great-aunts first. Ash walked into the hall.

"Mr. Dash!" the innkeeper said, professional smile appearing. "You'll be back for your cape, then, sir."

"No, I'm back for my great-aunts. I discovered that Lady Thalia and Lady Calliope Trayce are here. Since they seem to be cast up by the storm, I feel I should succor them."

The smile wavered. "But it isn't storming, sir."

Ash reined in a temptation to do the man violence. "A figure of speech only. If you could direct me to their rooms? And I will stay the night."

The smile disappeared entirely. "Sir! I am distraught, but I have just given my last rooms to that couple. A brother and sister, you see."

"No room at the inn? How seasonally appropriate, but there is always one to be found." Ash took a guinea out of his pocket.

"Truly, sir. I have given up my own bedchamber to the lady—"

Ash gave him the coin. "You'll think of something. Now, take me to my great-aunts."

The innkeeper shook his head, but he led the way down a corridor. At a door, he paused. "You said your name was Dash, sir."

"I said I was here to meet Mrs. Dash, which, as I'm sure you recognize, is an entirely different matter."

The man's face stiffened, but he turned to the door and knocked.

Chapter Four

*G*enova had accepted that they must take care of the baby for the night at least, so she'd requested that a mattress be set up in Thalia's parlor for the pair. Then she ordered one of the three Trayce maids in the entourage to help the girl bathe. Another was to arrange the laundering of as much of the baby's and nursemaid's clothing as possible.

Laundry was difficult in December, but Genova knew anything could be achieved with the promise of generous vails. It was Trayce money she was spending, however, so she went down to explain to Lady Calliope and Thalia.

When she'd finished an edited account, Lady Calliope scowled. "What are we to do with these waifs, Genova?"

She glowered out of shawls and rugs, her bald head covered by a fur-lined cap. Her abundant red wig lay on the floor nearby, looking for all the world like a ginger cat.

"Perhaps the parents will recollect their duty."

"If those two are married, I'm a stuffed goose!"

Genova had come to the same conclusion. "But if 'Mrs. Dash' is trying to foist a bastard on 'Mr. Dash,' why would she think he'd take-it? And how utterly heartless to dump her child on complete strangers."

"The world's full of heartless opportunists. This promises to be a plaguey mess!"

Genova soothed the old lady, knowing how hard this journey was for her. The most luxurious coach couldn't smooth roads rutted and frozen by the weather, and even with her own sheets and pillows, Lady Calliope hated strange beds.

"I suppose there's nothing to be done tonight," Lady Calliope muttered, "but—" She broke off because of a knock on the door. "What now?"

Genova went to open it, praying that by some miracle it was Mrs. Dash, but she found Lynchbold, who looked uneasy.

"Excuse me, ma'am. This gentleman claims to be a relative of the ladies and wishes to be of assistance to them."

He stepped aside and a man moved forward.

Mr. Dash!

Genova gaped at the man's gall, and he seemed as shocked to see her. Had she spoiled some new game? She dearly hoped so.

Before she could speak, Thalia said, "A relative? How delightful. Who?" She fluttered over to Genova's side. "Ashart! My dear boy. Come in, come in!"

Ashart!

The man inclined his head to the gawking innkeeper and obeyed, removing Genova from his path.

She would have loved to block the way again—and more effectively this time—but Thalia couldn't be doubted. Nor could Lady Calliope, who was greeting the scoundrel with remarkable warmth.

The wolf was the Marquess of Ashart?

This man was owner of that decadently luxurious coach?

That deceiving portrait must date from his youth. Even powdered, patched, and painted for the most formal court event, this man could never look so harmless.

He kissed Thalia's cheek and moved on to Lady Calliope. "Callie, my darling."

Callie! Lady Calliope's sisters sometimes used that girlish name, but on this man's lips it sounded unnatural.

"What the devil are you doing here?" Lady Calliope asked, not managing to sound severe. "Up to no good, I'll be damned."

"Brought by the angels to succor you, dear heart. I happened to halt here and learned you were making an unplanned stop at this inferior hostelry. I assume my people will have an adequate explanation."

"Don't bully them. It was our choice. And if you want to cut up sweet with a lady, flirt with someone younger."

Lady Calliope beckoned, so Genova had to go. What should she do? Spill the truth and break the old ladies' hearts? Over three months' acquaintance, she'd learned that they doted on the marquess.

"Permit me to present Miss Smith, Ashart. Genova, this is my devil's-spawn great-nephew, Ashart."

He looked at her—a flick up and down that his great-aunts couldn't see but that made her long for her pistol. "Enchanted, Miss Smith," he lied, bowing. "Astonishing to meet a real Smith. It is real, I assume?"

"Only an idiot would take Smith as a false name, my lord."

"Or a cunning villain who expected people to think that way. To add *Genova*, however, was a touch of brilliance."

Genova dipped a belated curtsy that was as icy as the air outside. "My lord. For some reason, I expected your name to be Dash."

"Dash?" He showed not a sign of guilt. "Perhaps you have powers of prognostication, Miss Smith. My intimates call me Ash."

"Do you have powers, Genova?" Thalia exclaimed. "How exciting! Do you use tea leaves? Cards . . . ?"

"I think that would be a more lowly form of fortune-telling, Thalia," the marquess said. "Doubtless Miss Smith simply knows things."

"Do you, Genova? Do, please, tell me something you know. Will our journey go smoothly? Will our reception be kind?"

Genova wanted to glare at the marquess, but she smiled at Thalia. "Yes to both, but that is because I will make sure the journey goes smoothly, and no one could be anything but kind to you and Lady Calliope."

"I am compelled to point out," said the marquess, producing a porcelain snuffbox, "that Miss Smith's abilities are not precise. She did predict *Dash* rather than *Ash*."

He offered the open box to Lady Calliope, who helped herself. Then he took an elegant pinch himself. "As for your journey, my dears, *I* will be your escort and protector."

Thalia clapped her hands. "How wonderful! And, dear me, you've just arrived, dear boy? You must be famished! Young men are always hungry. It is time for our supper, I'm sure. Genova, ring the bell, do."

Genova obeyed, almost gnashing her teeth. She should do something about this, but what? The wolf clearly was the Marquess of Ashart. These were his great-aunts. What's more, they were traveling in his coaches, with his servants, and quite probably at his expense. Presumably he could even dismiss her if he took a mind to.

And thus, she realized with a chill, he had power over the baby. Was that why he'd returned?

She turned back to find that he'd taken a seat between the two doting old ladies. "I gather your journey has been eventful, my sweets."

"Mostly it's been flat tedium," Lady Calliope stated, "but yes, we had an interesting encounter. Tell the story, Genova!"

Genova obeyed, including the arrival and departure of Mr. Dash. Not a trace of guilt showed on his face.

"And Genova thought you were this Mr. Dash," Thalia said. "How droll!"

"Very." The marquess smiled at Genova. She returned it, falsely.

A maid entered and went to get their supper. The Trayce ladies began to hash over possible explanations for the situation, and the marquess took part, as innocent as an angel.

To help her hold her tongue until she'd decided what to do, Genova picked up her embroidery. She was attempting to reproduce the beautiful cloth that went under her *presepe*, her Nativity scene. The old one was showing wear, but she had only a little more work to do on the replacement. When they arrived at Rothgar Abbey, she would be able to set the *presepe* up as it had always been at Christmas. It would be in her room rather than in pride of place, but it would suffice.

She kept part of her mind on the discussion, so wasn't startled when Lord Ashart addressed her. "Wiser, perhaps, not to have intervened, Miss Smith."

He was lounging insolently—if a marquess could ever be said to be insolent. That and his tone, and the look in his eye, all put Genova's teeth on edge.

She met his eyes, placing a stitch in order to look composed. "You would have passed by on the other side of the road, my lord?"

"I don't have the reputation of being a Good Samaritan."

"Or of being a good *father*, either."

His brows rose. "I don't have any kind of reputation as a father, Miss Smith."

"Surprising for a rake."

It slipped out, and cold fury flared in his eyes. Genova braced for retaliation, realizing that she hungered for another bout—one that she would win.

But he dismissed her. "I see you know nothing of the world, Miss Smith."

"Oh, you're wrong there!" Thalia exclaimed. "Genova has been everywhere and had so many adventures!"

The cold eyes assessed her again. "I am not at all surprised."

That carried so many insulting implications that Genova stabbed herself with her needle. She hissed and quickly moved her embroidery to suck a finger.

"Pricked yourself, Miss Smith?" the devil said. "And bled? Surprising—for an adventuress."

Genova inhaled to give him the full weight of her opinion, but the door opened and their food arrived. After a few cooling moments, she knew she'd been saved from disaster, but her anger still seethed.

He thought her a harlot!

Why would he think that?

Because of that kiss? He'd forced it on her!

While two maids laid the meal on the table, Genova put away her needlework and gathered as much composure as she could. She could not afford a battle. This man could get rid of her as if she were a gnat, leaving the baby unprotected. She couldn't depend on the Trayce ladies taking care of Charlie. Thalia was flighty, and Lady Calliope did not have a tender heart.

Genova thought of the maid upstairs and announced that she would take her some food. Carrying a laden plate upstairs gave her a chance to regroup and assess the situation.

Chapter Five

*L*ord Ashart's wolf fur cloak was as good as a warning hung around a villain's neck, she decided. She didn't for one moment think his previous visit had been coincidence. *Dash*, after all, was too close to *Ash*. He doubtless used the name for rakish assignations—assignations that led to embarrassments like a baby.

What frightened her was the way she was responding. She did have a weakness for a certain sort of man. A bold, virile man who fired her body and challenged her wits.

There'd been an Italian called Casanova, reputed to be fatally attractive to women, and she'd felt that power in him. She'd enjoyed a flirtation, but been in no danger of going further than that.

More strangely, she'd reacted to the bearded leader of some Barbary pirates. An alarming comparison.

Especially as she'd shot him.

She couldn't shoot this one, but she did have a weapon. She could tell his doting great-aunts that he was Mr. Dash, cruel abandoner of innocents. That would scuttle him.

She paused at the upstairs parlor door, suddenly realizing that he might not have expected to meet her in Lady Calliope's room. He'd tricked her in one inn parlor, then been taken to another. Oh, she wished she had that encounter at Lady Calliope's door to live through again and relish.

Genova entered Lady Thalia's parlor to find it empty, so she continued into the bedroom. The Irish

maid was still in the bath in front of the fire, alone
except for the baby, sleeping on the bed. Regeanne
must be eating in the servants' area.

The bathwater would be cool, but the fire roared
and towels hung ready. The maid would leave the bath
when it grew too cold for comfort, or when the baby
awoke.

Genova pulled a chair over by the tub and put the
food there.

Sheena smiled and presumably thanked her, looking
sweetly trusting and surprisingly young. Of course,
young women could become mothers, but it was still
a shock. She looked as innocent and vulnerable as
the baby.

"Everything will be all right," Genova promised,
but she added, "If will and strength can make it so."
She valued a promise, and what could she do to force
a marquess to bend to her will?

She returned downstairs to find that the inn servants
had been dismissed. The marquess and the Trayce ladies had almost finished their soup, so she sat to hers,
listening to chat about fashionable circles. The marquess was sharing risqué stories but his great-aunts
didn't appear to mind. In fact they hung on his every
word like elderly houris in a harem.

When Genova had finished, she collected the soup
plates, put them on the sideboard, then brought the
other dishes across.

"So," she heard Ashart say, "time to tell me what
you're about, my dears. Where are you jaunting off
to in late December?"

She shook her head, remembered Lady Calliope's
reaction when Genova had said how kind the marquess was to provide for their journey so well.

*"No need to credit him with kindness. Doubtless
tossed the letter to his secretary and went back to his
wenches and wild living."*

How right she had been.

"Why, to Rothgar Abbey, of course!" Thalia exclaimed. "We're going to dear Beowulf's Christmas gathering."

"*What?*"

Genova was watching the marquess, so got to enjoy his shock. She placed dishes on the table, trying not to smirk.

"There could be no question," Lady Calliope said. "Not with Sophia issuing orders."

Three weeks ago, the Trayce ladies had received a startling invitation to spend Christmas at Rothgar Abbey, the country home of their other great-nephew, the Marquess of Rothgar. In the subsequent flurry, Genova had learned that they'd not seen him for over thirty years because of some unspecified family disagreement.

She'd not been living with the Trayce ladies, but she'd often escaped her stepmother's house by visiting them, so she'd been part of the long, wandering discussions about whether they should accept or not.

There was another Trayce sister, Lady Urania, but she was a widow and always spent Christmas at the home of her oldest son. She, however, thought the other two should go if they were up to the journey. Lady Calliope thought it would be madness. Thalia fluttered between longings and vague murmurs about "poor Augusta."

Genova had longed to know more about "poor Augusta" but felt unable to ask. In the end, the sisters had decided to decline, but then their sister-in-law, the Dowager Marchioness of Ashart, had written forbidding them to go. That had changed everything. In naval parlance, the Trayce ladies hated the woman's putrefying guts.

Presumably the marquess was in agreement with the dowager, but if he tried to enforce her orders, Genova would make sure he failed. She placed a pie in the center of the table, and a ham directly in front of him.

"I do *so* look forward to seeing dear Beowulf again," Thalia was saying. "Whatever happened in the

past, those involved are long dead. Genova pointed
that out."

Genova placed two more dishes on the table,
prickling under the marquess's grim gaze. She remembered making that comment, but it had been casual.

As she sat down, Lord Ashart said, "A forgiving
nature, Miss Smith?"

"That is the Christian way, is it not, my lord? Pie?"

He ignored the offer. "Forgive so that we shall be
forgiven?"

She cut into it and placed a piece on Thalia's raised
plate. "I hope not to be so self-serving, my lord. It is
possible to forgive simply because it is right."

"But I'm sure you have sins that require
forgiveness."

She served Lady Calliope. "None of us are without
sin, my lord." Silently, she added, *Especially you.*

"Anyone who is not a total bore, certainly."

Genova cut pie for herself and accepted potatoes
from Thalia. "You think virtue dull, my lord?"

"You don't? Ah, but then, you admitted to requiring forgiveness. All that . . . er . . . pricking."

Genova almost dropped her plate. "That is not—!"

She bit off her reaction, which he was surely goad-
ing for. She glanced at the others to find Thalia watching, bright-eyed, as if at an amusing play, and Lady
Calliope stolidly eating. Genova put a slice of pie on
the marquess's empty plate, whether he wanted it or
not.

"Ah, pigeon. You have a taste for it, Miss Smith?"

Since *pigeon* was slang for *dupe*, it was another
insult.

Addressing no one in particular, Genova said, "I
hope the weather will be warmer tomorrow. The poor
men suffered so today, and it slowed us."

"Weather," the marquess murmured. "Refuge of
the dull . . . or the nervous."

She knew she shouldn't, but she looked straight at
him. "I am not nervous of you, Lord Ashart."

"But you should be, Miss Smith. You definitely should be."

Genova raised her plate. "May I have some *ham*, my lord?"

He served her. "You think I act? Don't."

Genova felt the danger, as if a storm raged or enemy guns blasted, and her blood sang. "I don't question that you are a marquess, my lord, a character of great power and influence."

"Character? And what are you in this play?"

She cut into her meat. "Merely the poor companion, my lord."

"Then you need acting lessons."

Genova felt a very real temptation to jab her fork into his elegant hand, which lay on the tablecloth so close to her, displaying an emerald that could support little Charles for life.

"My lord, you must be very bored to be amusing yourself with me. I'm merely a naval officer's daughter, and companion to two elderly ladies."

"I can vouch for that," Lady Calliope said, seeming amused. "Turn your agile mind to the problem of Mr. and Mrs. Dash's misbegotten babe, Ashart. What are we to do with him, eh?"

"Put him on the parish." He finally began to eat.

"The baby needs the wet nurse," Genova pointed out.

"Then put both of them on the parish."

The heartless wretch! "And what do you think would happen to them?"

He gave her a bored look that did finally remind her of that portrait. "They would be fed and housed while the errant Mrs. Dash is tracked down."

"To the meanest degree. No parish wants the poor and desperate from elsewhere. And who will fund that search? You?"

"Why the devil should I?"

"Language, sir!"

"No one else minds."

"And Genova, dear," interrupted Thalia, "you said that you'd heard everything when on board ship."

Lord Ashart gave her a look as if he'd scored a winning point. Genova seethed as she forced herself to eat the excessive amount of food she seemed to have acquired. Pistol point it would have to be.

As she ate and the others gossiped, she regretfully concluded that even gunpoint wouldn't work. She recognized stiff-necked pride when she saw it, and she doubted the marquess would back down at death's door. Would persuasion do any good? Surely there must be a scrap of Christian charity in him. He was kind to his great-aunts.

At a gap in the conversation, she returned to the subject. "What are we to do about the baby? To be put on the parish would likely be death for him."

Ashart sighed. "I'll leave funds, Miss Smith. Will that suffice?"

"And when the money runs out?"

"If this Mrs. Dash isn't found by then, she likely never will be. I can hardly be expected to provide for the child for life."

Why not? she silently demanded.

He met her eyes, daring her to insist.

So be it.

Genova turned to the two old ladies. "The marquess is the man who came here as 'Mr. Dash.' He is the baby's father."

Chapter Six

So the weapons are finally unsheathed, Ash thought.

"I most certainly am not."

The brazen hussy stood her ground. "You are, at least, the man the mother came to meet. You can't deny that, my lord."

"No."

"So you know who she is. You can return the baby to her."

Now where was that supposed to lead? He raised his wineglass and took a sip, but could see no reason not to tell the truth.

"I assume that the lady you met was Molly Carew. Lady Booth Carew, widow." He addressed his great-aunts, who would know the scandal. "I am not the father of that child."

" 'Course not," Great-aunt Calliope said. "A gentleman takes care of his bastards."

"If he can keep count of them." Miss Smith muttered it, but she intended him to hear.

She was outrageous, but that could be spice of its own.

"I pay a clerk to record the tally, Miss Smith."

She flashed him a startled look, clearly unsure what to believe of a "rake."

"Then it will make little difference to add another to the total, will it?"

"It would set a disastrous precedent. My doorstep would be crowded with hopeful bundles."

"True," said Great-aunt Calliope.

Ash managed not to grin as the hussy regrouped. "My lord, this Lady Molly—"

"Lady Booth," he corrected.

"Lady Booth, then. She left the baby for *you*. There had to be a reason."

"Stubbornness, which as Sophocles pointed out, is sister to stupidity."

"Stubbornness?"

"Precisely." She must know the details, but he would play by her rules—for a while, at least. "Lady Booth Carew, widow, has been trying to foist a baby onto me for nearly a year. Or, to be precise, she's been trying to force a wedding. This, I assume, is her final cat scratch—unless there were twins and she has one in reserve."

"I don't believe this absurd saga!"

"You doubt my word?"

Her look flamed him, but of course, she retreated. To accuse him of lying would be to overstep a fatal line.

"No, my lord," she said without a scrap of sincerity. "So, the baby is not yours?"

"It is not mine."

"Can you prove it?"

Damn the woman! "My word is sufficient, Miss Smith."

"It might be if any man could be sure of such a thing."

He used the tone that could make strong men tremble. "You go too far, Miss Smith. Especially when you must know the truth, being Molly's confidante."

Her shock was brilliant. *"What?* I never met the woman before today!"

"Can *you* prove *that?"*

She stared at him, then turned to the great-aunts. "Thalia?"

The old dears were observing as if at a play. Thalia cocked her head. "I'm sure you're honest, dear, but in strict fact I cannot swear that you've not known Lady Booth before. We only met three months ago, don't you remember? When you gave that talk about life with the navy?"

Ash turned the blade. "You see? It is entirely possible that you wormed your way into my great-aunts' confidence with exactly this plan in mind."

"No, it isn't! I moved to Tunbridge Wells when my father retired from the navy and married a widow from there. Lady Calliope and Lady Thalia are on this journey because of the Marquess of Rothgar's invitation and Lady Ashart's ban on attending. I had no control over any of this!"

"A point, Ashart," Lady Calliope said, like a judge at a fencing match.

She, however, would not suspect Rothgar's hand behind all of this.

Could Rothgar have insinuated Miss Smith into the great-aunts' house, then sent the invitation to get them on the road? It would have been child's play to track their journey and arrange for Molly to intercept them.

Ash had taken Molly's bait and turned up here on cue. Yes, it was possible, but what was the purpose? When would the blade fall?

Miss Smith interrupted his thoughts. "Perhaps we could make some provision for the baby and debate these improbabilities later."

"Such an admirably tenacious mind," Ash said, playing with his snuffbox. "What, pray, do you suggest?"

This, presumably, would be when he heard the true plan.

"You could send them to one of your estates, my lord."

That brat wasn't ending up under any roof of his, but he offered around the snuff as he considered. "The nearest is Cheynings, which is ruled over by my grandmother. I doubt she would be welcoming."

"She would hardly murder an innocent child."

He snapped the box shut, suppressing a smile of satisfaction. "A mistake, Miss Smith. You clearly don't know the cause of our family discord."

She looked around. "No, my lord."

"The murder of an innocent child," he told her, watching her every reaction. "Nearly forty years ago, my aunt, Lady Augusta Trayce, a sweet and lively young lady of sixteen, married Lord Grafton, heir to the Marquess of Rothgar."

He saw no start of guilt.

"Four years later, surely as a result of extreme cruelty, she went mad and murdered her newborn babe. She died herself not long after—which was convenient for her husband, who could marry again."

Miss Smith looked to the old ladies for confirmation. Surely even the greatest actress could not turn pale on command.

"Such a bright and beautiful girl," Lady Thalia sighed.

"Too pretty by far, and a wild piece," Lady Calliope said, "but she didn't deserve such treatment."

"But if Lord Rothgar is your great-nephew," Miss Smith said, "he must be this Lady Augusta's child."

Thalia answered that. "Augusta's firstborn, dear. *Such* a sweet child, and so very clever! I remember that he enjoyed apricot crisps, so I have brought some for him."

Ash almost laughed. He'd give a fortune to see Rothgar's face then!

"But surely," Miss Smith said, in battle order again, "if there was wrongdoing, the Marquess of Rothgar would be as keen for justice for his mother as her own family."

"Yet the matter gives him no obvious unease," Ashart replied. "True, he put around a rumor that he would not marry because of the madness in his blood—his Trayce blood. That helped protect his father's memory for years. But behold, he is now married without a qualm. Proof, wouldn't you say?"

"No. What of love?"

"What of it?"

"Come, come, my lord. History is full of crowns and even lives lost for love."

"Lust, perhaps, Miss Smith, not love. And lust, of course, does not require marriage."

She flinched. Devil take it, could she be telling the truth? Could she be an innocent Samaritan?

"About the baby," she said, rather desperately.

Thalia sat up straighter. "I know. We will take him to Rothgar Abbey!"

He wasn't the only one struck dumb by the notion. "Arrive at Rothgar Abbey with a misbegotten infant in train?" But then Ash laughed. "Well, why not? It is Christmas, after all. Do I need to provide an ass?"

Miss Smith shot him a look that clearly said that they already had one. Him.

Outrage turned instantly to amusement and arousal. Devil take it, but she was an exciting woman. Whatever the truth of her situation here, she clearly was no angel. She was too ripe, too bold, too responsive to a kiss. Sparks flew from her, igniting fires in him, and she knew it.

What a pity he couldn't stay at Rothgar Abbey to investigate Miss Smith at leisure, not to mention witness his haughty cousin's handling of the return of his pawn and his reception of nursery treats. It would also make it easier to assess exactly how to use his weapon.

It wouldn't do, though. It would look as if he was accepting the invitation, as if he was ready to sue for peace. He probably shouldn't return the pawn, either. Devil alone knew what Rothgar would do with it next. Cheynings would be a better option, but Thalia would be hard to convince.

Snares and entanglements. He raised his glass and wryly toasted the three ladies. "To Christmas, and all merriment of the season."

Chapter Seven

*G*enova returned the toast, but she recognized malicious enjoyment behind it. She should be wary, if not afraid, yet something was firing her blood as it had not been in an age.

Not something. Someone. The Marquess of Ashart. In the year since her father's retirement, she'd learned that she missed action and adventure. Now she was engaged in a duel with a formidable opponent, and the zest of it sparkled in her blood.

She was determined that he support his child, and he was determined to resist. It would be a glorious battle.

Thalia broke the moment. "Good, that's settled! Now we can have a nice game of whist. Genova, dear, ring for the servants to clear the table."

Genova did so. This hardly seemed the moment for a game, but Thalia adored whist and went after what she adored with the purpose of a willful child.

As they waited for the servants, Genova tried again to pin down practical details. "How are we to transport the baby and his maid? We can't fit five adults in the main coach, and the secondary ones are packed."

"Five?" asked Thalia, already with her cards in hand. "Oh, Ashart will ride. Won't you, dear?"

"Always," said the marquess.

Genova remembered his arrival in that ominous cloak. The outriders had ridden all day for two days, but that a marquess should choose to do so in such bitter weather seemed . . . unnatural.

The essential problem in the Trayce family was a

woman who'd murdered her baby. Did insanity, or at least instability, run in the blood? Thalia, dear though she was, was dotty.

Now that Genova thought of it, wasn't the mad-woman's son, Lord Rothgar, sometimes called the Dark Marquess? She seemed to remember reading of a duel not long ago in which he'd killed his opponent. The Portsmouth paper had regarded it as scandalous, and hinted that only royal favor had saved the mar-quess from dire consequences.

Caution chilled excitement. What was she blindly sailing into? What was she blindly carrying two inno-cents into? As the servants arrived and set to work, she said, "Perhaps we should think of some other plan—"

"Stop fussing, Genova," Lady Calliope growled. "We have space in the coach, and you've arranged for a bed."

"Which I haven't." Ashart caught the attention of one of the servants. "Tell the innkeeper I wish to see him."

The man bowed and left.

As soon as the table was clear, Thalia sat and dealt the cards. They had finished the first hand when the innkeeper arrived, looking distressed.

"Milord, milord, I spoke the truth. This close to Christmas, many are on the roads, and with the weather so bad many stopped early. The arrival of such a large party as this . . ."

"So? Do you expect me to turn holy and sleep in the stables?"

Lynchbold winced at the tone. "No, no, milord! If you would be so gracious, there is a mattress already set up in the lady's parlor upstairs. I gather it was for a maid, but it's a good thick mattress, milord, and a maid can sleep in the kitchens."

Genova braced herself for a tantrum, but the mar-quess sighed. "It will have to do."

The innkeeper left, almost quaking with relief. Ge-nova was weary of battle but had to make one more foray. "Would it be possible for Sheena to sleep with us, Thalia? With her speaking no English, it would be frightening for her to be put among strangers."

"She's already among strangers," Lady Calliope snapped. "Stop pampering her. She probably sleeps in an earth-floor hovel in Ireland."

Lord Ashart looked wry. "You truly do think I should sleep in the stables, don't you, Miss Smith?"

"No, my lord, but . . ."

"But the girl can share the trundle bed with Regeanne," said Thalia with a careless flutter of her hand. "Enough interruptions. Back to the game!"

The trundle bed was almost as big as the one it fit under, but Regeanne would not like it. It was the better option, however, so Genova dealt the next hand.

Ashart, however, rose. "Your indulgence, my dears, but I must check tomorrow's arrangements. I'll be back shortly."

Thalia didn't pout. Instead she beamed after him. "Isn't he the dearest boy?"

Genova couldn't stop herself. "He's a rake, and he's Charlie's father, and he plans to abandon him like a worn-out shoe!"

Thalia looked at her, eyes wide and serious. "Oh, no, dear. A Trayce would never abandon his responsibilities."

"And you said yourself that the supposed Mrs. Dash was not a reliable woman," Lady Calliope pointed out. "Why believe her?"

"A point," Genova conceded, frowning, "but what mother would abandon her child to strangers in this way?"

"It's exactly what she has done, though, isn't it? Whatever the truth behind this story, Lady Booth Carew is not here."

Genova couldn't argue with that.

Thalia gathered in the cards and laid out a game of patience, though her manner could not be called patient. She twitched for whist like a whippet eager for a walk. Genova felt more like a ship caught in a maelstrom, spinning out of control.

They would arrive at Rothgar Abbey, home of the possibly deranged and murderous Dark Marquess, with a mysterious, misbegotten baby in the party. And, she now realized, with Lord Rothgar's cousin Ashart, who was apparently his mortal enemy!

She looked at the two old ladies, wishing she could see their unconcern as reassuring. Instead, it seemed like further evidence of family insanity.

Ashart returned and the game resumed. Seeing no alternative, Genova focused her mind on the cards. The one thing guaranteed to irritate was careless play. After a while, Ashart ordered rum punch. It was delicious but Genova only sipped at it. She had no intention of growing tipsy in this company.

Both old ladies drank deeply, but it had no noticeable effect until Lady Calliope slipped into sleep between one trick and the next. Genova sent for her menservants to carry her chair into her bedroom, relieved that the evening was finally over.

But then she recalled that Ashart would be coming upstairs with her and Thalia. Could he not sleep in this parlor? A question revealed that Lady Calliope's two menservants slept here in order to be to hand.

That left no choice. A nobleman would not deign to sleep with lowly servants. While Ashart helped tipsy Thalia up the stairs, Genova followed with assorted items.

They entered the parlor, which was now a bedroom. A plain mattress was made up with sheets and blankets. A punch bowl and glasses sat on the hearth. Lynchbold was doing his best to make up for the inadequate room, but Genova didn't think anyone needed more spirits.

The table had been turned into a washstand, with bowl, mirror, and towels. Leather saddlebags lay nearby, and the great cloak was spread over a chair, damp fur giving a predatory presence.

Thalia wove toward the table. "Three-handed whist?"

Oh, no. Genova dumped the things in her hands in order to steer Thalia into the bedchamber. When she finally shut the door, she sagged against it in relief.

Ridiculous to think she was in danger. Be he wicked as Lucifer, the marquess would not try to rape her in his great-aunt's bed. But that wasn't the peril, and she knew it. The danger came from the sizzle in her blood, from the way she responded to even a look, from the way she lusted for another fight.

Regeanne came over to help Thalia to bed and, thank heavens, didn't look too put out over the baby. When the Frenchwoman whispered to be quiet, so as not to disturb the *petit ange*, Genova decided there might be hope of peace there, at least.

Sheena O'Leary and Charlie Carew were already fast asleep on the trundle, looking like innocent angels. But, Genova realized, a wet nurse could hardly be innocent. Sheena must have borne a child—and that baby had almost certainly died.

Some wet nurses fed two. Some gave their child to another mother's care in order to earn the higher wages given to a nurse who devoted herself to her employer's baby. Neither seemed likely here, and Genova's heart clenched with pity.

It seemed unlikely that Sheena was married, so the poor girl must have suffered the shame of carrying an illegitimate baby, then the grief of losing it.

No wonder she'd seized the chance to escape and earn her keep this way. Poor, poor Sheena, especially as she seemed to have transferred all her mother love to little Charlie.

That left Genova no choice. She vowed that Lord Ashart's innocent son and Sheena would be safe and together, even if she had to use her pistol.

Chapter Eight

*T*he baby's catlike warble woke Genova for the second time. She was hard to disturb from sleep, but something about the cry of a baby could do it. A soft Gaelic murmur beyond the closed bed-curtains would be accompanied by the presentation of a milk-filled breast. Peace returned.

Genova settled back, but this time sleep eluded her. She shifted, trying to find a comfortable position on the pillow. She needed sleep if she was to have her wits tomorrow, and she would need all her wits to deal with Lord Ashart.

A distant clock struck three—the goblin hour, when dark monsters invade even the most tranquil mind, and her mind was not tranquil. Her fretting bounced from journey to baby to marquess, then with a leaden thud to her deeper problem, her life now her father had remarried.

She tried to smother it, but goblins have no mercy.

If only her mother had lived.

Mary Smith had been carried from health to death in a day by a sudden internal bleeding. It had happened in the middle of the Atlantic and she'd been buried at sea, which had been a particularly painful blow. Genova was practical by nature, but even so, pain burst in her every time she remembered her mother's bundled body hitting the water with a splash.

Thrown away. Like bad food and waste.

She'd give anything to have a grave that she could tend. She'd been waiting for the right moment to sug-

gest a headstone for her mother in Tunbridge Wells,
or a memorial plaque in the parish church. It seemed
simple enough, but she'd sensed it would be awkward,
though how her stepmother could object she couldn't
imagine.

Her stepmother. Hester Poole as was, Hester Smith
now.

If Genova could dislike Hester it might be easier,
but she recognized a kind and gracious woman. Captain Smith would choose no less. Hester and Genova
were simply different.

It was a puzzle why her father had chosen a woman
so unlike his free-spirited, lively Mary, but perhaps
that was the point. A complete break, just as he'd
broken from the past by first retiring, then moving to
Hester's house in Tunbridge Wells, far from the sea.

Genova hadn't thought the move would be so very
difficult, but after three months she was ready to gnaw
through walls to escape. Hester's house was a very
conventional house; her family and friends a very conventional circle. If not for the Trayce ladies, Genova
felt she might already be stark, staring mad.

It had all come to a head on December 13 over a
superficially simple matter—the *presepe*.

The Italian Nativity scene was a family tradition.
All Genova's life it had been set up on December 13
to wait for the Christ child on Christmas Eve. Perhaps
it was particularly important to Genova because
Christmas Eve was her birthday. She'd not realized
how important, however, until Hester had gently refused to have the *presepe* on display in her drawing
room.

"Forgive me, Genova dear, but it is a little *popish*,
don't you think? And a little *shabby*? Some of the
finest people in the Wells pass through my house at
Christmas."

Shabby? Genova could still feel the sting of that,
especially as she'd seen it was true. The *presepe* was
gilded for her by a lifetime's memories, but the paint
on the wooden figures had faded, and the gold was

flaking in places. The embroidered white linen it sat on, which her mother had called the flowers-in-the-snow, had yellowed with age, and even become spotted with mildew. Some of the embroidery had frayed into tufts.

She'd touched up the paint and was making a new cloth, but Hester's words still hurt.

She'd bundled it away, fighting tears, but the deepest hurt had been because her father had made no protest at all. He'd helped her, and even apologized after a fashion, but she'd known then that the *presepe* was something else he'd like to leave behind. And that the same thing might apply to her. He still loved her—she didn't doubt that—but she was a cuckoo in his new nest. . . .

Genova jerked out of a restless sleep and sat up.

The flowers-in-the-snow! The new one. She'd left it in the parlor.

Before turning Thalia toward the bedroom, she'd dropped everything in her hands on the table, close by the washing bowl. What if it was already stained? She couldn't lie here and wonder. She had to go and retrieve it. It was still dark, still the middle of the night.

When she slipped out though the bed-curtains, however, she found that the fire had been started. It was only just beginning to catch the logs, so someone had crept in to light it not long ago. Perhaps that had woken her.

Though dark, it was almost morning.

She pushed her feet into her slippers and pulled her woolen robe from under the eiderdown, where she'd put it to keep it warm. Once wrapped in it, she found her timepiece and tilted it to catch the firelight. Ten minutes past eight! An hour later than they'd risen the other two days. Someone must have ordered a later start.

She'd like to blame the marquess for doing it out of laziness, but in fact it was sensible. In these short winter days, they'd had less than eight hours of travel light and had been forced to rise early. Today would be a short day, so they could afford to lie in.

She peeped through the window curtains, and scraped a clear spot through the frost on a pane. The pale light of dawn glinted off white on the ground. Heavy frost, not snow, thank heavens, but it promised another harsh day.

She turned to look at the adjoining door. If she was up, the marquess might be up. She was not a highly skilled needlewoman, however, and the new *presepe* cloth had taken weeks of work. There was certainly no time to do it over again.

It would do no harm to check. He might still be asleep.

She crept over to the door, listened, then eased it open. By the light of the new fire, she saw a still figure on the mattress, covers pulled high against the cold. It looked as if he'd added his wolf cloak on top for extra warmth.

Being a fair woman, she granted that he'd made little fuss over his situation. Whatever else he was, the Marquess of Ashart was not a pampered fop.

Moving carefully, she eased into the room. The fire gave enough light to show her embroidery frame, still on the table, still next to the washbowl and jug. It looked unharmed, but it would be safer in her possession.

She stepped carefully across the room, picked up her work, then checked the marquess again. The cloak was fur side up, which could be why the planes of his face looked so strong in the firelight. The line of his dark lashes seemed almost too delicate for that setting, like the sweep of a skillful Chinese brush.

His hair was loose, and one long tendril lay along his jaw, close to his slightly parted lips. Her hand moved as if to clear it, though she went no closer. Deep, earthy longings stirred between her thighs.

She'd retained both virtue and virginity, but her body had learned passion. She'd been engaged to marry, and had allowed Walsingham some license.

They'd been in the Mediterranean at the time. In summer. Burning days and long sultry nights—a combination that always seemed perilous to English propriety, perhaps because common sense dictated the lightest possible clothing.

But this man was covered by layers of cloth, so she could see only hair and the elegant bones of his face. How could they have such a potent effect?

When his lashes flickered, she was caught staring.

A pistol appeared in his hand, pointed at her.

Genova stepped back, caught her slipper on something, and sat on the floor with a thump.

They sat there for a heartbeat, staring at one another.

Then he shook himself and put the pistol down, uncocking it.

He'd *cocked* it?

Had she been a hair's breadth from death?

He pushed tumbling hair off his face, sparks flashing from his emerald ring and gold earring. "I'm sorry if I alarmed you, Miss Smith. You require something?"

His nightshirt gaped open in a vee down his chest. Any woman who spends time on board ship sees men's naked torsos. Most are not constructed in heroic style, but she knows a fine one when she sees it.

Genova moistened her mouth. "No, my lord. Except my needlework, that is." She waved it as feeble excuse.

"Isn't the light poor for stitchery?"

Perhaps it was the cloak that stole her wits. His admirable torso rose from fire-gilded fur like some sea-god from the foam.

She was running mad! She could weep, however, to be in her plain, practical nightclothes, her hair in a dull plait.

She was in her *nightclothes*!

What must he be thinking?

She scrambled to her feet, almost falling again as her slippers tangled with her robe. She grabbed a chair back for balance.

"What is that?"

"What?" Dazed, she followed his eyes and saw the hoop and cloth in her hand. She grasped the answer as if it could explain everything. "My needlework."

"Yes, but what is it? I was admiring it last night, but it's not a handkerchief. All that gold thread in the middle would scrape a nose raw."

He was sitting there, one knee raised, an arm resting on it, as if talking to a night-clad lady in his bedroom was nothing.

What had she expected?

He was a rake.

"It's the cloth for beneath a *presepe*, my lord. A *presepe* is a Nativity scene. The gold represents straw."

He rubbed his eyes. "Ah, yes. I saw such in Italy."

They might have met in Italy?

Hot Mediterranean sun.

Long sultry nights.

That earring winked at her in the firelight like a wicked invitation.

Chapter Nine

*H*e frowned at her, seeming puzzled. *Of course he's puzzled. He's wondering why you're standing here like a statue!*

"Is there any connection between you and Molly Carew?"

"What?" It was as much a bump as when she'd tumbled. He still thought her a wicked schemer? "None except *your* baby, my lord."

"It isn't mine. I mean," he went on with edged patience, "did you know of her existence before yesterday?"

Fury certainly cleared the wits. "Are you still on that road, my lord? Just because you're a villain doesn't mean that I must be, too!"

"I am not a villain!"

"You want to cast that innocent baby on the parish," she hissed, waving her embroidery frame toward the other room, but remembered to lower her voice.

"I thought we'd settled that. If I can believe you about Molly—"

"If?"

"All right! I believe you." He was almost shouting, too, but managing to keep the noise level low. "In which case she is the enemy, and we are allies."

Genova wanted to deny it, but as far as the baby went, he might be right. "Perhaps, my lord."

"Stop *my lord*ing me. I'm sure it chokes you. Why, Miss Smith, do you dislike me so?"

"You assaulted me, sir!"

"Oh, that."

Genova looked for the chamber pot. She'd upturn it over his wretched head!

"It was a stratagem, Miss Smith. As they say, 'All strategies are allowed in love and in war.' Then, we were at war. Now . . ."

" . . . we are playing at love?" she completed sweetly. And most unwisely. She knew that when the look in his eye changed.

"What a delightful thought." He held out an elegant hand. "Come, join me."

She met his eyes. "My lord, I would rather hang."

His brows rose, and his lips—damn him—twitched. "Truly?"

Unconquerable common sense ruled. "Very well, no. But by Hades, you would suffer from it as much as I."

"Are you a virgin, then?"

Genova felt her color flare. "That has nothing to do with it!"

"I doubt you'd suffer in my bed otherwise. But if you're not inclined to dalliance, let's continue with plain alliance. You must help me persuade Thalia not to take that baby to Rothgar Abbey."

"Must?" she asked, deliberately imitating his tone from yesterday.

A full smile touched his lips. "Touché. My dear Miss Smith, I humbly request your assistance in persuading Thalia not to take that baby to Rothgar Abbey."

"But what would become of him?"

"I will reunite him with his mother."

"The woman abandoned him!"

"She left him to my tender care."

"Which proves her insanity."

He surged out of the bed. "You unreasonable termagant! Whatever you're up to, you're completely unsuited to be companion to my great-aunts. God knows what your plan is there."

"Plan! My only plan is to take care of them. What is yours, my lord?"

"To rid them of weevils like you."

"Weevils!" Infuriated, Genova pushed him away

with all her strength. He toppled, but he grabbed the
front of her robe as he fell, taking her with him back
onto his mattress. Genova thumped on top of him,
hearing her tambour frame crack.

As soon as she had her breath back, she hit him
over the head with the sagging halves of it. "Plague
take you, you poxy knave!"

Laughing, he snatched it, tossed it, then cinched her
to him for a sizzling kiss, turning them as he did so,
so she was under him.

Genova fought and he released her lips, still laughing. For the first time in her life she understood the
urge to scratch someone's eyes out, but the vile man
had her trapped.

And she was on fur. On the deep wolf fur of his cloak
that she felt sliding beneath her, even through clothes.
Somehow, she'd lost her slippers, so when she tried to
use her feet to escape him, silky fur fought her.

"I'm sorry about your needlework frame," he murmured in apparent seriousness, though something not
so sober danced in his eyes.

"Let me go so I can see what damage you've done."

"You pushed me."

"With provocation."

"Perhaps." Smiling, he nuzzled her cheek. "Or is
this what you wanted all along?"

She heaved at him again, but he hardly moved. "Let
me up or I'll scream."

"Do you really want to be forced to marry me?"

"I'll see you hang for rape."

"Unlikely, don't you think?"

His confidence was as unshakable as his body, and
probably with reason.

"You're a fascinating woman, Miss Genova Smith,"
he whispered against her cheek, so she had to fight
for sanity.

"And you are a rakish reprobate, Lord Ashart."

If she could get a hand free, could she reach his
pistol? She wriggled. His response was to press down
more heavily, amused eyes on hers.

"Does it take one to know one? You're an adventuress, my spicy *pandolce*, and if you want adventure . . ."

He lowered his lips to hers and somehow she could not bring herself to fight as she should. *Pandolce.* The Christmas sweet bread of Genova in Italy. Sweet as his lips on hers.

It had been so long since she'd blended her mouth with a man's like this, felt a strong body over hers. She sighed and surrendered, knowing she'd wanted this since she'd met him. And dear heaven, how he could kiss. . . .

"Ash! Molly! Oh, by Jupiter, I do beg your pardon."

Genova wrenched her lips free and stared over the marquess's shoulder. A man and woman in outer clothes stood in the open doorway. If she was stunned, so were they. They were staring at her as if she were a three-headed monster.

"I say . . ." said the man, a smirk starting.

Ashart was off her, standing, and she was somehow standing beside him in a movement so swift she could hardly comprehend it. But she comprehended disaster. She'd been discovered in a man's bedroom in her nightclothes. On his bed. Under him.

Kissing him!

For the first time in her life she wanted to throw a fit of the vapors.

"Miss Smith fell," Ashart said, as if bored.

Genova glanced, praying that some magical transformation had dressed him, at least in a robe. He was still in his long nightgown open down his chest, his feet bare.

"How dare you burst into my room, Brokesby?"

The thin-faced man with small eyes laughed nervously. "I say, Ash. Arranged to meet Molly here. Assumed she'd be with you. This is a turn up for the books, though."

A maidservant passed by in the corridor behind the couple and stopped to boggle.

Ashart swept up a silky gray robe and put it on as he walked to the door and shut it, the couple inside.

Genova could feel the fury in him as if it were a heat, but what good would fury do?

"Permit me to make this situation clear, Brokesby, so that you and your sister will be in no danger of displeasing me with your tattle."

Brokesby and his equally thin-faced sister went still, but Genova wasn't sure even Ashart's fury could silence them. There was something in the sister's eyes that already relished the whispering of this tale.

"This parlor is part of the rooms taken by my great-aunt Lady Thalia Trayce, and this lady is her companion. I spent the night here because there was no other bed. She came into the room to retrieve her needlework and fell in the dark."

Genova looked around, picked up her cracked tambour frame, and dangled it as hopeful evidence. One splinter had pierced the cloth, and she anxiously eased the work off it.

"Of course, Ash. Of course! But what of Molly?"

"We thought she was here," the woman said.

"And why, Tess, would you think that?"

Alerted by menace, Genova looked up. The marquess's expression was merely cold, but color flared in the woman's face.

"She did say she might . . ."

"She did say she might to me, too. To be precise, she made an appointment to meet me here, which is why I have spent a devilish night in an uncomfortable bed. She never arrived and I am considerably displeased with her. I hope," Ashart added, in a tone that sparked prickles on Genova's skin, "not to be displeased with you, too."

The couple seemed to have the same reaction. They backed toward the door spouting reassurance.

Then the adjoining door opened and Thalia came in, smiling brightly in her ruffled pink robe. "Ashart, Genova! How naughty of you to tryst in *déshabillé*, but love will be love." She beamed at the Brokesbys. "I see you've discovered our little secret. Ashart and dear Genova are engaged to marry!"

Chapter Ten

*E*veryone seemed suddenly turned to statues. Unsure how to react, Genova, too, did nothing, praying without hope that this was all a dream. After a few seconds, she flicked a glance at the marquess. In a rare show of unguarded emotion, he had a hand to his face.

He lowered it. "Dear Thalia, you know that was a secret."

Thalia seemed completely unaware of danger. "You would not want to keep it secret at the expense of Genova's reputation, dear. Sometimes you young people do not think."

She turned her guileless smile on the Brokesbys. "I'm sure you are both the soul of discretion, but things do slip out, don't they? So hard to remember what one should and shouldn't say. The announcement will soon be made, but no one would want scandal to touch the happy union, I'm sure."

"No, no, of course not!" said Miss Brokesby with all the confusion Thalia seemed able to create. She did not, however, seem to doubt the story, nor did her brother. Who would think Lady Thalia Trayce party to impropriety?

Ashart opened the door. "I'm sure you wish to be on your way. If you see Lady Booth, oblige me by giving her this news. I'm sure it will interest her."

The woman tittered as the pair left.

Ashart shut the door. "And with luck, choke her on her own bile." But then he turned to his great-aunt. "Why did you do that, Thalia?"

She looked up at him, eyes wide. "For the reason I gave, dear. You would not want scandal."

"I do not want . . ."

"I know, dear. Men hate to have their hand forced, but when I saw you kissing Genova like that, I knew you'd recognized the bond between you. It was clear to me from your first meeting!"

Ashart looked at Genova as if this had been a plot. "Our first meeting, Thalia, was less than a day ago."

"But it can happen like that! It was so with my dearest Richard, and I have always regretted proceeding at the tempo of propriety. For then, you know, we would have had a little time as man and wife. Indeed, the whole pattern of our fates might have been different."

Genova went to her. "Thalia, I'm so sorry. I didn't know you'd lost a lover."

"It was a long time ago, dear. A lifetime ago. I hope to be reunited with Richard after death. But the Bible says that in heaven we do not grow old." She looked up at Genova, brow furrowed. "What will he think of me now?"

Genova knew then why Thalia dressed in a youthful style, but couldn't think of anything to say except, "With God, all things are possible."

Thalia chuckled. "Apparently that is what dear Beowulf says—'With a Malloren, all things are possible.' Naughty boy. But I was touched when his grandfather named his London development Marlborough Square. Richard was a great admirer of Marlborough."

Tangled in familiar confusion, Genova looked to the marquess for help but saw only hard-held patience.

"And now God's omnipotence is proved by your finding each other! But"—Thalia waggled a finger at both of them—"it was not clever to behave like that before the vows are said. I will leave you here for a minute or two, Genova, but no longer. I remember the passions of youthful ardor. There is no reason for you to delay the wedding, but until the vows are said, you must behave yourselves."

As she returned to the bedroom, Genova thought she heard her say, "A Christmas wedding. How nice. . . ."

She turned to Ashart, who seemed at this moment to be the only other sane person in the universe. He walked to the window and flung back the curtains. Dawn was now a bloody band on the horizon.

"Swear if you wish," she said. "I've lived on board ship."

He laughed. It was short, but it was a laugh, and it released some of the tension. "So I gather from your imprecations when your embroidery frame broke." He turned to her. "Is your work damaged?"

She looked at the frame, a thing awkwardly limp like a broken bird. "Only a little hole and some pulled threads. I should be able to conceal them." She looked up at him again. "My lord, what are we to do? Thalia *saw* us! How did she see us?"

He rubbed the back of his neck. "I assume our fall woke her and she came to see what had happened. Then she returned to her room, leaving us to our 'passion,' perhaps with the door ajar out of concern for you."

A frown lingered in his eyes that was more than annoyance at the situation.

"I could not have arranged for your friends to interrupt us," she pointed out.

"Did I say you had? And they are no friends of mine."

"At least you know them. I'd never seen them before! That means they can't know who I am—" But then she groaned. "Thalia. Do you think she really believes we are in love?"

"Oh, yes. In many ways she has a childlike view of the world."

Genova wasn't so sure. Thalia's eccentricities clearly grew out of her lost love, but Genova had thought for some time that the old lady acted the child to get what she wanted. But why should Thalia want her greatnephew to make such a poor match? Merely to secure a good whist player in the family? Whatever her motives, she was quite capable of playing her cards to achieve that end.

Genova could deal with Thalia, but she was growing worried about the marquess. He wasn't reacting as she

expected. She was beginning to take seriously the idea
that all the Trayces were mad.

"Who were those people, and what did they want?"

"Sir Pelham Brokesby and his sister, Tess. What did
they want? To catch me in bed with Molly, I assume."

He muttered something, and on the whole Genova
was relieved not to hear it.

"Why?"

"The devil alone knows. Molly must have thought
that being found here with me and the baby would
finally prove something. She's demented."

"It would seem so. But if that was her plan, why
did she flee?"

"Finally came to her wits?"

Genova truly felt surrounded by lunatics. "And
abandoned her baby on you, even though you insist
you are not the father? *That* is to come to her wits?"

She saw every feature tense. "That baby is not mine."

"I cannot believe that."

"And I care not one whit."

Genova inhaled and tamped down her temper. If
he had no shame, she could never win that battle. "To
return to more pressing matters, my lord, I cannot
marry you."

He relaxed and leaned back against the windowsill,
gray silk robe loose over his white nightshirt, his elegant feet still bare. A normal human should be cold,
but he didn't look it.

"Already married?"

"Of course not. But it's impossible."

"Not strictly speaking."

"In all practical senses. My lord, we have no connection at all."

"Thalia?"

"I'm her servant!"

"Nonsense, but I take your point. We must keep up
the pretense for a little while, however."

"What? Arrive at Rothgar Abbey as a betrothed
couple? It will be around society in days!"

"It will be around society in days anyway. Tess

Brokesby is generally known as Tattling Tess. Even if she sewed her lips shut, the urge to tell someone about this would win."

Genova put a hand to her mouth. "Dear heaven."

He came over and lowered it, quite gently. "No need for dramatics, Miss Smith. A betrothal is not binding before the law. Over a few days at Rothgar Abbey, I'm sure we'll find occasion to demonstrate that this was a hasty and improvident commitment. Thus, no one will be surprised when you give me my dismissal."

I might be, she thought, dizzied by the mere touch of his hand. It was purely physical, of course, but still powerful as a hurricane. "Everyone will think we anticipated the wedding."

"People may wonder, but they'll have the continued approval of my great-aunts to put in the balance. You may, of course, gain a reputation for passion."

"That's as bad!"

A smile warmed his eyes, and his thumb brushed her hand. "Not always . . ."

She snatched free. "You merely prove my point! I am as good as ruined."

"Nonsense. If there are repercussions, Trayce power and influence will brush them away. My word on it, Miss Smith. You will not suffer."

He was brushing her concerns away, and she almost spat out her opinion of his word. Wisdom won the battle, however, and she was glad. She must not stir the wolf now, when she felt too vulnerable, too shaken, for the fight. Bitter though it was to admit it, she might need his support to come through this intact.

"So," he continued, "we have only to play this game a little, then disengage, preferably in a public and spectacular manner. At least no one will be surprised that I momentarily lost my head over you."

"Is that supposed to be flattering, my lord?"

"I'm known for my fine taste in women."

"Lady Booth Carew?" she asked sweetly and, with relish, saw it hit.

He recovered. "She's a beauty with a magnificent figure and appealing talents. Come, Miss Smith, you must know you're an uncommon woman."

"But not that my uncommon assets are gold coin in the marriage market."

"Talk not of gold, but of fire." Not touching her, standing feet away from her, he caused heat to flare in her with a look. "Fire to warm. Fire to burn. I kissed you because I wanted to, Miss Smith, and one day, before we so sadly part, you will respond fully to a kiss of mine. My word on it."

After a moment, his brows rose. "Is it so impossible to imagine?"

Thanking heaven that he took her shattered silence for disdain, Genova glared at him. "Only think over your recent behavior, my lord. Remember, pray, my earlier words. I would not marry you if it was you or the hangman, and if you fail to sort this out, you will rue it to your deathbed!"

With that she marched into the bedroom. Unfortunately, she slammed the door.

The baby came off the breast and began to wail.

Milk spurted across the room.

Regeanne put her hands on her hips and glared. "Miss Smith!"

Genova collapsed in a chair and gripped her head in her hands. She wished she were a baby and could wail, too.

But then she sat straight, recalling some words that had flown past her in the fraught exchange. *"Over a few days at Rothgar Abbey . . ."*

He planned to *stay*? She'd assumed that he would escort them to the door, then ride away.

She might have to deal with the tormenting wretch for *days*?

Ash began to dress, considering the changed situation.

The last thing he needed at this moment was another scandal, but this absurd betrothal gave him an excuse to invade Rothgar's lair, if he cared to use it. How could he abandon his beloved so soon?

Though he and Rothgar were both courtiers, had seats in the Lords, and moved through fashionable London for a large part of the year, they were skilled at avoiding each other. All battles had been fought at a distance.

No longer.

If Rothgar was behind Molly Carew, then Ash was ready to take the battle to him, and he had the weapons needed to win. He would force his cousin to exonerate him, and that would change everything.

He'd been acting and reacting to strings pulled from the past, and in the process permitting the decline of his inheritance. During his minority, he'd not had power to change things, but he'd been in control of his property for five years now without breaking free.

It was time, but the Mallorens stood in his way, as shown by the affair with Molly. It was time to end the duel, but carefully, without getting his throat cut or being stabbed in the back.

The first essential step, however, was to clear his name with the king. Without access to the inner rooms of power, he'd achieve nothing. So, Rothgar—and where better to deal with him than in his home, where guards might be down, and weaknesses revealed.

He pulled a leather notecase out of his saddlebag and wrote instructions for Fitz. Ash would need suitable clothes and jewels at Rothgar Abbey. Magnificent clothes and jewels, so he would be armed if necessary.

He heated wax with a candle and sealed the letter, considering other possibilities. This also meant time to explore Miss Genova Smith. Perhaps she was innocently involved. That, too, should become clear when they arrived at the Abbey. Innocent or not, he had no doubt that they'd fight again. If the fates were kind, they would fight their way into bed.

It did indeed promise to be a very merry Christmas.

Chapter Eleven

*G*enova winced at Thalia's delight about events, but gave thanks she didn't mention Christmas weddings again. Once dressed, Thalia chirruped, "Breakfast is ready below, dear, so dress quickly!" and hurried off, doubtless to tell her sister all about it.

Genova dreaded to think what Lady Calliope would have to say.

She hurried into her traveling dress, but lingered to help Regeanne pack, putting off the moment. Sheena was feeding the baby, occasionally looking around the room uncertainly. She seemed in much better spirits, however, and when an inn servant arrived with the pile of clean laundry, her delight showed she hadn't been dirty by choice.

Lady Booth Carew, Genova decided, was a despicable woman, and her lover was low by association. She knew that having to frame that thought showed a weakness as dire as the hole in the hull of a ship.

She helped Sheena to pack her bundle. Everything was plain and cheap, including the baby's cloths and gowns. Genova contrasted that with the mother's velvet and fur and shook her head.

It was soon done, however, leaving no more excuse, so Genova braced herself and went downstairs. Ashart was already at the table.

Lady Calliope greeted her with a cynical gleam in her eye. "I gather you're to become one of the family. Don't know whether to congratulate you or wonder at your wits. Sit and eat. You're late."

Genova apologized and took some bread and meat, though she wasn't sure she could swallow.

"That's what comes of all this disorder," Lady Calliope grumbled. "Babies, then Ashart, now this. You'll be of use to neither man nor beast with your head in the flowers."

Genova almost objected, but she caught a warning look from her false beloved. She bit vengefully into cold beef.

"That Cupid is a damned awkward fellow," Ashart said. "Here he is, preventing me from leaving Rothgar's lair as soon as you are safe there."

Genova swallowed a mouthful in a lump in order to argue, but Thalia exclaimed, "You will stay, Ashart? How delightful that will be! And it will give you and Beowulf a chance to make peace. Old disagreements should be put to rest."

Ashart grimaced. "Don't build your hopes, Thalia," he said gently. "The problem has grown like a fungus in damp. Rothgar and I clash regularly over preferments at court, seats in Parliament, legislation, even purchases of art."

Genova seized on that. "Then perhaps you shouldn't come, my lord." With a languishing look, she added, "Though of course it will pain me to part."

Without disturbing his cool sophistication, Ashart managed to mirror her expression. "You are hardier than I, *pandolcetta mia*. To be apart from you would be more than I could bear."

Little sweet bread, she thought with amusement. "But your presence might cause discord, dearest."

"Fear not, beloved. Rothgar and I are experts at frigid navigation."

Genova shivered at that image. She sipped coffee, searching for ways to change his mind. Impossible with Thalia, resilient as always, fighting on the other side. Even Lady Calliope was making no objection.

When word came that the coaches were ready, Genova accepted her fate. She saw one bright aspect. If the marquess stayed at Rothgar Abbey, she'd have time to persuade him to accept his duties. And after all, she wasn't an inexperienced girl to be constantly a-tremor over a rake's tricks.

Servants hurried in to swathe them all for the chilly moment between inn and coach. Ashart supplanted the maid waiting to assist Genova.

She could see no way to object, even when he stepped close behind her—closer than any servant would. He draped the cloak over her shoulders, sliding his hands forward to put the clasp into her hands close to her throat.

She swallowed, able to imagine herself wavering like a person seen through baking hot air.

A rake's tricks!

She took the clasp and stepped away, fumbling in her attempt to fasten it. Only when she'd managed it did she turn.

A footman—one of his own, she reminded herself— was assisting Ashart with his riding cloak. Ashart clasped it at his neck, transforming before her eyes into the predatory stranger.

Danger. That awareness did not make him one jot less exciting. Quite the opposite, in fact. How could the physical be so at odds with the mind?

He pulled on leather gauntlets and escorted her out of the room and into the warm coach. Everyone was in place, including Sheena and the baby, who was awake and at his charming best.

Genova watched Ashart swing onto his horse, his cloak falling behind him. The breath of both horse and rider misted in the crisp morning air, which was hardly surprising. Only her disordered imagination saw the picture as hellish.

"So, shall we have a Christmas wedding?"

Oh, Lord. Genova turned to Thalia, feeling beleaguered by Trayces. "It's too early to think about that."

"Oh no, dear. Delay is such a mistake, and Christmas weddings are supposed to be blessed by good fortune."

"I could never marry without my father present."

"He could come! We could send this coach—which, as you see, is most comfortable—to bring him and your stepmother to the Abbey."

"I believe my stepmother has seasonal entertainments—"

"Oh, fie on that! What could be more important than a wedding?"

Genova looked to Lady Calliope for help.

"Now, now, Thalia. We know your concerns, but you mustn't press Genova so fiercely. She and Ashart have only just met."

Thalia looked at her sister, appearing very young. "I only want them to be happy, Callie."

"Yes, dear, I know. But you mustn't meddle any further just yet."

Genova relaxed, but she hadn't missed that *just yet*.

Surely Lady Calliope could no more want such a misalliance than Ashart—but then, who could understand the Trayce family?

The head of the family rode in the bitterest weather. It was so cold that he'd pulled up the hood of his cloak, but he could have commanded a place inside this coach with a snap of his fingers. Sheena could be with the servants, or he could even have hired an additional vehicle.

It wasn't natural. Hooded, she noted with a shiver, he looked positively ominous. Was that why she kept an eye on him all day between reading to the old ladies and playing whist?

No.

He rode ahead at one point. When they stopped shortly afterward to change horses and hot bricks, she realized that he'd taken the place of the running footman who usually went ahead to alert the next hostelry to be ready for them.

The same thing happened at the next stop, where they halted long enough for everyone to leave the coach and use the chamber pots. They lingered over cups of hot tea, in part to give the outside servants time to warm themselves. And the marquess, if he needed such human comforts.

She remembered her own words when Lynchbold had fretted about him. *"The devil looks after his own."*

Hyperbole, but still, he was extraordinary. He dismounted at each stop as smoothly as he mounted, as if frigid air was nectar to him.

When they returned to the coach, Genova was alarmed to see him on the box, complex reins in hand. She halted, thinking to protest, but could imagine how much good that would do. She settled in the coach braced for disaster. Men often fancied themselves as coachmen, but managing a coach and six was a challenging business.

She recognized his type now. For all his lazy sophistication, the Marquess of Ashart flared with excess energy. In battle such men were generally magnificent, but in dull times they could be a menace.

She prayed for a smooth road free of unexpected hazards. Whatever the cause, the party came to no harm, and stopped at the Sun at Mull Green for midday dinner no worse for noble steering.

Ashart dropped lightly down from the driving seat and escorted them into the inn. "Relieved to find yourself safe from the ditch, my dear?"

It was as if he could read her mind. Genova hurried after Thalia into a warm parlor and shed her cloak into waiting hands. As soon as Lady Calliope was carried in and settled at the table, they all set to, starting with oxtail soup.

"How much longer to our destination?" Lady Calliope asked, sounding weary. If she was letting it show, she must be feeling it deeply.

"Two hours if all goes well. We should arrive before dark, love." Ashart sounded concerned, too.

He was genuinely fond of the old ladies, which was to his credit, but Genova knew that people could divide the world into boxes—some to love, some to hate, some to cherish, some to kill.

Ashart apparently put the Mallorens in the hate box, or at least into the category of those he would harm if he could. The story of Lady Augusta was very sad, but it should not be causing such bitterness a generation later. She disliked seeing lives disrupted by such a thing.

At a break in the conversation, she probed a little. "Since your families are so at odds, my lord, how do you think Lord Rothgar will react to your arrival? I hope there will be no unpleasantness."

"Banish dull care, beloved. The nobility are trained in self-control. It is frowned upon to even sneeze in the royal presence."

"It's possible not to?" Genova asked, rising to get the main course.

"Oh, yes," said Thalia. "It's not easy, however. I remember Lady Millicent Ffoulks. She had a cold, but Queen Anne would not excuse her. She stuffed lumps of wool up her nose in the hope they would suppress a sneeze, but instead, when a sneeze overtook her, they shot across the room like pistol balls! Poor Millicent was banished from court—though I think perhaps she didn't mind."

Genova put down a chicken fricassee, then a dish of stewed peas. "I'm surprised that any but the desperate are willing to serve."

Ashart raised a brow at her. "What if your father's rise to admiral depended upon it?"

"Rank isn't purchased in the navy as it is in the army."

"But progress is often greased."

She added a platter of fried potatoes to the table and sat, silently giving him that point. Her father's career had been assisted by his second cousin, a viscount.

Talk progressed to other court matters, and Genova learned that both Trayce ladies had spent time as ladies-in-waiting, and that it had indeed been part of their duty to their family to try to be close to the monarch and promote Trayce interests.

She admitted to herself that such practices existed at all levels of society. There'd been many times when she and her mother had strained to please some high-ranking official or his wife because he could affect her father's career.

She'd found it hard and gave thanks that court service and intrigue was not in her future—unless, she suddenly worried, the establishment of the great Marquess of Rothgar was a court of its own. Oh, Lord, would she have to back out of his presence, stand and curtsy whenever he entered a room, and stifle the natural need to sneeze?

Genova had known lesser nobles who demanded almost as much, and the idea was one burden too many. She spent the rest of the journey with tension winding tight around her head.

Chapter Twelve

*T*he first warning of arrival was the sight of the
running footman passing, the setting sun glinting
off his gold-knobbed staff. He was speeding ahead to
announce their arrival, and this time Ashart did not
supplant him. He rode beside the main coach, looking
straight ahead, face still.

Was he braced for battle or intent on causing it?

What, Genova suddenly wondered, was his true purpose in planning to stay? She knew their betrothal
was merely an excuse, but one he'd seized on.

As they trundled through open gates, a horn blasted
to alert the great house just visible through bare-
branched trees. Rothgar Abbey was probably built of
pale stone, but sunset's fire turned it gold and gilded
roofs and chimneys. The same magic washed over roll-
ing hills, stands of evergreens, lawns, lakes, and pictur-
esque classical delights.

She recognized a park carefully created for delight,
but the effect was of countryside in natural perfection.
Even so, Genova's tension didn't release.

Perhaps Sheena shared her feelings, for she clutched
Genova's hand. Genova was touched by her faith, but
feared she'd be a leaky lifeboat in these waters.

Thalia had no apparent concerns. "What a delightful park! Even in winter. An excellent balance of
evergreens and other trees. And deer. I do love deer!
Oh, look at that Chinese bridge. How *very* pleasing.
And a Grecian temple. I do hope the weather will be
mild enough to permit strolls!"

She turned to Genova. "I have never been here

before, you know, so this is such a treat. And for
Christmas. I have heard that dear Beowulf celebrates
Christmas in the grand manner."

That was what Genova feared.

"You'd better call him Rothgar, Thalia," Lady Calliope said. "He's a man now."

Thalia pouted. "Oh, I suppose you are right, but I
remember the sweet child." She looked at Genova.
"He was Lord Grafton then, of course, but I have
never thought it right to call a dear, sweet child by a
title. Such a smile he had! And so clever. His parents
doted on him. . . ."

Memories turned her eyes sad in the way only old
eyes can be. "Such a sorry business. And it happened here."

Genova looked at the approaching gilded house
with new trepidation.

"Don't stir old ghosts," Lady Calliope commanded.

"I'll try not to, Callie. But a *baby* . . ." Thalia leaned
over and patted the blankets around sleeping Charlie.
"Perhaps the fact that we bring one will help."

The coach halted at the base of a double sweep of
steps. Servants stood ready for them—maids in white
aprons and mobcaps, and footmen in blue-and-gold
livery and powdered hair. They must all have felt the
cold, but Genova couldn't see shivers. At least they
all wore gloves.

One of the footmen put down steps and opened the
coach door. Genova climbed out first, then stepped
aside so Thalia and Sheena could descend. Lady Calliope would have to wait for her chair and porters.

Sheena was clutching both baby and bundle despite
offers from servants to take one or both. Genova took
the bundle and stayed close, trying soothing words.
"It will be all right, Sheena."

But she didn't like to promise what she couldn't be
sure to provide.

"What a splendid journey, my dear boy! I am not
at all fatigued." Thalia was beaming at Ashart, who
had dismounted and joined them.

He looked at Genova. "And you, beloved?"

She wasn't imagining the danger. He was primed for battle, too.

And he, in his dark mood and his dark cloak, was framed against his frivolous, indulgent chariot. The contrast perplexed her and she had to ask, "That vehicle is truly yours, my lord?"

His brows rose. "You think I stole it?"

"No, but . . . Thalia says you never travel by coach."

"Rarely," he corrected. "That coach was my father's. He was a different sort of man."

A clear explanation released some of her tension. Perhaps she was overwrought because of nerves. "It was kind to give your great-aunts the use of it."

"I merely pay the bills."

"You could have refused."

He smiled slightly. "Refuse Thalia? Impossible."

That was true. Thalia was so sweet and good-natured, so *innocent,* that it was impossible to refuse her anything. Genova prayed the Dark Marquess would feel the same way.

Thalia exclaimed, "Callie is out at last! Come along, do, everyone, before we all freeze!"

She trotted toward the steps like an eager child, and Genova urged Sheena after. Perhaps she should have sent maid and baby around to the back with the coaches and other servants, but she hated to let the pair out of her sight until she was sure they were safe.

"Great-aunt Thalia."

Genova looked up to see that a man had come out of the house to greet them at the top of the steps.

Could this man in casual country style be the ominous Marquess of Rothgar? His breeches and jacket were of nut-brown cloth, his waistcoat buff. Only moderate lace showed at neck and wrists, and he wore his dark hair simply tied back.

What? Had she thought the high aristocracy wore robes and coronets every day?

No, but he lacked any hint of arrogance, madness, or deadly intent. Thalia went straight to him, gloved hands outstretched. "Beowulf! How splendidly you've grown!"

Was that a twitch of wild humor as Lord Rothgar took Thalia's hands and kissed both? Then he pulled her closer and bent to kiss her cheek.

"I'm sorry you missed the stages of it," he said, surely with a twinkle in his eye.

Genova could have laughed at her own folly. Where had all those dark dramas come from? But then Lord Rothgar's eyes swept over the rest of the party, and chilled at sight of Ashart.

Genova held her breath, praying. She suddenly realized that if Lord Rothgar barred his enemy from his house, the Trayce ladies might refuse to enter, too. It would break their hearts, but more to the point it might kill Lady Calliope, who needed rest and care.

After a still moment, Lord Rothgar bowed to Ashart, then escorted Thalia into the house. Genova thanked God. A host of problems still remained, but they could all stay.

They entered a grand chamber that rose up past gilded stairs and balustrades to a skylight in the roof, though which the last of the golden sun spilled to light a floor rich with inlaid woods. The walls held alcoves marked off by marble pillars of cream and gold. A pale classical statue stood in each, and Genova suspected the sculptures were truly from ancient times.

It was awe-inspiring, but the effect was shockingly disarmed by Christmas decorations. Colored cords and golden ornaments decorated balustrades and pillars, marble fireplace and carved picture frames. There must be bells, too, for the draft of their entrance had stirred a delicate chiming.

Dishes of gilded nuts and fruit, both fresh and dried, stood on all surfaces, as if guests must be offered instant hospitality. Logs crackled and roared in the huge marble fireplace, fighting the chill in the enormous space, but not quite succeeding. Even with a Malloren, apparently, not everything was possible.

However, a powerful sense of welcome helped Genova relax. This was certainly no rigid court. A glance showed that it was terrifying Sheena, however, so Genova stayed close, wondering what to do. Where in this house did such a child belong?

She looked for a suitable servant but saw only statuelike, liveried footmen. Then her eyes settled on the woman who was warmly greeting Thalia.

She must be the marchioness, but she, too, was in simple clothes—a blue gown with modest ruffles, and a large shawl. The lovely design and the way it draped told Genova it probably cost more than her own entire wardrobe. Even so, Lady Rothgar seemed as ordinary as her gown, being brown-haired and of average build.

As Genova observed her, however, she recognized a presence, an air of command. She remembered Thalia saying that Lord Rothgar had married that rarest of creatures, a countess in her own right. Perhaps Genova wouldn't approach her, either. Should she ask Thalia to raise the subject?

With a thump, Lady Calliope's chair was put down next to Genova, and Lord Rothgar came over to kiss the old lady's cheek. "You're a most redoubtable woman, Great-aunt Calliope."

The old lady looked shrunken, but she was gruff as usual. "Always have been. Stupid, though, to have let matters come to this pass."

"Folly all around." Lord Rothgar's eyes moved with a question to Genova and her charges, but then on. From his expression, she knew Ashart had come to her side.

Rothgar bowed. "Cousin, you are most welcome."

That was clear enough.

Ashart swept a bow of his own. "How could I resist, especially when I bring mysteries and complexities?"

Lord Rothgar smiled. "We thrive on mysteries and dine on complexities."

Despite the smile, a tingling tension clamped the back of Genova's neck. She last remembered feeling like this when their limping ship had caught sight of those Barbary corsairs.

Chapter Thirteen

*L*ord Rothgar turned then to look at Sheena and Charlie. "Speaking of mysteries, a baby, Great-aunt Calliope? At your age?"

A rumble of laughter rolled through Lady Calliope. "Foolish boy! We'll amuse you with the story later, but make known to you our companion and friend, Miss Smith."

Genova curtsied, warmed by the "friend," which raised her status a good deal.

"Welcome to Rothgar Abbey, Miss Smith." Lord Rothgar extended his hand, which gave her no choice but to surrender hers for a kiss brushed just above her glove. "How courageous of you to venture among Mallorens and Trayces."

"You make your families sound like Scylla and Charybdis, my lord."

Another brief smile touched his lips. "An apt construct—if you were a sailor."

Scylla and Charybdis were two of the challenges Ulysses had faced when sailing home to Ithaca.

"How clever you are!" Thalia declared. "Genova is a naval officer's daughter and has spent a vast amount of time at sea. She fought Barbary pirates!"

"Not quite," Genova tried to protest, but the marquess smiled fully.

"Then you are admirably qualified for this voyage. As long, of course, as you can decide which side is Scylla, the monster who desires to eat you, and which is Charybdis, the whirlpool that seeks to suck you into the depths."

Without thinking, Genova glanced at Lord Ashart and caught him looking at her. Muscles deep within her contracted, and her breath shortened. In public, when separated by, perhaps, four feet!

Someone chuckled.

She looked quickly, her color rising, but the marchioness was chuckling at something Thalia had said. Everyone seemed in merry Christmas spirit, but Genova wanted to hint that Lady Calliope needed a warm bed.

She hesitated to abandon Sheena, but went over to curtsy to Lady Rothgar. "Excuse me, my lady, but Lady Calliope is tired from the journey. I think she would welcome her bed."

Shrewd eyes took in the old lady. "Of course. We are caught up in excitement."

In moments a senior servant was taking Lady Calliope and her servants up the grand staircase, its banisters twined with red and green cords, while Lord Rothgar guided Thalia and Ashart toward a room off the hall.

Scylla and Charybdis. Should she be there with Thalia or here with Sheena? She couldn't abandon the girl now.

"So this is Lady Booth Carew's baby," Lady Rothgar said. "I gather some strange story attaches."

Genova knew she was blushing. "My lady, I'm very sorry—"

Lady Rothgar waved a hand. "I'm sure you could do nothing but bring the child here. Is he healthy?"

"Yes, mylady. And the nurse, too."

"Then come along. We have extensive nurseries and they are already in use."

She turned and walked briskly toward the staircase, her heels rapping on the wooden floor like the rat-a-tat-tat of a battle drum. Genova pushed that thought away and urged Sheena after, carrying the maid's bundle herself. At least one problem had evaporated. Sheena and Charlie were not to be thrown out. In fact they would have a place in the family's nursery, which was very generous.

As they climbed the stairs Genova found the bells. They hung from the cords wrapped around the banisters, and tinkled as she passed. Charming, but she could imagine the noise fraying the nerves.

They ascended a short flight to a half landing where the steps split to left and right. As they turned to the left, Lady Rothgar said, "Why don't you tell me some of this strange story as we go, Miss Smith? This is a large and somewhat mazelike house. It's been added to by every generation, and the last marquess inserted corridors all over the place. I don't *think* we've lost a guest, though a few have wandered for a while."

Genova quickly decided to keep Ashart's part to a minimum. Scylla and Charybdis didn't need any more problems. She began with the encounter with Lady Booth Carew. Then, as they walked down a long, carpeted corridor hung with works of art and set with tables and chests holding treasures, she framed Ashart's later arrival as coincidence.

"How very intriguing." The marchioness turned right into another corridor. "Odd, however, to abandon the baby with strangers."

"Indeed, my lady."

Her hostess stopped at another junction. "Is Ashart the father, do you think?"

Genova abandoned pretense. "He insists not."

"He was Lady Booth's lover about a year ago, which would make it possible." Lady Rothgar glanced at her. "Perhaps I shouldn't speak so frankly of such matters to an unmarried lady."

"I've spent most of my life in seafaring circles, Lady Rothgar. I'm not easily shocked."

The marchioness smiled. "As my husband said, you should fit in here excellently. But I must tell you that I choose to go by my own title of Arradale in all but the most formal situations. No, don't be embarrassed. You were quite correct. It is I who is out of order."

"You're very kind, Lady Arradale."

Genova meant it. Despite daunting grandeur and all
the other problems, she was ready to like the Dark
Marquess's wife.

"To be kind we must get our innocents to a simpler
and warmer setting. Come along."

Genova noticed then that Sheena was standing in
the center of the corridor, as far from anything as she
could get. She must be terrified of breaking something.

The countess led them around another corner into
a short corridor that appeared to go nowhere. She
opened a door and revealed a plain, narrow staircase,
whose sides brushed her wide skirts as she went up.

"Do you have a plan for dealing with the baby,
Miss Smith?"

Genova wished she could see Lady Arradale's face,
the better to judge the tone of the question. Was she
to be held solely responsible?

"Lady Booth must be found," she said, choosing
her words. "Lord Ashart will help, since he knows the
lady so well."

The "will" was her statement of intent, and that
was probably obvious. At the top of the stairs, Lady
Arradale flashed her a smile. "We will make sure he
does."

They had reached a plain but carpeted corridor, and
Lady Arradale seemed to hesitate, tapping her lips
with one finger. She wore rings worth a fortune, and
what's more, she wore one on every finger.

"I wasn't in London last winter, but Lady Booth's
scandal ran well into summer. She claimed all along
that she was with child by Ashart. When he wouldn't
marry her, she fled to Ireland, and eventually announced the birth of a son."

Disappointment stabbed Genova. "So it *is* his. And
now the poor woman is driven to extremes to force
him to accept his responsibilities."

"A singularly foolish way to go about it, wouldn't
you say? And . . . inconvenient. You burn for justice,
which I completely understand, but we'd prefer to at-

tempt peace rather than war over the next few days. We didn't expect Ashart to attend, you see, but now he's here, we wish to make best use of it."

"I understand, my lady."

And Genova did. Aristocratic peacemaking would come before justice for a baby. It was the way of the world, but it meant that Genova would be the only one to truly care about Sheena and Charlie.

Lady Arradale nodded, then continued along the corridor. Genova heard childish sounds nearby. The countess opened a door, and laughter danced out. Genova urged Sheena into a warm room of comfortable dimensions and closed the door after them. This, at least, was right.

The room could be the parlor of a modest house, and the fire, shielded by an ornate metal guard, banished all trace of cold. In her cloak, Genova was already too warm.

The walls were painted a pale green, the woodwork was white, and a Turkish carpet cushioned the floor. A spinet sat in one corner, a drum and some recorders on top of it. There were comfortable chairs, some child-sized, and an assortment of books and toys on shelves.

Two blond girls, in matching blue gowns open over white quilted petticoats, sat on the carpet to one side of the fire playing with dolls. A maid in a chair was keeping an eye on them while doing some plain sewing.

In the center of the room, two other mobcapped maids sat on the floor with a copper-haired toddler. The sturdy, dark-haired one of the pair sat back observing, while the slender one helped the child build with brightly colored blocks.

Both maids looked up.

Lady Arradale said, "Look what we have, Portia. A baby."

The slender maid was not a maid. Her copperish curls bubbled out from beneath a pretty, lace-trimmed cap rather than a servant's mobcap, and her gown was clearly of the finest quality. She scrambled to her feet, proving to be petite but close to Genova's age.

"How lovely. Whose?"

"Lady Booth Carew's."

"It's Ashart's, then?"

It was like a nail in his coffin.

Chapter Fourteen

"*H*e's here, by the way," the countess said. "Ashart. Came with the Tunbridge Wells greataunts."

"Oh, my! And yet I hear no distant sound of war."

"Children are kept up here so they won't be heard, but it works in reverse. They could be murdering each other and we wouldn't know. But Bey has matters in hand, I think, though it was quite a shock, as you can imagine."

Lady Arradale drew Genova forward. "Let me make known Miss Smith, Portia, companion to Lady Thalia and Lady Calliope. Miss Smith, this is my sister-in-law, Portia, Lady Arcenbryght Malloren, more commonly Lady Bryght. The late Marquess of Rothgar had an obsessive attachment to all things Anglo-Saxon, which is the cause of the names. You are spared Hilda, Brand, and Cynric, who are Christmasing elsewhere. Elfled—Lady Walgrave—is here, but not much in evidence since she expects a baby any day. We tease my husband that he's arranged a Christmas reenactment."

Genova dropped a curtsy, trying to take all this in.

"And this," the countess said, smiling at the child who had toddled over to hide in his mother's skirts, "is Master Francis Malloren."

Lady Bryght ruffled his hair. "Make your bow, Francis."

The child emerged enough to make a quite reasonable bow but then slid back into safety.

"He'll be all right soon," Lady Bryght said, picking

him up and kissing his round cheek. "He takes his time with strangers, don't you, poppet? And very wise, too. See, Francis, a baby. What's his name?" she asked Genova.

"Charlie, my lady, and the maid's name is Sheena. Sheena O'Leary, but that's about as far as we've progressed. She speaks virtually no English." She turned to Lady Arradale. "Is there anyone here who speaks Gaelic?"

"My goodness. I'm not aware of any Irish servants, but there must be some in the neighborhood. That will wait and you must all be so tired. Let's make arrangements for little Charlie and then you can refresh yourself."

She sent the maid to find a Mrs. Harbinger, and soon an older woman appeared. She was heavy-boned and could have looked glowering, but her eyes lit at the sight of the baby.

"Ah, the precious!" She came forward with the clear intention of taking Charlie. Sheena stepped back.

"She's afraid," Genova said quickly. "She doesn't speak English, and I don't think she understands what's happening to her, poor girl."

"This is Mrs. Harbinger, the nursery governess," the countess explained. "She's in charge of this part of the house." She gave the nursery governess a vague explanation of Charlie's arrival. It implied an accident on the road without actually telling lies.

The woman was all sympathy. "It's only a matter of airing the baby nursery, my lady, and bringing another maid up here, with your permission. You can leave it all to me."

"I know I can. I'll see if there's anyone in the area who speaks Gaelic, but in the meantime, I know you'll be understanding with poor Miss O'Leary, who must feel very ill at ease."

"Of course, my lady." The woman wrapped an arm around Sheena's shoulders and drew her to a chair near the fire, murmuring comfort all the while. The

Irish girl looked desperately at Genova for a moment, but then relaxed and even smiled at her new protector.

Genova felt a burden rise from her shoulders. That, at least, was all right.

Lady Arradale moved toward the door, and Lady Bryght kissed her son and gave him to the maid. She swept up a large shawl and wrapped it around herself. "I must come and see what's happening. Ashart here. My stars!"

Soon the three of them were heading back down the stairs and through the maze of corridors. Genova was sure that by herself she'd be one of the wandering guests. After a number of turns, the countess opened a door to a fine bedchamber.

Genova saw some of her possessions, including the *presepe* box. This was her room? The splendor shocked her. She would have much preferred something simpler.

"We'd normally give you a room for yourself," Lady Arradale said, "but over Christmas, every space will be required."

Genova noticed then that various items belonged to Thalia. That explained the grandeur, but she'd hoped for a place of her own, no matter how plain. She'd not realized until the past three days how much she relished her privacy.

However, she said, "I'm accustomed to sharing a room with Lady Thalia."

"She is delightful, isn't she? Such a shame that Rothgar's been cut off from his great-aunts all these years. Now the ice is broken, things will be different."

Genova recalled a scene she'd witnessed once—ice breaking and people falling through it to their deaths. It was a strange saying, all in all.

The brisk countess opened an adjoining door. "There's a closet attached, with a bed for the maid."

It was a narrow dressing room, just large enough for a huge armoire, a chest of drawers, and a small bed. Even so, Genova envied Regeanne, who was putting things away. The maid looked around, startled, then dipped a curtsy.

Lady Arradale waved for her to continue her work and closed the door again. "I gather Ashart visits the great-aunts in Tunbridge Wells?"

"A few times a year, I understand, my lady, but not while I've known them."

The countess cocked her head and Genova was aware of being studied. "A handsome rascal, is he not?"

"We've only just met, my lady."

"A moment tells us if a man is handsome or not, Miss Smith."

Genova knew she was blushing and shed her fur-lined cloak as excuse. "He's certainly handsome in that way, my lady. But handsome is that handsome does, and his behavior toward his poor child isn't handsome at all."

"Molly Carew's behavior would drive a saint to distraction," Lady Bryght said. "Such folly to think a man like Ashart would marry her under pressure, and I do believe she started the affair with just that in mind."

That fired Genova's sense of justice. "It was certainly wrong of her to become his mistress, but wasn't it equally wrong of him to take one?"

Both ladies gave her an identical look.

"We're speaking of folly rather than virtue," the countess said, not unkindly. "Virtue, they say, is its own reward, and as such, it provides a thin cloak in winter. Seek also to be wise, Miss Smith."

"There's nothing between myself and Lord Ashart."

Lady Bryght chuckled. "Very unwise. Keep your clothes between you at all times."

"Portia!" laughed the countess, but she added, "It's good advice, Miss Smith. He's an infamous rascal."

Genova remembered the ridiculous betrothal. What would these ladies think of her words when they heard? What could she possibly say to make things better now?

Oh, I forgot. I do know he's a rascal. That's why I'm engaged to marry him. . . .

"I heard Molly Carew left Lady Knatchbull's masquerade with Ashart without a hint of shame," Lady Bryght said. "She was dressed as Salome."

"What?" asked the countess. "In the seven veils?"

"And not a stitch on underneath."

"The result is a lesson to all wise women." Lady Arradale went to the washstand. "There should be hot water." She raised the linen covering a jug, and steam rose. "Good."

She indicated a bellpull by the fireplace. "That rings in the servants' quarters and will bring somebody at any time. Please make yourself comfortable, Miss Smith, and join us in the Tapestry Room when you're ready. We have a few guests already with us, but most will arrive tomorrow. I'll send a footman to wait by your door to guide you. Please treat Rothgar Abbey as your home."

The two ladies left and Genova put a hand to her head as if that could stop its whirling. This had seemed such a simple voyage once. It had presented escape from her stepmother's house, along with an opportunity to mingle with the great and observe their follies.

She had not planned to be a folly, stuck like a fly in the center of a gilded web.

But no, she was not so helpless as that. She would think of herself as a ship navigating between Scylla and Charybdis. Scylla, the many-headed monster was an excellent image for the Malloren family, and Ashart enswirled her like a whirlpool.

She felt the effect even now, when she knew he was exactly the heartless rake she'd thought. Even if Lady Booth Carew had set out to seduce him, he'd let himself be seduced and was now denying responsibility for the innocent result.

Thank heavens there was no danger of her falling into the same trap.

She caught sight of the *presepe* box and went to it. She needed to preserve the traditions and the memories it carried. The Nativity scene should have been up ten days ago.

She unlocked and opened the box, but then realized she must wait. For all the pleasantries about treating this house as her home, she would be expected below in short order. Despite the mock betrothal, despite hospitable kindness, she was merely the Trayce ladies' attendant, and should be attending.

She quickly washed her hands and face and tidied her hair, commanding herself to keep to her place and out of noble matters as much as possible. Then she found her warmest shawl, sucked in a deep breath, and sailed out to navigate between monster and whirlpool.

Chapter Fifteen

*T*he promised footman waited outside the door like a sentry—far more finely turned out than Genova was. She followed him, making herself relax enough to appreciate the passing objets d'art and to try and remember the route. She might need Theseus's ball of twine.

Soon they descended the grand staircase and crossed the gleaming floor. Genova summoned the image of herself as a flagship, cruising into hazardous waters, hoping for peace, but with guns primed and ready to fire.

The footman opened the door and she sailed through.

But if there were hazards here, they were deep below the surface.

In this awe-inspiring house, this room could be called cozy. It was twice as large as the drawing room at Trayce House, but no more than that, and a large fireplace triumphed over chill. The high ceiling was decorated with fine plasterwork, but the medieval tapestries that covered all available walls gave a welcoming warmth. The furnishings were grand, but they had the look of pieces chosen for comfort and well used over generations. Two cats and two dogs formed a carpet in front of the hearth.

Twenty or so people were taking tea in two groups, with no sign of servants. Lady Arradale presided over a tray from one sofa, while Thalia shared a sofa opposite with an extremely enceinte lady. Genova remembered that one of the family was expecting to be confined any day. Lady Bryght presided over another group that included Lord Rothgar.

Genova paused, unsure which group to join. She'd choose the one without Ashart, but he was in neither. Then she saw him on the far side of the room, apparently investigating a folio of maps.

Apart.

He looked up, and their eyes locked. She raised her chin, refusing to be cowed. After a moment, he bowed as if in acknowledgment, and began to walk toward her.

"Genova! Come sit by me, do!"

Thalia's voice snapped Genova's entrancement, and she hurried to take the empty place on the sofa, hoping she didn't look as flustered as she felt. She willingly surrendered to the distraction of introductions.

Lord Bryght Malloren, tall and dark, was easily recognizable as Lord Rothgar's brother. Half brother, she reminded herself. The expectant lady was the Countess of Walgrave, and Lord Rothgar's sister. She didn't resemble him, being russet-haired and sunny.

"Call me Lady Elf," she said. "Everyone still does here."

The handsome man who rose from a chair beside Lady Elf to carry Genova's tea to her was the Earl of Walgrave.

Genova had never before been in a room with so many titled people. She was grateful for two men who were ordinary both in looks and status—Dr. Egan, Lord Rothgar's librarian and archivist, and Dr. Marshall, curator of Anglo-Saxon antiquities. Dr. Egan was thin, sallow, and dominated by a large nose. Dr. Marshall was rotund, with a shiny, glowing face.

Ashart appeared in her line of sight and accepted a cup of tea from the countess. Was it his first?

". . . don't you think, dear?"

Genova jerked her attention away and said, "Yes, of course, Thalia," hoping she wasn't agreeing that the moon was made of cheese.

Apparently not. Only that winter walks were especially bracing.

As others chatted, Thalia pointed out some of the people in the other group. "That young man is Mr. Stackenhull, Beowulf's music master. And the older lady is Mrs. Lely, the countess's secretary. Such a trial to have property to manage. The couple are the Inchcliffs, and the glowering man is Lord Henry Malloren. He courted me once, but he's never known how to please." Thalia leaned closer and whispered, "When offered tea, he complained it wasn't good honest ale."

Like most confidential whispers, this was heard by others, but they seemed amused, and Lord Henry was too far away to hear. He might not mind, anyway. He had the lean, weather-beaten look of a "damn your eyes" type.

"The dumpy woman with Lord Henry is his wife. Never opens her mouth except to eat."

Genova saw twitching lips and wondered how she could stop Thalia saying these things.

Then the door opened and a young woman came in. Genova noticed Ash startle and looked at the new arrival again. A little tall, slim, and with a straight-backed confidence that implied she belonged here.

She didn't look like a Malloren, however, having mouse brown hair and rather commonplace features. That was the only word that came to mind. Commonplace, perhaps even a little plain, but saved by bright eyes, a wide smile, and an impression of being very pleased with her world.

Genova glanced at Ash again, but he was talking to Dr. Egan.

The young woman turned toward their group, but Lord Henry called out, "Damaris! There you are at last. Make yourself useful, girl. Play us a tune!"

The young woman stopped, smile fixed, and Genova thought she would refuse, but she curtsied—"Of course, Lord Henry"—and went to a harpsichord. A lowly companion? Or a tyrannized daughter?

Lady Arradale spoke in a voice designed to carry.
"How kind, Miss Myddleton." She turned to Genova.
"Miss Myddleton is Lord Henry's ward, and we are
so fortunate to have her here. She plays beautifully."

Notes began to tinkle out, rapid and precise.

"She does, doesn't she?" Genova said.

"She sings beautifully, too."

Expensively trained, Genova assumed. *Ward* probably meant money, which might be why confidence
overshadowed a lack of looks. Genova thought she
might like Miss Myddleton, especially as the young
woman was playing for the company as if that were
her greatest joy. Sulking never served.

And presumably, Miss Myddleton wasn't any sort
of Malloren. An outsider, like herself.

Then she saw the smile the young woman shot at
Ashart. Those long-lidded eyes were, in fact, catlike—
slightly slanted, and predatory. How dare she look at
Ashart like that!

The stab of jealousy was irrational but real. While
playing her part in the conversation, Genova studied
Ashart's response. After a slight bow he seemed to
ignore Miss Myddleton, but he was aware of her. Genova was sure of that.

She knew she had no proprietary rights, but by
heaven, if she had to play the besotted betrothed, she
would not have her supposed beloved ogling other
women!

"Another cake, Miss Smith?"

Genova found Lady Elf offering the plate and looking quizzical. Had her thoughts shown? To cover that,
she plunged back into the conversation, not looking
at Ashart at all, but irritatingly aware of the fluent
notes spilling out of the harpsichord.

Then Lord Rothgar joined their group. "I think it is
time to discuss the mysteries and complexities." Lady
Bryght had come with him, and Dr. Egan and Dr.
Marshall discreetly excused themselves.

So, this was family business, except for herself. She
was a key witness. She glanced at Ashart, who seemed

blandly uninterested, as if none of these events concerned him.

When called upon, she gave a carefully edited account of the acquiring of the baby, again leaving out anything to pin down Ashart's part in it.

"How strange it is," Lady Arradale said. "What should we do now?"

"Why, reunite little Charlie with his parents!" Thalia announced. "It will be in the spirit of Christmas. Perhaps it's a case similar to when Christ was mislaid in the Temple."

Genova almost choked on a crumb. "Reunion would be excellent, Thalia, but Lady Booth must know where her baby is." She looked at Ashart. "Wouldn't you agree, my lord?"

He met her gaze as tranquilly as an innocent angel. "She has that regrettable sense of direction, my dear."

Genova kept her smile in place. "Then we must find and redirect her, my lord. I believe you were to try."

"I was distracted"—his eyes said how—"but it shouldn't be difficult. She has a house in Ireland."

"She clearly is not there now."

"But she must return there, or join fashionable circles in January—like a frog returning to its pond."

This time Genova almost choked on a laugh. She put down the delicious lemon cake for the duration of battle. "In *January*, my lord? Your frog analogy is not quite apt."

"Poetic license. I am," he added, "ardently in favor of license."

She spotted a target and fired at it. "A *marriage* license, you mean?"

"But of course!" Perdition, she'd forgotten the betrothal again. "A necessary evil in these reformed days. Once, we gentlemen could simply ride off with brides of wealth, nobility, and beauty."

As he spoke, however, he turned from Genova to Lady Arradale and bowed slightly. Genova almost choked on air. Surely he wouldn't take that line of attack? It could lead straight to a duel.

The countess parried his sultry look with one declaring that he was talking nonsense. Lord Rothgar seemed oblivious.

"A marriage license!" declared Thalia. "We'll need one for a Christmas wedding. How is that done?"

"We're in no hurry," Ashart said quickly, calm cracking, "and Genova prefers banns."

"You do, dear? Why?"

Genova thought of giving him the lie, but it wouldn't serve. "I believe in traditional ways, Thalia."

"Then we share that interest, Miss Smith," Lord Rothgar said. "We celebrate Christmas here with all the old customs, as you will see. As for the missing mother, the weather is sharp and Christmas approaches. I will not send servants on an errand that isn't urgent. Later will be soon enough to hunt her down."

It was said pleasantly, but an image of baying hounds cracked the elegant hospitality.

"Miss Smith. Your cup is empty." Lady Arradale smiled at Ashart. "Please bring Miss Smith's cup to be refilled."

Tense from the previous exchange, Genova expected Ashart to refuse the command. After a moment he obeyed, but she was sure this noble informality seemed as strange to him as it did to her. Probably in his own home he never lifted a finger to do anything.

Lady Arradale poured. "It would help to be able to communicate with the maid. Do we have any Gaelic speakers, Bey?"

"Not to my knowledge, but I'll inquire."

Genova paused in the act of taking back her cup. Extraordinary that a highborn lady call her husband by a familiar name in public, but no one here seemed surprised.

"That does strike me as strange, however," Lord Rothgar added. "Ashart, does Lady Booth speak Gaelic?"

"I've seen no sign of it. I gather the Anglo-Irish can get by without."

"So why hire a wet nurse with whom she couldn't communicate? Would she have lacked choice? Was there perhaps another servant who could interpret?"

"Or," Ashart said, "with this plan in mind, did she want a servant who could tell no tales?"

A connection clicked between the cousins, but Genova couldn't tell if it was a meeting of minds or the tap of steel blades.

"Precisely." Lord Rothgar almost purred it. "We must find a translator. Alas, that truth will probably have to wait a few days."

Ashart took out his snuffbox. "Alas, indeed, but truth, like gold, never decays. Thus it lurks, like a keg of gunpowder beneath a house."

Genova heard her cup rattle and held it to stop the noise. Her sudden tremble wasn't because of the words, which meant nothing to her, but because of the reaction she'd glimpsed on Lord Rothgar's face.

Ashart had said something crucial, and Lord Rothgar had moved *en garde*. What? Guy Fawkes had attempted to blow up King James I using gunpowder stored below Parliament, but that was ancient history now.

The fleeting disturbance was gone without a trace. Lord Rothgar accepted a pinch of snuff from his cousin. "Marcus Aurelius was predictably naive when he claimed that no one was ever hurt by the truth."

Ash offered snuff to Lord Bryght, who declined. "Doesn't the Bible say that truth will set us free?"

"But is it worth the price?" Rothgar asked. "Freedom is never free. We must be willing to pay everything for it."

"Seneca." Ashart inclined his head, as if acknowledging a point scored. "He also said there is no genius without madness."

Madness.

Instead of showing alarm, Lord Rothgar smiled. "I

am merely Daedalus, creator of mazes. Are we somewhat lost?"

"A maze?" interrupted Thalia. "Do you have a maze here, Beowulf? How delightful! I should love to try it."

The ice of danger shattered.

"Alas, my dear, I do not. How could I have been so thoughtless?"

Thalia gave a little pout, but then smiled again. "It would doubtless not have been pleasant in winter. This has been so delightful, my dear boy, but now I need to retire. Such a long day."

Lord Rothgar was there first, but Genova hurried to Thalia's side, grateful for escape, and that Thalia had cut short that exchange, surely on purpose. Even so, she still prickled with awareness of a circling storm.

As they followed a footman upstairs, Thalia chattered of apricot crisps and tapestries and mazes and nothings. Genova was shocked by an urge to scream at her to shut up.

Oh, for a private space, no matter how mean, and peace and quiet in which to think!

Chapter Sixteen .

*A*sh followed Thalia and Miss Smith out of the
room, but not up the stairs. He had no desire for
talk or scrutiny, though Thalia's intervention had been
as well. A duel to the death, even a verbal one, would
be inconvenient.

"Are you accepting the olive branch?"

He turned to find Rothgar behind him. "Was the
invitation here an olive branch?"

"What else?"

"A call to battle?"

One of the elegant hounds had accompanied its
master, and Rothgar idly stroked its silky ears. "The
enmity has always come from the Trayce side."

"Has it? What was your purpose in inviting my family here?"

"How distressing," Rothgar said, apparently to the
dog, "to have a reputation that makes an invitation
to Christmas revelries a matter for suspicion." He
looked up. "This is Boudicca, by the way."

Ash was aware of being given a breathing moment,
but took it. "What sort of dog is she?"

"A Persian gazelle hound. We have persuaded her
and Zeno not to pursue the deer. It doubtless causes
them frustration, but in a civilized world we cannot
follow our rude natures. Perhaps you would like a pup
from the next litter."

After a moment, Rothgar added, "I make that offer
only to people I believe know how to value a gift."

Ash snapped his guards in place. "You cannot know
me well enough to judge."

"I have observed you. Having—I apologize for the unfairness—over ten years advantage on you, I have witnessed many stages."

"So you baited your hook, and I took it." Damnation. He was being pushed into leaving.

Rothgar's brows rose. "I sent an invitation. I didn't think you would come."

"I wouldn't have except for Genova, and the great-aunts." Ash launched a dart. "You could have visited them anytime during the past thirty years."

"I confess, I never thought of it. Given their fond memories, I'm slain with remorse."

"Not apparently."

"Perhaps I'm a walking corpse. How would you know?"

"I could stab you to see if you bleed."

"But how embarrassing if I did." Rothgar picked up a crystal dish from a nearby table and offered it. "Apricot crisp?"

Bemused, Ash picked one up and nibbled. "Very tasty."

"And I haven't had any since I was a child. You see how the disagreements between our families harm us all. You can have more if you stay. Having breached the portals it would be a shame, don't you think, to leave with treats as yet untasted?"

Ash felt as if he was being entangled in gilded whimsy. "What if I'm here to seek out your weaknesses and use them against you?"

"Like Loki?"

Ash started at the apt reference to the Norse god of discord and destruction.

Rothgar spread his hands in apparent invitation. "Please, tell me first. I will follow the Bible and pluck them out. That excepts, of course, my family, especially my wife."

At last, the blade. "My grandmother thought Lady Arradale would be an ideal wife for me."

"The Dowager Marchioness of Ashart, as always, was wrong, but at least her taste is excellent. You should not let her ride and spur you, you know."

"I'm her only surviving descendant."

"She has grandchildren in Scotland and a daughter in a French convent. And of course," Rothgar added, "she has me."

This surprised a laugh, which Ash instantly regretted. He took a step back, a physical disengagement. "I'm welcome to stay?"

"You were invited, Cousin, but an invitation was never necessary. My relatives are always welcome in my homes."

"Perhaps I should encourage our grandmother to come here, too."

Ash expected at least a twitch of resistance, but Rothgar appeared completely unperturbed. "I would be charmed if you could arrange it."

Thwarted, Ash turned and went up to his room. Rothgar had revealed nothing when he'd seen the baby and Miss Smith, nor when Ash had tossed a hint of the threat he held at his throat. It was frustrating, but exhilarating. He hadn't known until now how he'd hungered to bring the contest into the open.

He had been raised to see the Mallorens as his enemy, as a cunning evil to be destroyed. In his grandmother's eyes they were not only the cause of her daughter's death, but of her husband's, and possibly of two sons. She'd blame Aunt Harriet's death from smallpox on them if she could.

It had burgeoned out of all reason, but suggestion of softening threw his grandmother into a tempest of rage and hurt, and certainly Rothgar was no long-suffering saint.

Could his apparent moves toward peace be trusted? The proof of that could be his willingness to clear away Molly's mess, but that alone would require negotiations as complex and delicate as the Peace of Paris.

Which, as John Wilkes had remarked, "is like the Peace of God. It passeth all understanding."

Bryght Malloren came out of the Tapestry Room to find his brother in an unusual state of contemplation. "He escaped unharmed?"

"Of course." Rothgar led away from the hall to his office. Once the door shut, he asked, "Why do you think he came?"

"A chance meeting with his great-aunts?"

"If I'd known he merely needed an excuse, I would have provided one years ago. No, there's been a change of some sort. The question is, how do we use it to reform him?"

"Struth, you plan to turn him virtuous?"

"I have little interest in his virtue. I plan to turn him into a proper cousin."

"Bey, some family rifts cannot be healed."

"With a Malloren, are not all things possible?"

"No," Bryght said bluntly.

Rothgar smiled and shrugged. "Perhaps, but this is worth an attempt. So, what do we have that can hold him?"

"Whatever reason brought him here. What was all that about truth?"

"Interesting, wasn't it? I suspect he holds some evidence that he believes could be a mistletoe branch."

"Don't you mean an olive branch?"

Rothgar shook his head. "I did try to have you educated well. Balder, Norse god of light, was impervious to all weapons except those made of mistletoe. When Loki, god of discord, discovered his weakness, he used it to kill him."

Bryght's hand twitched to where a sword might be. "You think Loki comes bearing weapons that could slay you? What?"

"An interesting question."

"Bey!"

Rothgar smiled at him. "I merely seek to spare you anxiety. He will not succeed."

"Ashart's a ne'er-do-well in some ways, but he doesn't make idle threats."

"I should hope not. Since I have no desire to destroy him, we shall have to convince him to love us."

"For Zeus's sake!"

"What do you think of Miss Smith?"

Bryght frowned at the switch of topic. "You think she's Ashart's ally?"

"If so, she acts the opponent well. I thought it a most interesting exchange. Shall I play Cupid?"

"Ashart and a paid companion?"

"She's the daughter, apparently, of a naval officer."

"Even so."

Rothgar tut-tutted. "You in particular should know that the right wife is more valuable than rubies, that personal qualities matter more than aristocratic bloodlines and a large dowry."

"Says he who married a peeress who owns a large bite of the north of England."

"You think that was an *easy* choice? Next year, by the way, we Christmas in Yorkshire."

Bryght shuddered. "In that case, my family will celebrate the season in our own, southern home."

"As you will. According to Lady Thalia, Ashart and Miss Smith are already betrothed."

Bryght stared. "She is somewhat dotty."

"I suspect she's as dotty as she cares to be, but it's true that they don't seem besotted. It has, however, provided Ashart with an excuse to stay. Is that its sole purpose? Another mystery to amuse us over the holidays. Delightful, wouldn't you say?"

Instead, Bryght Malloren said something rude.

Chapter Seventeen

*W*hen Genova and Thalia reached their room, the old lady sat rather heavily. Regeanne rushed to put a footstool under her feet and fuss.

"Are you all right?" Genova asked.

Thalia sighed. "In prime twig for my age, dear, and delighted with the company. Dear Beowulf. I gave him the apricot crisps and he was touched that I remembered."

Yes, he probably had been. He seemed honestly warm to his family, but the Dark Marquess was still there. It had been he who'd crossed swords with Ashart, and she couldn't forget that he had killed.

"Thalia, do you know what Rothgar and Ashart were talking about down there? About truth, and explosives?"

"Oh, no, dear. How could I? It's a very shifty sort of thing, though, truth."

"Explosives aren't. Look at Guy Fawkes."

"But he was stopped, dear, so that was all right. You mustn't worry about these matters. Men sort them out for themselves. Now, I'm going early to bed, but you must rejoin the company and enjoy yourself."

"I couldn't—"

"Now, now, this matter of you being a companion is mostly fiction. You're here to have pleasure and," Thalia added with a romantic smile, "you will want to spend more time with dear Ashart."

Dear Ashart, my foot! "I'm tired, too, Thalia. It's been a long day, and I didn't sleep well last night."

Thalia pouted. "Oh, very well, but I will not have you hiding away! Or hovering over Callie and me."

"I won't." Genova meant that. She'd pay guineas for moments alone.

"What is that lovely box, dear?"

Genova turned to look. "It holds my *presepe*. That's an Italian Nativity scene—the stable and figures. My family always set it up for Christmas wherever we were."

We. An entity that was gone forever.

"Then you must set it up here, dear!"

Genova smiled at the dear lady. "I admit, I had hoped to."

Despite her former claim of tiredness, Thalia bounced out of her chair and over to the box. "Excellent. I long to see it!"

She waited, eager as a child, as Genova turned the key and raised the lid. As always, Thalia's open pleasure was contagious and drove away lingering concerns.

Genova took out the folded cloth on top and opened it. "My mother called this the flowers-in-the-snow. It was very grand once, but it's sadly shabby now."

She used Hester's word deliberately. Sometimes wounds needed to be opened for them to heal. "I have a new one, the one I've been embroidering."

She smoothed the new cloth on a small, square table. She'd managed to set the last stitches today without her frame, including the ones necessary to hide the damage done that morning in the fight with Ashart.

That fight.

That kiss·. . .

"Oh, I see now what you were doing." Thalia compared the two cloths, then touched the old one. "Well-worn, but it was lovely work once."

A knot inside Genova loosened. She folded the old cloth gently and put it aside, then took out the first rag-wrapped bundles and began to undo them. "These are the pieces of the stable. I must set this up first."

"What fun!"

Thalia took over the unwrapping, watching as Genova slotted together the pieces of wood. Genova set it up on the cloth on the table, but then she looked at the fireplace.

"We've always put it on a mantelpiece when possible," she said.

"Then you must here, too!"

Thalia moved the gilt, lyre-form clock to the end of the mantelpiece, and Genova spread the cloth in the center. Her work was not as fine as the original, but the gold shone in the candlelight, and the flowers bloomed afresh. Then she set the assembled stable in the center.

Regeanne returned with a restoring tisane. With cries of alarm and scowls at Genova, she tried to get Thalia back into her chair. Thalia took the tisane but brushed the rest aside.

"See, Regeanne. We are going to set up a Nativity scene. A *presepe*, Genova calls it."

"Une crèche." Regeanne nodded, mellowing a little. "It will be very nice to have. If you do not need me, milady, may I visit the nurseries to see how the *petit ange* goes on?"

Thalia gave her blessing, and Regeanne left. Thalia returned to the box, clearly longing to discover it all. She reminded Genova of her own excitement as a child, bringing a smile and some of the old magic.

"Yes, we can add some of the figures. You unwrap, and I'll put them in place."

Thalia set to. "Oh, an ox! How very well made. And a sheep and lamb. How lovely!" She exclaimed with delight at each discovery, banishing every taint and shadow.

"What's that song, dear? A carol?"

Genova realized she'd been humming the song she and her parents had always sung as they set up the

presepe. She hesitated because she didn't have a strong
voice, but then began to sing.

> *In the stable, in the wild,*
> *Came the mother, Mary mild.*
> *Came the star as bright as day,*
> *Came the angels, lutes to play.*
> *Lutes to play, joy a-ringing,*
> *At the sound of angels singing.*
> *Joy, joy, joy, joy. . . .*

She smiled at Thalia. "It's a round that works well
with three voices."

"Teach it to me."

Genova had never heard Thalia sing before, but she
had a sweet if thin voice. She soon learned the song and
they wove their voices together as they put in more
animals. Genova and her father had sung it with just two
voices last year, missing the third voice, her mother's. . . .

Thalia stopped singing and took her hand. "My
poor dear. Sad memories?"

Genova couldn't deny it. Tears were blurring her
vision. "Just two Christmases ago, we were all together. Now everything is changed."

She managed not to say that she was alone, which
might offend, but that's how she felt. Thalia was a
dear, but she wasn't family. Genova's only real family
was her father, and he wasn't hers anymore now that
he'd remarried.

Thalia patted her hand. "There, there, dear. We all
miss a mother's love, but soon you'll be a mother
yourself. That will fill the void, and Ashart needs
that, too."

Create a child with Lord Ashart? Horror collided
with something else.

Thalia opened the locket that she always wore
pinned to her gown. "I understand loss, dear."

Genova looked at the miniature of a gentleman in
the age of the long, full wig. He was upside-down to

her, but he would be right side up to Thalia whenever she opened it. Thalia's Richard looked young and merry. Genova had known a number of young, merry men who were now dead.

"I'm very sorry, Thalia."

"It's long ago now, dear, and Richard did so enjoy going to war. He idolized the Duke of Marlborough. Such a splendid man he was. Marlborough, I mean, though Richard would have been, too, had he lived. Twenty-six," she sighed. "At the very beginning of life. The same age as Ashart."

Genova hadn't known the marquess's age, and would have thought him a little older. The price of a wicked life.

Thalia looked at the picture again, then snapped the locket closed. "You probably both feel old enough to be past folly, but you're not. You have your lives before you. Please don't take the wrong path."

Genova guessed what Thalia meant and distracted her with more figures. What would Thalia do to promote her scheme, though? Genova told herself she couldn't be trapped. All she needed to escape was open disagreements, and judging from their exchange downstairs, that would be easy.

Soon the *presepe* was at the stage her family had always created on December 13—an ordinary, ramshackle stable with farmyard animals in and around. At the far end of the mantelpiece, Joseph and Mary-on-the-donkey were on their way to Bethlehem.

That had been another problem for Hester. The *presepe* had two Marys. One was the heavily pregnant figure on the donkey. The other was slender and formed to kneel by the manger. Genova had always loved that magical transformation on Christmas Eve, but Hester had pursed her lips and said that such an obviously *fruitful* Mother of God was not suitable for her grandchildren.

And Genova's father had not said a word.

Thalia, blessed Thalia, only said, "How hard it must have been to travel in that condition. I have always been thankful not to be a saint. So demanding."

Genova chuckled.

"There are still some figures to unwrap." Thalia was hovering near the box and Genova remembered how she, too, had always found it hard to ration out this treat. This time there was no need. Tomorrow was Christmas Eve.

"If you unwrap the rest," she said, "we can set them along the mantelpiece, waiting."

Thalia plunged in, and Genova took shepherds, angels, and extra animals, ready to talk of what this meant to her.

"My parents bought the *presepe* in Naples just before I was born. My father always says that if I'd been a little speedier, I might have been called Napolia."

"Genova is much prettier, dear."

"Perhaps that's why I waited. Then, when I was born, one of the sailors carved a little lamb to add to the Nativity scene. It started a tradition. Every year on Christmas Eve my father would add an animal."

Just in time, she managed not to say that it was a birthday gift. The last thing she needed was the attention that might bring.

"Over time, they became stranger and stranger. How my mother laughed at the tiger! This one," Genova said, holding up the gaudy Chinese dragon, "was the last before my mother died. A Chinese dragon is supposed to bring good fortune. . . ."

Thalia patted her arm. "Your mother is happier in a higher place, dear, and watching over you."

Genova smiled, but she couldn't help wondering what Mary Smith thought. She pushed bitterness aside. She knew her mother would be delighted that her dear William had found new comfort.

Then all the animals were around the stable, and the shepherds, angels, and glorious kings stood ready at a distance. Thalia picked up the baby Jesus and moved to put him in the manger. Genova took the figure and tucked it out of sight behind the stable along with the Mother Mary figure, the slender one.

"Not until Christmas Eve," she said, remembering

her mother doing and saying the same thing to her. Act and reaction had become a ritual along with so many other steps of this tradition.

Thalia peered into the box, clearly hoping for one more treat, but then closed it. "All done." She stepped back and cocked her head. "It looks very well and is a delightful tradition. Now, dear, as you're going downstairs again, you must dress."

Genova had hoped she'd forgotten. "I'm *tired*, Thalia."

"Nonsense. Ashart will be missing you!"

Genova tried to argue, but then noticed that her friend did look worn yet seemed unable to rest with company around. This shared room was going to create many problems, but she could solve this one by leaving for a while.

As if to settle the matter, Regeanne returned and took Thalia's side. Genova allowed the two women to arrange her as if for a play. Regeanne went into the dressing room and returned with a blue *gros de Naples* gown.

It was three years old, but Mrs. Rimshaw, the Trayce ladies' mantua maker, had refurbished it quite magically with embroidery and seed pearls. It was open from the waist down to reveal a new petticoat of white figured silk.

Genova had four new shifts, as well, each with ruffles to show at the neckline and elbow. They were in addition to three entirely new gowns that were gifts from the Trayce ladies. Genova had protested, but they had insisted, saying that they were return for her kindness in agreeing to be their companion on this visit.

"The embroidered net ruffles tonight," said Thalia, picking a shift. "Nothing too grand for a family evening, dear. But your hair must be redressed in a more relaxed style."

Genova hadn't known that Regeanne was a truly skilled lady's maid until she went to work on her. Her hair was rearranged and paint delicately applied to her face.

Genova had never learned skill with maquillage, and she stared, impressed by the effect.

Regeanne smirked. "Me, I have not forgotten how to make a young lady look her best."

"No, you haven't. Thank you, Regeanne."

The maid inclined her head. "Some young ladies use the heavy paint. It is folly. The old use the paint to look like the young!"

"Twenty-two is not so young as that," said Genova, standing, "though perhaps I feel young at this moment." She put her hand on her stomach, which felt full of flutters. "What do I do?"

"Don't worry, dear. Good hosts take care of their guests, and I'm sure dear Beowulf and Diana are excellent hosts. And Ashart will take especial care of you."

"Oh, Thalia . . ." Genova hated to live this lie.

"Now, now, dear, I doubt he'll feel it a burden, and you cannot tell me you didn't enjoy exchanging words with him! Your eyes sparkled, and your color was pretty without use of the rouge pot."

Genova didn't know what to say but tried to prepare Thalia for the future. "I do worry about our different stations in life. I'm not the sort to be a grand lady."

"Oh, fie! Love doesn't count such things. Beowulf and Diana seem quite as devoted as I would wish, and I want no less for Ashart."

"Lady Arradale is rich and noble."

"Which has nothing to do with it, dear."

Genova slipped the ribbon of her fan onto her wrist. "You never call Ashart by his Christian name."

Thalia pulled a face. "The dowager is quite ferocious about formality. She threatened not to let me see him if I called him Charles. Now, it doesn't feel right."

"Charles," Genova echoed.

"The Trayce family has a tradition of using only Stuart names. No Hanoverian Georges or Fredericks among us. Thank heavens no one thought to put action to the thought and support the Jacobite risings. We were all in a quake at the time, I assure you! The Stuarts have always had a fatal charm. There is a rumor that Sophia's father was Charles II. She does have the look, and Ashart has it, too."

Sophia was the dowager Lady Ashart, Thalia's sister-in-law.

"Royal blood?" Genova gasped.

"But safely on the wrong side of the blanket. Off you go and enjoy yourself, but behave! You can marry as soon as you wish, so there's no need for impatience. Are you sure you want banns, dear . . . ?"

Regeanne was draping Genova's merino shawl around her shoulders. Genova gathered it and escaped before Thalia pinned her down to day and minute.

Chapter Eighteen

*A*s Genova shut the door behind her, shivering slightly in the cooler air, she realized that no footman waited. Perhaps she hadn't been expected to return downstairs, or perhaps she should have rung for service. Whatever the cause, her reaction was delight.

She looked up and down the corridor. The coast was clear. She had freedom, which as Lord Rothgar had pointed out, was beyond price. Before it could be snatched away, she hurried off in the opposite direction to the main staircase.

Perhaps it was scandalously impolite to wander a house in which she was a guest, but she wouldn't enter any rooms. She just wanted some peace and quiet in which to think.

She turned into another corridor where dim light suggested lack of current use. The light came from occasional candles well guarded with glass that provided only enough illumination to prevent accidents.

As a result, Genova felt she progressed into a mystery, but one blessed with solitude. And not only solitude but the opportunity for exercise! Even in Tunbridge Wells, constrained by Hester's ideas of what was suitable, she had managed walks to shops, church, and the lending library. In the past few days her only walks had been from vehicle to inn.

She followed whatever turn took her fancy, setting a brisk pace and swinging her arms until she'd shaken the misery from her bones. Probably much of her blue-deviled mood had been simply need for this.

Heart beating, skin tingling, she paused to stretch,

reaching out on either side to walls still far away, then up, up, to the shadowy ceiling. Then she carried on, regretting that tomorrow guests would pour in, filling the house.

She stopped. What an ingrate she was. She'd thrilled to the idea of a grand house party but now wanted to be alone. She'd been desperate to escape Hester's house, but now she almost wished she were back there, where the trials were familiar. She continued her walk, pondering this.

As she'd left childhood, she'd grown weary of the hardships of navy life. Even the best ships stank down below, where—if you were lucky—poor animals were confined to provide milk and meat for the voyage. Transporting cavalry horses was even worse.

On a long voyage food was often limited, and sometimes barely edible. Knocking weevils out of biscuits and scraping mold off cheese were everyday matters.

Weevils. She directed a baleful thought at Ashart, wherever he was.

In fine weather the sea could be beautiful, but in foul, it was hell. Then, no part of the ship could be completely dry, and those not needed to fight the storm huddled in misery in places awash with sloshing seawater and worse.

Life ashore had been a delight by comparison. With the thoughtless selfishness of youth, she'd sometimes prayed for battles, because then she and her mother were left in the nearest port. Often she'd wished for a permanent home back in England, and fate had given it to her. When her mother died, her father had retired, and they'd settled in a pleasant house overlooking Portsmouth.

Had she been happy?

No, but how could she be with her father so miserable? He'd seemed to need her company, perhaps as substitute for that of his Mary, but hadn't welcomed guests. She'd made some friends, but had little opportunity to spend time with them.

Then Hester Poole, the widowed sister of a fellow officer, had come into their lives. Her father had found joy again. The move to Tunbridge Wells had not appeared to be a problem, since Genova hadn't set down deep roots in Portsmouth.

Now, within months, she'd seized this chance to escape, and the thought of returning there filled her with panic. It wasn't just that she found her new home oppressive; she feared what she would do. A screaming match with Hester would break her father's heart. Her suppressed unhappiness was already wounding it.

After the distressing confrontation over the *presepe*, her father had helped her pack it away, trying to make light of the problem. As they'd closed the box, he'd said, "We always made a *presepe* wish, didn't we?"

Past tense. Past tense.

She'd pointed out that they did that on Christmas Eve, but he hadn't seemed to care. "This is my wish for you, Genni-love. A fine husband and a babe in your arms by next Christmas. Then you'll have your own home in which to set up the *presepe*, and a child to share it with."

She'd smiled to cover pain, because the wish was as much for him as for her. He did love her and want the best for her, but he wanted peace in his new nest, too. This journey had been her escape, but after just three days in a coach with the Trayce ladies, she fretted for solitude.

She realized she'd come to a halt and hurried on again. Was she impossible to please? Was she one of those people who could never be content, no matter where they were? Surely not. She'd been blessed with much happiness and knew how to appreciate it.

She was simply upset by today's events, but they would set a saint on edge. As a result, she was in no state to think clearly about anything. What she needed was a good night's sleep. With luck, Thalia would be tucked up and snoring by now.

She turned to retrace her steps, but realized she had no sense of where she was. Which way? How embarrassing to become the first truly lost guest.

She picked a direction, trying to steer a straight line

through random corridors, then turned a corner and saw light. It was cool and pale, so must be moonlight through a window. She headed for it, sure she could get her bearings from a look outside. She could even, she thought with amusement, navigate by the stars.

The light spilled through an archway, not a window, an archway into a long room moonlit by a wall of tall windows. She walked in and turned, not surprised to see ranks of pictures. This was the Malloren portrait gallery.

The wash of light turned the ancestral faces a ghostly gray, which seemed disturbingly appropriate, as if any of them might step out of a frame to haunt her. Facing her, however, was a portrait of someone very much alive—the current marquess.

He stood in formal dress, haughty and austere, young but very much the magnate. He seemed unoffended by her invasion, but his direct gaze was so perceptive that she shivered. She looked away—and saw another marquess.

Lord Ashart lounged on a window seat, long legs stretched before him, hands in the pockets of his breeches. He was studying her in a manner chillingly like that of his cousin.

Disregarding courtesy, he did not rise. "Is this a damsel which I see before me?" he said, misquoting Shakespeare. "Come, let me clutch thee."

She hesitated, as much from sizzling response as from fear. She was in no state for another encounter, but pride would not let her turn and run away.

She replied from the same speech of Macbeth's. "Perhaps I am but a damsel of the mind, my lord."

"The worst sort. What are you doing here, Miss Smith?"

"If marquesses may wander in the night, may not we lowly commoners do the same?"

"Ah, you're fleeing Mallorens, too, are you? Then flee this room. It's full of them."

"In fact, my lord, I'm fleeing Trayces."

"Still a mistake. You've found me. And"—he gestured lazily—"my infamous aunt."

Genova couldn't resist. She walked closer to him until she could turn and study the picture on the opposite wall.

She shivered at a truly ghostly effect—the features floated into nothing. Then she realized it was a sketch for a portrait either hung elsewhere or never completed. The picture showed head and shoulders of a girl in Grecian costume, arms bare, holding a lyre, her dark hair tumbling around her laughing face.

"She doesn't look mad," Genova said.

"But madness is mad itself, and can come and go."

"Do you truly think her husband drove her mad?"

He gestured to a portrait beside the sketch. "There he is."

Genova studied a formal portrait of a powdered-haired man with a mild, amiable face. Beyond that was one of a lady who looked both lovely and sweet-natured. There was a matched kindness and poise that made Lady Augusta seem wild.

"Portraits can lie," she said.

"But generally to conceal fat and warts, not soul."

"I've seen the one of you the Trayce ladies have."

"Ah, that. I remember being deadly bored. But that is the condition of man, is it not? Inconstancy, anxiety, and boredom."

She turned to study him. "Are you drunk, my lord?"

His heavy-lidded eyes could give a deceptively sleepy appearance. "Don't people say, 'drunk as a lord'? It's clearly my duty to be drunk, and of course, noblesse obliges. May I oblige you?"

Genova sighed audibly to cover a shiver of foolish temptation. His proposition gave her an excuse to leave, however, pride intact.

Before she could move he said, "Come, sit with me, Miss Smith. I promise not to offend, and we should plan our strategic disengagement."

Willpower can stretch only so far before it breaks. Genova joined him on the seat, but left enough space between them for one or two imaginary chaperones. They were necessary. Moonlight flowed down his virile body, making him seem half light, half dark, and breathtaking.

"Strategy, my lord? We seem to have no difficulty in finding disputes."

"True, peace might be more difficult, but perhaps we should try it. We need to be besotted for a day or two to lend credence to our commitment."

Genova's skin tingled with anticipation and alarm. "Why?"

"Come now, you're not dull-witted. If Tess Brokesby is tattling, guests will arrive tomorrow pregnant with gossip and watching our every look. If we are already at sword's point, the betrothal will look spurious, or at least forced. If they witness a day or two of devotion, you'll emerge as victim of my callousness."

"I don't care to be seen as any sort of victim!"

A smile moved the corner of his lips. "Then I'm sure we can portray it as a triumph of virtue over vice."

Not if you smile at me like that.

Genova flicked open her fan to provide a shield. "Very well, my lord. I will try to pretend devotion for a day or two, but the dramatically enjoyable separation will be my reward."

That smile deepened. "Can I interest you in a dramatically enjoyable joining first?"

Parts of her trembled, but Genova was not such a fool as that. "If you seduce me, my lord, I will not release you from this engagement."

That wiped the smile away. "A worthy opponent. So be it. When shall we two part again? Not, at least, until after Christmas. We don't want discord to disturb the season of joy and peace."

She studied him, cursing the uncertain light. "Don't we? I assumed you were here to do precisely that."

"Why?"

The air suddenly felt colder. She should brush past the subject, but for survival's sake she needed to know what was going on. "Truth," she said.

"Ah, yes. I am Loki at this feast."

"Loki?"

"The Norse god of discord."

"Talk sense, my lord! What do you plan?"

"It's no concern of yours."

He was right, but it wasn't in Genova's nature to back away from a just cause. "If it threatens your great-aunts, it is. I won't let you hurt them."

"You may trust me with their welfare, Miss Smith."

She wanted to protest, but she recognized one of those lines a sensible person did not cross.

"You look," he said, "as if you are biting your tongue."

A touch of wry humor gave her courage to persist. "Are you really planning havoc, my lord, because of a tragedy nearly forty years old?"

"Ah, don't, *pandolcetta*. Don't meddle there."

The sobriety of the warning raised the hairs on her neck.

Chapter Nineteen

"*W*e have more interesting conflicts," he said with false lightness. "We must bill and coo."

Genova wanted to resist his warning and his deflection, but her courage failed her. She preferred to think of her cowardice as sensible caution.

"Only in public," she said.

"I don't remember that proviso."

She looked at him over her fan. "Why would you want to bill and coo in private, my lord? We are nothing to each other."

The smile was back, the wicked one that threatened impossible, mouthwatering delights. "I wouldn't say that."

"About the Mallorens . . ." She raised it deliberately as defense.

"About our attraction."

"Our *pretended* attraction."

"Our passion."

"Our problem."

"Our love."

"Our war," she retorted.

He laughed. "Very well, I will stage *amor*, and you will stage war, though I warn you, I lack experience in my role."

She raised her brows in disbelief, and he said, "We'd need another word."

"You won't shock me, my lord. I know them all."

"How interesting."

She recognized that her retort, though true, had been unwise. It had given him a wrong impression.

But at least he wouldn't presume that he was dealing with a naive miss.

"So, let us plan war," she said, "since that is unambiguous."

"Is it? You will need provocation. Shall I let you find me in another woman's bed?"

"It would give me cause," she agreed, hating the thought. "But wouldn't you end up at the altar?"

"Not if the lady was married."

She was caught unawares by that. "Then at sword's point with her husband? I'll have no blood spilled over this, my lord. I must have your word on that."

"Must," he echoed. "You have a too commanding disposition, Miss Smith."

"You're probably correct, but I mean what I say. I will not be a cause of bloodshed. You *must* avoid that."

He sighed and held out a hand. "Come here."

Her heart thumped. "Why?"

"To pay your forfeit."

"I agreed to no forfeit."

"Even so."

She licked her lips, knowing she should ignore him, should rise and walk away, but it was as if she was snared—by the exhilaration of the fight, by the razor-edge of danger, by him. She knew she'd taunted him, hoping for something like this.

"You cannot force this, my lord."

"No?"

"Very well, you *will* not. It would be the action of a knave."

He was watching her in a way that would send a sensible woman screaming into the night. "I grant you a counterforfeit, then."

"What?"

"You may choose something for which I must pay a forfeit in turn."

"You *are* drunk."

At last she stood, but too late. He caught her wrist and tugged her back down, closer on the seat. She tried to pull free, but he tightened his grip. She didn't fight very hard. Her blood was singing in mad delight.

"You're cold," he said, sounding surprised.

Of course the man who'd voluntarily ridden outside all day did not feel the cold like a normal person. He let her go and clasped her hands in wonderfully warm ones, gently massaging them. She suppressed a groan at the pleasure of it.

"Come, Genova," he murmured, "I propose a game, no more. Christmas is time for games, and it will help us play our parts."

"Your game seems more like a challenge to me." But she was melting so much under his warm touch that she was surprised she wasn't sliding off the seat into a puddle.

"An easy challenge." He raised her hands to blow first into one palm, then into the other. "To avoid penalty, you have only to avoid giving me orders. And, of course, you have only to command me if you want a kiss."

The confident glint in his eyes should have given her strength to resist, but instead it made her want this game more. "What if I make your forfeit for you kissing me?"

"Somewhat circular, but why not? What shall I pay? More kisses? A circle of delights. No, a spiral, like a whirlpool . . ."

Alarmed by that image, she pulled free. "Guineas."

He stared, all humor wiped away. "I did not think you mercenary."

She put distance and cool air between them. "I see no reason why I shouldn't be, but as it happens, the guineas won't be for me, but for the baby."

She saw him react with sharp impatience, and her shiver was not of pleasure this time.

She raised her chin. "I may not be able to force you to admit your responsibility and provide for Charlie, my lord, but now I can compel you to provide the funds. Anytime I *must*."

After a moment he laughed. "Very well, my Amazon. A guinea a kiss. How many guineas, I wonder, are needed to support a child for life? A hundred? A thousand?" His voice mellowed into a seductive purr. "In how many days?"

Her mouth and throat dried.

No wonder he'd laughed.

"We have an agreement, Miss Smith?"

Kisses were only kisses. It rang hollow in her mind, but she would not, could not, back down. This would all be under her control.

She stirred moisture in her mouth and swallowed. "Yes, my lord."

He captured her hand again, sliding closer. "Then come let us start our account."

Every scrap of sense screamed a warning, but the rest of Genova sank willingly into the whirlpool so that his last word was murmured against her lips and sealed them. Need for this had been building since their morning kiss, had been mounting to fiery heat during their debate, and was crowned by his mastery now.

His hands, clever hands, traveled over her, and hers were doing the same. She slid one beneath his jacket, savoring the hot, hard lines of ribs and hip and spine. Another cradled his head, holding him close, as if he might try to escape before she'd had her fill.

It had been so long, too long, since she'd kissed a man like this.

She'd never kissed a man like this.

Never a man like this . . .

His mouth was hot and skilled, with a taste still new, but remembered from the morning and already delicious. It stirred fires in her she'd never imagined. Soon her whole body burned for him, rubbed against him as if layers of clothing could melt away and bring them, as she scandalously longed to be, skin to searing skin. . . .

It was he who broke the kiss, he who put space between them.

For pride's sake, Genova stopped herself from pursuing. At least he looked as wild as she felt, eyes dark, breaths deep. His disordered coat, hair, and cravat were, she knew, entirely her work.

She had to say something, something that would cover the way she felt. "I think that's more than a guinea's worth, my lord."

"What's the price for a night, then?"

After a devastated moment, she slapped him.

She surged to her feet to run, but he caught her to him. "I apologize. I apologize! I didn't mean it like that." Then he laughed. "Yes, I did, but I meant no slur. Lord," he groaned, "I can't even make sense."

She pushed and he let her go. She gathered herself as best she could. "I accept the apology, my lord. I think we were both a little carried away."

"A little . . ."

She had to conceal how strongly she'd been affected. If he knew, he'd pursue and she'd drown in the flames. Could one drown in flames . . . ?

"There must be no more of this," she said, proud of her flat voice.

"Must," he repeated softly.

She put out a hand to hold him off, though he hadn't made a move.

"Yet we must act the lovers for a day or two, Genova."

"Not like that!"

"No, alas. Not like that."

She was braced for attack and afraid she would succumb, but he turned and picked up something from the window seat. It was the pins and combs that had held her hair in place. She put up a hand and found it in wild disorder. It was thick and heavy and must look a tawdry mess.

She gathered it with shaking hands into a tight knot and took a proffered pin to skewer it in place. Then another, and another, reassembling Genova Smith, woman of sense. The combs were decorative, and she thrust them in last. Her hair could look nothing like

Regeanne's skillful arrangement, but it would look vaguely as she was used to wearing it.

He was watching her, his face shadowed, for his back was to the light. Could he hear her pounding heart? Could he smell her perfume as she smelled a spicy, subtle scent from him?

She tried to hold him off with words. "Remember, my lord, if you seduce me, I will hold you to the betrothal."

After a moment, he nodded. "Then be strong for both of us, Genova Smith, for we will be dancing very close to the flames."

He picked up her shawl, clearly intending to wrap it around her, but she grabbed it and backed toward the arch. "There's no need to escort me, my lord."

He stayed where he was, all cool, disordered, desirable elegance in the moonlight. "Perhaps I was hoping you knew the way back."

"Back to where?"

"Ah, an interesting question. For we're not where we were when you entered this room, are we?"

Breath caught by that, Genova turned and walked out of the gallery.

Ash watched the place where he'd last glimpsed Genova Smith, his body still hot with desire for her, with dangerous, irrational physical need.

The woman was magnificent, but terrifying. She seemed to accept no boundaries, and he did not want her hurt by whatever happened here. He wanted her, but that way would lead to a disastrous marriage. She was not the bride he needed.

He remembered his coarse, appalling words and groaned. When had he last said anything so clumsy?

Perhaps never.

Why? Why had those words escaped?

Because he'd been thinking them. Thinking them in his mind, in his blood, in his throbbing cock. Hades! She could inflame him like spark to tinder. He pushed his hands against his temples. Once was enough. No other woman was going to rip his life apart with rich curves and wicked, knowing eyes.

His fingers touched his hair and he realized the destruction the woman had wrought. He pulled the loosened ribbon free, memory rippling through him. If Genova Smith had been insinuated into the great-aunts' household with this in mind, Rothgar had chosen his weapon well.

He walked to confront his cousin's austere portrait. "My bane, as always," he said under his breath. "Are you behind Molly's plot? Is Genova Smith your tool? This time you won't win, not even with a siren on your side."

A siren that didn't sing but argued.

Havoc.

A good word. The ancient battle cry that swept away all rules of war and set free rape, slaughter, and destruction. "Cry havoc and let loose the dogs of war."

Dogs. A Persian gazelle hound that had been trained not to go after the quarry it had been bred to kill.

There hadn't been a single word between him and Rothgar without meaning.

"You should not let her ride and spur you."

Ash cursed at the portrait and strode out of the room.

Genova entered her bedchamber quietly. Three candles and firelight made it welcoming, but the bed-curtains were open and the bed was empty. For a moment her overwrought nerves threw up wild scenarios of murder or kidnapping.

By the next breath she knew what had happened. Thalia had rested a little, then realized that a game of whist was possible and that had been enough.

Regeanne helped Genova out of her gown, hoops, and stays, but then Genova said she would do the rest herself. She wasn't used to a lady's maid.

She washed and put on her nightgown, which was warm from hanging before the fire. The bed would be cozy, too, for the handles of two warming pans stuck out of the covers. She moved one over to Thalia's side, drew the heavy curtains all around, then settled into the haven.

Warmth, however, did not soothe unwelcome heat.

Was it truly unwelcome?

How was it even possible that she feel this way? She and the marquess were strangers in every way.

She might as well protest that rock cannot burn. She'd seen lava flow, as hot and molten as the desire that had erupted between her a stranger on a moonlit window seat.

Chapter Twenty

*S*leep came slowly, so that exhaustion caused Genova to wake later than usual. When she emerged from the bed in the morning, the fire was well established and the room warm. The gilded clock said nearly nine, but Thalia was still asleep, each breath a soft whistle, her frilly bed cap over one eye.

With a smile, Genova quietly redrew the bedcurtains, then added another piece of wood to the fire. She tenderly rearranged some of the figures in the *presepe*. It was Christmas Eve—both her birthday and the beginning of her favorite season. She wouldn't let other events steal that from her.

Here, at last, she would experience a true English Christmas.

On ships and in ports around the world, English people tried to re-create Christmas, but it was never quite right. Hot climates did not suit the food, and the mounding snow of Canada or the Baltic seemed too lush. Last Christmas had been shadowed by grief.

Traveling here, she'd realized the truth. An English Christmas needed cold but a starker setting and the afternoon death of the light.

She went to the window and looked through frost feathers at the right sort of setting. The frosted grass of the park became in the distance black fields streaked with white. Old trees made crooked skeletons against a steely sky.

In this setting rich foods and evergreens would be carols of hope, and the Yule log would promise the return of long sunny days.

Contrasts and necessities. Winter darkness could make fire precious. Starvation made a dry crust taste like *pandolce*.

Pandolcetta mia . . .

Her stomach rumbled.

Genova laughed, glad that her wanton body still paid attention to honest hungers.

So, clothes. If Christmas traditions were followed here, today was for gathering greenery to bring into the house. Warm clothes, then.

Genova tapped on the closet door, then opened it, but Regeanne wasn't there. She could dress herself in her simplest gowns and did so. She chose a plain closed dress of fawn-colored wool, adding warm woolen stockings and an extra flannel petticoat.

She gathered her hair into a simple knot, pushing aside the memory of last night, of Ashart holding pins in his beautiful hand. Of the touch of that hand . . .

Perish the man!

She fixed the knot, then pinned a small cap on top, thrusting one pin so hard she pricked herself. Tears threatened, and they weren't from the pain.

Her stomach rumbled again. Hunger explained her weakness. How did she obtain breakfast in this house?

She eyed the bellpull, but she wasn't familiar with that modern convenience. Besides, if she ordered breakfast here, she'd wake Thalia. She was reluctant to venture out into the strange house, but food must be available somewhere, and she would not be a timid mouse.

She wrapped her warm everyday shawl around her shoulders and left the room. If she didn't find breakfast, she'd seek out the kitchens. She was close to a servant, after all, and bread and cheese would do.

She turned left. To her delight she remembered the way and soon arrived at the main staircase. The house seemed quiet, but she thought she could smell food somewhere and hear faint voices and rattles.

She went downstairs, fighting the feeling of being an intruder, wincing when her skirts brushed the banisters and stirred the tiny bells. She couldn't help thinking of a cat being belled to stop it from pouncing on unwary birds.

At the bottom she looked around and noticed a powdered, liveried footman outside a door. He bowed. "Breakfast is served in here, mistress."

She walked toward him, noticing that he wore gloves and a thick, quilted waistcoat. Lord Rothgar was a considerate master.

The footman opened the door at just the right moment so she could enter without much warm air escaping. A modest table was laid, and one man sat there, cup in hand, reading a magazine. The Marquess of Rothgar.

Groaning at her faux pas, Genova made to retreat, but he rose, smiling. "Miss Smith. Another early riser. Join me, please."

Genova curtsied. "I'm sorry if I intrude, my lord."

"The table is laid for a reason, and I prefer conversation, if it is available, to reading at breakfast. Of course," he added, holding out the chair next to him in invitation, "if you cannot bear the thought, I shall have some reading matter brought for you."

Genova sat, both unnerved and flattered. It was simple courtesy, of course, an obligation to make guests at ease, but she felt as if she was truly brightening his day.

He took his seat, ringing a golden bell by his plate. A footman appeared from the corner of the room as if by magic. Genova realized that there was a service entrance concealed by the paneling. There would be a serving pantry, and probably stairs from there to the kitchens. Beyond the magnificent scale of this house lay another world necessary for its functioning.

She requested eggs and chocolate. A platter of rolls already sat on the table, so she took one and buttered it.

Once the footman left, Rothgar said, "Tell me, Miss Smith, what is your opinion of Lady Booth Carew?"

Genova had expected polite talk about the weather, not this. "It is not my place. . . ."

"Come now, didn't you fight Barbary pirates? I'd think you could wield sharp-edged truth."

She could hardly refuse, and owed Lady Booth Carew no charity. "Very well, my lord, she seemed a thoughtless, selfish woman. Even so, I'm shocked that she abandoned her baby to strangers."

"Not all mothers are devoted, and of course, she may not have thought the child would end up with strangers."

Delicately put, but the inference was familiar. "Lord Ashart."

"Quite. He supports at least three bastards that I know of, but Lady Booth was optimistic if she thought he would support hers."

The footman returned then, saving Genova from an immediate response. So, Lord Rothgar kept himself informed about his cousin. Sadly, her mind was stumbling over the fact that Ashart was known to have bastards. Ridiculous to be shocked or offended. He was a libertine and a rake, and at least he did support them.

"What do you suppose Lady Booth thought would happen?" Rothgar asked, pouring chocolate for her.

Genova hadn't considered that question before, and sipped as she did so. "I think she's a very stupid woman."

"But not insane."

"I can only assume that she thought Lord Ashart would take care of the baby, and be embarrassed by that. Which suggests that she doesn't know him well at all."

"Or perhaps that she had some other plan. We will discover the truth eventually."

Wasn't there a saying about the mills of the gods grinding slowly but being impossible to evade?

"In the meantime," Rothgar said, "her baby and maid seem settled in the nurseries, and I've alerted the neighborhood for a Gaelic speaker. Have you celebrated Christmas in England before, Miss Smith?"

Some time later, Genova realized that she'd been skillfully drawn out to talk about her life. She remembered discussion of foreign parts, her hopes for the Christmas season, and even mention of her mother's death and her father's sickness and retirement. She didn't think she'd revealed her discomfort in her stepmother's house, but she couldn't be entirely sure.

The conversation broke when Lady Arradale came in, sat opposite Genova, and ordered coffee. Her smile seemed to indicate that nothing could make her day more perfect than to find Genova Smith sharing the breakfast table with her husband.

Talk turned to Christmas plans.

"Most of the guests will arrive by two," Lady Arradale told Genova, "which will allow us a couple of daylight hours to ravage the countryside. It adds to the pleasure to return to the house as darkness falls."

"It certainly makes the mulled wine and spiced ale welcome," Rothgar commented, "which leads to celebratory spirits."

"Quite." The countess thanked the footman for the coffee, then smiled at Genova. "I found Christmas in great disorder here, with evergreens brought into the house before Christmas Eve. Can you imagine!"

The marquess seemed merely amused. "I have previously held Christmas festivities a little earlier, Miss Smith. I now understand that I've been dicing with fate."

Lady Arradale frowned at him. "Everyone knows it brings bad luck."

"And yet, we have survived."

"By the skin of your teeth."

"Do teeth have skin?"

"Only when revoltingly unclean."

Lord Rothgar winced theatrically. "Not at the breakfast table, I pray, my love."

Lady Arradale laughed and apologized to Genova, who was pondering the strange question herself.

"I have imposed good order," the countess stated, "which means that Christmas will be celebrated at Christmas, and begin today."

"Thus demanding a mostly family gathering," Lord Rothgar explained. "Most people wish to spend Christmas in their own homes, so no one has been invited who is not connected to the family tree."

"I'm not." Genova instantly wished she could take the words back. She'd not been invited at all.

"But you are betrothed to my cousin."

She'd managed to forget that detail.

Lady Arradale poured herself more coffee. "I'm told Old Barnabas promises mild temperatures for the afternoon, and even some sunny skies."

"Old Barnabas," said Rothgar, "remembers when he's right and forgets when he's wrong."

Lady Arradale swatted his arm. "He will be right because I wish it so."

"Ah, in that case the sun will shine as in July."

A flicker of such sweet intimacy passed between them that Genova felt intrusive. She rose. "I must go and see if Lady Thalia is awake, and how Lady Calliope does."

Rothgar stood to assist her. "Thank you for your company, Miss Smith. And please, don't curtail your enjoyment to fret over my great-aunts. It is my honor and pleasure to provide them with all the attendants they require."

"But it's my reason for being here, my lord."

"Your reason for coming here, perhaps, but now you are one of my guests. Thus your raison d'être is to have pleasure, full to the brim and overflowing, so that I may be a contented host."

Feeling attacked, Genova said, "Whether I want to or not?"

Two pairs of surprised eyes studied her.

"We can probably find a dank cell and a hair shirt if you insist, Miss Smith."

"Don't tease, Bey. Miss Smith, you must do just as you wish. That is all we ask."

Mortified by her idiotic reaction, Genova dropped a curtsy and escaped.

"I was maladroit," said Rothgar in some surprise.

"With a Malloren all things are possible, even mistakes. But she is interestingly prickly, isn't she?"

He sat down and refilled their cups. "Especially for a lady recently betrothed to one of the most eligible men in England."

"Do you think that's true?"

"Oh, yes. The question is, is it real?"

"Why invent it?"

"To give him a reason to be here, perhaps. It would, however, serve us well to have Ashart bound to a sensible woman."

"Bound? That sounds unpleasant, Bey."

He took her hand and kissed it. "But it isn't, is it? It could distract him from more pointless pursuits."

"What pointless pursuits?"

"He believes that he has the means to harm me."

"What?"

"D'Eon, I think. The letters I had forged that appeared to be from the French king."

Her hand tightened on his. "How could he know about that?"

"Frailties and leaks. They can never be entirely prevented."

"But why? Does the animosity run as deep as that? If the king learns what you did, the consequences could be dire."

"Don't frown," he said, smoothing her brow. "We will woo him to family fondness and thus end all danger. But in the meantime, it suits us well to have him distracted."

"By Miss Smith? Bey, is that fair to her?"

"She might make him an excellent wife."

"A naval captain's daughter?"

"You're as high-nosed as Bryght. Naval warfare would be excellent training for any woman becoming granddaughter-in-law of the Dowager Lady Ashart."

Chapter Twenty-one

*F*eeling out of her depth, Genova escaped up to the nurseries, realizing by the time she arrived that the visit might be useful. She was entangled in things that could harm her. The more she understood, the better.

Ashart persisted in claiming that he was not Charlie's father. Rothgar said he supported some bastards. Sheena might know something that would help clarify matters. If Ashart was speaking the truth, it would make a difference.

The parlor was empty, but she followed noises and found the nursery dining room. Little Francis Malloren was eating some sort of gruel with the assistance of his nursemaid, and the two Misses Inchcliff were breakfasting on buttered bread and cups of chocolate.

Genova greeted them all, then asked for Sheena. She was directed to a room across the corridor, where she found the baby nursery. It was small so as to be easily kept warm, and the walls were whitewashed, while the floor was bare wood. A nursery had to be readily cleaned.

There were two small beds with tall, railed sides, and two ornate cradles, one hung with cream silk, the other with blue. The blue one was clearly in use, but the baby was on Sheena's lap, dressed in a long flannel gown.

Charlie was waving hands and feet and making happy noises. Sheena was beaming with proud love and looking a different girl. Someone had provided a sturdy dress in a pink-striped material with narrow

ruffles at neck and sleeve. Her fichu and cap were
bright white cotton.

She looked up, then gathered the baby, clearly intending to stand, but Genova waved her down. "No,
please."

"Good morning, Miss Smith," the girl said carefully.

Progress. Genova walked closer. "Charlie looks
well."

Sheena's blank and slightly worried look showed
they hadn't reached the stage of conversation.

Genova smiled and shook her head. "It doesn't
matter."

But she had to try. She pointed at the baby and said,
"Father?" Then, "Papa? *Pater?*" Weren't the Irish all
Catholics, used to Latin?

Sheena simply stared, looking anxious.

Genova smiled again, but it was so frustrating.
Sheena must know something. Probably not who
Charlie's father was, though, she realized. The baby
had been conceived in England.

Without the mother's evidence it was impossible to
prove who the father of any child was, and some
women didn't even know. Was that Ashart's ratio-
nale? Genova didn't approve. Even if he knew other
men might be the father, he couldn't know he wasn't,
and it would take so little of his wealth to provide for
the child.

She studied the infant for some resemblance, but a
baby is a baby. He seemed to be staring at her with
fascination, so she leaned closer, smiling. "Good
morning, Charlie-boy. Are you fed and happy?"

The baby stretched his mouth and squawked as if
he was trying to reply. He was delightful when clean
and happy.

Sheena stood, offering him. Hesitantly, Genova
gathered the bundle to herself, still looking down at
the fascinating face. He was heavier than she'd expected, a solid item, full of the energy to grow.

She walked the room with him, but it offered little
for those curious eyes, so she turned to the window.

From this height, they looked out to woodland and distant villages, and a river glinting in the brightening sun.

"A world to be explored, Charlie."

The baby was looking up at her, not out, so she shifted him. When he faced the window his arms waved as if he was trying to reach the glass, or perhaps that world beyond.

Genova remembered the matter of commands, kisses, and guineas. A silly thing in one way, a perilous one in others. Crucial for this child. As Ashart had said, however, how many guineas would it take? How many kisses? More than a hundred. Perhaps a thousand.

A thousand kisses? In days?

Ridiculous, but dizzyingly delightful to her wickedest parts.

The baby squawked again, and she was glad of the distraction. "What are we going to do with you, Charlie, when you have your guineas? Would you like to go back to Ireland?"

But that wouldn't do. She couldn't simply give a girl like Sheena a large sum of money and wave farewell. She'd have to arrange some kind of supervision. Guardians, trustees. It was a morass of complications that daunted even her.

"You're a problem, true enough," she murmured against the baby's quilted cap. "But I can't regret taking care of you."

Genova gave the baby back to Sheena.

"How old are you?" Genova asked. She pointed at the baby, holding up one bent finger, since he must be less than six months old. "Charlie."

Then she pointed to herself and spread her hands twice for twenty, then held up two fingers. "Twenty-two." A second later she realized it should be twenty-three today, but that would only confuse.

She pointed at Sheena. "You? How old? How many years?"

Sheena frowned for a moment, but then she spread one plump hand three times, then held up one finger.

Sixteen. As young as Genova feared. What was she to do?

Mrs. Harbinger walked in. "Miss Smith," she said, with a small curtsy.

Genova gave the lady a similarly small curtsy, hoping it established equality. "Thank you for taking such good care of Sheena and the baby."

"That is my job, Miss Smith."

"These are lovely cradles," Genova said, to continue the conversation.

"That they are. The blue is over a hundred years old, but the cream was made to match when the late marchioness gave birth to twins. The marquess's youngest brother and sister," she explained. "Lord Cynric and Lady Elfled. And for all that they called her Elf, she was as much of a hellion as he. We'll use her cradle for her baby."

"This nursery must have been very busy in those days."

"That it was. And a blessing after what came before."

Remembering, Genova was hard-pressed not to shiver. This might be the very room in which the murder had taken place.

As if forced into action, Mrs. Harbinger bustled over to Sheena and patted her shoulder. "He looks very well, dear."

Genova looked around the plain room, but if ghosts lingered, they didn't speak to her. As Ashart had said two days ago, however, the problems between his family and the Mallorens had started with the murder of a baby, here.

She had no effective way to intervene between two marquesses in present times, but did a key lie in the past? It would be arrogant to imagine that she could uncover a different story, but if she understood better, she might find something she could use.

She decided to pretend total ignorance. "What came before? What can you mean, Mrs. Harbinger?"

The woman looked at her, appearing the picture of

reluctance, but as Genova had guessed, at heart she was a gossip. "We had a tragedy here in the past, Miss Smith," she said in low-voiced solemnity. "I tell no secrets, since the whole world knows of it."

"I'm afraid I don't, Mrs. Harbinger. I've spent most of my life abroad."

"So I heard." That clearly wasn't a point in Genova's favor, but even so, the woman went on.

"I was only the undermaid here. Thirteen, I was, and hired because her ladyship was expecting her second child. Everything went well and there was such rejoicing, even though it was a girl this time. I myself saw the marquess come into this room to smile at little Edith with all the love in the world, and little Lord Grafton adored her."

The man who was now Marquess of Rothgar.

"What happened?" Genova prompted.

The woman pulled a face. "Her ladyship wouldn't feed her, you see. She'd fed Lord Grafton for a while, but not Lady Edith. She didn't even want the baby with her. We had a good wet nurse, but she was a timid woman. When she was told to go, she went."

"Lady Rothgar told her to go?"

"Her wits turned. That's all anyone can say."

Genova tried a blunt question. "What happened?"

Mrs. Harbinger put a hand over her mouth, then spoke. "She murdered the little innocent to stop her crying."

Genova didn't have to pretend horror. "To stop her *crying*?"

The woman nodded. "So she said. So she said."

"You witnessed it?"

"Oh, dear, no! Do you think I would have stood by, young as I was?"

"No, of course not. I'm sorry. It is all just so terrible to contemplate."

"That it is. It still bothers me in the night sometimes, to think that if I'd returned with some excuse, I might have saved the precious child. Mrs. Leigh, who was nursery governess at the time, blamed herself most bitterly. She left her position shortly after and I heard she drank herself to death. But what could she have done when her ladyship wanted to be alone with her children?"

Genova wished she hadn't stirred all this pain. "I'm sure no one could have expected such a terrible outcome." She had one important question. "Unless the marchioness had always been . . . unbalanced?"

"She *was* wild," Mrs. Harbinger said, beginning to show discomfort with the conversation, "but not in a lunatic way. She was just young. Young in her ways. She doted on little Lord Grafton—the marquess now. Dressed him in fine clothes. Played hide-and-seek with him. Carelessly, though. Enough to say, Miss Smith," she added with a return to starchy briskness, "that she was the sort of mother who needs a nursery staff if her children are to thrive. This Mrs. Dash sounds like another of the same. But anyone would have expected that the innocents would suffer from carelessness, not . . ."

She broke off there, unable to say the word *murder.* "Now we have a new marchioness, and in time, we'll have a full nursery. That will chase the ghosts away."

Genova agreed, smiling, but something jangled in her mind. "You said the marchioness wanted to be with her children. Was her son present when she killed her daughter?"

Mrs. Harbinger's mouth pursed as if to hold back words, but then they escaped. "Ran screaming for help, poor mite, but we couldn't tell what he was saying. We went to him, not her. . . ." She shook her head. "The crying of a tiny babe upsets the marquess still, Miss Smith. It's better, but it still bothers him. I tell you that only because Charlie must stay out of his sight, since nothing can stop a baby crying."

Nothing, thought Genova, except a hand cutting off all breath.

What a terrible legacy. What would happen when Lord Rothgar had children of his own? It was impossible to convey to Sheena that she must avoid him, but it didn't matter. There would be no reason for her and Charlie to mingle with the family again.

Genova left the room weighed down by the old tragedy and unable to see how to tear away the tendrils that poisoned the present. Had the young mother's wits truly been turned by cruelty?

She sighed and shook her head. She would try to find out more, but her true concerns were the Trayce ladies and Sheena and the baby. For the moment, they seemed well taken care of, and it was Christmas Eve.

Chapter Twenty-two

Genova headed back toward activities, but where to go?

She peeped into her own room, but Thalia was up and away. She knocked on Lady Calliope's door but found that she, too, was elsewhere.

Genova was still nervous in this house where she knew hardly anyone. That realization was enough to stiffen her spine. She wasn't going to skulk, so the Tapestry Room seemed the most likely place to mingle.

She was approaching the door when someone called, "Miss Smith!"

She turned to see Lady Bryght coming into the hall, her arms full of a tangle of green and red. "Could I impose upon you to help me untangle all this?"

Genova could hardly refuse, and she would enjoy being useful. That was another problem, she realized. Before her father's retirement, and even in Portsmouth, she'd been busy, active, and productive.

Lady Bryght looked around, wrinkling her brow. "I think I'll take it up to the library to spread on one of the big tables there. Come along."

They went up to a magnificent room. Lit by tall windows, the long room gleamed with gilded wood, flaunted elaborate carvings, and clasped thousands of leather-bound books behind glass-paneled doors.

Down the center, three long oak tables were set with chairs and held branches of candles ready for use, each with polished reflectors to focus the light on the page. Newspapers and magazines were spread invitingly, and in the center of each table a book lay open on a book stand.

She noted a tall lectern chair beneath each window—the sort seen in medieval illustrations. These chairs could well date from that time, especially as they each had an ancient book chained in place. She'd heard that was the practice when books were handwritten and precious.

A fireplace blazed at one end of the room and a rich carpet covered the floor, but there were no upholstered chairs. This was a room intended for study, not napping or chatter. She wondered if the scribes and philosophers painted on the ceiling disapproved of Lady Bryght's invasion with a mundane task.

Lady Bryght spilled the mess of green and red at one end of the center table without apparent concern. She sat in one chair and Genova took another, eying the mess dubiously.

"This was used to tie bundles of greenery last year," Lady Bryght said, "but it wasn't put away properly. Diana wants to reuse it, but I don't know how much will be salvageable."

Genova poked at the ribbons. "It's astonishing how things can become so thoroughly tangled."

"If there were merchants nearby, it would be easier to buy new." Then Lady Bryght looked up with a smile. "That's a very Malloren way of thinking. I was raised to be frugal."

Genova chuckled, relaxing. "So was I. I've unpicked trimmings, unstrung beads, and made useful items out of scraps. Let's try, at least." She chose a green end and began to trace it back to free more of the ribbon.

Lady Bryght started on a piece of red. "Tell me more about life with the navy, Miss Smith. It must be fascinating."

"In parts." Genova was happy to entertain with her stories, however.

Lady Bryght didn't only listen, so Genova learned a lot about the Malloren family. It was particularly interesting because it was an outsider's view. Lady

Bryght, as she'd implied, came from a family that owned only a modest manor.

"Sometimes the Mallorens act as if they're gods," she remarked at one point. "Especially Rothgar. Don't let him bully you."

"He seems kind."

"Oh, he is, but like all of us, he has many sides." Genova was thinking about portraits when Lady Bryght added, "He killed a man in a duel earlier in the year."

Genova said, "I read about it in the paper."

She hoped for more detail, something to make it a noble act, but Lady Bryght frowned at the yard of creased red ribbon she'd freed. "I don't think this has to be in very long lengths." She produced small scissors from her pocket and snipped it. "Now that," she said, "is a very Malloren solution."

"With blades?"

"Sometimes."

Genova met the other woman's eyes. Lady Bryght might claim to be ordinary, but she was a Malloren. "Is that a warning, my lady?"

Fair freckled skin blushes easily. "Don't let my chatter upset you, Miss Smith. Oh, we must not be so formal. May I call you Genova? I do wish you to call me Portia."

It was all a move in a game, but again, Genova could hardly refuse. "Of course."

"Excellent." Portia began to wrap her length of ribbon around her fingers. "I probably understand how you feel here. My only touch with greatness before I met Bryght was that our property sat close to Walgrave Towers and we knew the family. And now Fort—Lord Walgrave—is my brother-in-law, which I never would have imagined. His father and Rothgar were dire enemies."

"But they made peace?"

Was that a message of hope?

Portia's hands stilled. "He died."

"How?"

Portia's eyes were wide, and Genova thought she wouldn't answer, but then she said, "Suicide. Here, as it happens. Everyone knows about it."

Despite that, Genova knew that revelation hadn't been planned. She had the strange notion that a true Malloren would have handled it better.

"Elf—Lady Walgrave—is hoping for a Christmas baby," Portia said, too brightly. "The midwife is in residence, but nothing is happening yet."

It was a clumsy change of subject, but gave an opening for a question that had been puzzling Genova. "Isn't it strange to expect an *accouchement* during a house party?"

"Elf has always spent Christmas here and wished to again. And they're making changes at Walgrave Towers."

Was that adequate explanation? Especially when Lord Walgrave's father had committed suicide here. She teased free a bit more ribbon while trying to frame a question about that.

"Of course Rothgar is pleased to have Elf here at this time," Portia chattered. "Men do worry. Poor Bryght was in agonies because I'm so small, but Francis gave me no trouble at all." Then she looked up, wide-eyed again. "I'm sorry. Married ladies aren't supposed to discuss such matters with unmarried ones, but talking to you feels . . . different."

"Different, I am," Genova agreed wryly. "Being raised in ports and on naval ships has its effect."

"But it's delightful! I can see why Ashart was bowled over."

"Almost literally," Genova muttered, then felt herself blush.

"I'm sorry?"

"I mean it was doubtless very rash of us."

"Which doesn't mean it was unwise." Portia tugged on her length of ribbon, tightening a central knot of red and green.

"Stop!" Genova exclaimed, then said, "I'm sorry. . . ."

Portia laughed. "No matter. I lack patience with tasks like this. I surrender that Gordian section to you." She chose another loose end. "Ashart is quite fascinating, isn't he?"

So they were back to that. Safer, no doubt, than other subjects. "To every woman?" Genova asked, concentrating on loosening red from green.

"He has rank and charm and knows how to use it."

"Then he'd make the devil of a husband."

"Doubts already?"

"A million of them." No harm in admitting that. A woman would have to be feather witted not to worry about marrying a man like the Marquess of Ashart.

Portia cocked her head. "But a man like that is a very rewarding husband if he is a true one."

"Faithful, you mean? I doubt—"

"More than faithful. A friend. A friend of the heart. Sharer of strength and secrets, even in winter. Especially," Portia added, "in winter."

Genova responded to that deep within, but was it another pointed message? If the Mallorens wanted the betrothal to become real, she doubted it was for her benefit.

"Ashart and I have nothing like that," she said.

"I believe you only met two days ago. Within two days of meeting Bryght I had no idea of what we could be."

Genova hesitated, but she was tired of fighting tangles and the simplest way to cut through this was with truth.

"This is different," she said. "The betrothal is false. Ashart and I argued. Some people interrupted. . . ." Too late she realized that the telling might be embarrassing. "It appeared that we were behaving improperly. Then Thalia arrived and said we were betrothed, in order to save my reputation. We intend to break it soon."

Portia's main reaction seemed to be fascination. "How improperly?"

"Portia!"

"It's a salient point."

"We fell to the floor. In the argument. Then he kissed me. On his bed."

Portia's eyes went wide. "You were in his *bedroom*?"

"No!" Genova knew her cheeks were flaming. "We were in the parlor, but he was sleeping there. On a mattress on the floor."

She looked to the sages on the painted ceiling for help, but they frowned severely back at her. "It wasn't so very bad. But we were both in our nightwear."

Portia broke into laughter. "Oh, my. It is quite in the family tradition!"

"I just wanted to get my needlework."

"Oh, I'm sure." Portia waved a hand. "But it's delightful. Bryght broke into the house where I was staying and I tried to shoot him."

"Broke in?" The Mallorens were as mad as the Trayces.

"There was something hidden there that Rothgar wanted, and they thought the house was empty." Portia seemed to think that was explanation enough. "Who saw you?"

"What?"

"You said someone interrupted. Who was it?"

"A man called Brokesby and his sister."

Portia winced. "Tattling Tess? No wonder Thalia intervened. And her presence would help. Despite their eccentricities, the Trayce ladies are beyond reproach. Even though the story will be ricocheting around England, embellished by Christmas cheer, it will only be amusement. Passion between a betrothed couple is naughty but not ruinous."

"Even when the engagement is broken?"

"Even then."

Genova looked down at the impossible tangle of ribbons. "I do worry about my reputation. Lord Ashart said that we should act the lovers for a day or two to seal the story."

"He's right. First convince the world the attraction

is real, then show that the bond cannot last. Unlike this one." She gave up on another knot and snipped some ribbon free.

The flash of sharp blades made Genova shudder. "There's no cause for a duel between Rothgar and Ashart, is there?"

"Rothgar doesn't permit duels in the family, and he considers Ashart one of the family."

"I doubt Ashart agrees."

"Even so, it would be hard for him to push Rothgar that far."

Hard, but not impossible. Was that Ashart's plan—to push Rothgar into a deadly duel? He had made that dangerous remark about Lady Arradale.

"I gather Lord Rothgar is a skilled swordsman."

"They all are," Portia said. "Rothgar trained them quite brutally, from what Bryght has said, because he wanted to be sure they couldn't fall victim to the sort of bully who uses sword skill to murder. Bryght says he'll do the same with Francis and any other sons we have. Pistols *and* swords." Her brow wrinkled. "I suppose it will be for the best."

"It probably is. I've seen good men hurt or cowed that way. The whole matter of dueling should be made illegal!"

"I gather it is in a way, but it's rarely enforced. Men have their own brutal code." Portia looked at Genova. "That was the kind of man Curry was—the swordsman Rothgar defeated. He'd killed a number of men in duels. According to Bryght, he'd been paid to kill Rothgar that way, and almost succeeded."

This could be an attempt to glorify, but Genova suspected it was true. She'd find it hard to see Rothgar as a cold-blooded murderer. It didn't reassure her much, however, to know that he could be a cold-blooded executioner.

How was she to enjoy Christmas in the midst of this?

Portia looked at the tangle of ribbons. "This is carrying frugality too far. I shall take it back to Diana and say so." She gathered the mess into her arms, keeping the liberated streamers safe. Genova caught a straggler and wound it on top, suspecting that ribbons had been a pretext to slide her some information and warn her of danger.

Portia headed for the door and Genova opened it for her, unready to mingle with others now. "Will it be all right for me to stay here?"

"Yes, of course! It is magnificent, isn't it? And I hear the horn, which means arrivals. Best to be out of the way."

She left Genova with an image of being trodden under a stampede of Malloren feet. That was whimsy, but other problems were not. Behind this jovial Christmas cheer lay altogether too many deaths.

Chapter Twenty-three

Genova started to count. Baby Edith. Lady Augusta. Lady Augusta's husband and his second wife must have died quite young. More recently—the Earl of Walgrave and a professional duelist called Curry.

Curry sounded like the sort of man someone had to kill, however, and people did commit suicide. What's more, the earl's son had married a Malloren and was awaiting the birth of his first child here. There could be no dark secret there.

She shook her head. For some reason, her imagination was running away with her. Ashart and Rothgar were at odds, but not to the extent of murder. It simply wasn't possible, even for aristocrats. Earl Ferrers had been hanged not many years ago for the murder of his steward.

A duel, though? Only with words.

She put aside her morbid thoughts and considered the ranks of books. What could she do in a library that would be useful? She was no scholar. Her education had been broad but haphazard, mainly drawing on places her family had visited and whatever books came to hand.

There could be a history of the Malloren family here. Most great families commissioned such a thing, and any extra information might help her navigate these tricky waters.

After some searching, she found the history section. It seemed to be arranged in chronological order, but when she read the spines of the most recent books they looked like dry analyses of legislation and for-eign affairs.

What else would be useful to know?

Loki. She would definitely like to know more about Loki.

She'd seen books on mythology and returned there, but they all seemed to be about Greek and Roman legends, many in Greek or Latin. She spoke a little Greek but couldn't read it, and modern Italian was not Latin. Neither would help with the legends of northern Europe.

Feeling a dunce, she turned to leave the library but paused by one of the books invitingly open on the tables. It was a great Bible, open appropriately to Saint Luke's account of the Christmas story, to the Magnificat.

She read through, coming to the lines

He hath scattered the proud in the imagination of their hearts.
He hath put down the mighty from their seats, and exalted them of low degree.
He hath filled the hungry with good things; and the rich he hath sent empty away.

My! Was Dr. Egan responsible for turning the pages to ones appropriate for the day? Would he be dis-missed for choosing these?

She moved to the next table, which displayed a quite small book. At the top of the open pages it read, *A History of the Malloren Family.*

She started at having her search so easily solved, but then realized the book would be on display during a family gathering. And of course it would tell nothing unpleasant about them.

She expected something a little more exciting than what she read on the open pages, however. They told of a crusading ancestor, and apart from that one fact, nothing interesting had happened to William de Malloren. He'd died at age seventy in his bed, his children, grandchildren, and great-grandchildren around him.

What was Dr. Egan's message there? That great houses were built with plain bricks?

She moved on to the last book, anticipating some other subtle commentary on the great, then stared at it as if it were a striking snake. The top of the page carried one word.

Loki.

She looked around as if someone might be watching, but she was still alone. She partly closed the book to read the spine. *Tales of the Norse Gods.* Feeling as if another message was being fed to her, she began to read.

Loki was described as beautiful, fickle, clever, and malicious. He deliberately created problems for the other gods, then showed his superiority by solving them. Among the problems were his three children— a wolf, a serpent, and Hel, or death.

Was Ashart's wolf cloak deliberate? Why in heaven's name would he link himself to a mythical character as unpleasant as this?

The story on the page was about destructive Fenris, the wolf, whom the gods eventually tricked into letting himself be bound with a magical rope called Gleipnir. The mighty wolf was suspicious, however, and wouldn't submit until one of the gods put his hand in its mouth. So Tyr, god of battle, did so. The wolf was bound, but it bit off Tyr's hand.

She saw the message in that. Those who sought to defeat evil must be willing to sacrifice, perhaps everything. Hadn't Lord Rothgar said something similar yesterday—to Ashart?

She turned the page, seeking more about Loki, but arms snared her from behind. "I gather I'm to chop down trees for you, my love."

Something—a step, perhaps, or even a smell—had given Genova a second's warning, so she managed to conceal the sudden rush of energy within her.

She turned, and Loki allowed it, though he didn't

draw back. They were so close that every breath brushed body against body, igniting desire despite everything she knew about him.

"What do you mean?" she asked, trying to appear unmoved.

He pressed a tiny bit closer. "As Rothgar said, he keeps to the old traditions, so we are to go like laborers to harvest evergreens and the Yule log. Or rather, the men labor and the ladies applaud."

She shifted slightly away, but this pressed her hips closer. Heat rose in her. "It's always a pleasure to watch men sweat."

His eyes sparkled, suggesting another meaning entirely.

"Have you arranged for another gossip to interrupt, my lord?" she said desperately, praying for something to brace her willpower.

"No, why?"

"Then why play at *amor*? Let me go."

She pressed forward but he didn't move. She raised her hands between them. "What do you want, Ashart?"

He lowered his head to breathe against her neck. "To sweat?"

Every nerve jumped. "On a library table?"

Too late, she knew he would find that no impediment—and neither did she. She'd never even imagined such a thing but now she did. She saw it, felt it, wanted it. Sharp aches rippled up her thighs.

Impossible!

She pushed again, turning her head away from his teasing lips, but that exposed her throat and he bit it. Lightly, but she felt his teeth, thought of wolves, and swayed back, suddenly boneless with desire.

He lifted her to the table. Her heart gave a great thump of warning, but she didn't stop him, couldn't stop herself, not even when he pressed between her thighs, her two thick petticoats seeming no protection at all.

The rippling aches were piercing her there, demanding satisfaction. She heard herself moan, but she only deepened the kiss, driven by a frantic hunger she knew was insane.

She felt his strong hand on her naked thigh, spreading it wider, was aware of his other strong arm supporting her swaying body. She rolled her head back, opening her mouth to gasp in air, and her eyes in search of sanity—and saw the stern disapproving faces of the sages on high.

A different kind of jolt shot through her. What was she *doing*?

She pushed at his shoulders, trying to close her legs. "No! For pity's sake, anyone could come in here!"

Their eyes locked and the expression in his froze her passion. He was flushed, dazed, dark eyes darker still, but beneath he was watchful. Was this what a rake was like? Clever, calculating, doing and saying all the right things to get what he wanted?

"No," she said again, chills shaking her. "Release me, my lord."

After a moment he eased back, rearranging her skirts and then flowing into a bow with a skill no honest man would possess. She shivered as she slid off the table, refusing to fuss with her clothes. "We agreed we wouldn't do this."

"I don't believe so."

"Then you should! Anyone could have discovered us. If not a guest, sooner or later a servant must come to build up the fire. Why risk having to marry me, my lord, when it must be the last thing you wish?"

She heard her voice rise to a shout, and covered her mouth with her hand.

"Hardly the last," he said, infuriatingly unmoved. "I'd certainly marry you rather than hang. And isn't a *should* as good as a *must*?"

She tried to push past him. "This is not a game!"

He blocked her way, gripping her arms. "Are you claiming not to have wanted that? Saying you don't want more even now?"

Lying would demean her. Eyes fixed on the door,

she said, "No. But I won't be trapped by this, Ashart. You'd make the devil of a husband."

Did he flinch, or was it just anger?

"I'm sure you're right." He let her go, then took a guinea out of his pocket and held it out.

It was their bargain. There was no reason to feel outrage, but it took every scrap of will not to slap it away, or slap him. Instead, Genova took the coin and slipped it into her pocket. "On Charlie's behalf, I thank you, my lord."

"It will buy him a sucket or two." Then he held out his hand in formal style. "Come, Miss Smith. I believe I heard the dinner gong."

Had she been as deaf to the world as that? She wanted to sweep out and ignore him. She wanted to run to her room and hide. Neither would serve in the long run. Better by far to convince him that he had no deep effect on her.

She put her hand in his, blocking the power of his touch, and let him lead her from the room.

Chapter Twenty-four

*A*shart led Genova Smith downstairs, gathering control or he'd be in no state to deal with Rothgar.

He'd woken early in the grand bedchamber that had been found for him despite his unexpected arrival, and he'd suddenly needed to escape. He'd found the stables and his horse, and ridden fast around the frostily beautiful estate.

Every elegant curve of land, every classical delight, felt like a taunt. *See what I can afford*, they said, *and you cannot*.

Devil take his grandmother for pouring money into ways to attack the Mallorens. No, devil take him for allowing it. For the past five years, at least, he could have been in command of his own affairs. He hadn't insisted on that, or resisted her urging to be more and more glorious at court.

Diamond buttons, for Zeus's sake.

He slowed Zampira and surveyed his cousin's domain. It was impressive and elegant, but Ash didn't particularly desire its like. What he desired was hearty fields and tenants, and a house without crumbling plaster in damp corners.

He'd spent his life blaming the Mallorens for any problems, but most of his current ones were not their fault. He knew Fitz had brought about some of the change. His friend's casual observations had shaken Ash's world until the realization had seeped in that a life of attack and retaliation was not what he wanted.

It had been too late. He'd already taken Molly Carew

home from the Knatchbull masquerade. Was that a
Malloren plot? His predicament would be easier if it
was, but he'd ridden back here hoping it wasn't.

He'd returned to the house and breakfasted in his
room, having used the bellpull, a modern development
that he would like to install in his homes. Then he'd
wandered Rothgar Abbey, talking casually to servants
when he could, but for the most part simply absorbing
history and present truths from the walls.

He wasn't sure he'd learned anything of use, though
he'd spent some time amid Rothgar's collection of
clockworks. He'd known of the interest. He'd been
present at court when Rothgar and the Chevalier
D'Eon had conducted a duel of sorts with automata.

The acting French ambassador had presented the
king with a showy dove of peace, all silver, pearl, and
jewels, but with a very simple mechanism that picked
up an olive branch and spread its wings.

Rothgar's automaton could be seen by the foolish
as simple, since it consisted of a shepherd and shep-
herdess kissing beneath a tree, but it was exquisitely
made. The movements were smooth and complex as
the two lovers turned, looked, and kissed, the shepherd's hand rising to touch his beloved's cheek. At
the same time, birds in the tree above broke into song,
heads moving, wings spreading.

It had been easy to see the mechanical room as
sign of Rothgar the great manipulator, but Ash had
recognized taste, and also interests that could mesh
with his own. Clocks were part of astronomy, after all,
and telescopes needed complex mechanisms.

Such subjects were also excellent antidotes to inconvenient passion, but he couldn't say they were working
now. He was sharply aware of Genova Smith's soft
hand in his, of her generous body moving gracefully
beside him, of the delicate perfume she wore, and of
a deeper, spicier one that had stirred in the library.

Her hair had not come down, which was a shame.
His dreams had been haunted by her hair. She'd been
right to stop him, though, and thank the gods for her

willpower. Anyone could have come in, and if they'd been caught it would have sealed their fate.

How had passion slipped loose when he'd only meant to see how far she would go to distract him?

If that was her purpose.

If she was Rothgar's tool.

If she didn't drive him as crazy as poor Aunt Augusta. Perhaps the very air here was toxic to Trayces.

He and Miss Smith entered the dining room to find the table increased to seat thirty or so. All seats were filled except two at Rothgar's right hand.

Ash recognized that his cousin had little choice. Everyone here would know of the family strife, and any lower honor could be seen as a slight. They were almost exactly equal in status, though the marquessate of Rothgar had been created a few years before the Ashart one.

As he led Miss Smith to pride of place, he noted a slight nervous clutch of her fingers. For the first time it occurred to him that if she was involved in his affairs by accident, this must all be very difficult for her.

As they sat, he assessed those nearby. Sir Rolo and Lady Knightsholme sat opposite. He was bluff and honest, and she bold, as the smile she flashed Ashart showed. She was the Malloren connection, though distantly.

On his right, Miss Charlotte Malloren, middle-aged spinster and gossip, her eyes bright, her ears doubtless perked for juicy tidbits.

Rothgar offered bisque from the tureen before him, indicating what others were available down the table. Footmen stood ready to ferry dishes around.

Miss Smith took bisque in the way of one who doesn't want to draw attention to herself. Ash declined, annoyed that her boldness had been so easily tamed.

Rothgar said, "I understand you have been enjoying my library, Miss Smith."

Ash saw her almost drop her spoon into her soup, and braced to intervene, but she collected herself. "Yes, my lord."

"Did you enjoy anything in particular?"

Ash had to fight to hide amusement.

"I found the open books intriguing, my lord," she said and he silently applauded.

"I try to choose pages to stimulate thought."

"You!" It escaped and she blushed, but it seemed to bring her to life. What had been in those open books? Ash wondered.

"I was surprised to see a biblical selection preaching against the rich and mighty, my lord."

"The rich and mighty should always remember the perils of their situation. Don't you agree, Ashart?"

Despite a smile, the question was pointed. "Is it not the gods' way, to bring low anything that threatens them in greatness?" Ash responded.

"And vengeance is mine, saith the Lord. Bread, Miss Smith?"

She declined, but was bold enough now to redirect the discussion. "I found Lord William de Malloren interesting, Lord Rothgar, if only because nothing unusual seemed to happen to him. We so rarely hear from the quiet voices of history."

"And thus may have a false impression of the past."

So, thought Ash. Was that supposed to mean that their family history was wrong?

"Stories about ordinary people would be tedious reading, wouldn't they?" Maddie Knightsholme asked as the soup plates were taken away. She always liked to be the center of attention.

During the serving of the main courses, Ash had to deflect nosy questions from Miss Charlotte. Oyster stew, turbot, battalia pie. Beans. When he turned back, Miss Smith, Rothgar, and the Knightsholmes were talking about Italy.

"To think," Ash said as he forked an oyster, "we might have met in Venice, my sweet. I was there in 'fifty-five."

She looked at him, amused. "So was I, my lord, but I was only fourteen."

"I'm sure you were delightful at fourteen."

"I was a lanky tomboy."

"Then at least I can say that you have improved with time."

"A clever recovery, sir. And you? What were you like at eighteen?"

Maddie Knightsholme laughed at that. "Already a breaker of hearts, Miss Smith! We encountered Ashart in Naples, didn't we, Rolo? Lethal, I assure you, in that Mediterranean heat." She turned a sultry look on Rothgar. "I gather you, too, cut a swath through Europe in your day."

"Maddie, you make me feel ancient. Even Ashart must be feeling the frost of time."

"And we can't have that. What would the world be without Ashart's scandalous goings-on to amuse us?"

Maddie Knightsholme was a menace.

Miss Charlotte tittered. "Why, yes. I heard—"

Ash cut her off ruthlessly. "We could dine on stories about the Chevalier D'Eon."

Maddie Knightsholme's brows rose at his tone, but she addressed herself to her food. Miss Charlotte fell silent, too. Ash's attention was on Rothgar. How would he react to that?

Sir Rolo, damn him, interrupted. "Aye, quite a state of things. I hear the new ambassador threw him out, but he refuses to go back to France, the impudent jackanapes. Be glad to see the back of him. Too much closeness to Their Majesties."

Ash saw that Genova was looking puzzled and slightly shocked.

"You look confused, my dear. The Chevalier D'Eon was acting French ambassador until recently. He's a most intriguing fellow and became a great favorite at court—especially with the queen."

"Quite innocently," Rothgar said in a warning tone.

"Oh, of course. However much in favor he was here, the same cannot be said of France, where he seems to have made enemies. Unwise, when he appears to have been misappropriating embassy funds.

Strange," Ash added, watching Rothgar, who he now knew had been the cause of the man's downfall, "he seemed a clever fellow."

"Clever enough to cut himself!" Sir Rolo declared, apparently oblivious to undercurrents. "Always the same with these fancy, tricksy ones. Give me bluff honesty. Gads, I heard the man wears dresses!"

The look on Genova's face was priceless, and the moment to catch Rothgar unawares had passed.

"It's true," Ash told her. "I remember him at a ball in a stylish blue sacque, and in the park demure in gray and white."

"Some say *he* is in fact a *she*," said Miss Charlotte.

"Yet he was a dashing war hero," Rothgar pointed out, "and decorated for bravery. Not that I would ever suggest that women cannot be brave."

"I know no woman who is brilliant with a sword," Ash said, "and D'Eon is that. Perhaps the best of our age. Rumor whispers," he added to Rothgar, "that you fought him."

It was a matter of some moment. Ash did not intend to come to swords with his cousin, but if he did, he wanted to be the victor.

"Informally," Rothgar said.

"Who won?"

Rothgar smiled slightly. "We decided it would be diplomatic to call it a draw. And you?"

"I have never had the honor."

"You should seek him out. To fence against a master clarifies the mind."

"If one lives to appreciate it."

"I'm sure a clear mind is of use in heaven, too."

"But especially in hell."

"Which is where that Wilkes deserves to be!" Sir Rolo interjected, and launched into his opinion of political scandal.

Ash did his part when necessary, knowing he had been given a warning. He was probably outclassed with a blade and should avoid that course. It had been years since he'd dreamed of bringing the vile Mallorens to account by defeating Rothgar in a duel, but he wished he believed he could.

He noticed Genova Smith frowning. "Wilkes is a boring fellow, isn't he?" he said, but felt compelled to add, "Don't let our family tensions weigh on you. There is nothing you can do."

She met his eyes. "Do you think it is as easy as that?"

Chapter Twenty-five

*G*enova saw Ashart mirror her frown as if he wanted to argue with her, but then the older lady on his other side demanded his attention.

She wished she could ignore the battle, for she was developing a headache, but it was hard when sitting between the combatants. This D'Eon was important, and the matters to do with him were connected to court, kings, and even treason.

Ashart and Rothgar had been tapping swords again, seeking out weaknesses. She hadn't missed the point that Rothgar was almost certainly the more skilled in duello.

She took a deep drink of wine, glancing around at a table that seemed unaware of strife. Because she was looking for trouble, she caught an expression on the face of Miss Myddleton.

The heiress was seated between Lord Walgrave and a young man in a scarlet uniform. She appeared to be enjoying the company, but she shot a look up the table at Ashart that reminded Genova of a cat eying dinner on the wing.

He's no bird for your stalking, she thought, but she knew it wasn't true. A well-born heiress was precisely the sort of bride Ashart would choose.

The girl's catlike eyes met Genova's and Miss Myddleton smiled, apparently in polite query. The false betrothal allowed Genova to fire back a warning, and she enjoyed doing it. For the next few days, Ashart was hers and the heiress could keep her claws to herself.

The Wilkes affair had progressed to Russian art, and main dishes were being replaced by savories and sweets.

Simply to claim Ashart in front of the heiress, Genova covered his hand with hers. "Have you traveled to Russia, my lord?"

After a surprised glance, he raised her hand and kissed it. "Call me Ash, beloved. It's what most of my intimates use."

Genova knew Miss Myddleton's eyes were upon her. "Ash, then. Even though it does unfortunately recall dead fires."

A brow rose and a finger tickled her palm. "If you want proof that the fires are not dead, my sweet, you need only command."

Heat rushed through her, but she was saved by Lady Arradale rising and commanding everyone's attention. "My friends, Christmas gaiety is upon us already, I see, but first we must bring in the greenery."

Others had been playing flirtatious games, and now there were shouts about greens and greenery that raised laughter. They were a euphemism for love play. A "lady with a green gown" was thought to have been with a lover in the grass.

Much time spent with Ashart, and that would be her fate.

"And mistletoe, of course!" called the young officer, winking at Miss Myddleton. She smiled, but her eyes slid again to Ashart.

The officer tried song.

> *Hey, ho, the mistletoe,*
> *It's off to the greenwood we do go.*
> *My lady fine and I.*

Other men joined in, singing to their partner. Miss Myddleton had to respond appropriately, as did Genova. She was helped by the fact that Ashart had an excellent baritone voice.

Hey, ho, the mistletoe bough,
That a daring lass stands under now
To tempt the man in her eye.

Hey, ho, the mistletoe kiss
That leads many men to wedded bliss
To a lady by and by.

"There'll be mistletoe enough," the countess assured everyone, laughing. "It only requires harvesting, and so, to work!"

"Not everyone is conscripted for hard labor," Rothgar said as the company rose. "But we insist on the young bachelors taking part. The felling and handling of the Yule log requires their vigor."

"Vigor?" Ashart queried.

"My lady tells me that in the north they believe that the more virile bachelors bring in the log, the more strength it bestows on the house in which it burns."

"Then I wonder if I should contribute."

An uneasy stillness rippled out from the two men. Despite high spirits, clearly everyone was aware of the enmity.

"I have wondered," Rothgar said, "why this custom assumes that virile bachelors are preserving their vigor."

Laughter shattered tension, and even Ashart smiled. "Then I will contribute my little all."

Good humor restored, everyone flowed into the hall in a stream of chatter and laughter. Beneath it, however, ran the same sort of fever Genova had tasted once in Venice, during one of the wild festivals there. She remembered behaving then with a little less caution than she should.

She didn't want to do this. She feared taking part in what was, in effect, a pagan ritual, where she'd be paired, she knew, with Ashart. She glanced around and hurried after the Trayce ladies, who were entering the Tapestry Room.

Thalia spotted her and shooed her away. "Genova, what are you doing? You must go out with the young people!"

"I'm here to look after you—"

"Fie on that! There's a footman near every door. Away with you."

Genova retreated. She considered slipping away until everyone left, but she could imagine the result. Someone, probably Ashart, would start a hunt, and he'd know she was hiding specifically from him.

She went upstairs for her outdoor clothing, taking her time in the hope that the party might leave without her. When she returned to the stairs, however, people were still milling about in the hall.

Ah well, she thought as she went down, pulling on her gloves, she had guineas to earn and had thought of a way to speed the process.

Most of the ladies now wore cloaks or heavy caraco jackets. Most of the gentlemen wore long redingote coats. Everyone wore hats, gloves, and sturdy footwear. None of them looked the slightest like country laborers.

Genova was probably the one here most familiar with hard work, which might be why she didn't feel as if she belonged. She hovered, pretending to admire a classical statue until she realized that studying a naked man could not improve her reputation.

She turned away, looking for Portia, or even Lady Arradale, and saw Ashart coming down at last, but with Damaris Myddleton on his arm. The heiress's eyes seemed to seek out Genova's so she could signal her triumph.

Ashart had added only gloves and hat. Perhaps he had no extra layer other than his riding cloak, which would be too heavy for a stroll. Would a marquess spend Christmas with only the contents of a saddlebag? More Trayce eccentricity.

Miss Myddleton's waist-length cape was trimmed, and probably lined, with fur. Genova guessed mink. She hoped the heiress was wearing woolen stockings and an extra petticoat or two. Such a shame if she got chilblains.

Trying not to think catty thoughts, Genova strolled over to meet the two at the bottom of the stairs, to claim Ashart's other arm. He raised her gloved hand and kissed it.

"A guinea, please," she said.

With a cocked brow, he produced one and gave it to her.

"You *charge* him for kisses, Miss Smith?" Miss Myddleton asked.

"In a game." Ashart's eyes never left Genova. "Something like the mistletoe bough. Does that really count as a kiss, Miss Smith?"

"If you need lessons, sir . . ."

"A definition, perhaps?"

"That would be as difficult as defining a true husband."

"Vows said before a minister," inserted Miss Myddleton, tightening her paw—hand—on Ashart's sleeve.

Genova suddenly felt sorry for the young woman. "What if the vows are broken, Miss Myddleton? The law doesn't allow a lady to end a marriage for that."

"It's remarkably hard for a gentleman," Ashart said. "Thus, the bonds are best considered binding, no matter what becomes of the vows."

"Is that why you're not bound, Ashart?" Miss Myddleton demanded.

"But I am. To Miss Smith. My word is given and will be kept unless she insists on her freedom."

It was cruel as a blade, and Genova winced. Miss Myddleton snatched away her hand, a spot of angry color in each cheek. Had she not heard before? Or chosen not to believe.

"I must wish you both happy then," she said, pitch too high.

"Must," Ashart echoed, eyes on Genova.

"Must," Genova replied.

When the heiress marched off to talk to others Genova said, "That was unnecessarily cruel."

He dropped the amorous manner. "Is your soft heart touched? Damaris Myddleton wouldn't be trying to sink cat's claws into plain Mr. Dash."

"I wonder."

He was probably right, however. Miss Myddleton might be attracted to handsome Mr. Dash, but she wouldn't invest her fortune in him.

The young officer came over. "We're planning the correct handling of the Yule log, Ashart. Hoping you'll give your advice."

He'd probably been sent to drag in the unwilling bachelor. With a bow to Genova, Ashart went to join the other men.

Lady Arradale and Portia had not come down yet. It was possible they wouldn't be joining the party at all, since traditionally only unmarried people brought in the greenery. Lord Bryght seemed to be part of it, however, and she saw Lord Rothgar join the men.

"Miss Smith."

Genova turned to find Damaris Myddleton approaching and suppressed a sigh.

"I understand you've spent time at sea," the young woman said. "How fascinating. I hope to hear some of your stories."

Genova recognized a masterly tactic. Open rivalry would get Miss Myddleton nowhere, so now she angled to become a confidante.

When the stars fell into the sea.

"I would be delighted to share them," she said politely, "but your life would be as fascinating to me, Miss Myddleton."

"Then I will trade stories of fashionable circles for your stories of foreign parts."

Miss Myddleton's smile was an excellent simulation of warmth, but there was acid in the word *foreign*. Genova, it was made clear, did not belong. The fact that she knew it did not improve her temper.

"I'm sure that will be delightful." She did not try to sound sincere.

The slanted eyes narrowed. "Lady Thalia said you fought off Barbary pirates."

"She does tend to exaggerate."

"But not by much, I think. She also says you are redoubtable. I'm sure you are. I must tell you, however, that I intend to marry Ashart, and I believe I can get what I want."

Perhaps a better woman would tell the truth, but Genova fired back, "You're welcome to try."

"Oh, I will. I have his grandmother's approval."

That was a heavy gun and Miss Myddleton clearly knew it.

"I didn't expect to meet him here, of course," she went on, looking at her quarry across the room, "but it seems an excellent opportunity to settle matters."

Genova found herself fascinated and even admiring in a way. Most well-bred women were trained to take the indirect path, to get their way by coyness and wiles, or to depend on a man to win them what they wanted. She had to like one who fired directly at her target.

"Will it not be difficult for you to marry into a family so at odds with the Mallorens?"

Miss Myddleton looked back at her. "I'm not a Malloren, and anyway, with Ashart here, the feud must be over."

"It isn't. Don't do anything to create more difficulties."

The young woman studied Genova, looking alert and intelligent. She might even make Ashart a good marchioness, especially if she drew back and made him hunt her and her fortune.

"Difficulties for whom?"

"For everyone, but particularly for Ash."

The intimate term slipped out and shattered any hope of accord.

"I will never create any kind of difficulty for Ashart, which is more than can be said of you, Miss Smith. One bitter rift may be ending here, but the wrong marriage will create another. You will alienate Ashart from his grandmother, from the woman who raised him. They are devoted to one another."

With that salvo, Miss Myddleton stalked away and Genova struggled not to show the effect of her words. The hunting cat, damn her, was probably right.

Then she came to her senses. None of this mattered because this betrothal was *false*. Ashart probably would marry Damaris Myddleton, and at least the heiress had spine enough to stand up to him. He needed that.

The doors were flung open then for them to leave. Fresh, cool air and sunshine were a brisk relief.

Ashart came over. "Are you all right?"

"Yes, of course," she said composedly, linking her arm with his. "Perhaps a little dull from food and wine."

It was time to put her plan into action. She didn't think she could endure this mock betrothal much longer.

"Some brisk exercise in the open air will be just the *must*ard," she said.

With a laugh he kissed her quickly and slipped the guinea into her pocket, out of sight of others but in a sliding touch that she could not ignore.

She almost faltered, but pursued her plan. "I'm so grateful that Englishmen don't wear *must*aches," she said as they went down the steps. "So ticklish."

"Vast experience, I gather." But he stopped her midflight and kissed her more thoroughly, the slide into her pocket firmer and more challenging. "You're cheating, my pet."

"We established no rules." As they continued down the steps, Genova saw that all eyes were on them, but the mood seemed indulgent. "So you *must* not object. Am I taxing your fortune?"

"Oh, don't worry," he said as they reached the gravel and he drew her into his arms. "I can *must*er the price."

As his lips met hers, Genova recognized a familiarity. Her own lips, her body, shaped themselves to his without thought. She'd come to this stage with Walsingham. It had taken weeks.

She pulled away. "You stole one I'd prepared, but that doesn't matter. It only needs the word. *Must, must, must, must, must!*"

She danced away as she said it. He pursued and captured her, his eyes bright. This would, she realized, work perfectly to convince everyone they were besotted lovers.

She waited for five more kisses.

He kissed her hand, then up her sleeve to brush the last kiss against her sensitive neck. It seemed time paused for a heartbeat at the sweetness of it.

"To spill out guineas might raise questions," he whispered near her ear. "What *must* I do?"

Genova disengaged, adjusting the set of her cloak. "I will remember what you owe me."

He smiled. "I'm sure you will."

"It's a lovely day," Genova said, taking a step away and looking around at the sun-gilded estate. She needed recovery before the next foray. "Exercise in the fresh air is so invigorating."

"Indeed."

With memories of Malta, she understood his innuendo. She gave him a look. "Not in England in December, sir."

"But you give me hope for summer."

"By summer, I gather you will be married to Miss Myddleton."

His brows rose. "Do you? I look to you for defense."

"Come now. You want to continue this mock betrothal for six months?" It would shatter her. No, melt her. Evaporate her.

"Why not?" he asked. "A suit of armor is always useful."

"I'm afraid I can't oblige. I have a mind to marry, and soon."

"Why?"

"I'm twenty-three years old."

"But hardly desperate."

She saw no harm in telling him the truth. "My father has remarried and I'd like a home of my own. In fact, I hoped to meet suitable gentlemen here."

"And I'm in your way. I see, but selfish aristocrat that I am, I intend to hold you to your bond."

It caused a frisson, but of course he meant only for the next few days. Genova saw Miss Myddleton eyeing them and prayed she never let her hungers show like that.

"Don't marry Miss Myddleton unless you love her, Ash."

Now, where did that completely inappropriate statement come from?

He seemed to be wondering the same thing. "She wouldn't thank you for that."

"She might. One day."

"Does it not occur to you that I would try to be a good husband?"

Surprised by his sharp tone, she studied him. "I'm sorry. But she'll fall in love with you, you see. Don't you understand the powers of your attractions?"

"I must marry. What solution do you present, O fount of wisdom?"

His tone stung, so she stung back. "Pray for love, my lord, but in the meantime, try chastity."

He laughed. "I think that would more likely engender desperation. And then what folly might I tumble into?"

Unfortunately, Genova knew exactly what he meant.

The group was finally in order and were being marshaled to walk across the lawn toward a distant stand of trees. For some reason, perhaps romantic tact, she and Ash had not been shepherded along with the rest.

That would not do. Genova hurried after them.

Chapter Twenty-six

*B*reath still misted a little in the air, but the sun was warm on her skin. The air was sharply fresh as it never was in summer. Genova inhaled, trying to clear her mind of madness. The cause of her madness fell into step beside her.

"Running away? Were nine kisses too much for you? Do you want to end the game?"

"I will end the game if you agree to support . . . that child." Diplomatically, she avoided saying "your child."

When he didn't reply, she glanced at him. "Why not? I know you already support other bastards."

"Who the devil told you that?"

"Does it matter?"

"Probably not. I can't take responsibility for Molly Carew's child."

She stopped to confront him. *"Why not?"*

She saw anger flare. "Because to do so would be seen as an admission that Molly was telling the truth. That the child is mine. And he is not."

"How can you *possibly* be sure?"

"I have no intention of explaining myself to you, Miss Smith. You must simply take my word."

If the thought wasn't ridiculous, she'd want to shake him. "You needn't protect my innocence. I know the ways men seek to avoid fathering a child."

At his look of shock, she wished the words unsaid, but why did the world insist that unmarried meant abysmally ignorant?

"How?" he asked.

She turned and marched on. "I have no intention of explaining myself to you, my lord. You must simply take my word that I am not a ruined woman."

He fell into step beside her. "I said nothing about ruin. If you're not a maiden, Genova, the next few days could be a great deal more interesting, and you must know it."

"Must?"

"I pay no forfeit for that, but you, on the other hand, do."

He stopped her, kissed his own gloved fingers then brushed them across her lips. "Seven owed," he said.

How could that touch be as devastating as a passionate embrace?

Genova turned and hurried on. She'd given him a wrong impression and now felt as if armor had been stripped away. Heaven knows what he'd do next, or how she'd respond.

"It's quite enlivening to be thought a wicked woman," she said to correct things, "when I've spent my life enshrined in virtue."

"A saint doesn't kiss as you do, Genova."

"Not even if married?"

"You're a widow?"

She heard shock and was tempted to let him think that. It wouldn't do. "I was engaged to marry."

He stopped her again, gently, looking truly compassionate. "He died?"

She turned her head away, staring blindly at a gnarled and leafless tree. Look what she'd done now. She didn't want to talk about Walsingham.

"He lives. I broke it off." Then the words tumbled out. "And thus I broke his heart. You see what a wicked woman I am." She had never before admitted the shame she felt at having treated Walsingham so cruelly.

"Why did you end it?"

Why couldn't she rebuff his quiet question?

"Because I didn't love him," she said with a sigh.

"Because I believed that marriage should be made for love."

"Believed?"

"Believe," she corrected, compelled to turn and face him, because she did still believe, despite everything.

"Remarkable. I suppose your parents were idyllically besotted."

She raised her chin at his tone. "They were in love. It's not so unusual a situation."

"No?"

"Lord Rothgar and Lady Arradale are in love."

She expected flippancy, but he said, "Perhaps."

"And Lord and Lady Bryght."

"And I would have thought him as cynical a bastard as I am. I grant you your point. The same goes for Walgrave as best I can tell, and he and I used to hunt in the same pack."

"And consider Thalia. In love after sixty years."

"Maybe," he said.

"You can doubt that?"

"Doesn't love have to be tested by reality and time, or else isn't it only a dream?"

She blinked at him. "You're right."

"I am, occasionally. And for the most part, love fails under the test."

"You're not right about that. I gather your parents were not devoted."

"Oh, intensely, but not to each other." He tucked her hand in the crook of his arm, and they headed toward the others, who were now a dangerous distance ahead. "My father was devoted to wine and dice—an unfortunate combination, you must admit. My mother loved another but was compelled to marry my father. Upon his death, she married her true love and moved abroad."

"A sorry tale, but she did love."

"But pity the poor child who perhaps hoped he was loved, too." He stopped. "Though devil alone knows why it should matter. I hardly ever saw her before my father died."

A loud crash rocked the earth beneath their feet.

"Alack and alas," he said, "they've conquered the Yule log without my vigor. Will the house of Rothgar fall with an equally earth-shaking crack? Come, before we miss the drama."

He grabbed her gloved hand and pulled her toward the trees at a run. She picked up her skirts and went, still dazed by his words. They were true, painful, and perhaps words he had never spoken to another.

He probably wished them unsaid, but for all those reasons and many others, Genova was storing them in her heart and her mind like a precious treasure.

They ran into the woodland and she almost tripped on a branch. He put an arm around her, sweeping her along, up over a rotting boll, down under a low branch.

"Stop!" she cried, gasping.

He swept her into his arms and carried her. "What have you been doing with your vigor, Genova, my sweet?"

She laughed into his shoulder, still having to suck in breaths. It was that or cry. It was as if the earth had cracked and they'd fallen into another, deeper world.

His wicked earring twinkled before her eyes. His fine jaw, slightly darkened, was close enough to touch, close enough to kiss. His smell could already make her head swim.

He looked down at her, then stilled, reflecting, surely, her bewildered thoughts. The world receded and Genova trembled, with fear as much as anything. She did not want to feel like this. Not about this man. Not when nothing connected them but artificial threads.

But was that true?

He looked away and strode forward.

"At last!"

Genova turned her head and saw they'd entered a clearing where everyone was observing them with an amused expression. Except Damaris Myddleton, of course.

It had been Lord Rothgar who'd spoken. To Genova's astonishment, he was stripped down to his waistcoat and shirtsleeves, and his wife was playing the servant by carrying his outer clothes.

Some other men were in the same casual state, and other women were loaded with clothing. Despite the crisp air, some of the men had taken off their cravats, as well, so that their shirts stood open. One had rolled up his shirtsleeves.

The gentlemen were playing woodsmen for the day. The real woodsmen, fully dressed in rougher clothing and heavy boots, observed the games with good humor. It would be a treat for them to have the lords doing the work.

A tree trunk two or more feet in diameter lay across the space. It was cut roughly at one end, but more neatly at the other, and without side branches. Even Genova's inexpert eye could tell that this tree was long dead and had been carefully prepared for the ceremonial felling.

Ash slid Genova to her feet in a way that caused a ripple of shock, and not just in her. She pushed him away in reproof, and he fell back farther than she pushed.

Despite his smile, the wolf was back. She knew it was recoil because of what he had revealed, but she frowned at him anyway. It was the only appropriate response.

"I hope you have enough vigor left for the sawing," Lord Rothgar said, indicating the big two-handed saw. Two guests—Lord Theo Dacre and Mr. Thomas Malloren, Genova thought—picked it up and set to, pushing and pulling the big saw so it bit into the wood.

Ash shrugged out of his coat with a slight air of disdain and held it out to Genova. She took it, resisting a need to snuggle it close and inhale his scent.

"I suspect I can play the maid more easily than you can play the carpenter, my lord."

"*Play* the maid?" He unpinned his cravat and unwrapped the length of soft, lace-trimmed cloth. He draped it around Genova's neck and fixed the jeweled pin through the ends, his fingers brushing against her throat. "I thought you claimed to be pure," he murmured, his eyes coldly rakish.

She ignored his comment.

"Carpenter is a noble calling, though," he said. "Even saintly."

He unfastened the placket of his shirt, then undid his cuffs and rolled up his sleeves, exposing long, strong muscles. It was as if he had her snared. She couldn't look away from arms, throat, and the chest she could envision all too well.

"I daren't attempt saintly," he said, "but I'm adept at noble."

Genova broke the entrancement and saw Miss Myddleton across the clearing, burdened with Lieutenant Ormsby's scarlet and watching Ash with a hungry frown. *Beware!* Genova wanted to call out to her. *Beware the wolf who will eat you whole.*

When she looked back, Ash was strolling over to the log. One of the men there said something, grinning. Ash laughed and replied in kind.

Genova hugged his jacket to her, fearful that they were laughing at her, though she knew they would not be so coarse. Not where she could hear it, at least.

She struggled to show nothing, wishing she was half the actor he was. Wishing she wasn't tumbling in love with an impossible man.

Chapter Twenty-seven

Genova saw Miss Myddleton approaching and groaned. *Not now.*

"I see you love him," Miss Myddleton said.

Genova defended by instinct. "That would be normal when two people plan to marry."

"Would it?" Miss Myddleton turned to watch the sawing. "People marry for practical purposes all the time."

"Which you plan to?"

"I plan to marry Ashart."

Genova wanted to shake her. "You can't marry a man without his cooperation."

The heiress's eyes were fixed on her quarry. "No?"

Genova wasn't sure if she was impelled by concern for Ashart or the young woman, but she had to warn. "Miss Myddleton, it wouldn't be wise to marry a man who is not willing. It could naturally incline him to be unpleasant."

Damaris Myddleton frowned. Was she hearing and understanding? "Men can be very stupid."

"Certainly, but so can women. Consider Lady Booth Carew."

The cat's eyes flickered to her. "A vain lackwit."

"Precisely, because forcing a marriage with Ashart, if it could be achieved, would be like locking oneself in a cage with a hungry wolf."

Those eyes widened, but not, perhaps, entirely with alarm. Unfortunately, Genova understood. Sanity said to keep as far from Ash as possible, but very little of her seemed ruled by sanity these days.

The first pair of men stepped back sweating and offered the saw to others. Ash immediately took one end. Genova saw Lieutenant Ormsby move to take the other, and Lord Rothgar stop him and take the place.

"What about the untapped vigor?" Ash asked.

"Mere rank must lend us strength."

The two men set to work, pushing and pulling so the saw ate into the wood. Given the family strife, it should have been a competition, but that was impossible. To achieve anything, they had to work in harmony.

Genova prayed that Ash take the lesson, but doubted it. Neglected by feckless parents, raised by a bitter grandmother, spoiled by rank and wealth, he might be exactly the sort to revel in chaos.

Lieutenant Ormsby demanded his turn, his look at Damaris Myddleton showing that he wanted to impress her. He was a fine figure of a man, but his cause was hopeless. He was as good as invisible in Ash's bright light.

Breathing deeply, looking glorious, Ash was returning. Genova unpinned his cravat and wiped his sweaty brow with it, aware of the ancient instinct to both cherish and claim. She could tell herself she was trying to deter Miss Myddleton from folly, but she was simply succumbing to a force as natural and irresistible as a hurricane or tidal wave.

He responded with a wicked smile that weakened her knees, even though she knew it was artifice. He draped the cravat around his neck, drew her to him with one arm, and paid her with a kiss.

It took all Genova's will not to cinch him close and demand the sort of kiss she hungered for.

"I believe that's eight guineas you owe."

"Still far short of your needs, though, isn't it?"

He strolled away to help use ropes and pulleys to load the log into a waiting cart. She watched, not caring what others saw. The beauty of their false betrothal was that she was allowed to drink in the sight of his muscular body stretching and applying force like a magnificent animal.

For sanity's sake she glanced away and saw the grinning woodsmen. They were enjoying the occasion, but there was nothing malicious there. The Bible said that you could judge a tree by the fruit it bears, something she'd always thought sound. In the navy, you could always judge a captain by his ship. Judged by his land, his servants, and his tenants, the Marquess of Rothgar was a good lord.

What of the Marquess of Ashart?

Once the log was on the cart, a long-necked jug of something went the rounds of the sweating gentlemen. Ash drank deep, his head thrown back, his strong neck rippling.

The jug ended with the woodsmen, who took hearty swigs and called, "God bless ye, merry gentlemen at Christmastide!" They took it with them as they climbed up on the cart and traveled off with the log toward the house.

The men began to reclaim clothing. When Ash strolled back to her side, Genova gave up his coat and gloves, and posed the question that concerned her. "Shouldn't you be at your own estate for Christmas?"

"My grandmother takes care of everything there."

"That isn't an answer to my question."

His look was all marquess. "Your question was impertinent."

"Tell me anyway."

He shook his head, looking astonished. Genova wasn't daunted. In their new world, he wasn't a marquess. He was a man, no different from the young naval officers who'd been her friends.

"My grandmother thrives on the work. She'd sink into a decline if I interfered."

"But how did that come about?"

With an air of one humoring a lunatic, he said, "She married my grandfather sixty years ago, Miss Smith. Cheynings has been her life ever since. Grandfather apparently had little interest in estate management. He was a soldier and courtier. My uncle and father cared nothing for their properties beyond the income they provided."

"Your grandmother had the raising of her sons. She could have trained them to their tasks."

"Do you never respect boundaries?"

She didn't flinch. "Not with friends."

Something—a frown?—flickered across his face and he looked away. "We're being armed with weapons and baskets."

Conscious of having said more than she'd intended, Genova went to pick up one of the baskets. When she turned, Ash was close beside her, a sheathed pruning knife in his hand.

"I don't know how my uncle was raised," he said, "but my father was never expected to inherit the title. His career was the army." After a moment, he added, "I was only eight when my father died. It was as well that my grandmother was skilled at managing my properties."

But the Dowager Lady Ashart hadn't raised Ash to supplant her any more than she'd raised her sons to do so.

Genova phrased a careful question. "Does she not tire of the work? She must be Thalia's age."

"She thrives on it. What impossible thing are you thinking now, Genova Smith?"

She had to give him the truth. "That it's time for you to relieve her of her labors."

She was braced for dismissal, even for anger, but instead he looked away and she heard him say softly, "What if it's like stealing her breath?"

Her understanding of him shifted deeper, as it had been shifting all afternoon. She wanted to take him in her arms. She wanted to sit and talk about these things until everything was resolved. She wanted . . .

Lady Arradale cut into her thoughts like a blade through silk. "And now for greenery!"

Genova looked around slightly dazed, even sick, as

if she'd been out in the hot sun too long. All the ladies had baskets, all the men had knives. She thought vaguely that armed men could be dangerous.

She couldn't bear any suggestion of danger to Ash. If she could, she'd wrap him in flannel and never let him take a risk again. She was mad.

People spread through the trees, stripping long lengths of ivy, and snipping holly. Genova did her part but felt distanced, as if she had a fever. Ash joked, teased, and flirted as if among friends.

Everyone wanted to get to the mistletoe, but Lady Arradale stood firm until the cart was full. "Now," she said, "we can go on to the orchard."

There was a great cheer and someone started the mistletoe song again.

> Hey, ho, the mistletoe,
> It's off to the greenwood we do
>   go. . . .

"But beware," said Ash when the song died, "for the mistletoe can slay even invincible heroes."

They were emerging from the wood by then, in small, laughing groups. The house stood massive some distance away, and they would have to go partly around it to reach the orchards and kitchen gardens.

Genova and Ash were with Lord Rothgar, Damaris Myddleton, and the ever-hopeful Lieutenant Ormsby. Genova was again between two marquesses. Was she unbalanced to be braced for danger? It was probably the effect of evening creeping early upon them.

The sky had darkened, and somewhere behind the clouds the sun was beginning to set. She didn't think she was imagining that the air had turned colder, that a damp chill was creeping through shoes and under cloaks.

Or perhaps the shiver on her skin was because of Ashart's comment about dead heroes and the tone in which he'd spoken.

"Because it's poisonous?" she asked.

Lord Rothgar answered. "Because the mistletoe killed Balder, and he was not a mere hero but a god. That's what you meant, isn't it, Ashart?"

"Precisely. But one could say that Balder was killed because of the actions of his mother."

Mother. Genova knew then that a new duel had begun.

"What actions?" demanded Miss Myddleton, who had placed herself on Ash's other side.

"First Balder's mother begged the gods to let her swear every living thing not to hurt him."

"How could that be bad?" Genova asked. "Any mother would do that if she could."

"But she ignored the mistletoe because she thought it too feeble to be dangerous. Typical female idiocy."

"And on idle evenings," Rothgar said, "the gods amused themselves by trying to kill him. Typical male idiocy."

"What happened?" Genova asked, wondering what hidden dangers this conversation held.

"Imagine if you will," Rothgar said, a raconteur amusing an audience, "a night in Asgard, Hall of the Gods. Mead flows and spirits soar. Lacking better amusement, the gods fire arrows at the fortunate one, and even hack at him with sharp blades."

Ash laughed. "How reminiscent of the Court of St. James."

"Hush." But surely Lord Rothgar's lips twitched. "Balder does not suffer—"

"May I express doubt?"

"—until Loki, envious of Balder's good fortune . . ."

Loki. Genova almost gasped.

"The good fortune, note," said Ash, "of being subject to constant attack. How very like the life of a favorite at court."

"The fortunate must always be on guard," Rothgar agreed. "Balder lacked this insight, and see what became of it. Loki—I believe you remember Loki, whose sole purpose was to ferment strife . . . ?"

"We all recognize the type."

"Name no names, cousin."

Genova's head was whirling.

"Loki cut a mistletoe branch and shaped a spear of it. Did he intend to kill, or was he ruled only by mischief?"

"But," Genova interrupted, "no one could make a spear out of mistletoe. It's a vine."

"Relentlessly practical," said Ash. "This was before the modern age, before Christ. One story says that the Cross was made from the mistletoe tree, which was then cursed into its present feeble state, required to suck life from other trees."

"In that case, Balder's mother wouldn't have ignored it."

"*Relentlessly* practical. The point of the story won't be affected by logic, Genova."

She had been arguing because she sensed something unpleasant coming. She made herself stay silent.

"Loki made his weapon," said Rothgar, "but he did not launch it himself. Instead he persuaded Balder's blind brother to do it by telling Hodur that Balder wanted him to be part of the game. Then he guided his arm. Balder died, and all the gods wept into their mead."

"None considering, we assume, that the disaster rose entirely from their own foolish actions."

"Who ever does?" Lord Rothgar asked. "Instead they turned on Loki."

"It was his fault," Genova pointed out.

"But sometimes an action has deep roots, Miss Smith, and the final hand is not the only guilty one. As for Loki, the gods hunted him down, then chained him beneath a serpent whose scalding venom drips on his face for eternity. There are none so harsh as those weighed down by guilt."

Guilt? Whose guilt? Rothgar's mother's? His father's? This wasn't all about ancient myth.

A silence ran and in the end Genova couldn't stand it. "Why are mythological mothers so careless? Achilles' mother left his heel unprotected. Balder's mother neglected the mistletoe. A little thoroughness would have solved all."

Ash gave her a "relentlessly practical" look, and she wished she'd held her tongue.

"Thoroughness would give us invincible heroes," Lord Rothgar said, "and it's our vincibilities that make us human."

"Or perhaps," said Ash, "it is merely that since Cain and Abel, children have borne the burden of the sins of their parents."

"It would explain a great deal," Rothgar said, apparently unaffected by the reference, "but the cruel gods are dead, and we live in the reign of the Prince of Peace. He who commands us to forgive our enemies."

That was direct.

Ash made no response. Did he really see himself as Loki? Was he threatening to destroy Rothgar with some mysterious weapon?

They had crossed the meadow with her scarcely aware of it, and come to the orchard, protected from the deer by a fence.

"Onward to mistletoe," Rothgar said, opening the gate. "In these enlightened times it can only slay us through kisses."

Ash guided Genova through and closed the gate behind them. "But remember," he said, "that the Prince of Peace was betrayed unto death by a kiss."

Chapter Twenty-eight

Genova expected something more, some climax, even a violent one. Part of her wanted it as one longs for the storm that will break oppressive weather. Lord Rothgar left them, however, to chat to other guests, taking Miss Myddleton and Ormsby with him.

She frowned at Ash, wishing she could drag his thoughts out of him like rope out of a hold. All sense of knowing him had gone. He was an enigma.

It was Christmas, time of peace, but she'd lived among war and knew how it could run mad in the blood. She'd seen men attack others simply for their nationality, or uniform, or name, as if hatred for certain groups was burned into their soul.

"Aha," Ash said.

Genova looked up and saw a lushly berried branch of mistletoe almost brushing her head. She couldn't believe he was trying to play games now and stepped back.

He sighed. "I warned you not to get involved."

"How can I help it?"

He cut the sprig and gave it to her. "Let me arm you, at least. I'm sure you know my vincibilities by now."

She put it carefully in her basket, preserving the berries. "I will never hurt you if I can help it, Ash. Please believe that."

"But as we've seen, the best intentions can be disastrous."

He used a ladder propped against the tree to harvest it with brutal efficiency. "This stuff's a parasite, you know. It lives off the tree. If allowed, it will suck all life out of it, and thus die itself. A very stupid plant."

"Tell me a clever one."

He looked down at her, startled, then laughed. "You will never let me get away with an idiocy, will you, Genova?"

She should make a light rejoinder, but she said, "I'll try not to."

He cut the last branch of mistletoe and climbed down. "A penny for your thoughts."

"A guinea. No, ten."

"Agreed."

She glanced at him, then across the misty, darkening orchard, where laughter and chatter were clear, but where everyone but Ash beside her looked like a wraith.

"I was thinking that I feel on an edge. Scarce able to hold my balance. I don't even know what the edge is, what lies to either side." She pulled a wry face at him. "These wanderings are not worth even a penny."

But he was looking at her seriously. "I know what you mean about an edge. Sometimes it feels that I live on the edge of a sharp sword."

She shivered, but said, "Not for me. For me the danger comes from what's on either side. Often everything is shrouded in mist, so it's unclear which side is safe, which is dangerous."

"But do we always want the safe side?"

"Ah." She inhaled it, understanding at last why she'd felt such turmoil. "No, not always. It feels wrong not to want safety, but the edge is where everything happens. The edge is where things change. It's decision, and action, and creation. It's birth and death. It's life. Doesn't everyone live on the edge, anyway?"

"Probably wise people try not to."

"Then I don't think I'm wise," she whispered.

"Nor I. But it doesn't need to be dramatic, I don't think. A man can live on the edge in one room, studying the stars, like Galileo."

She turned to him, surprised by this whole conversation, but especially that he'd understood her unformed problem. "So he can. I was worried for a moment that I'd have to go traveling again or die."

"One room and an idea will suffice. Everyone's leaving at last," he said, taking her basket and touching her to guide her across to the other side of the orchard.

"For you?" she asked.

"I am compelled to walk the perilous edge through many rooms. It is my destiny. I have to admit that I often enjoy the thrill."

This let her say, "So do I. I have enjoyed much of my life, despite hardship and war. I am finding my new life tedious."

"Really?" he asked, and she laughed.

"Not the last few days, I must admit."

"Good. Above all, I would hate to be boring."

"I need to find the edge," she said, as much to herself as to him. "To do useful things and see tangible results."

"Relentlessly practical." There was no sting in it now.

"And you're not?"

"Genova, my sweet, I'm a creature of whimsy and artifice of no practical use at all."

"Rosemary!" someone called ahead in the gloom. A hinge creaked.

"Ah, rosemary," he said, as they quickened their steps. "Sacred to Venus and reputed to replenish male vigor. Useful at this point."

He'd slid from their discussion, and Genova knew it was wise. The conversation was another pearl, however, that she would consider deeply when she had time.

"Christmas is taking on a most unholy aura when seen through your eyes," she said.

"But of course. Christ's birthday was pasted on top of the Roman feast of Saturnalia, a time for wild revels. Add the Norse Yule, festival of light, and what can we do but be wild? Rothgar must be demented to play these games.''

"He wasn't expecting you," she pointed out.

"How true. Do you think I should make peace?"

For a moment she didn't understand him. When she did, she tried to read his expression in the vague, deceptive light. In the end she said, "Yes."

"Without knowing the cause and details of the war?"

"Peace is always better than war."

"A simplistic assessment."

Sudden rage flamed in her and she stopped. "What do you know of war and peace, you creature of whimsy and artifice? Assist at an amputation, or try to hold a man's body together as he cries for his mother before you speak lightly of war to me!"

His hand moved toward her, faltered.

Behind him, lights in the great house began to spring to life in random windows. They had reached the afternoon death of the light.

Genova whirled and almost ran after the group, into a walled herb garden, aromatic even in winter. Her shoes clipped on a stone path as she hurried to press in among the others.

She realized she had neither basket nor knife.

Ash appeared at her side and returned her basket. Then he cut sprigs. The pungent smell stung her nose.

" 'Here's rosemary for remembrance,' " he said, passing a bundle over.

"And it means true love and weddings!" a woman cried.

"And fidelity," said Damaris Myddleton, appearing at their side. "Here, Ashart, dare you wear a sprig of it?"

Genova thanked heaven she didn't have a sharp knife in her hand. The great house glowed brighter and brighter, promising warmth, safety, and civilized restraint.

"It's time to go," Genova said, turning and leading

the way out of the garden, even though it wasn't her place to do so.

Damaris Myddleton would drive her to violence, but the deeper pain was because Miss Myddleton would probably end up in the cage with the wolf. Despite all logic, Genova envied her that.

Why had she said what she'd said? People far from war never wanted to know what it was really like. War was a part of the edge that most people avoided, a part red with blood.

She'd simply been infuriated that someone with the chance of peace should contemplate throwing it away, and she still was.

Chapter Twenty-nine

*E*veryone caught up with her and she let herself be enveloped by the merry group as they entered through the main doors. She laughed with them, teased and flirted, as they all piled their mistletoe and herbs with the holly and ivy near the Yule log.

The marble hall was brilliant with vibrant life. Excited voices seemed to bounce off the walls and return threefold, and the light from hundreds of candles blazed off crystal chandeliers. A servant took Genova's outerwear, and it was certainly warm enough with so many people and so many candles, even though the grate was empty, awaiting the log.

She accepted a mug of mulled cider and warmed her hands on it, blocking all thoughts of what had happened out there, but she couldn't keep her eyes off Ash.

He stood near the log, drinking, laughing, presumably debating how to get the log off its felt cloth and into the fireplace. He was so good at masking his feelings. It was probably the result of lifelong training for court, where a person wasn't allowed to even sneeze. Of a life, as he'd said, lived on the edge.

How could she know the real man when he wore so many layers of artifice?

She knew, however, that at moments today he'd revealed the truth.

Damaris Myddleton, hovering near Ash, was not good at masking her feelings. Perhaps she was what he needed, though. Someone who would be satisfied with lord and husband, and wouldn't drag him to the edge of the emotions.

Emotions, oceans. She suddenly saw the edge like the place where the oceans kissed the earth. Not apparently dramatic, and yet a complete change . . .

"Genova! Genova, dear!"

She turned to see Thalia waving from across the hall. Lady Calliope was with her, pushed by a footman. Genova hurried toward a safe haven.

"How splendid!" Thalia exclaimed. "And mistletoe. Plenty of berries, too! Always a good sign."

"Sign of a harsh winter," grumbled Lady Calliope. "Steer some of that punch over here, Genova."

Genova beckoned one of the footmen carrying trays of glasses and passed two drinks over. "Christmas blessings," she said, raising her own glass.

"And many of them!" Thalia declared, draining half in a gulp.

Lady Calliope drank but didn't say anything.

"Is something the matter, Lady Calliope?" Genova asked. "Are you in pain?"

"No more than usual." She looked up. "Ashart's not for you, Genova, so don't do anything foolish."

Genova couldn't stop her face flaming.

Thalia exclaimed, "Callie!"

"Of course he isn't," Genova said, as calmly as she could.

"I'd say this betrothal was a folly of Thalia's making except that the Oliphants heard the story on their way here. Fat, red-nosed fellow over there and his gaunt wife. Encountered the Brokesbys in London and heard the wondrous tale of Ashart's betrothal to his great-aunts' companion, along with hints of lewdness. Probably all the worse for being vague."

Genova looked at the middle-aged couple, wishing them to Hades.

"No one will think *too* much of it, dear," said Thalia, "now you are engaged to marry."

"And when that ends, I'll be a fool who permitted too many liberties."

"It'll blow over," Lady Calliope said brusquely, "and it'll be a feather in your cap to have interested him at all. As long as you don't fall into folly over it."

Genova knew exactly what she meant, but said, "I am not the sort to fall into folly."

"No, thank Zeus. Unlike that Miss Myddleton. Silly piglet. But he might as well let her catch him. She's from a good enough family and rich."

"I do think it a shame," Thalia said with a pout.

"There's a light in the darkness." Lady Calliope looked up at Genova. "We're hoping we can persuade you to live in our house in Tunbridge Wells, dear. To continue as companion. You'll have a room of your own, and a maid, and all comforts. I'm sure it won't last past the spring, when the Wells is alive with eligible gentlemen, but we would enjoy your company."

Genova looked away, swallowing tears, touched but embarrassed. This was an offer made out of pity, a salve to her wounded heart. She must have been as transparent as Damaris Myddleton, and she hated that.

What's more, she couldn't take the kind offer. She couldn't live where she might meet Ash, perhaps even be expected to dance at his wedding.

She was saved from having to respond by a bump on her leg. She steadied little Francis Malloren, who seemed intent on Lady Calliope's chair. He toddled on and arrived at the old lady's blanketed knees.

"G'day," he said, beaming, with no hint of shyness.

A flustered maid rushed after. "I'm so sorry, milady! This is Master Francis Malloren, milady."

Genova braced to deal with harshness, but Lady Calliope looked the boy in the eye. "And what attracts you to an old crone, Master Francis Malloren, when there are mince pies and sugarplums to be had?"

The boy patted her lap. "Up!"

A chuckle rumbled. "A Malloren through and through. Lift him up then, girl, and we'll tour this mayhem together. Off you go, Genova, and enjoy yourself. But take care."

Thalia linked arms with Genova. "Do let's help with the mistletoe, dear!"

Genova might have tried to slip to the edges of the room—another sort of edge—but Thalia headed straight for the middle, where the ladies were making bundles of greenery to place around the hall. Genova noted that they were tying it up with new ribbons, so frugality had lost that battle. But then, that had only been a pretext.

During that chat with Portia, she'd been informed that the Mallorens were ordinary people beneath the glitter, but that Lord Rothgar was ruthless in protecting them and their interests. Why inform *her,* however? Did they overestimate her influence to that extent?

No longer. She'd told Portia the truth about the engagement. Thank heavens for that. She would not be a pawn in this game.

"Perhaps I might even get a kiss," Thalia said, looking up at a huge bouquet of mistletoe that had just been hung from the central chandelier, low enough for the gentlemen to pluck the berries. "I'm sure Richard wouldn't mind."

Genova steered Thalia under there, looking for a suitable gentleman. Her eyes fixed on Ash because she caught him looking at her. Her heart skipped a beat, with no conscious control at all.

After a still moment, she mimed her request.

He looked puzzled, but then came toward them, smiling. He still wore the plain riding clothes in which she'd first seen him, but he was all beau, all courtier, as he bowed. He could have been in powder, satin, and lace.

"Why, Thalia, if you don't want to be thoroughly kissed, this is most careless of you."

Thalia laughed with delight. "You naughty boy, but I am caught, indeed I am!"

She presented a cheek, but he swept her into his arms and planted a kiss solidly on her lips. She emerged with high color that was entirely natural, and with a beaming smile that was brighter than any Genova had seen on her.

She feared her own smile was as wide. No matter what his faults, the Marquess of Ashart could be exceedingly kind.

As he plucked a berry from the bunch, Thalia said, "What a charming rascal you are, Ashart!" But then she tugged Genova under the branch. "And here is your reward."

Genova could hardly resist. They were the center of all eyes, including the Oliphants'. She wanted to refuse, though. Mistletoe kisses seemed sour when put against her confused but profound feelings.

He took her hand, but only to pull her away from the bough. "A man needs no excuse to kiss his future bride, Thalia, so I'll preserve the berries for less fortunate gentlemen."

A buzz said some had not heard the news. People nearby congratulated them, wishing them well, but Genova saw much astonishment. She hoped her blushes were taken for maidenly delight and was grateful when Ash drew her away from the hub.

"I hate this," she said.

"Do you want to break it off now? It's too early, but we can cope."

He was serious. She shook her head. "As you say, it's too early. We might as well play the game to its end. This feels like a lie, though. I don't like to lie."

He took her hand. "Then consider us betrothed for a little while. I certainly haven't promised anyone here that I'll actually marry you. Have you sworn to marry me?"

He was making her smile. "No."

"You see. All is easy."

Easy? Hardly, but good humor made it easier to express her thoughts. "I'm sorry for what I said earlier. It was unfair."

"No, it wasn't. I should have realized what your experiences might have been. You awe me."

She shook her head. "Don't. There's nothing extraordinary about my life."

"Perhaps I have lost touch with what women can be."

"Any woman, Ash. Don't forget, the edge can be found in the simplest places. In a room with an idea. In a kitchen with a pot, in a nursery with a child. Women who fight Barbary pirates aren't better than those who tend their families at home."

"But you," he said simply, "are you."

She looked at him, breathless, but then it was as if a shutter closed. He looked away, then said, "There's the maid and baby."

Chapter Thirty

Genova turned and saw Sheena with Charlie in her arms. A glance around showed many servants present, some helping, some merely looking on and even enjoying the Christmas delicacies and drinks. It had to be with permission.

Ash was already heading across the hall toward the Irish girl. Genova hurried after him, thinking that he, too, was concerned that Charlie might cry, but then realized that he probably didn't know about his cousin's weakness.

She was caught and kissed by three other men. She managed to laugh and flirt to the required degree, but her reaction was only impatience. She needed to keep up with Ash, but also, no kisses other than his mattered now.

She saw Sheena bob a curtsy, face sinking into sullenness. Was close enough to hear her say, "Good day, milord," as if she spoke English well. The girl was clever, which would be a good thing.

"Good day, Sheena," Ash said, as Genova arrived at his side. "Lady Booth Carew?"

The girl's eyes widened, but she nodded.

"Where is she?"

Sheena's eyes hunted around for help.

"Where is Charlie's mother, Sheena?"

"Stop!" Genova put herself between them. "You're frightening her."

"If I'm to make peace," he said sharply, "I have to sort out my affairs, especially those relating to Molly

Carew. Sheena is clearly not stupid and she understands a bit of English. Names do not change much from language to language, and nor does the word for mother."

"But why would she know anything of use to you? She's simply a wet nurse."

"Don't you want to find the truth?"

"Yes, of course, but not like this!"

His dark eyes studied her. "You admit there is a truth to be found?"

She hadn't meant that, but challenged, she opened her mind. She now felt sure that he would not lie to her.

"Yes. I believe you," she said. "I don't understand how you can be sure you're not Charlie's father, but I believe that you are. Sure, that is."

"Somewhat guarded, but thank you. If I can discover the real father, it will solve many of my problems."

"Lady Booth's the one to ask, isn't she?"

"She seems to have slipped away."

"Slipped away?"

"A friend was with me at the Lion and Unicorn. He went after her, but lost the trail."

Genova kept an eye on Sheena and the baby but was absorbed by this discussion. They were talking, directly and practically, and it felt completely natural, as if they had known each other a long time.

And as if they trusted each other. It was as if a cloud of insubstantial delights had coalesced into a pearl, something real that could be held and cherished.

It made it easy to put a hand on his arm. "As you said, she can't disappear entirely, Ash. There'll be time enough to talk to Lady Booth after Christmas."

He covered her hand with his own. "I think you could keep me sane, Genova."

"Is your sanity in doubt?"

"Constantly. Especially recently."

He put his finger beneath her chin, and when she

didn't resist, he kissed her. It was light and simple, but perhaps the sweetest kiss they'd shared. She didn't request a guinea, and he didn't offer one.

"I should be doing my duty to the Yule log," he said, with a last glance at Sheena. "Will you try to find out what she knows?"

"Of course, but she really does understand virtually no English."

He grimaced, then walked away.

Genova turned back to Sheena, who was still looking wary. To soothe the girl, Genova plucked a cake from a passing tray.

Sheena brightened immediately and consumed it. The baby slept on, but he could awaken at any moment. Genova hated to spoil Sheena's treat, but she had to. "You must return to the nurseries," pointing toward the great stairs.

Sheena shook her head, but Genova insisted and began to steer her that way. Genova went slowly, however, and chose various delicacies for the girl along the way.

To allow Sheena to enjoy them, Genova took the baby for a while and found comfort for herself in the bundle. There was something about a baby that brought the world into perspective.

When they reached the stairs, singing started over near the Yule log. Sheena stopped to listen, and since the baby was still fast asleep, Genova took the girl up three steps so they'd have a better view.

A group of gentlemen, including Ash, was singing a Christmas round about spiced ale and cheer. It would probably be called a glee, and once Genova would have thought glee and Ash uncomfortable partners. No longer. There was a joyous man in him, and he might be breaking free.

Then some ladies sang "The Holly and the Ivy," led by Damaris Myddleton, who did have a lovely voice. Everyone began to join in.

Genova rocked the baby, praying the swelling sound wouldn't wake him. A twitch of the bowed lips was

almost like a smile. A deep need stirred then, a powerful need to have children of her own. To bear one
man's children.

She looked across at Ash. Her heart was given.

It was a strange recognition. Not dramatic, but calm
and certain. This wasn't a fit of wild lust or a passing infatuation.

Well, then. What was she going to do about it?

She was no grand lady, but she could be a good
wife for him, she was sure. They were equals in all
the ways that mattered. Hadn't he just said that she
could be his sanity?

She didn't know all she would need to know, but
that would have been true if she'd encouraged the
courtship of Hester's neighbor, a wine merchant. She
could learn. She would enjoy learning. She would even
learn how not to sneeze in the royal presence.

And love must weigh in the balance, especially a
love like this, which she thought he shared. Only
thought, but surely that would become clear.

Then there was the physical. Yes, indeed, there was
the physical, not to be discounted when it came to
marriage. A happy bed was the heart of that. She
could certainly be happy in his bed, and she hoped
she could make him happy in turn.

Make a rake happy enough to be faithful?

She remembered him saying he intended to be a
good husband. He might not have meant fidelity, but
it was a start.

She allowed herself to watch him a little longer,
absorbing the change in everything. Her new thoughts
and feelings were as frightening as naked blades, but
as exciting. Yes, she was someone who needed to live
on the edge.

The song ended in laughter and chatter, and a little
noise pulled her out of thought. Charlie wasn't crying,
or about to, thank heavens, but his big eyes were wide
and alert. It was time to get him away from here.

She put the baby in Sheena's arms. "Charlie's
awake. You must take him back upstairs."

She pointed upstairs, but Sheena shook her head.

Genova was about to insist when the girl pointed toward the back of the house, saying something equally firmly. Of course. By now she'd have learned to use the servants' stairs.

Genova watched the pair leave, thinking that Sheena might have a clearer idea of her place in this world than she had. What sort of madness said that she could marry a marquess?

She climbed the elegant stairs to the half landing to observe again. This in-between spot was more in keeping with her position. Ash was down in the heart of things, near the fireplace, where the log was now in place. She was apart, up here.

She remembered leaning on the balustrade in the Lion and Unicorn, admiring a virile stranger.

He was still a stranger in some ways, but she knew him. She knew him deep in her heart, soul, and gut.

Then she realized that being up here felt like being on the bridge of one of her father's ships. She'd been blessed by good parents and an interesting life. What would her father have to say about her strange new adventures if he knew?

Keep a solid ship beneath your feet, Genni-love, and you can ride out the wildest storms.

Fanciful dreams did not form a solid ship, but surely the connection forged between her and Ash today did.

Chapter Thirty-one

Genova saw Damaris Myddleton heading back toward Ash and went down the stairs. It was time to roll out the guns and do battle for the prize. Though she'd like to have sailed a direct course, discretion forced her to tack, chatting, flirting, and being kissed a few more times.

If all the men were paying her guineas, Charlie's account would be growing nicely.

She was almost at the fireplace when she noticed Lady Walgrave—Lady Elf—frowning and rubbing her massive belly.

"Are you all right, my lady?"

Lady Elf looked at her, then smiled. "Oh, yes, just feeling restless. I have always done this, you see."

Genova did. "It's strange to pass things over to others. You have your own home now, however."

"Yes, and I intend to do something as splendid in time. Walgrave Towers was a rather chilly house, so it's being drastically renovated. That's why we're here at such a time. I didn't want to give birth in town."

Was this chatter, or more information being fed to her? Lady Elf, after all, was a true Malloren.

Genova could see Ash, and Damaris Myddleton was in the same group. She needed to ask a question of Lord Rothgar's sister, however. "Do you think your brother wants peace with Lord Ashart?"

Lady Elf looked at her, surprised. "Yes, of course. Is it possible?"

Negotiation through intermediaries? Genova hesitated, for Ash certainly hadn't appointed her to the position. "Yes, I think it is. But there must be many grievances to be dealt with on both sides."

Lady Elf looked around, clearly making sure no one was listening. "There are, yes," she said quietly, "and the most serious are to do with family. I gather the Dowager Lady Ashart truly believes that the Mallorens were responsible for the death of her husband as well as her daughter. He died, you see, because of Lady Augusta's tragedy. At least, he died not long afterward, and she chooses to see cause and effect."

"It could be so. My mother's death caused a great change in my father."

"But it still requires that my father caused his first wife to murder her baby. No one who knew him believes it."

"Can't Lady Ashart be convinced of this?"

"Apparently not. As for our wounds, she has tried many times to harm us." Lady Elf glanced around again. "She paid a man to try to seduce me."

"My heaven! What happened to him?"

"Rothgar called him out."

That's what Genova feared. "And killed him?"

"No. But he has little use of his right arm."

In a way it seemed worse than death. It sounded so coldly calculated, but Lady Elf seemed to think it completely normal.

"My brother's vigilance has kept us safe," Lady Elf said, "despite the dowager's machinations. Things have been better recently. Rothgar's growing power deters, and I gather the Trayce fortune is severely depleted."

"The sooner peace is settled, the better."

"We agree entirely."

We.

Genova glanced at Ash. He was about to kiss Miss Myddleton beneath the mistletoe!

Before Genova could excuse herself, Lord Walgrave came over to his wife. "You must be tired, love. Come and sit down."

"Don't fuss. If anything I'm restless. If my hips didn't ache, I'd go for a long walk."

"Heaven help us, isn't that typical of a Malloren?" Lord Walgrave addressed that humorously to Genova, making it hard for her to move away, and if she did, what could she do?

"They say my mother walked miles every day when she was carrying children," Lady Elf protested, "and she bore them without trouble, even Cyn and I." She put a hand to her back. "I must say I hoped to be sharing Christmas with my baby, rather than with a sore back and hips."

"My mother said she felt the same about me," Genova said, stealing glances at the mild kiss, "and it came true."

"You were a Christmas baby?"

Genova realized what she'd done and tried to think of an evasion.

"When's your birthday?"

She could hardly lie. "Today, just. A half hour before midnight, or so I am told."

Lady Elf clapped her hands. "Diana! It's Genova's birthday. We must have a birthday ball!"

Genova tried to protest, but was ignored.

"But of course!" said Lady Arradale, coming over. "I intended an informal hop once the work is done, but this will make it special. To the ballroom, everybody!"

Genova could do nothing but allow herself to be swept by the company up the stairs and into a grand ballroom already transformed. She gaped at a miraculous illusion of a village in the mountains.

The open floor was dusted with chalk, which gave the look of snow, and surrounded by small, steep-roofed cottages. They would be big enough only for a couple to sit in, but in proportion to everything else, they looked full-size.

Miniature fir trees in pots created the effect of forest around the cottages, and that was continued by trees painted on cloths hung on the walls, cloths that ended in white peaks, like mountains. They sparkled in the light of three chandeliers, as if they truly were snowcapped.

"It's amazing," Genova said.

"It has worked out well, hasn't it?" Lady Arradale was beside her. "The true ball will be tomorrow, Christmas Day, but everyone deserves some merriment now."

Music started. Genova saw that six musicians had taken their places in a greenery-hung gallery. Lord Rothgar took Genova's hand and led her into the center of the room. "This is Miss Smith's birthday ball, so she must call the first dance and choose her partner."

Pinned firmly at the very heart of this artificial, glittering world, Genova was struck by panic. Lady Arradale had talked of an informal hop, but this seemed very formal to her. She didn't know what dances were suitable here. She was going to embarrass herself.

And she'd dreamed she could fit in!

"I will drink poison if you choose anyone but me, beloved," Ash said, coming forward to take her hand. "Especially as you have stationed yourself beneath some mistletoe."

Genova looked up and realized that she was exactly under a mistletoe bough that hung from the central chandelier—and that Lord Rothgar had placed her there. She shot him a glance before moving into Ash's arms.

He drew her close, but just before his lips touched hers, he murmured, "Call for the 'Merry Dancers.'"

She kissed him back, her love greater because of gratitude. He'd realized her predicament and solved it.

Her doubts fled. This had to be right.

She tried to read his expression, but it could mean anything or nothing. He reached up and plucked a berry, but then took something out of his pocket.

A guinea, here?

"A gift for a kiss," he said, "and what better for you, my love, than a ring."

Light flared on a diamond. A large diamond. He took her left hand but she pulled back. Diamonds had become popular for betrothal rings because the stone was so resistant to damage and would endure. A beautiful thought, but until she won Ash's love it would be as false as the mountains on the wall.

He raised his brows and she surrendered. What else could she do but let him slide the ring onto her finger? It was a little loose, but only a little, and candlelight sparked rainbows from the magnificent stone.

Everyone applauded. Genova smiled, but she could only think how lovely this would be if real.

"You must call the dance, Miss Smith," Lady Arradale reminded her.

Looking at Ash, Genova said, "The 'Merry Dancers.'" It was a simple one that she knew. If he'd suggested it, it would be appropriate. She could trust him that far. No, she could trust him much further than that. He had never promised more than he could fulfill and he had warned her not to get involved.

If this broke her heart, it would not be his fault.

The music started up, and Ash led her into place. She would at least have this, a dance with him. She knew she would count all these little things like pearls knotted one by one onto silk, and carry them with her if she lost this fight and lost him.

She was glad of the lively line dance that allowed little opportunity for conversation or thought. As always, it became impossible to be gloomy when in a dance.

She passed down the line and touched hands with all the ladies, including the older Miss Inchcliff, whose eyes were brilliant with excitement. The younger people were here, including small children in a line dance of their own, giggling as they bumped and hurtled up and down.

Genova turned with a girl—Miss Yardley?—who must almost be of age to be presented at court. She was flirting with all the men like a puppy testing its teeth on a thrown leather ball. Miss Yardley ignored a couple of young lads who, though old enough for the adult dance, looked uncertain as to whether this was a treat or penance.

They were all in training for their purpose, Genova realized, even here at an impromptu celebration. Training to be courtiers, to amuse, to flirt, to promote their family's interests, to progress in a career or marry well.

She was trained, too. Her parents had not neglected manners and etiquette, but her practical experience had been somewhat more varied. Did knowledge of how to eat from a communal dish of spicy lamb stew that included eyeballs count?

It might, she thought. She knew well the lesson that a guest must adapt to the host, whether it be at a house or in a country.

The first set ended, and punch and other drinks were carried in. Ash led Genova over for refreshment, and she thought he hadn't escaped the magic of the dance.

"Exercise becomes you," he said.

"You mean that I'm flushed and hearty?"

"I mean that you are beautiful. Like a rich, spicy dish."

"Complete with sheep's eyes?" The joke escaped, but of course he couldn't see the connection.

"What?"

So she told him, describing a feast in Morocco and how the British had been trying to slip the eyeballs into their pockets.

"That must have created an interesting discovery for your maid."

"Oh, I ate mine."

"Why am I not surprised?"

"I had the distinct impression that our host knew the eyes would upset us and was enjoying the fuss."

He laughed, his eyes admiring. Another pearl, but she was wincing inside. Why had she talked about sheep's eyes? It might be interesting, even admirable, but it wasn't a recommendation as a marchioness.

But then, as she danced with Captain Dalby, a naval officer, she knew nothing good could come of pretense. If she tricked Ash into marriage with an artificial Genova Smith, that would surely lead to disaster.

Captain Dalby turned out to know her father, which was delightful, and with some prompting she remembered a few encounters over the years. She came to see that he was an admirer, and could even be a suitor. Once she might have at least flirted, even though she didn't want the navy life. Now she gently discouraged.

Lord Bryght claimed her next, then Dr. Egan. She never lacked a partner, and she danced with Ash twice more. More pearls on her string. Then, sooner than she could have imagined, clocks chimed twelve.

"It's Christmas Day!" people cried out, and, "Merry Christmas!"

Everyone mingled, kissing cheeks and offering good wishes, and then they were all swept out and down to the hall where the great Yule log awaited. Genova watched from Ash's side. Another pearl.

Within moments, a dignified, gray-haired servant marched out from the back of the house with a burning tinder in his hand. "The Yule light, milord!"

It was the fragment of last year's log, preserved until now to provide continuity of light and warmth. Rothgar took it and applied it to the tinder. The tinder caught, then flames began to lick at the dry bark. Soon the great fire roared. Christmas had arrived.

Genova saw Ash observing the flames with an unreadable expression and knew he was thinking of vigor, still torn between allegiances. She took his hand. After a moment, his fingers wove with hers.

That gave her courage to say, "Peace is always the best choice."

"If it can be achieved with honor," he said.

She swallowed an ache caused by his doubts, but said, "You're right. That is essential. Some wars are justified."

She didn't add the obvious coda—*Is yours?* He was already struggling with that question.

Chapter Thirty-two

"Genova, dear."

Thalia was by her side, bright-eyed. "Isn't it time for *presepe*?"

How could she have forgotten? "Yes, of course. We must go up right now to do it."

Genova hoped to slip away, but Thalia called out, "Beowulf, dear, Genova has a most *charming* Nativity in our room. We are off to give birth to the baby Jesus!"

Laughter rippled around the room.

Before Thalia could invite everyone along, Genova linked arms with her. "Come, then, Thalia. It won't take a moment."

"Miss Smith."

Genova turned with foreboding to Lord Rothgar.

"Lady Thalia has described your *presepe*, and I remember seeing such collections in Italy. Alas, I lacked the foresight to bring one home with me, but I would be honored if you'd allow us to display yours here. It should, I think, be in pride of place."

Panic churned inside. "It's a simple thing, my lord, and . . . and has traveled."

She would not use the word *shabby*.

"So have you, and so have I. So have we all in our various ways. None of us are the less for it."

Genova realized that Hester's words had etched deeper than she'd thought. She would *not* be ashamed of the *presepe*.

"Very well, my lord, and thank you. I'll need some extra hands to carry down the parts."

"I'll go," said Lady Arradale, and Portia came over with her.

Thalia agreed to remain below when promised that she would put the baby Jesus in the manger.

Genova and the two other women hurried upstairs and into the room where the empty stable sat waiting. Genova was wound tight with anxiety over her companions' reaction. She still feared wrinkled noses.

"Oh, how lovely!" Portia exclaimed.

Lady Arradale touched the stable gently. "Isn't it? We must obtain one of our own. Now, how best to move it?"

"I can carry the stable in one piece," Genova said, smiling with relief, "but perhaps the rest should go back in the box."

Portia raised her upper skirt to make a sling. "If we carry the figures like this, I think they'll be safe. We'll be careful." She picked up the nearest animal and put it in the cloth.

Lady Arradale did the same. It was the sort of thing a countrywoman would do, gathering rosehips from a hedge, and their underpetticoats reached almost as low as their skirts. Even so, Genova was astonished that great ladies would do such a thing.

As she helped to collect the figures, she considered that her companions were countrywomen. Portia had described her home as a simple country manor. Lady Arradale's Yorkshire home could hardly be simple, but various comments had made it clear that she involved herself in the affairs of her tenants and other local people.

Real people. In many ways like her.

The figures were all safely stowed, so she took the baby Jesus and the Mother Mary and put one in each pocket. Then she picked up the stable and cloth and led the way out of the room.

When they arrived back in the hall, Lord Rothgar gestured toward a table set not far from the fire. "I gather the mantle would be more traditional, but it

should be low enough for the children to see. I'll sta-
tion a servant to make sure it isn't harmed."

Genova saw that some of the older children were
still up, fidgety, but expectant. She went to the table
and Ash stepped beside her. "Can I help?"

Another pearl.

"My hands are full, so could you spread the cloth?"

He took it and did so, smoothing it. Genova tried
not to remember the fall that had broken her embroidery frame. It was hard, especially with her attention
drawn to his beautiful hands, which made her think
of his touch, his taste, his . . .

He stood back and she placed the stable on top,
centering it carefully, blinking back tears. If only her
mother were here.

She stepped back then, giving Thalia the pleasure
of taking figures from the ladies' skirts and placing
them in their places. It didn't matter if some were not
quite where they normally went. It was time to let go
of the past.

Someone took her hand. She knew without looking
that it was Ash. Though her throat ached, she curled
her fingers around his. Another pearl to be with him
at this moment.

Thalia had half the figures in place when she said,
"Each one has a story! Genova, what did you say this
one was?"

Genova had to swallow to clear her throat. "A
llama, from South America."

"Ah, yes, and here's the lovely dragon!" Then she
paused and looked at Genova. "We must sing the
song."

"Oh, no . . ."

Ash squeezed her hand. "Teach us the song."

She looked at him. "But my voice isn't very good."

"You clearly taught Thalia. Sing. I'll help."

Genova bit her lip, but she began to sing. She hated
to raise her voice in this great chamber, but the acous-
tics helped and Thalia joined in with the second part.

Then Ash picked it up, but not to sing the third round.
He added his voice to Genova's, carrying her to places
she'd never reached in song.

The third round wove in, and she realized that
Damaris Myddleton was leading that with her strong,
trained voice. Then everyone was singing, and the simple tune became a grand chorale.

> *In the stable, in the wild,*
> *Came the mother, Mary mild.*
> *Came the star as bright as day,*
> *Came the angels, lutes to play.*
> *Lutes to play, joy a-ringing,*
> *At the sound of angels singing.*
> *Joy, joy, joy, joy,*
> *Joy, joy, joy, joy,*
> *Joy, joy, joy, joy. . . .*

The cascade of "joy, joy, joy" rang as rich as the
bells of Rome.

Genova claimed the angel Gabriel, wings gleaming
freshly gold, and attached the figure to the peak of the
stable—the last step before the miracle of Christmas.
Without her having to guide, everyone ended their
song until the last "joy" faded into silence.

She moved Mary-on-the-donkey behind the stable.
Then she took out the baby Jesus and gave it to
Thalia, who seemed as filled with wonder and excite-
ment as Genova had always been.

The children were shifting closer, eyes wide. Heart
swelling at their pleasure, Genova put the ass into the
stable with Joseph and the Mother Mary in place.
Then she stepped aside to let Thalia put the chubby
baby on the straw.

"And now," said Genova, as her father had always
done, her voice choked, "it is Christmas. Peace to all."

Everyone applauded and cried, "Peace to all!" and
turned to greet and kiss those nearby.

Tears were pouring down Genova's cheeks and she

couldn't seem to stop them. Ash pressed a handkerchief into her hand. Silk, finely embroidered, and edged with precious lace.

When she'd dried her eyes, he dropped a kiss on her lips. "May all your Christmases be blessed with peace, Genova."

Something in his eyes suggested more, but then Lady Walgrave spoke.

"I know that it's quite disgustingly apropos, but I do think this baby is beginning to make its appearance."

Chapter Thirty-three

Amid exclamations, the company split into action. Lord Walgrave insisted on carrying his wife upstairs, despite her laughing protests. Orders were given and the ladies of the family hurried off to varied preparations.

Children were swept off to bed, but Lord Rothgar encouraged the rest of the company to continue the festivities. Some returned to the ballroom for more dancing. Others went to the drawing room for cards and chatter.

Genova, who'd waited through some births, doubted the baby would arrive before morning, but she, too, was in no mood for sleep. She lingered by the *presepe*, journeying through its lifetime of memories.

"It means a great deal to you," Ash said.

"It's home. I hadn't realized, but everything in my life was changeable except this one thing. The *presepe* changed only by being enriched every year."

"Enriched?"

"My father always gave me a new animal on my birthday, a new worshiper at the manger." She touched the Chinese dragon. "This was the last one before my mother died."

"A dangerous guest at the feast."

"Not really. In many cultures dragons are predators, but the Chinese dragon is a harbinger of good fortune. Ironic, isn't it?"

He picked up the brilliantly colored figure, its scales picked out with gold. "So a dragon doesn't have to breathe fire and eat people."

She waited, hopefully, for him to develop the point, but he put the little figure down. "Even Chinese dragons must eat. What," he asked her, "if not unwilling victims?"

She pulled a face at him. "What does anyone eat but unwilling victims?"

"Genova, you're a cynic!" He took her hand. "Come back to the ballroom and dance your bile away."

To dance the night away with him would be heaven, but she shook her head. "No, I'm sorry."

"You're for bed? The night is young."

She knew she should just slip away, but she couldn't lie to him. "I have to find the Christmas Star. It's part of the tradition."

He laughed, puzzled. "You can't think that Elf Malloren is about to give birth to a new Messiah."

"Of course not! It's always in the sky at Christmas, and I have to make a wish on it."

He shook his head, but with a smile. "Show me. Do we go outside?"

"That's best." She didn't want him to laugh at part of her traditions, but she couldn't deny herself his company.

They went to the great doors, and he swept up someone's abandoned shawl for her in passing. The solitary footman hurried to open the doors, blankly uncritical of the insanity of venturing outside in the middle of a winter's night.

As they stepped out onto the terrace at the top of the double curve of stairs, icy air shocked Genova's skin. But then Ash wrapped the shawl around her shoulders, creating a whole string of pearls with his touch alone.

Here, in the dark beneath the stars, she felt they were truly alone together for the first time.

He looked up, breathing in as if relishing fresh air. It was a still, peaceful night, and not bitterly cold. Genova inhaled, too, searching the brilliantly starry sky. She pointed. "There it is!"

"My dear Genova, that is Jupiter."

She smiled up at the bright spot. "I know, but to-night it's the Christmas Star."

She felt his hand warm and companionable on her back. "The Star of Bethlehem was probably a comet, I'm afraid."

She turned her back to the stone balustrade, looking at him rather than the planet. "Did you see Halley's comet in 1758?"

"Of course. Where were you?" Then his mouth twitched up in a smile. "I mean, where in the world? How strange to ask a lady that."

"Ladies staying safely home in England? Your experience is somewhat limited, sir."

He touched her cheek. "There aren't many who would think that."

Heat uncoiled inside her so that the mist of her breath could almost be steam. "Halifax," she blurted. "In Nova Scotia. Where were you?"

"London. Or rather, at a house I maintain near Greenwich."

"Near the observatory?" What a puzzle box he was. Each exchange revealed something new, and she was already addicted to discovery. "You have an interest in stars?"

"You make me sound like a dreamer."

"You forget that you're talking to a naval captain's daughter."

"Yes, of course. Can you navigate?"

"I know something of the art. My father taught me many things when he had the time."

Her thoughts slipped to her father, and the sadness of change. Ash brought her back with a touch on her cheek.

"Shall I buy you a ship so you can sail into your dreams?"

"I thought you were hard-pressed for money?"

"Only on the scale of a marquessate. I have an interest in some voyages being planned to record the transit of Venus in 1768. Would you like to go?"

She laughed in perplexity. "I've no idea what you're talking about, but they'd never take a woman. And no, I've done with the oceans. Will you go?"

He looked past her, then, to the horizon and the stars. "It's not my destiny. Like most of my ancestors, I send others in my place, to adventure and to war."

She took his hand, offering comfort as he had offered it to her earlier. "I heard a rumor that one of your ancestors was Charles II. He traveled and fought."

"Unwillingly." His thumb rubbed gently against her palm. "He's reputed to have refused to convert to Roman Catholicism because he'd no mind to go wandering again."

"*Is* he your ancestor? I'm quite awed at the thought of royal blood."

He shrugged. "Family legend says that he was my great-grandfather, but as we've established, it's impossible to ever be certain who fathered whom."

She freed her hand and traced his jaw, his nose. "There is perhaps some resemblance. Not so much to Charles II, but to his brother King James, and his father, Charles I."

He captured her fingers and used them to seal her own lips. "Hush. In former times, royal blood could have my head on the block."

"And not so former. It's less than twenty years since men lost their heads for supporting a Stuart pretender!"

He shook his head at her alarm. "Whatever the truth, I'm safely on the wrong side of the blanket, love."

Love.

He used it casually, but it was another pearl.

He released her hand and slid his fingers into her hair. She leaned into the cup of his hand, thinking this one short night might give her pearls enough to last a lifetime.

"Why not sail in search of Venus, Ash? What's to stop you?"

"Some would say I seek out Venus far too often."

"Be serious."

He nuzzled her neck. "I'm always serious about such matters."

She smiled but waited.

"Duty, then. That's what ties me. My duty to manage my estates, to make laws, to shape a nation."

She understood. "Your marquessate is your ship. No one else can captain it."

"My ship is likely to sink for lack of tar, or whatever it is keeps ships afloat. I have to marry, Genova, and I have to marry money."

She knew, she thought she knew, why he was telling her that. It hurt, but it hurt less because he was honest. "If you must, you must. Only promise me that you'll be a good captain."

He drew her into his arms, into an embrace more tender than any they'd shared. Her head rested perfectly on his broad shoulder.

"I'll do my best," he said. "I know it's time to take over my properties from my grandmother. I would have done it already if not for other problems."

"Molly Carew." She was relishing the hard heat of his body and a steady strength she wouldn't have expected to find in him just a few days before. Inhaling his scent, she said, "Can you tell me about that? I'm not easily embarrassed."

His hands moved on her back slightly, in a tender touch that might even have been unconscious. "It's a ridiculous tale."

She moved back to look at him. "Ridiculous?"

His smile was rueful. "Isn't that what we all fear the most, to be ridiculous? Are you too cold to stay out here for a sorry saga?"

"No."

He drew her close again, sliding her arms around him beneath his coat, and tucking her shawl securely. "Listen, then. Last February I attended Lady Knatchbull's masquerade. It is not noted for taste and sobriety. I went as an Indian brave, largely naked. . . ."

Genova hummed with approval against his chest and felt his chuckle.

"Molly Carew went as Salome, in seven extremely transparent veils. I am not a saint."

"I think I noticed that."

"Not shocked yet?"

"No, impatient to get to the point."

"I might as well confess all my sins. I had been Molly's lover in the past, when Booth Carew was still alive."

He paused, obviously expecting comment.

"That's *all* your sins?" she asked.

He laughed again. "No."

"I didn't think so. Go on. I'm anxious to know how you can be so sure that Charlie is not your son." She made certain that no hint of doubt lingered in her words.

He let out a breath. "To edit drastically, then, I left the masquerade with Molly, not attempting to be discreet, but I never did that for which *amor* is not the right word."

It was her turn to chuckle. "I told you I knew them all, but *swived* will do."

"Rather too matrimonial, but if you wish, I did not swive Molly Carew."

She moved slightly so she could look at him. "If you are about to confess to being a eunuch, I will be much surprised."

He rubbed his cheek against hers. "You have only to explore, *pandolcetta mia*, to correct that impression."

She stirred, sensing the truth despite layers of skirts. A deep ache trembled, but she said, "So why?"

"Because I realized she was trying to hook me. It was just a sense, an instinct, but as we traveled to my house in my coach, and she pleasured me in ways she knows well, I knew. I remembered that she was a widow who might have different intentions from when she'd been a wife, so though I returned the pleasure, it was not in the way that might create a child. And then I took her to her home."

"But then . . . ," Genova said. "She made it all up?"

"Not entirely. I assume she was already pregnant, but not by a man who could marry her, or perhaps not a man she wanted to marry. It's typical of her boldness that she pursued her plan anyway. Perhaps she thought I was too drunk to know."

"Were you?"

"No."

His tone was a friendly rebuke and she said, "Sorry," knowing her smile would sound in her voice.

It was a scandalous tale, but she loved that he was telling it to her, and that he was somewhat uncomfortable about it.

This was the man, not the marquess.

They were friends.

Chapter Thirty-four

"The devil of it was," he said, "that when I denied it no one believed me. Was I supposed to protest and plead? I certainly couldn't prove my account. I ignored the woman, assuming she would give up. She never did."

"Even to abandoning another man's baby on you. Perhaps she's the Loki in this tale."

He brushed his lips against hers. "You are a remarkable woman."

"Because I'm not shocked by your tale? Some of the younger officers were like brothers to me, and because we'd been on ships together, the barriers were down. They often came to me with tales of woe, and most of them were to do with women." She shook her head. "It must all have been infuriating."

"Especially as one cannot prove a negative. I need to, though. I need to force Molly to tell the truth, or . . ."

"Or?" she asked, freeing a hand to touch his face, to guide it so he looked at her.

"Or force Rothgar to use his influence with the king. His Majesty would probably believe him, especially as our enmity is well known."

She flexed her hand against his warm skin, feeling the slight roughness of his beard. "That wasn't the whole truth."

"You're a terrifying woman."

"Tell me."

He moved slightly against her hand. She thought it

was a shake of the head, but then he said, "I have
long assumed that Rothgar was behind this plan, and
that Molly was his puppet. The plan had a suitably
devious design. If I succumbed, then I would end up
married to a woman I had come to dislike, accepting
as my child, possibly my heir, a baby who wasn't mine.
If I resisted, I would offend the king, perhaps even to
the point of being cast into the darkness, from where
I could trouble Rothgar no more. I came here prepared to force him to right the wrong."

"With what?"

"That, Genova, you do not want to know."

"The mistletoe bough?" she asked, wishing he'd tell
her. When he stayed silent, she said, "And if he had
nothing to do with it?"

"Then I need to get my hands on Molly Carew."

"Until then?"

He touched his nose to hers. "Enjoy Christmas. Try
to understand my cousin more. Test the air. Be betrothed to you. . . . So, Genova Smith, what do you
think of me now?"

She cradled his head in both hands. "I think you
are an honest man, Ash, and there is nothing more
noble than that."

She kissed him, turning her head to find just the
right angle, exploring and tasting as if for the first
time. The passion was there, the passion that had
burned from the first, but their new closeness was
more powerful than showy flames and sparks. It
glowed in the deeps, under control.

Then denying that belief, her whole body clenched,
a shaft of need piercing her. He murmured, "Genova," and pressed closer, a hand claiming a breast
through cloth and stays.

She teetered, trembling, then found strength to put
a hand to his chest and push. "No, Ash, don't.
Please. . . ." He stilled, and she added, "It's not because I don't want it."

He laughed shakily. "I know that, love."

He straightened, restoring her shawl, breathing as deeply as she. His hands lingered near her breasts as he gathered the shawl together there.

They had talked at length and in depth, and he had revealed himself to her as to no other woman, she was sure, but he had been honest about everything, including his belief that he could not marry her.

Whatever she did about that, she needed to end this encounter. "I'm cold," she lied. "Time to go inside."

He didn't protest, but opened the door for her.

The once chilly hall seemed hot in a way the glowing Yule log couldn't explain. Brandy, spices, and oranges played games with Genova's senses, and merry music spilled out from the magical ballroom.

He took her hand and led her across the hall and up to the doors. "The night is young," he said softly. "We can dance."

Through the doors, Genova saw illusion. Cottages with cozily lit windows nestled among trees at the base of glittering mountains. Couples danced and laughed beneath the great chandelier. If she stepped in there, she knew, she was lost.

"I'm ready for bed."

Wrong words! Wrong words!

She saw him register them and let them pass, but he raised her left hand and kissed her knuckles by the ring.

She pulled free. "I wish you hadn't given me this."

"It seemed a necessary part of the play."

"It's wrong."

"Cast away scruples. There's no reverence attached. That ring was my mother's. She wore it under protest and abandoned it when she left. When you reject me, you can keep it. In fact, why not put it to the baby's care."

She saw the implications of that. "No more kisses?"

"It seems safer. Remember, Genova, I'm not a saint." He kissed her hand. "Good night, my dear, and may Christmas bring you joy."

Genova looked down at the quiet hall, where the

Yule log burned steadily and the *presepe* sat beside it, in pride of place as it was meant to be. She hadn't made her wish on the *presepe*, or on the Christmas Star.

There were many things she could wish for, but one spilled out and would not be denied. *Let this man find peace and joy, and strength to be the man he's meant to be.*

She looked at him once more, then hurried upstairs and away.

Without Genova, the ballroom held no appeal. Ash returned to his room and found Fitz lounging at his ease, enjoying Rothgar's brandy.

"Ah, the answer to all puzzles arrives!"

"Where?" Ash asked, pouring for himself. "It certainly isn't me."

"So how did you end up in the devil's lair? Your archenemy seems remarkably untouched."

"You can't have expected us to fall to blows like Italian braggadocios. We are being perfectly civil while circling for the kill."

Ash listened to himself prating the sort of words he'd spoken all his life, trained like a parrot.

"I'm working toward peace," he corrected, and took a mouthful of brandy. "This is superb. Clear evidence of my cousin's wealth."

"Peace," Fitz reminded him. "I certainly approve."

"You probably started the rot."

"Then my life is worthwhile."

Ash studied him. "It's true, you know. You don't say what I want to hear like all the toadeaters. You've been a mirror of sorts, exposing folly. But my grandmother won't approve."

"Let the bounteous Miss Smith deal with her."

Ash drank more brandy. "It's nothing to do with her."

"Your future bride?"

"It's all sham. You must have realized that."

"It did seem rather sudden. When I received your

note asking me to collect the ring from Cheynings, I assumed it would be for Miss Myddleton. When I encountered her here, I was sure of it."

"It probably will be, in time."

"You can't give her that ring now."

"I never planned to. I suspect it's cursed."

"A shame to put it on Miss Smith's finger, then."

Ash considered that with disquiet. "It's only for a couple of days. I've told her that when she rejects me she can keep it."

Fitz whistled.

Ash sat wearily in the other chair. "She's insisting that someone has to support Molly Carew's brat. Since it can't be me directly, it's a way out of that mess."

"It'll make him a little gentleman."

"His mother is superficially a lady, and as you say, Damaris Myddleton will never wear it now."

"You could have it recut."

"It's Genova's to do with as she wishes. It will preserve her from harm, as well as the baby."

Fitz pulled a thoughtful face, but said, "Miss Myddleton is not best pleased with you, you know."

"Of course I know."

"So what are you going to do there? You need to marry, and soon."

"Dammit, I know. It's only been three days since this exploded, Fitz! And things have become . . . complicated."

From the way Fitz looked, Ash suspected his friend knew the complication he meant. "Look, draw off Damaris Myddleton for a few days. She's stalking me like a lynx, and if I give in to my irritation, it won't pave the way to a good marriage."

"If she has any spirit, it won't pave the way to marriage at all. Which might be a good thing."

"Title for wealth is a fair trade. I mean her no harm."

Fitz shook his head. "Go to bed. You must have been having a trying time. It will look different in the morning."

Ash drained his glass. "I'm not sure that would be a blessing."

He was weary, however, he who sometimes danced or gamed through the night. He rose and began to undress.

"By the way," said Fitz, "what happened to Molly's baby?"

"Oh, it's here. In the Malloren nurseries. We're all one big happy family."

Fitz slid lower in his chair, laughing.

Chapter Thirty-five

Genova spent long hours of the night reliving kisses and trying to think of ways to sort out Ash's problems. She tried to be objective, but monkeylike, her mind took its own ways, throwing up scenarios in which the solution was to marry him.

She woke, poorly rested, trying to remember the folly of locking herself in a cage with a wolf. He wasn't unwilling, though—that was the frustrating part.

He believed he needed to marry money to carry out his duties. How true was that? She lay there, going round and round this. The reality was that poverty bred poverty, and wealth bred wealth. But hard work and talents succeeded, too.

Did she have any talents to put against a fortune? She still winced at the memory of talking about sheep's eyes.

She thought at first that the noise was a dream. Then she realized there really was loud singing and bell ringing outside the window.

"What . . . ?"

Grumbling, she climbed out of bed, thankful that Thalia was a little deaf and hadn't been disturbed. She pulled her robe around her and peered around the edge of the window curtains. Countrypeople, some in strange costumes, seemed to be marching around the house in a long procession, ringing bells and singing. As she made out the words, she realized they were wishing the household a merry Christmas—and begging for pennies.

"Oh, wassailers," said Thalia amid a rattling of curtain rings. "How splendid!" She poked her head out, yawning, cap lopsided.

Genova had heard of wassailing. It was a custom more charming in the telling than in the experience, waking people up at the crack of dawn. Well—she glanced at the clock—at nine o'clock.

Her eye was startled by a flash and she looked at the huge diamond with distaste. She couldn't connect the showy stone with the rich, deep warmth of her emotions.

Like lava, she thought, remembering Vesuvius—no cooler for being deep. Quite the opposite.

She put another piece of wood on the fading fire, watched it flame in a merry, careless way. She could no longer tell what was selfish and what was noble.

Ash must feel the same way, unsure whether his impulse toward peace was strength or weakness. Whether his intention to marry money was noble self-sacrifice or foolish greed.

Thalia rang the little bell by the bed and Regeanne came to ask what they wished to wear for Christmas Day.

Genova remembered Lady Elf. "The baby?"

"He is well, Miss Smith."

"No, I mean Lady Walgrave."

"Ah, not yet. But there seems no deep concern."

Eight hours was not so long, but Genova sent up a sincere prayer.

"What should I wear?" she asked. She longed to wear one of her new, fine dresses, but didn't want to be out of place.

As if in answer to another prayer, Thalia said, "Dress finely, dear. Today will be one grand entertainment!"

Genova chose her favorite of her new gowns, a dusky pink silk figured with silver and trimmed with silk lace. It was certainly not her warmest, but she couldn't resist.

The gown had a sacque fall at the back in the latest style and required wide hoops. She would wear it over a silk shift, trimmed at the elbows with a deep fall of fine lace.

As they started to dress, a maid arrived with a chocolate tray, including sweet rolls, and with the news that Sunday service would take place in the chapel at ten and that everyone would dine at one.

"Oh, it's both Sunday and Christmas!" Thalia exclaimed. "How lovely. Warm shawl, Genova. Perhaps two!"

Genova chuckled. Despite ruffles and bows, Thalia was as sharp as a new needle.

When they were dressed, Thalia took something out of her jewelry box and said, "Close your eyes and hold out your hand!"

Genova obeyed, knowing the sweet lady was going to give her a trinket to wear. Her own jewelry was modest. She was wearing only pearl earrings and a silver cross on a ribbon around her neck.

She felt beads and opened her eyes to see . . . a string of pearls. "Oh, Thalia. Thank you! I'll take good care of them."

Thalia closed her hand over them. "They're your Christmas birthday gift, dear."

"I can't, Thalia. They're far too valuable."

"I shall sulk if you don't take them! It's quite a simple string and perhaps a little girlish for me now. But they will go perfectly with that gown. I know Ashart will admire them."

Ash would probably think they should go to him when Thalia died, but Genova clasped them around her neck, loving the way they glowed against her skin. Surely she now looked like a candidate for marchioness.

Unsteady with hope, she left the room with Thalia.

The double shawls were certainly welcome as the route to the chapel took them into an old part of the house which might even date from the original abbey. It was as if the new house had grown around it like barnacles around a wrecked ship.

Eventually they entered a stone chapel that was

definitely centuries old. It was of modest size and
would surely not hold all the guests if they chose to
attend. Not seated, at least. The gentlemen, as colorful
and bright as the ladies, were obviously going to have
to stand.

As she and Thalia waited for a line of ladies to
settle into chairs, Genova looked around for Ash. He
hadn't arrived yet. Surely he would come. She couldn't
wait to see him again.

The musicians who had played for dancing the night
before began to play for worship on wind instruments
and drum. It was an old, haunting tune that suggested
ancient times, and the altar was backed by a medieval
triptych in which gilded angels prayed around Christ
in the manger.

Genova felt as if she'd stepped back in time, as if
she might look around and see men in long, furred
gowns and ladies in strange headdresses. A brilliance
caught her eye like a flame. She turned, and there was
Ash, entering the chapel.

She almost laughed aloud, even as her hopes
crumbled.

He shone like an angel made of ivory and gold. She
blinked away that strange vision, but his pale suit was
still lushly embroidered in brilliant colors and golden
threads, and his buttons on coat and waistcoat flashed
fire like diamonds.

They probably were diamonds.

His possessions had clearly arrived, revealing the
truth. This must be the sort of clothing he wore at
court, and she was sure he'd chosen his most splendid
outfit as a statement to his cousin.

She glanced around and found Lord Rothgar near
the altar. His was a quieter magnificence, but it was
of crimson and gold. Lady Arradale stood beside him
in matching crimson, large rubies around her neck.

How could she find humor in loss of hope? And yet
she did. She and these people lived on different scales.

She looked back—how could she not?—and Ash's
eyes met hers as if he had been watching her. A slight

smile flickered. She couldn't help but return it. Her love hadn't altered.

He began to come to her, but then they were all asked to settle for the service. She took her seat and opened her prayer book.

Dr. Egan led the lovely, traditional Christmas prayers and readings. Genova sank into them, praying for peace. In the night she had regretted her spilled words on war, but no longer. They might have helped move Ash's mind toward reconciliation, and that was the truly important thing.

Mr. Stackenhull, the music master, led the hymns, but Genova was more aware of Ash's voice. She sang quietly, as she always did, but hearing afresh the words.

> *A great and mighty wonder,*
> *A full and blessed cure!*
> *The rose has come to blossom*
> *Which shall forever endure.*

Then later:

> *Hark, how all the welkin rings!*
> *Glory to the King of Kings,*
> *Peace on earth and mercy mild,*
> *God and sinners reconciled.*

During the last verse of the last hymn she looked at Ash.

> *Join then, all hearts that are not stone,*
> *And all our voices prove,*
> *To celebrate this holy one,*
> *The God of peace and love.*

She and Ash came together as everyone filed out, as inevitably, Genova felt, as the sea kissing the shore.

"Hail, glorious morn. You look like sunrise, Genova."

She knew she blushed, and then blushed more because of it. "And you look like a seraphim."

"What?" His eyes lit with laughter. "No one's called me an angel since I was a child."

She told him of her first impression, admiring the truly beautiful work in the flowers that bordered the front of his ivory velvet coat to a depth of at least eight inches.

"You put my flowers-in-the-snow to shame." Then she had to explain that, which led to thoughts of her embroidery and their meeting. But they shared the memories silently with looks.

"I'm surprised anyone but an angel dares wear such an outfit."

He glanced down at himself. "Why?"

"A mere human might spill a spot of gravy down it."

He laughed. "I would simply command the addition of another blossom. Lush embroidery is very practical, even economical, you see."

It was as if he knew that in the night, she'd thought that frugality and economy could substitute for a fortune. A laughable notion now.

He tucked her arm in his, and gave his other to Thalia. They joined the procession back to the main part of the house, accompanied by Thalia's inconsequential chatter.

Genova didn't mind that. Everything that needed to be said flowed between her and Ash without words, the delicious and the bitter. She felt it so strongly that she was surprised it wasn't obvious to all.

Thalia separated from them in the hall, chattering off to old friends. Genova saw Portia, in rich moss green velvet and some yellow jewels, and went over there with Ash to ask for news of Lady Elf. That was a business that all the money and the power in the world could not smooth.

Portia pulled a face. "Is truly laboring mightily, but there don't seem to be any problems. I wish it were over for everyone's sake."

Ash let the women talk about birth and tussled with the problem of Genova Smith. He shouldn't have smiled at her like that in the chapel, but how could he not when she looked as splendid as the dawn?

He shouldn't have said that, either. He should have resisted the pull to go to her, but could the tides resist the moon, or the moon the sun? And besides, they had this damnable betrothal to act out.

He'd already learned that she was magnificent, but now she looked it—elegant, dignified, graceful, pink, silver, and pearl. The diamond was a discordant note, but she needed gold, he thought. Perhaps even topaz to reflect her hair. Yes, a rich parure of gold, pearls, and topaz. . . .

Lady Bryght left and Genova turned to him. "You're very quiet."

"Women's matters. A wise man retreats."

"Are you saying you wouldn't have a care while your wife labored to birth your child?"

A sudden vision of Genova in labor assailed him. He knew nothing of the mysteries, but he could still imagine her, sweaty and magnificent. . . .

His.

"I'd probably run away and get drunk. What's happening now?"

People were shifting into different groups.

Her look expressed surprise. Clearly some announcement had been made.

"We're offered the usual hospitality until dinner, but also tours of the house. The gallery." She glanced at him, knowing what thoughts that would stir, the wicked woman. "An Anglo-Saxon display. The Malloren names are all Anglo-Saxon, you know."

"Yes."

"Of course you do."

She seemed embarrassed, so he said, "One generation only. Bryght's son is Francis, and Lord Cyn's is John. Lady Hilda, who's married to Steen, has used ordinary names, too. A Charles and Sarah, I think."

"A detail about the Mallorens that isn't etched into your mind?"

He should be offended, but he delighted in her sharpness. "We know the gallery and old English pots don't appeal. What else?"

"Chinese prints and porcelain. A harp recital. Oh, and Lord Rothgar is willing to show people his mechanical room, whatever that is."

Ash's interest stirred. "He famously enjoys clocks and automata." He took her hand. "Shall we go there? It never hurts to know how someone's gears work."

How pleasant, he thought as they joined Rothgar and three other guests, to be a machine. To smoothly perform a designed function, without the inconvenience of a heart.

Chapter Thirty-six

*A*sh's unusually withdrawn mood worried Genova. She was trying to hide her feelings so as not to disturb him. She knew he'd care.

Or was it nothing to do with her? Was he backsliding, turning against peace and reaching again for the weapon that could hurt his cousin?

As they entered a plain room noisy with the ticking of clocks, she tried to assess the feelings between the two men. They might as well have been automata themselves.

Apart from a fire, the room was starkly simple, lined with workbenches and containing a long table in the middle that held a large, shrouded object. Windows along one wall gave light, but there were candles as well, some with complex lenses to focus the light.

Clocks had always interested her, as time was so important at sea, so she walked down the room looking at them. Most were silent and presumably awaiting repair. Did Lord Rothgar involve himself in that or was he simply a patron? No craftsman was here at the moment, but the place looked as if two or three people regularly worked here.

Some clocks were already in pieces, spread on a part of the bench. Drawings and diagrams were pinned on the wall above them. What was the purpose here? Simply mending clocks because they were broken?

Rothgar, in his velvet and gold, looked out of place, but he moved around the room with ease and familiarity. As soon as he started to explain various pieces of special interest, she knew that his involvement here was not only as patron.

And Ash apparently interested himself in the stars. The cousins had more in common than they had differences. In fact, they had no significant differences apart from those fabricated by a previous generation.

Rothgar showed them tiny mechanisms arranged beneath magnifying glasses, and large ones methodically moving through their purpose. He explained the breaks in some and how they could be repaired. He demonstrated beautiful precision implements, including a tiny lathe.

Genova had always been interested in machines. Far more than she'd been interested in fancy needlework. Machines were *useful*. They created something solid and necessary. Even a dress wasn't necessary. Many people in the world clothed themselves in a wrapped cloth.

Rothgar pointed to a model of a fireplace with a cat curled in front of it. "There's a switch there, Miss Smith. Why don't you move it?"

Genova did so. A cheerful tune started and simulated flames rose from the log and moved. The cat waved its tail, and the clock on the mantelpiece ticked.

"It's charming!"

"A simple thing," he said, as it wound down, "but it was broken and we have brought it to life again. Will you take it as a birthday gift, Miss Smith? You have shown that you know how to take care of treasures."

Genova felt flustered, but she thanked him. Was he referring to the *presepe* or to Charlie? Or to both? Or even, perhaps, to Ash?

Rothgar moved on to a bench spread with a hundred pieces of metal on a white cloth. They were all shapes and sizes. Genova could see that the drawing pinned on the wall behind was a design or map of where all these pieces went, but it made no sense to her.

She remembered how confusing sea charts had looked when her father had first taught her about them, and how clear they had become in time.

Rothgar pointed to a place on the drawing and then picked up five pieces. He deftly linked them together and pushed a pin through. Holding the pin in place with his fingers, he moved one piece, and another piece moved twice.

He split them apart and put them down. "You may try if you wish."

Genova looked around. Ash stood nearby, but the other three guests were wandering, switching on various devices that had been put out for exploration.

Genova looked back at the master of machines and wondered just how she was being wound up, but she couldn't resist. "It's easy because you've left the pieces in order."

She picked them up, repeating what he'd done, glancing once at the drawing when uncertain. That bit of it made sense to her now. Then she pushed in the pin and moved the delicate extension of metal. The other piece responded, in double time.

She laughed with delight out of all proportion to the simple task, then looked at Ash, feeling as if he might disapprove. He looked only surprised.

"It was easy," she said.

"No," he responded.

She looked back at Lord Rothgar.

"Easy to us, maybe. Are you, too, one who needs to make the world run smoothly, Miss Smith? I warn you, it will break your heart at times."

"I wouldn't be so arrogant," she said, then bit her lip.

He smiled. "We are all arrogant in our passions, whether our world is a globe or a small cell."

"What is this?" Ash asked, indicating the shrouded shape in the middle of the room.

Rothgar lifted the cloth. Genova was not the only one to gasp in admiration at a huge dove with wings of pearl, tipped with diamonds.

"You're trying to improve on peace?" Ash said.

Now, when she wasn't braced for it, Genova felt the rank stink of strife.

Rothgar folded the cloth and put it aside. "His Majesty agreed with me that it was less than it could be."

Genova longed to understand, and as if she'd asked, Ash turned to her. "This was a gift from the acting

French ambassador to the king. All show and little substance. But then," he added, "D'Eon is perhaps all show and little substance."

D'Eon.

"Unwise to underestimate him that far," Rothgar said and turned to the machine. "The mechanism is simple and couldn't be changed, but it gave no illusion of nature. If you saw it in operation before, Cousin, judge it now."

Rothgar moved a lever, and the bird came to life. It turned its head, flexing a little, then lowered its beak and picked an olive branch from among greenery and raised it. Genova was caught in the illusion that the dove had selected it, that the bird was real.

"There was only the one branch before," Ash said, "and there was a click when the bird's beak grasped it."

"There's still a slight click, but the branches rattle a little and hide it. Distraction is a powerful device."

Then the bird spread its wings to reveal words written in gold beneath. PEACE. PAIX. They were glimpsed for a moment before the wings settled again with the slight ripple of a bird adjusting its feathers.

Everyone applauded, and someone demanded that it run again. Rothgar showed the man how to wind it up and set it in action and stepped back to join Ash and Genova.

"It stayed open before," Ash said.

"And took skill to reset. A serious miscalculation in design. When it closes, as now, the natural impulse is to want to see it open again, and it only needs winding. Before, it stayed open, and that was that. But then D'Eon had reached the stage of miscalculation in many things. I am tempted," he said, considering the dove, "to strip away pearl and diamonds and substitute feathers."

"To make peace real?" Ash asked.

Rothgar looked at him. "Precisely."

And Ash said, "So be it."

Genova looked between the two cool, dispassionate men and wasn't sure what she'd just witnessed, but she prayed it was what she thought.

Problems would still remain, but surely Rothgar would help his reconciled cousin regain the king's favor. Hope stirred on her own behalf, but she knew one issue didn't really connect with the other.

She turned back to the various mechanisms displayed on the bench. If people were machines, everything would be a great deal easier.

Rothgar joined her, demonstrating what each did, then encouraging her to take one clock apart, explaining what each piece did as she freed it.

When she thought to look around, everyone else had gone, even Ash. She rose quickly from the stool she was sitting on. "Oh, I'm sorry!"

"There's no need to apologize for sharing an obsession, Miss Smith, though Ashart was perhaps surprised when you didn't notice him leave." His lips were twitching, but he added, "Don't let guilt even touch your mind. Even the deepest devotion should not lock us away from the wider world. I hope he knows that."

She looked back at the clock she'd investigated, accepting that she was reluctant to leave it half explored. "Is it something a woman can do?"

"There are few things a woman cannot do, though many that are made difficult for them. It might be hard if you tried to set up shop, but not for private work, especially as an amateur."

"How would I learn? As an amusement only," she added, unready to admit the grip this had on her.

"You may stay here and explore the mysteries if you wish. I employ two craftsmen."

She looked at him, startled.

"Or if your destiny carries you elsewhere, I know others who will be pleased to share their knowledge."

It seemed her ambitions would never stay within reasonable bounds. "What if I wanted to earn my living this way? I may have to."

He didn't seem shocked. "Private commissions would be possible. It would take time to learn, however."

"I have a portion that could support me for many

years." Then she shook her head. "This is idiotic. I had no notion of this an hour ago!"

"But that is often how it is, isn't it?"

She knew what he meant. She recognized also that he had not argued with her assumption that she might be free to learn a trade and possibly earn a living with it. In other words, unmarried.

As she carefully picked up her artificial hearth, she tried to let that settle in her mind.

She left the room with Lord Rothgar, coming to terms with another change. Once she had been in awe of this man. She didn't think him any less grand, but now she could talk to him almost as easily as she could talk to Ash, perhaps because of a shared desire to make things work. To burnish away rust and corrosion, apply grease, and see order restored.

An inveterate need to meddle, in other words, she thought with a wry smile. She felt free to ask a question. "There is peace between you and Ashart?"

"Of a sort, but loosely pinned."

"It could fall apart again? Because of his grandmother?"

"She will certainly do her best."

"Doesn't that all hinge on"—she hesitated, realizing she was about to speak about his mother—"Lady Augusta? If it could be shown that her actions were nothing to do with the late marquess, wouldn't that help?"

He looked at her. "I warned you about trying to make the world run smoothly, Miss Smith. And how can my family have had nothing to do with it? How can those around a tragedy not have contributed in some way, if only by what they failed to do?"

They had arrived back at the hall, where in a real fireplace, the Yule log crackled. Candles blazed, and the distant notes of a harp trickled through the great chamber, hinting at life elsewhere. The only other person, however, was a still, silent footman. Rothgar summoned him and the man carried her present up to her room.

"You wish to heal the Trayce family wounds," he said, "and so do I. But alas, people are not clockwork."

"He carries such a burden of hate."

"He carries the burden of the dowager marchioness and her hate. Did he tell you that he was raised by her?"

She considered him warily, unsure if it was right to discuss Ash with him. "Yes."

"It's reasonable, even noble, that he feel allegiance to her, and I suspect she loves him like a mother. Not all mothers, however, are benign. She raised him to be a weapon. Or more precisely, to fire the ones of her making."

"I think he sees himself more as Loki than Loki's blind brother."

"We all prefer to be the wielder rather than the tool."

Something caught his eye, and Genova turned to see brilliance. Ash was watching them.

Genova knew now who Loki was. The Dowager Marchioness of Ashart.

"Ah, Ashart," Rothgar said easily, leading Genova across the hall. The click of heels and the rustle of her own silk skirts seemed loud to her.

She expected to simply be handed over, but Rothgar said, "I have some things that might interest you, Ashart. Could I persuade you to accompany me?"

Ash looked wary, as well he might. What now? But then he bowed. "I am at your command."

"Do you want Miss Smith to accompany us?"

Ash glanced at her, frowning slightly, but said, "It can only add to my delight."

Rothgar took them upstairs and to a room beside the library. It was a library of sorts itself, but much smaller and in plain form, with the lower level composed entirely of drawers.

"The muniment room," Rothgar said.

Genova's interest sharpened. This room housed the family records and archives. Most would concern business and politics, but there could be letters and other such personal documents.

What had Ash been brought here to see? What had *she* been brought to see? Rothgar had included her in a way that would have been hard for Ash to avoid.

There couldn't be an easy solution here. If there were, the Mallorens would have produced it a generation ago.

One long table sat in the middle with just two chairs by it, though two others sat against the wall beneath the window. There was no fireplace, but she thought the room shared a section of wall with the library chimney, taking off the chill. Even so, it was cold enough to make her shiver in her silks, and she wished she still had two shawls instead of just one.

Rothgar opened a wide shallow drawer. "These are my mother's papers. There are no startling revelations, no accusations or vindications, but you may want to read them."

Genova saw some bundles of papers and two books or folios.

"Why were they not returned to Cheynings?" Ash asked, unmoving.

"At your family's request, my father returned everything that my mother had brought with her, but he kept anything from after the marriage. By then, my mother was a Malloren. The dowager has always been welcome to come here and inspect them if she wished."

"But you knew she'd never do that."

"I was a child of four when my mother died."

Genova saw Ash flinch at that reminder. No, his mind still wasn't free of long training.

"But you say there's nothing of importance there," he said.

"That's not precisely what I said. You have over an hour until dinner."

Rothgar left, and Genova wondered what her part in this was. If she could help, she would be glad to do so.

For long moments, Ash made no move. Then, slowly, resistantly, he walked to the open drawer. "Anything that casts a shadow on the Mallorens will have been destroyed long ago."

"It will do no harm to look."

"Isn't that what Pandora said?" He touched a bundle. "Are these letters she received, or did she make drafts? Or even use a secretary? And what are these?"

He untied a gray ribbon around marbled boards, revealing that it had once been red. When he turned back the top board, Genova saw a sketch of a Grecian temple, adequately but not brilliantly executed in pen and ink. He flipped through the sheets. "Her art? Do pretty pictures of false ornaments show the soul?"

He closed the folio and picked up the other bound boards. No, it was a book. He untied the ribbon and turned to the first page. Even from by his side, Genova could read the well-trained but overlarge writing.

June 14th, 1724. I am now the Marchioness of Rothgar and vastly pleased with my new state. . . .

"Unless that's a forgery," Genova pointed out, "she was a happy bride."

"If a rather silly one."

"She was only sixteen, I understand."

"Wicked, wouldn't you say?"

"Many girls marry at sixteen."

"And some are ready to."

She pulled a face. "You can't blame the Mallorens for that, Ash. Her parents could have forbidden the banns."

"Not so easily. The rules were loose before 1753. If a girl was willing to run away with a cur, there was little her parents could do about it, short of locking her up. But as best I know, everyone approved of this match." He closed the book and handed it to her. "If you're interested, you read it."

Genova kept her hands by her side. "No. You must."

"Must?"

"We're done with that game."

"Pity." He looked at the book. "Why am I so reluctant to read this? Because I fear disappointment, or fear breaking free of chains that support me?"

"Chains bind rather than support."

"But we can still become dependent on them."

He gestured to the table. "If I'm to read this, you will sit and read those letters."

Chapter Thirty-seven

*S*haring his wariness, Genova gathered the three bundles of papers and the portfolio of drawings and seated herself at the table. Ash sat down opposite, flipping the richly embroidered skirts of his coat out of the way. Then he began to read.

She watched for a moment, looking for a change of expression, but seeing none she started with the simplest part of her collection and flipped through the drawings, wishing her hands weren't already chilled.

Lady Augusta had been well trained but lacked talent. The pictures all seemed to be dutiful sketches made around Rothgar Abbey. Then Genova paused.

In a recognizable sketch of the Tapestry Room, Augusta had drawn a man sitting in a chair reading a book. The figure was wooden with a poorly drawn head, but surely it was her husband. Would a wife try such a picture of a husband she feared?

She found two others, one a disastrous attempt at a man on horseback. Disastrous in technique, but again without indication of malice. Part of the disaster came from the attempt to show a wide smile. No normal human showed quite so many teeth.

Then Genova came across a series of pictures of a child, of an infant just beginning to sit up. Perhaps Lady Augusta had taken more lessons, for the attempt was a little better. Or perhaps the drawing master had done more than instruct. Many a lady's portfolio of sketches was the work of her drawing master, not herself.

Whatever the explanation, the solid roundness of the infant was clear, and the positions seemed natural.

The head was in proportion to the body. Surely the many pictures of her firstborn child were not the work of a trapped, unhappy woman. Mrs. Harbinger had said she doted on her firstborn. But carelessly.

Genova remembered that this was Lord Rothgar as an infant. What was it like to grow up in awareness of such a troubled mother? To witness her at her worst. Was that why he'd developed an obsession with machines, which could be controlled, could be made right?

What did that say of herself? Perhaps her own interest in machines was as insignificant as a preference for cherries over plums, or perhaps it sprang from a rootless life often at the mercy of chaotic elements. Or even from her mother's shocking, inexplicable death.

She shivered.

Ash looked up. "You're cold?"

He rose and walked around the table, shrugging out of his embroidered coat. With some difficulty, she noticed. It was made to fit without a ripple.

He put it warm around her shoulders.

She could make a number of polite protests, but she gathered it close. "Thank you."

He sent her a look that was troubled but caring, then sat again to his book. He'd read through over half of the journal, but she still could see no reaction.

She allowed herself a moment to admire him in his fine lawn shirt and embroidered silk waistcoat, and another to savor the delicious sense of him that encircled her from his coat. She peered at the buttons. She thought they really were diamond, but close to, she saw they were composed of many small stones.

She'd progressed far into absurdity if she could be relieved at that.

She settled back to work.

She put the pictures of husband and child to one side and closed the folio, then began on the letters. She untied another faded ribbon, red again. Lady Augusta had clearly liked red. Did her son's fondness for it come in the blood?

She found a mix of letters to the Marchioness of Rothgar, and drafts or copies of letters Augusta had sent. They were in order, so someone had organized them. Of course they had. Two Marquesses of Rothgar must have searched these documents for evidence of Augusta's motives.

Genova settled to read, holding Ash's coat close, and admitting to some guilty pleasure at having an excuse to peer into private lives.

She skimmed letters from Lady Augusta's mother, which were doting, but often included admonishments to cease being so wild and reminders that Augusta was a great lady now and must act with dignity.

Augusta's letters to her mother were stilted and dutiful. The ones to her sisters and brothers were more relaxed but revealed no secrets. There were occasional letters back, and the sisters at least clearly envied Augusta her amiable, indulgent husband.

If Augusta had problems, to whom would she confide them?

Friends?

There were a few letters from friends, but by the time Genova started on the second bundle, she was struck by their rarity.

She herself was in the same situation, but it was because of her wandering life. She'd made and left a hundred friends. Sometimes she'd tried to keep up the connection through correspondence, but mail was slow and unreliable and she wasn't an eager letter writer.

She glanced at Ash again. Perhaps one of the unusual skills she'd developed was the ability to judge people rapidly, and develop a friendship quickly. Someone met in a port might leave in weeks or even days.

Was it that friendships, like love, needed the test of time? Could she trust her rapid, passionate response to him? Was he, perhaps, wise to fix his eye on steadier goals?

She sighed at that, and he looked up. "This is tedious, isn't it?"

He began to close his book, so she said, "No, it's not that. Just a thought. I'll tell you later."

Maybe, she added silently as he settled again.

She returned to Augusta and friends. Lady Augusta Trayce hadn't led a wandering life, so her circle of acquaintance would have been stable. Yet Genova found no sign of a regular correspondence with one particular friend.

Of course, those letters could have been destroyed. If so, what might they have contained?

No. To follow that path was to join the Dowager Lady Ashart in her obsession. Genova had to believe that these papers were as complete as they could be. She kept reading, hoping for a glimmer of something among the banal.

A distant bell began to ring.

"That must be the dinner bell," Ash said, seeming pulled from elsewhere. "Well? Revelations that escaped Rothgar?"

Genova refolded the letter she'd been reading. "I don't think so, but you might like to look at these drawings." She pushed them over.

He spread them. "Not very good, was she?"

Genova didn't mention her thoughts. She wanted to see what he made of them.

"We have none of her drawings at Cheynings as far as I know. I wonder if Grandy destroyed them."

Genova started at the affectionate name for the woman she had begun to think of as Loki incarnate. "Why would she do that?"

"Nothing can be allowed to tarnish the angel's halo."

"Lady Augusta?" Genova couldn't keep the astonishment out of her voice.

"Aren't mothers supposed to dote? Anything else?"

Genova desperately wanted his account of the journal, but she gave him her impression of the letters, uncomfortable about judging the long-dead woman who had been younger than herself.

"The journal?" she asked at last.

He placed the drawings in the book to mark his place. "Flighty, self-centered, spoiled. At first all is honey, but she's beginning to complain of his unkindness."

Genova felt a chill. "Does she explain the cause?"

"Clearly. He scolds if she overspends her pin money. He spends too much time on estate matters. He expects her to read to his boring mother."

"Oh."

He stood. "She was a child. Why the devil did he marry her?"

"Perhaps he saw the girl in the sketch in the portrait gallery."

"I wonder how quickly he regretted it. And," he added, "how he behaved then."

Genova wanted to argue, but she could imagine Augusta driving a sensible man to distraction. To violence, even. But to persistent cruelty that would break her mind?

The bell was still ringing, clearly being carried about the house to catch everyone's attention.

"We are summoned to celebrate," Ash said. "I'll take everything to my room for further study."

Genova felt some reluctance in giving over the letters with some unread, but she bridled her nosiness. She gave back his coat, and they left the room.

They detoured to his bedchamber so he could leave the papers there. Genova insisted on waiting outside. She still had some willpower.

He emerged moments later with his blond friend who had arrived yesterday. So, she would have been safe from weakness anyway.

Genova was trying to remember the name when Ash provided it. "Do you remember Fitzroger, Genova?"

Ash's friend bowed, she curtsied, and she walked down the corridor between them, but with a feeling of being studied. Did Mr. Fitzroger not approve? Perhaps he, too, thought Ash should marry money, and didn't know the betrothal was sham.

Chapter Thirty-eight

*T*hey had just reached the bottom of the grand staircase when people began to look upward. Genova turned and saw Lord Rothgar on the landing.

"My friends, rejoice! I have the best possible Christmas news. My sister is safely delivered of a son, and all is well."

Cheers and applause carried everyone toward the glittering dining room, but Genova was mostly struck by the true joy she'd seen on Lord Rothgar's face. As he'd talked of clockworks, as he'd worked for peace, he must have been pressingly aware that some human events could not be made to work perfectly, no matter how hard one tried.

She sent up a prayer of thanks, and another that the baby thrive, and went on with the rest to the dining room. The table was now long enough for the whole company, and was spread with a splendid feast on platters of china, silver, and even gold.

Lord Rothgar and Lady Arradale sat together this time, in the middle of one side, with the great-aunts bracketing them. Ash and Genova were seated opposite. Unfortunately Miss Myddleton was on Ash's other side, doubtless ready to try to monopolize his attention, but Genova felt that was a minor threat.

Except that she did envy the heiress's emerald necklace, probably chosen to match Ash's ring. Pearls were all very well, but they were unfortunately demure.

Music started, and she realized the musicians, including singers now, were performing in the hall to provide a background for this. Again, the music selected seemed old, more ethereal than modern compositions, as if designed to carry them all away from reality.

It was still daylight but on a dull day, and hundreds of candles lit the room, sparkling off crystal, gold, and flashing jewelry. Finger bowls by each person stirred perfumes when used.

Genova balanced her attention between Ash and Lord Henry Malloren on her other side. He was a gruff, sinewy man with little to say, though at one point he grumbled that he'd hoped to get Damaris off his hands by now.

"Regular golden peach, she is," he said, tucking into goose. "Father was a merchant captain. Bit of a privateer, if you ask me. Fell afoul of some pirates in the South China Sea and left me guardian. Imposition, but I've done my duty by her."

"I'm sure you have," Genova said, feeling a little sorry for Miss Myddleton. She didn't miss that the heiress was also a sea captain's daughter. It really was a shame that a man had come between them.

"Thought things might be settled," Lord Henry added with a scowl at Genova.

"Really?" she said, angling her hand to show the large ring.

He made a sound like a growl and settled back to food.

Poor Damaris, who must have lost both parents, not just one, and found herself in the power of this unpleasant, resentful man. How had that come about? When Genova found herself trying to think of ways to rearrange Miss Myddleton's life, she suppressed a laugh and attended to her dinner and light conversation all around.

Rich course followed rich course until Genova found herself unable to eat another bite. She contented herself with sipping wine, even though she'd done that too much as well.

As the meal flowed merrily toward its end, darkness fell and she realized there were no lights in the room except firelight and the candles on and above the table. It made the gathering like a bright island in a dark ocean.

Some of the diners were drunk, but no one had slid under the table yet. Conveniences had been arranged in adjoining rooms for ladies and gentlemen. Genova used the ladies' room at one point, startled to find her balance unreliable when she stood. No more wine, she decided, or heaven knew what she might do.

When she returned, Ash's fingers twined with hers beneath the table. It seemed completely natural, though she did check that he wasn't fondling Miss Myddleton's at the same time. No, his other lay near his glass.

Ash raised her hand and kissed it. "We could probably slide under the table and make love there with no one the wiser."

She could imagine it so vividly, she tingled. "Have you ever?"

"Yes."

She giggled, and then she couldn't stop. He swallowed her laughter in a kiss, a kiss that went on far too long. She knew that when they separated to laughter and bawdy jokes.

Ash broke into song.

> *Oh, I gave her cakes and I gave her*
>   *ale,*
> *And I gave her sack and sherry!*
> *I kissed her once and I kissed her*
>   *twice,*
> *And we were wondrous merry.*

Knowing the song, Genova clapped her hand over his mouth, but others took it up and finished it in a grand chorus that had her blushing.

It was all in high spirits, however, and song followed song, many of them cause for a blush. She'd heard them all before, though, and could have contributed a few far bawdier if she'd been even drunker and lost to all shame.

At last the meal was over and dancing was announced. They all poured out and up the stairs to the ballroom. Or most.

Genova looked back and saw some guests snoring, including Lady Calliope, her red wig, topped with a diamond tiara, askew. Servants were beginning to take care of them. Genova supposed, with suppressed laughter, that one sleeper in a chair designed to be carried would make the work easier.

The ballroom was at its magical best, and music started up immediately. Lady Arradale called the first dance with her husband as partner, and Ash led out Genova.

The evening spun on like magic, even including a kissing dance where the couples progressed through a mistletoe arch. As the couples changed during the dance Genova ended up kissing Lord Rothgar, his chaplain, Dr. Egan, and Ash.

After that playful kiss, Ash snared her into a "snow-covered" bower designed to shield lovers from sight.

"How pretty this is," she said.

"Rothgar has a gift for entertainments."

She recognized the pull of the chains. "Peace, Ash."

He stroked her brow with a finger. "I feel like one of those hapless victims caught in a fairy circle. How do I know what is real and what is false? If I succumb, am I lost forever?"

"Quite likely, yes. But think what you'll have lost."

He laughed. "You give no quarter, do you?"

"No."

He played with her hand, then raised it to his lips. "Will you come up with me, then, and finish the reading of those papers?"

Time stopped, it seemed, giving Genova infinity to understand the likely outcome. But then she rose with him. "Of course."

They slipped out of the ballroom and upstairs, Genova's heart pounding with desire and alarm. If she hadn't drunk so much she might not be doing this, but in her present insane state, that only meant that she was glad to have drunk.

A victim of a fairy circle. Like such a victim, she could only surrender. She halted in a corridor and drew him to her for a kiss, an unwise kiss that threatened their reaching his room at all, but he ended it, shaking his head, eyes deep and dark.

He looked ahead, and his expression changed.

Genova turned. "What?" The corridor was empty.

"Stay here," he said.

She watched, braced to act if necessary, as he walked down the apparently deserted corridor to a junction. She'd left her shawl somewhere and was growing chilled, and this was not how she'd expected this adventure to go.

He looked around, then shook his head. "No one here, and this corridor is a cul-de-sac. I could have sworn I saw someone."

She joined him, aware of her footfalls on carpet, and the whisper of her skirts. "Someone like us?"

"No, a poorly dressed man."

"A servant?"

"The upstairs male servants are all in livery."

She looked down the empty corridor. "A thief?"

"A clever one, to invade tonight when most of the household is the worse for drink."

Then she realized where they were. "This leads to the nurseries."

"Kidnapping?"

A figure leaped up from behind a table and rushed at them.

Ash caught him, but was bowled over. They were tussling on the floor when Genova grabbed a queue of dirty hair and yanked the man's head back hard. He cried out and stopped struggling. Ash dragged him to his feet in a strong hold.

"Who are you, and what are you up to?"

The grubby young man, who looked hardly twenty

and ill nourished, shook his head in numb terror. Ash's scintillating garments were probably enough to strike the lad dumb on their own.

Genova remembered she was in fine clothes herself and resisted the need to wipe her hand on her skirts. Grease was the devil to get out of silk.

"You'll get nowhere by silence," she said, trying to sound reassuring. "If you've a reason to be here, tell us."

He looked between them again, then burst out in a heavy Irish accent, "You've my Sheena here! I know you do. You shan't keep her, you shan't!"

Ash must have relaxed his grip, for the man almost broke free and he had to tighten his hold to restrain him. The Irishman cried out.

"Don't hurt him!"

"I won't if he'll stop fighting," Ash snapped back. "Have done, man. If you know anything about Sheena O'Leary, we want to hear it."

"Where is she, then? What have you done with her?"

Genova saw the door to the nurseries crack open and Sheena peep out. The girl gasped, "Lawrence!" But then she shut the door and Genova heard footsteps pounding up the stairs.

She dashed to open the door. "Sheena, come back down here!"

Tone or words worked. The girl turned and crept back down, muttering something in Gaelic. Lawrence answered her and they started a rapid conversation.

"Silence!" Genova commanded. To Ash, she said, "We can't let them sort out their story before we've heard it. Bring him along."

"Aye, aye, captain, but where?"

She grinned at his reaction. "Your room is closest." Where they'd been going.

This had broken the spell that had allowed her to surrender. In time she'd be glad of it, and perhaps at last there'd be a key to Ash's problems.

Genova thought of something and addressed the

young man. "Ask Sheena if someone else is taking care of the nurseries."

His question was quick, and Sheena's reply clearly included Harbinger.

"You take them to your room," Genova said to Ash. "I'll come when I've made some sort of explanation to the ruler of the nursery domain. Don't start until I join you!"

He looked amused. "A definitely musty tyrant."

Genova blushed, but she had a commanding disposition and he might as well know it.

Chapter Thirty-nine

She hurried up the plain stairs, having to squeeze her hoops a little, and found Mrs. Harbinger looking for "that girl." Clearly Sheena was not a perfect servant. Genova simply said that a relative of Sheena's had arrived and they were allowing a meeting.

"Very well, Miss Smith, but I'll not have her loose in the house tonight. She's clearly not of a *careful* nature."

Genova had to agree. She hurried back down to Ash's bedchamber, then paused outside the door thinking of what might have been. It would not have been *careful* at all, but it hadn't seemed to matter at the time. She had no right to look down on Sheena's fall.

She went in to find Sheena sitting warily in an armchair and the young Irishman standing on guard by her side. He was short and thin, but wiry and well made.

Ash stood by the fireplace, his eye on them. He indicated the other chair for Genova and she took it, giving Sheena an encouraging smile because the girl was wringing her hands now.

"Now," Ash said, "tell us who you are, man, and the whole of this story."

The young man glanced at Sheena, then faced them. "M'name's Lawrence Carr, m'lord. I know Sheena from back in Annaghdown." Then he raised his chin. "I'm the father of her child, m'lord, and have the right to protect her."

The child that died. The poor couple. "Sheena's

safe," Genova assured him. "She's only here because her employer appears to have abandoned her."

"Lady Booth Carew." Lawrence almost spat it. "I tracked them across Ireland and almost to London, then realized Sheena wasn't with her anymore. I've been frantic since, but then heard that a lord here was seeking an Irish speaker, and that it was to do with a baby."

"Wiser to have presented yourself openly as the translator, wouldn't you say?" Ash remarked.

"I don't trust the big houses! When I found I could get in, I did. I'm not a housebreaker, m'lord. I'm not!"

He was standing bold, but shaking. It wasn't surprising. He could end up transported for that.

"That's all right," Genova soothed. "But we need you to ask Sheena about Lady Booth. We need to know why Lady Booth abandoned her and Charlie with us."

Lawrence Carr took Sheena's hand and asked her the questions.

Sheena looked around almost furtively, or perhaps like a trapped animal, then spilled a stream of Gaelic. There was an exchange that rose rapidly to an argument. Then Sheena burst into tears.

Genova was ready to shake the English out of the man. "What did she say?"

Lawrence Carr looked at them, angry and perhaps bewildered. "M'lord, ma'am, I can hardly make sense of it m'self. She tried to tell me our child died, but when I returned to Annaghdown, me own mam told me Sheena'd had a baby, and it was a fine boy. Boxed me ears, she did, for not writing so I'd know."

"You didn't know?" But then it sank in. "Charlie is Sheena's own baby?"

Of course, of course. So much made sense now. But some things, many things, still didn't.

"And Lady Booth's plan?" Ash asked, not showing any reaction.

"She doesn't know, m'lord. But Lady Booth promised her money if she'd come to England with her baby, and that the boy'd grow up to be a fine lord. The silly biddy to believe such a thing. But it was hard for her with an unwed babe and me being away. I was trying to make money so we could marry, m'lord! I don't have the writing, and I didn't want to spend money on someone to write for me when I'd nothing to say."

Nothing to say to the girl he'd made love to. How very like a man, and yet Lawrence Carr had been trying to do the right thing, to earn enough to marry his sweetheart.

"So the baby died," Ash said to no one in particular, "and Molly found a substitute."

"Or," Genova suggested, "there was never a baby at all."

"What?"

Ash looked dumbfounded. Genova wondered if it took a woman to follow a tangle that deep into the knot. "Mr. Carr, I gather your village is close to Lady Booth Carew's home?"

"That it is, ma'am. She was left her husband's place there, though she takes no care of it."

"So ask Sheena, if you please, whether Lady Booth carried and birthed a child there."

After an exchange he looked back, but Genova was already smiling, having understood Sheena's tone and some gestures.

"She says not, ma'am. Apparently Lady Booth went about with a growing belly, complaining of her ill-usage, which was a strange thing to everyone, for you'd think she'd want to hide in shame. But her maid laundered her cloths every month, and hung them out to dry."

She laughed aloud at that. "Never think anything can be hidden."

Ash was shaking his head.

"Swear if you want," Genova said, rising and going to his side to speak confidentially.

He laughed at that as he had once before.

"It should have occurred to me," he said. "She'd

been married to Carew for eight years without sign. But she risked her reputation."

"Or used it to try to force you. I suppose if you'd married her, she would have conveniently miscarried and hoped to truly quicken soon."

"Optimistic, given her history, and it would assume I could bring myself to . . . swive her." He smiled as he chose that word.

"Not necessarily," Genova pointed out.

"Zeus," he said. "She might not have cared. She'd have had what she wanted, a marchioness's coronet."

"And worn it in a cage with a wolf."

He raised a brow but seemed to catch her meaning. "I might well be tempted to bite in that situation, yes."

"But why the end play?" Genova asked. "Did she think evidence of a baby would change your mind at such a late date? He was born out of wedlock, so he could never be your heir."

Ash shook his head. "Impossible to understand a mind like hers. Perhaps she hoped that proof would crush me with guilt. Or that it might cause the king to insist I marry only her. I expect word of the king's ultimatum prompted her one last attack. We were to be found together, and the Brokesbys were to carry the tale around England."

"Then why flee at the last minute? I hate the pieces not fitting!"

"Like clockwork," he said with a look. "I'd like to think that she realized I'd throttle her, but we'll probably never know."

Genova smiled at him. "You'd never have touched her, Ash."

"No? I think you're deluded about my character."

"Am I? I don't forget that she left the baby for 'Mr. Dash.' "

"So?"

"There would have been no point unless she knew that you wouldn't be able to abandon him."

He took out his snuffbox, a mother-of-pearl and diamond one, and flipped it open. She was beginning to recognize a defensive move. "If you remember, I did my best to run."

"Because I was there, and you thought then that I was Molly's deputy."

"I tried to put him on the parish."

"And planned to leave money for his care. Despite what you said, I know you would have arranged to be informed about his welfare."

He inhaled a tiny amount. "You are often given to delusions? I am not known as a Good Samaritan."

"Let's put it to the test. What are we to do with these two?" She nodded toward Sheena and Lawrence, who were holding tight to each other's hands and waiting to hear their fate.

"Put them on the parish," Ash said, snapping his box shut.

She looked at him, and he added, lips twitching, "We could run away and leave them on Rothgar's hands."

Then he smiled in acknowledgment that he'd do neither. "Relentless," he said. "I suppose we should inform my cousin of these developments under his roof, though I look a fool."

"It would take a devious mind to see through this one."

"Are you saying I'm not devious?"

He seemed truly affronted, and she couldn't help but laugh. His smile became a grin and she knew it was sinking in that this finally cleared him.

It would take deft handling to smooth things with the king, but Ash's way was clear to what he wanted. He would finally take up his full position as Marquess of Ashart, and do it well.

He tugged the bellpull. "I need to have this arrangement installed at Cheynings. It spares us from servants hovering within earshot all the time."

"It takes longer to get service," she pointed out.

"You like the old ways?"

"I think a man short of money shouldn't be considering expensive renovations."

"Genova, sweetheart, don't nag."

A footman arrived and duly went off to find the marquess. They waited in silence, then. The Irish couple, relaxing, leaned close and murmured. Sheena began to smile and dabbed her eyes with her apron. Genova guessed they were beginning to plan their future, and longed to be doing the same thing.

Perhaps if she and Ash had made love, it would have changed his mind. But she'd never take that route to marriage.

When Rothgar came in, he looked around the room. "What have we here?"

In an attempt at a cool manner, Ash gestured to the Irish couple. "Mr. Lawrence Carr and Miss Sheena O'Leary, lovers, parents, now happily united. I thought it best to inform you."

"Parents?"

"Parents of the baby we arrived with. Charlie Carr, I assume we should call him now." Ash told the story.

"So Molly Carew was never with child. I felicitate you, Cousin."

Ash inclined his head. "It seems best to let the lad stay. In the stables with the grooms, perhaps?"

"We could build a bower in the hall and have a living *presepe*." But Rothgar was teasing. "Of course he may stay. Perhaps Mr. Carr might like to see his son before he leaves the house?"

Lawrence Carr bowed, touching his forelock. "Indeed I would, milord."

Rothgar turned to Genova. "Perhaps you could bring the infant down, Miss Smith. Mrs. Harbinger dislikes strangers in her domain, and Miss O'Leary looks a little unsteady still."

In fact, Sheena did not look deliriously happy. She was clinging to her lover's hand, but she looked as if the blow was yet to fall. Was there more to tell?

Genova hurried to the nurseries, wondering if Mrs.

Harbinger would welcome Charlie back when she knew he was Sheena's own child.

When Genova told the nursery governess the gist of the story, however, Mrs. Harbinger nodded. "I had begun to suspect as much, Miss Smith, and was in something of a puzzle over what to do about it. Strange goings-on."

She led Genova into the nursery where only one cradle remained, and scooped out the sleeping baby. She wrapped him in an extra blanket and passed him over. Genova carried him away, thinking she knew Sheena's concern. Life in her village was probably simple and poor, and having tasted better, she might want better for her child.

Genova navigated the stairs with care, since a baby and hooped skirts was a challenge. Distant music told that the Christmas revelry continued—a celebration all to do with a baby. Charlie stirred, his mouth working for a moment.

"Don't cry for food yet," Genova told him. "Especially since Lord Rothgar might still be there."

He settled, and she hummed the *presepe* song to keep him happy. She entered the room to find Ash alone with Sheena and Lawrence in a tense silence.

It broke as soon as Genova gave the baby to Sheena. Lawrence's open delight, the eagerness with which he took Charlie into his arms, eased some of Genova's concerns. But the story wouldn't end until they were comfortably settled somewhere.

Rothgar returned with a servant who was to take Lawrence to the grooms' area above the stables. As soon as he started to leave, Sheena clung to him, crying.

Genova had Lawrence explain to the girl. Sheena reluctantly let him go and left to return to the nurseries, but as if tragedy weighed on her head.

"I feel like a Capulet or Montague," Ash said. "I hope you've locked away the poison, Rothgar."

"This abbey is clear of meddling monks, at least. What will you do now?"

Ash moved around the room, pausing at the table holding decanters. "May I offer you some of your own brandy?"

Rothgar smiled and declined.

"It would be useful to find Molly and confront her with her sins, but perhaps cruel to make her confess them in public."

"You're more compassionate than I am," Rothgar said. "May I be of service in presenting this evidence to the king? I believe he would find this tale of Irish lovers interesting, perhaps even touching, if told aright. He could be persuaded that he has been less than just. It would be wise to marry, though. Kings hate to have it obvious that they have changed their mind."

Genova looked at her meaningless ring. She told herself that she didn't want Ash to marry her only because a rapid wedding would suit. Anyway, Damaris Myddleton would snap him up.

"It is time I married," Ash said, "though I doubt anything will convince the king that I'm a saint."

"He's pragmatic enough to realize that if he surrounds himself only with saints he will wander empty rooms, and lack some excellent advisers. His Majesty does persist, however, in believing that marriage can save a sinner. Have you read my mother's papers?"

Genova looked up and saw the cousins assessing each other.

"I haven't read all of the journal, but it doesn't paint a picture of cruelty."

"No, and I can pledge my conviction that my father was incapable of it. Perhaps he came to find her trying, however, so he may not have been a perfect husband."

"*I* found her trying and I was only reading her daily grievances."

Genova stood still, hardly breathing, not wanting to break this crucial dialogue.

Ash looked into the fire, then up. "Was she mad?"

"In the end, certainly. Whatever led her to believe that Edith must die cannot have been sane. Earlier?"

Rothgar shrugged. "We all walk an edge between sanity and insanity and can be pushed over by a powerful enough force."

Another edge, Genova thought.

"Some require very little pressure," Rothgar said. "I think you will have seen that she was unstable."

Ash turned to fully face his cousin. "Rumor said you would not marry because of the madness in your blood."

"We all walk that edge," Rothgar repeated. "I came to understand that I was my father's son as well as my mother's, that I had kept my balance through trying times, and that the factors forming future generations cannot be predicted. And I had fallen in love."

"Love. Are men like you and I allowed to indulge in that degree of insanity?"

Did Ash glance at her for a moment? Genova's mouth dried and her heart beat faster.

"It's an unjust world if we're not. Can we cry peace, Cousin?"

Ash looked into the distance for so long that Genova wanted to speak just to break the silence. Then slowly, he said, "Peace be with you, and upon your house be peace."

Genova tried to not even breathe as the cousins shook hands and gave each other the kiss of peace.

As they stepped apart, Ash said, "I would like to take the journal and some drawings to show to our grandmother."

Rothgar stilled. "I would prefer that they not be destroyed."

"I give you my word that they will return here safely."

"Then perhaps we could agree to an exchange of documents."

"For some that you would wish destroyed?" Ash asked, and Genova knew that was of great moment.

"Precisely. We have no more need of weapons, I think."

"Nor of defense, I hope. Very well. I will arrange

to have them delivered to you. Or perhaps you would trust me to destroy them and the supporting evidence. I will be thorough."

Now it was Rothgar who hesitated, but then he bowed. "My thanks. Now, excuse me but I should return to my guests."

He left the room and Genova exhaled.

"What was that about?" she asked.

Ash had turned to look into the fire. "The documents? I hold some work of his that in the right hands could destroy him."

She'd shared a more perilous edge than she'd known. "You would have used them?"

He looked at her. "I don't know. Do you approve of this peace?"

"It's not my place—"

"To hell with that. Do you approve? Did I do the right thing?"

"Yes, of course!"

He turned back to the fire. "How pleasant to be so sure of everything."

Genova bit her lip. "I'll leave you now," she said, and headed for the door.

He caught her hand as she passed. "Why? The night's still young."

"And you're in a mood best served by solitude."

"Foul, in other words."

"Yes."

He let go of her hand but stepped closer. "I might be improved by a taste of a sweet bread from Genova."

He lowered his head and nibbled gently at her lower lip.

Chapter Forty

*P*erhaps wine and spirits still raced in Genova's blood. Perhaps the solution of so many problems made her delirious. At the first touch of his mouth, reason evaporated and molten need exploded.

She pushed off his jacket as they kissed, unbuttoned his long waistcoat. A waistcoat button resisted and she wrenched it off so she could slide her arms around his strong torso, feel his heat beneath fine lawn.

Distantly she thought, *I just threw away diamonds!*

But her mind was all on him and the fire his mouth, his hands, his body, ignited. She'd wanted this for days—for a lifetime, it seemed—and she couldn't fight it anymore.

Their mouths slid apart and she explored his jaw, his ear, his throat, his wonderful taste and smell that made her purr deep in her throat.

His cravat. It was in the way.

She jerked out the jeweled pin, tossed it away, tugged loose the knot and discarded the length of silk and precious lace. To unbutton, to kiss, to nuzzle hot skin, to inhale him. Him. The only man to create this ecstasy in her.

He was laughing, murmuring, nuzzling, nibbling.

She dragged his shirt out of his breeches and he stepped back to pull it over his head and discard it.

She held him off with her hands over his flat nipples, letting her eyes feast. "Even to a woman who's seen many naked chests, yours is remarkable."

"Is it?" He put his hands to the front of her gown. "And you do not disappoint me, *pandolcetta*."

With a rake's skill he'd loosened her clothes as they kissed. Her gown slid off her arms at his touch, and her loosened petticoats fell to the floor. She was in her stays over her shift, and he stroked up her sides.

"You're magnificent, Genni."

"I want to be. For you."

She wanted to eat him whole, as if starving, but this was good, too. This moment of pulsing restraint.

She stood still as he dug into her hair and found pins, as she felt her hair tumble. He drew fingers through it, flaring it around her shoulders. Then he buried his face in it against her neck, inhaling like a drowning man bursting out of the water.

They wove toward the bed twined around each other, she licking his strong neck, he squeezing her tingling breast. He dragged back the covers, then picked her up and laid her on smooth sheets, sliding his arms away, watching her with hot, dark intensity.

She could imagine herself, mirror to her vision of him. Laughing, disordered, half naked, and crazed with desire. Slowly, loving every stormy look from those heavy-lidded eyes, she unhooked the front of her stays bottom to top, until her full breasts sprang free, now covered only by the delicate silk shift.

His eyes were fixed there, so she cradled her breasts in her hands and offered them. He fell, catching himself on his arms over her, then lowered his head to mouth first one nipple, then the other.

Heat shot through her thighs to burst in exquisite pain deep inside her, so she thrust up against him, seeking.

A flicker of caution stirred. Too late, too late, because she would not give this up now, not even at threat of the hangman's rope.

He switched to kneeling over her, pushing up her shift to reveal her nakedness. No man had ever seen her there, but it felt right in the passionate admiration of his gaze. She helped him lift her shift over her head, then lay back down, his, as he should desire.

Please.

He knelt before her, magnificent in candlelight and firelight, and unfastened his already bulging velvet breeches. Slowly, he opened them, watching, smiling, as she inhaled, exhaled, and licked her dry lips.

He rolled off the bed and stripped.

She turned to watch. "You put Rothgar's statues to shame."

He laughed. "I might be hard as stone, but I promise I'm anything but cold."

As he came back toward her, Genova realized she wasn't naked. She was still wearing her stockings. She reached for one black garter, but he said thickly, "Keep them on."

He crawled up onto the bed and over her, pinning her hands on the pillow as he lowered his head to suck at first one, then the other nipple.

Her body surged again, even more powerfully for being restrained. Still suckling, driving her wild, he put a knee between her legs, nudging her open. She spread herself willingly, wondering through fever if her virginity was going to spoil this.

Nothing must spoil this.

Surely she could hide the pain.

Could a man tell?

She heard her own deep-throated cry of need and then the hard pressure of him, there, against her burning hunger.

She was saying, "Yes, yes . . . ," and then she cried it—"Yes!"—as he thrust hard and deep.

Had there been a sting? It had been nothing, and she was tight and full. They were locked together now as she'd longed to be.

Then he pulled back and thrust even deeper, then again, and again. Startled by the force, Genova faltered for a moment, but then she matched it, loving it, exulting in the fast, slick pounding that allowed not a breathless moment for anything but pure, blinding sensation.

When she thought she'd reached her limit, he drove her on and fire exploded in her brain, searing away all reality except his body surging with hers, and then his shattering release.

Her head was still full of fireworks, and she had her teeth sunk in his shoulder. She released him as they tumbled slowly down, him heavy over her, her boneless, liquid, sated.

She stroked him, inhaling and exhaling as if breathing was a novelty. That had been insane. That had been wonderful. Having thrown herself into the ruinous flames, she wanted to do it again. She knew men needed time to recover. How much time?

They didn't have a night. Thalia would miss her, and Fitzroger would return here at some point.

She tensed. Had they locked the door?

As if he picked up her thought, he rolled to one side trailing kisses over her, then left the bed. As lordly naked as when in velvet and jewels, he strolled over to turn the key. Then he looked back at her as if she were the most beautiful object in the universe, and promised wordlessly that there would indeed be more.

He went to a small table and poured brandy into a glass. One glass? He brought it back to the bed with a look in his eyes that made her feel that she might swoon down through the bed into the room below.

"What?" she asked, and some instinct made her pull the sheet up over herself a bit.

Smiling, he sat on the edge of the bed, facing her, so at ease with his naked virility that she wanted to eat him. Her whole life seemed to have shrunk down to the present. To this.

He dipped a finger in the glass and traced her lips. Brandy magic teased her nose, and when she licked, it tantalized her tongue. He drank, then kissed her, sharing brandy heat.

Then he lowered the sheet and dribbled brandy just above her right garter, and licked it up.

"I wish my stockings were gossamer fine," she breathed, "clocked with flowers, and held up by lacy garters."

"They will be," he murmured there. "You'll take

off silk stockings for me. You'll swim naked with me in a warm Grecian bath."

He poured a tiny amount of brandy into her navel and tongued it. "We'll lick cream and honey off each other as we lick brandy now."

He collapsed onto his back beside her and upturned the glass to empty over his chest. She laughed for the madness of it and set to lick him clean.

"We'll have long nights of love in a bed," he said, hand playing in her hair and down her back. Playing, as a musician plays an instrument. "And we'll slip away from entertainments to enjoy quick, silent passion in an alcove within hearing of the throng. . . ."

Arousal rippled through her body at that thought.

"All in one night?" she asked unsteadily.

"Probably not."

She stilled, scarce daring to breathe. Her swimming mind couldn't quite comprehend what he was saying, but surely he'd just sketched out a life. A life together.

"We'll spend quiet times talking," he went on as his fingers slid between her thighs, opening them as if he'd touched a spring. The spring of her need. "In bed and out."

He found the place that made her arch, his touch teasing, tantalizing. "I talk with you as I never have with a woman, Genova Smith, and that is precious beyond rubies."

Wasn't there something about a good wife being more valuable than rubies?

"Be my sanity, Genni, please."

Delirious with happiness, Genova cradled his head in her hands and blended their brandied mouths. "Yes, of course, Ash. I will be yours, forever."

He rolled her under him—hers, miraculously hers!—and slid his hand between her thighs. Her body responded immediately. As he built her desire, she touched, tasted, stroked, bedazzled that he was hers forever.

Love and passion wound tight in her, and she wanted him in her again. She cried out, "Now!"

"Yes, now," he commanded, stroking harder, sucking harder. Tension shattered into pleasure that rolled on and on.

"And again," he said, thrusting into her still-shimmering body, and indeed, it happened again.

Perhaps she fainted. It seemed that she returned to reality from a great distance, from a dark, burning, airless, wonderful place.

But this was wonderful, too.

She stroked his hot, sweaty skin all the long length of his powerful body, from shoulder, down back, to thigh. No wonder empires had fallen for this.

And this, and he, was hers, till death did them part.

Fitz was strolling along a corridor toward bed when he heard, "Fitz! Oh, Fitz!"

He turned to see Ash's dotty Great-aunt Thalia trotting after him, quite out of breath.

"What is it, Lady Thalia? Is something the matter?"

"The matter? No, dear boy. But I do so want you to partner me at whist."

She hooked an arm around his, giving him no choice other than to turn with her and go back toward the festivities.

"It must be an age since we've been partners, dear boy. Come along. The night is young!"

In the face of this ancient sprightliness, he could hardly claim exhaustion, especially when it was not yet ten. In truth, he'd left the company to avoid Damaris Myddleton. He'd done as Ash wanted and distracted her, but it had left him out of sorts.

It was tiresome to be so obviously Ash's substitute, but Damaris could be clever and engaging. He knew her father had been something of a rogue, though a very successful one, and he glimpsed that in her at times. As he was something of a rogue himself, it appealed.

Most of the time, however, she tried to be the perfect lady—the perfect marchioness, in fact—and he wanted to shake her. He knew Ash probably would offer her marriage, even though he clearly loved Genova Smith. Ash would see it as his duty, and he had become resolved to do his duty, suppressing all natural urges as necessary.

That was Ash's grave, and he could lie in it, but Fitz hated to think of Miss Myddleton trapped there with him, innocent except for an ambition that had doubtless been trained into her.

Fitz had flirted with her and done his damnedest to distract her permanently, but though she played the game well, he knew her attention, like that of any predator, never truly wavered.

He'd eventually abandoned her to lovesick Ormsby and retired to the billiard room. He was better than the other players, however, which made it boring. He'd sat out for a while, chatting and drinking, then decided to give up on the night.

Now he was being dragged back.

"Dear Genova can foretell the future, you know," Lady Thalia said. "She's very good at it."

He didn't like the sound of that. He still wasn't convinced that Miss Smith wasn't an adventuress of some sort.

"Such people use tricks to make their predictions come true."

"Oh, no, dear," Lady Thalia said blithely. "I'm the one to do that!"

Lord save him from them all. But he let Lady Thalia tow him into the drawing room, where she dismissed Dr. Egan from the chair opposite her. Thank heavens the man seemed only amused. Perhaps, thought Fitz somewhat morosely, the librarian would like a peaceful early night.

Fitz settled down and sharpened his wits. Crazy though Lady Thalia was, she was a devil with the cards and had no patience with sloppy play.

Ash shifted slightly, his hand sliding up to her breast. "Pearl beyond price. My sweetest Genni . . ."

"That's my father's name for me."

He looked up. "Do you mind?"

"No, of course not." She told him then about her father, and Hester, the sweet and the sad. "It's not her fault. It's me."

"No, love, it's just a mismatch. It's good you'll be away from there, however, in a place of your own."

"It will be heaven." She pulled him close for a kiss. "Especially because I'll be with you. We can be happy, even if things aren't perfect. I'll prove it to you."

He nuzzled her. "There's nothing to prove. It will be as perfect as I can make it. You'll have everything you want. Jewels, silk, even clockworks, if that's truly an interest."

She laughed. Economy was going to take time. "I will want nothing but you."

"And food once in a while?"

"And food," she conceded, smiling.

"And perhaps a bit of wood in winter?"

"Yes, I suppose I'll need that."

"Just possibly a scrap of clothing?"

Laughing, she pushed him and they fell to tickling, tangling themselves in brandy-stained sheets.

When they came to rest again, he said, "I want to give you precious things, Genni. I want to give you the moon and the stars."

"And I want you to spend your money on your land and your people, but I'll try not to nag."

"I can think of nothing better than being nagged by you."

She shifted to stroke his chest. "Not even this?"

He smiled. "Yes, perhaps that."

She kissed him. "Or perhaps this? And this . . ." She slid her hand down and found him, delighting in the softness, smiling when it began to change beneath her hand.

"Certainly that," he said, lids lowered. "You win. You need never nag again. Speaking of nags . . ."

He shifted, encouraging her to straddle him.

Genova understood. Enjoying watching him, she rose and slowly guided him into her core, alert for signs that she might be doing something wrong. She couldn't imagine how when it felt so beautifully right to her.

She was deeply sensitive, but it still felt right. She settled slowly, filling herself again. "I'd certainly rather do this than nag," she said, her voice husky.

"I'll remember that." His lids were almost shut and she knew his attention was on one place only.

She leaned forward, testing the sensation deep inside, the shifting fullness, the pressure against sensitive places. Her hair fell forward and he cupped her breasts in the veil of it, thumbs working her nipples. She gasped and tightened around him, already hovering near ecstasy.

He slid his hands down to her hips and moved her up and down. She began the moist movement herself, slowly, watching him. His eyes shut tight.

"Perhaps I need to nag to provide contrast," she said, trailing her hair across his chest.

"Beloved, you could nag with a razor-sharp tongue and I wouldn't care right now."

She closed her own eyes and joined him in that hot, wet whirlpool of a place, loving doing it, controlling it, making it happen for him.

Later, sticky with sweat, she said, "I'm sure I can improve my skills. At nagging, I mean."

He simply laughed, and she knew how he felt. Too exhausted to even think. She never wanted to move, never wanted her skin to be separated from his. If only this night could last forever.

But there would be other nights.

An infinity of magical nights. She could hardly believe it yet, but it was true.

Perhaps they dozed. The clock chimed and she idly counted.

"Eleven!" she exclaimed, sitting up. "We'll have been missed."

Chapter Forty-one

*H*e pulled her back down. "Everyone's too drunk and merry to notice." When she frowned at him, he sighed. "All right, we can return if you want, love."

Since he was tracing circles on her belly, his words had little impact.

"I'm curious about something," he said.

"What?" She tensed, fearing something might break the magic.

"Barbary pirates."

Ah. She pushed him to his back and traced patterns on his belly to distract him. "It wasn't as daring as it sounds."

He captured her hand. "Tell me, Genova."

"A command?"

"I'll pay you with a kiss." But then he added, "Because you hesitate, I want to know. Tell me, love."

She pulled a face, but couldn't refuse him anything. "My mother and I were sailing on a merchant ship to join my father. It was well armed, however, and the corsairs would probably never have attempted an attack if we hadn't been limping after a storm. As it was, it only needed a little resolute resistance to drive them off."

"And your resolute resistance was?"

She didn't like to speak of it, because some people treated her as a heroine, and others considered her unwomanly. Thalia wouldn't have known about it if her father hadn't told the tale. He was one who thought it heroic.

"Well?" Ash asked.

"I shot one of the pirates who boarded." After a moment, she added, "I killed him. And I knew what I was doing. My father taught me to use a pistol and where to aim. I was frightened. The pirate looked at me and he wanted me. He was the captain, and he would have raped me." The words spilled out. "So I killed him."

He stroked her hair. "It's nothing to be ashamed of, love. Quite the opposite. Killing him probably broke the will of his crew."

"That's what my father said."

She was circling, deciding whether to tell him the final part. She knew from the steady look in his eyes that he guessed there was more.

She looked away. "I desired him," she whispered. "Something about him, bold and confident, exuding that power that such men have, made me breathless."

She looked back at him and told him the one thing she'd never shared with another.

"I thought he might not have to rape me, and it was intolerable. He was looking at me, grinning at me, as I raised the pistol. He *knew* how I was feeling and that was intolerable, too. And it let me kill him. He never moved. I can only suppose that he didn't believe that a woman who . . . lusted after him would shoot."

He gathered her into his arms. "It was brave and it was right. He was a villainous pirate who'd doubtless killed many and enslaved more. He would have raped you whether your body responded to him or not, then sold you into a harem. Rejoice, Genni, at being able to act when you need to."

The old burden of it shrank, then disappeared. "I love you, Ash."

"And I love you. I think."

She looked disapproval at him. "Only think?"

"It's a novel emotion." He was teasing, but he added seriously, "I want honesty between us, Genni. Complete honesty."

"Yes. Honesty." Unable to believe how things were getting even better, she sat up to face him. "As for love, I've never been in love before, either. Oh, I've felt something, and once or twice I've been besotted. But it wasn't like this. You've become the steady heartbeat of my world, Ash."

"And you of mine." He rubbed a tender hand along her thigh. "I'll try to mitigate the hurt."

"Hurt?"

"It won't be easy."

She recognized that honesty wasn't always easy, but that made what he was doing more precious. He was acknowledging the problems they faced.

Lady Calliope was opposed to the match, and she might not be the only one. The dowager marchioness would certainly fight it—she wanted him to marry Miss Myddleton's money. Most of his world would think him a fool to marry for love. Even the king might disapprove. Together, however, they could conquer all of this.

"You will be accepted at court again?" she asked.

"I presume Rothgar will work his magic."

"You resent that?" she asked. "Of course you do. A generation of conflict can't be smoothed away in a night."

"It certainly would have been pleasanter to force him to assist." But he pulled a humorous face at her. "I'm reformed, love, I promise."

"I like you as you are formed," she said, approving of his body with her hands. "What made the papers you hold so dangerous? Something to do with truth, I think, and possibly to do with that strange D'Eon?"

"You're too sharp by far, Genni. Forget it."

She stroked his cheek, his jaw. Disheveled, beard-shadowed, he was just a man. They were simply a man and a woman, naked in bed. The sinews of history, the bones of life.

"I hope you'll share things with me, Ash. All things. I can be trusted, but in any case, the marriage bed is sacrosanct. Wives can't testify against husbands."

"Wives? Genni . . ."

She knew. Without words, she saw it in his shocked face, and a lump of pain almost choked her.

"Oh, how silly! I'm carried away by this silly betrothal business. It's so late—"

She was half out of bed when he caught her arm and pulled her back.

"Genni, love! I would if I could. I have to marry money."

Bitterness exploded. "For *what*? For another set of diamond buttons? For your doxies and bastards? I slipped into the folly of thinking you meant it when you said we'd be together. I know better now." She pulled against his hold. "Let go of me!"

She fought him but he conquered her, pinning her down on the bed. "Listen to me. The jewels and the gold are necessary for court, and court is necessary for survival. We're on the brink of ruin, especially because of Molly Carew."

"Good for her!" she spat. "You probably promised her the earth, too."

"Blast your eyes, I did not! I've never promised a woman more than I will do. Including you. Genni, sweetheart"—his voice softened—"I hoped you'd become my mistress. A permanent mistress, with a house, a carriage—everything you could desire."

Her stomach rebelled. "What I desire, my lord, is a *husband*. A true husband, a loving home, a safe, secure world into which to bring *legitimate* children."

"I thought you a kindred spirit."

"You were wrong. Let me go."

He moved off her and she scrambled away, grabbing for clothing. She heard the curtain rings rattle and turned at bay as she struggled into her shift.

He'd pulled on his breeches. "Barbary pirates," he stated. "A wanton response to kisses. A familiarity with men's chests. A bold way with words. Don't claim to be a violated saint!"

Dear God, he saw her as another Molly Carew.

She managed to hook her stays up the front, which

wasn't easy with the laces still tight. "I'm sure you were dreadfully misled. This is all my fault. Just help me dress so I can get out of here. You don't need to be afraid," she threw at him. "I'm not a Molly Carew. I would die before trying to hold a man who doesn't want me."

He handed her the petticoat and she stepped into it and tied it at the waist. She was fighting tears, but one escaped, running down her cheek. She dashed it away.

He had her dress ready and she shrugged into it, fastening the clasp at the waist. She was still in her stockings. After all this, she was still in her stockings! She went to her shoes and put them on.

She turned to the mirror to see a blowsy wanton, her thick hair a tangle. She grabbed his comb and dragged it painfully through knots. She had to restore order. No one must ever know.

He took the comb from her and held her shoulders. "I'm truly very sorry if I misled you. Believe me, I care. More deeply than I should. I made a serious mistake, but I'll do my best to save you from disaster. Sit."

Genova obeyed, mostly because her knees were failing her. He began to gently tease the tangles out of her hair. That gentleness was perhaps the cruelest blow. He did care. But under his coldhearted code, that weighed very lightly in the balance.

She'd come here knowing this, but she'd put the blindfold on herself and raced to ruin.

She kept her eyes on her hands and rolled the ill-fated diamond. She longed to take it off, but even in her distracted state she knew that would be exactly the wrong thing to do. Their split must be in public, not here.

He was drawing the comb through her hair now. It was, as always, soothing. She swallowed tears, accepting her own responsibility.

She knew her free-spirited ways gave people an impression of improper boldness, and why on earth had

she said that about naked chests? What was a man to
think? He wouldn't consider shipboard life.

She'd responded to his kisses like a wicked woman
from the start, without a scrap of maidenly modesty.
He'd not forced her into his bed, or seduced her with
promises. She'd left the ballroom willing to make love
to him and he knew that.

He gathered her hair on the top of her head and
pushed pins in, as deftly as the finest maid. He even
found and added the discarded spray of silk roses. She
looked in the mirror. Not up to Regeanne's standards,
but it would do.

She stood, putting all her purpose into being calm.
She wouldn't flee this room like a devastated virgin,
even if she was one. Thank heaven, thank heaven, for
a fragile maidenhead.

She found her fan and slipped the ribbon on her
wrist, then checked that she'd left no other evidence.
Evidence! The rumpled bed and sweet, mysterious
smell would tell the servants someone had been his
lover.

Not who, however.

Though the thought choked her, she'd have to return to the party and hope no one had noticed their
absence.

"Genova."

She turned at the door.

"I'm very sorry."

She knew what he meant, but she deliberately
misunderstood.

"Please don't worry. I won't let this trap you."

Once outside, she hurried away, but all her willpower couldn't stop tears. She turned toward her
room and almost ran into it.

And there she wept until she was limp, until she
was drained of everything, even pain. For now. Grateful for generous hosts, she poured herself a glass of
the sweet ratafia Thalia liked.

Thank heavens it wasn't brandy. She might never
be able to drink brandy again.

As she drank, she became aware of her body, of soreness and lingering sensitivities. Then it struck her. What if she was with child?

She drained the glass, accepting that the possibility had been there all along. If she had conceived, it was his fault as much as hers, but she wouldn't make it into a chain to bind him.

He would never know, because if he did he probably would insist on marrying her. She was the antithesis of Lady Booth Carew. She could not bear the thought of marriage by force.

For now, she must do her best to undermine any suspicion. She checked her appearance again, then dabbed at her eyes with a cold cloth. She'd go to the dimly lit ballroom, where the ravages of the night might not show, and dance her cares away.

Chapter Forty-two

*A*sh stood in his room half dressed, feeling strangely at a loss. His earlier euphoria at being free of Molly's schemes, and the growing hope of an end to the conflict with the Mallorens, now seemed like dust.

Genova.

He had lost her.

No, he'd thrown her away.

After only a few days, he couldn't imagine life without her, but that was his course, it would seem.

She'd played such a crucial part in clearing his mind and clearing his name. Without her, he might not have broken free of hatred. Without her, he would not have learned the truth about Molly.

Despite her delusions, he would have left the child to the care of the parish charity in Hockham. He would have left money, certainly, but he wasn't sure he'd have given the child a thought thereafter. He certainly wouldn't have been around to discover the truth, that Molly had never been pregnant at all.

He should be celebrating. His life was now in order again. He would soon be able to move forward with his plans to restore his property and powers. Grandy would hate peace with the Mallorens, and perhaps resist his other plans, but he would deal with that.

He should be celebrating, but he felt dull in the extreme.

Or perhaps simply unhappy.

Devil take it—he smashed his hand into an oaken post of the bed—he couldn't marry Genova Smith!

The bed only shook, but his hand hurt like Hades. He welcomed that. He deserved that.

She brought nothing with her.

Except herself, her wits, and her courage.

How many women would have been able to make a dignified exit from this room? None that he knew.

And she'd shot a man. He should be grateful there were no pistols to hand here. But no. He corrected that flippant thought. She valued justice, his Genova.

His Genova.

Damn and blast!

He could smell her perfume, and her, but it wallowed amid the smell of lust, and devil take it, Fitz would be coming up here soon. He couldn't be expected to put up with this.

Ash tugged on the bellpull, frustrated by not being able to hear it ring. Pestilential idea. He yanked again and the wire came off in his hand, staggering him back.

"Hell and damnation!" He hurled the thing into a corner.

Henri, his valet, rushed in, jacket disordered, his powdered wig askew. "M'lord, I thought you with the dancing!" He looked around and Ash saw his expression. It said, *Not again.* "The sheets, they need changing, m'lord. I will see to it, m'lord. And your clothes . . ."

Henri went to the bell, then stared at the hole. "Your indulgence, m'lord," he said, bowing out to find servants the old-fashioned way.

Ash didn't want to be here when they arrived. He dressed himself and found a button missing from his waistcoat. He unbuttoned all the rest so it wouldn't show. There would be plenty of other disheveled revelers. He combed and tied his hair, his mind tangled in combing Genova's. . . .

After a quick check in the mirror, he escaped. He couldn't face company yet and went to the picture gallery, cold and quiet as it had been the last time.

"Is this a damsel that I see before me? . . ."

He didn't even have the excuse of meddling witches for the bloody mess he'd made of everything.

The moonlight was dulled by clouds, making the paintings more ghostly than before.

Damn your prosy faces! If you were my ancestors, you wouldn't want me to marry a penniless nobody. I'm trying to do the right thing. To do my duty!

The portrait of a young, wary Rothgar seemed to accuse him. Of what? Rothgar would laugh to see the Trayce family stuck in such folly.

Then Ash remembered peace. Damn peace.

It was all very well for Rothgar to disapprove. He had a thriving marquessate and a large, loving family.

There was a date on the scroll tumbling off the table by his cousin's pale hand. Ash went closer and read, *1744*. The year the Marquess of Rothgar and his wife had died of some virulent fever. The year Ash's cousin had inherited the title.

Ash knew the Malloren family tree as well as his own. Rothgar had inherited at nineteen, which was young, but not as young as inheriting a title at eight.

For the first time, however, Ash considered what that must have been like. Rothgar had had no grandparents to take care of everything. His mother's family had been alienated—were, in fact, active enemies. His paternal grandparents had been already dead. His stepmother's family was French.

Rothgar's half brothers and sisters would have been children, not support. Elf Malloren and Ash were of an age, so she and her twin brother would have been seven.

Ash remembered the day when the news had reached Cheynings that his grandmother's bête noire, her Malloren son-in-law, had died. She'd ordered a feast and sat Ash at the table to enjoy it. At last, she'd crowed, justice had fallen on the monster's head. The hand of God had struck, blasting him and his wife, leaving the house of Malloren in the hands of a wild youth.

She'd made Ash drink toasts, so even though they

had only been watered wine, he'd become woozy. He remembered being happy because she was happy. The Mallorens were evil and a blight upon the land. Anything that destroyed them was God's work.

Children believe what they are told.

When Grandy heard that the new marquess was insisting on keeping his half brothers and sisters in his care, she'd danced around the schoolroom with him, singing, "We've won, we've won! They're doomed."

Soon, however, his father's death had loomed larger than the affairs of the Mallorens, who were only names to him. He didn't miss his father, but he'd minded being moved from the schoolroom to the marquess's suite of rooms. At least he'd been allowed to bring his nursery governess down with him.

He'd had to go to court at eight to be presented to old George II, who'd pinched his cheeks and teased him about women. Grandy had pointed out Rothgar in a whisper of hate. Ash had seen a man looking very like this picture, and to an eight-year-old, Rothgar had seemed terrifyingly tall and adult.

"He's a devil," his grandmother had whispered, turning him away. He hadn't know then that Rothgar's success in holding his family together and continuing the Malloren prosperity was already burning into his grandmother like acid.

He hadn't known she was actively seeking to balk Rothgar's work until he was sixteen. His grandmother had rounded off a lecture about gaming with the gleeful news that Bryght Malloren had turned out to be a gamester and could be depended upon to ruin the family.

She hadn't said as much, but Ash had suspected then that she'd played a part. He'd thought it an excellent plan, the Mallorens being so despicable. And after all, if a man played to ruination, it was his own fault.

Ash had returned from his grand tour to find the Mallorens unruined and Grandy a bitter woman pouring guineas after guineas into a losing battle. Bryght Malloren was gambling with investments rather than dice, and winning. Brand Malloren was overseeing improvements in the estates. The youngest brother, Lord Cynric, had gone into the army, apparently against Rothgar's wishes, but was having brilliant success.

There'd been a brief moment of hope. King George II liked a rake, so Ash had become the sort of rake the king enjoyed, and had picked up plums and preferments by the handful.

But then George II had keeled over on his closestool one morning, and his grandson George III had ascended to the throne. The new king was young, shy, stiff, and ruled by his mother and the smooth Earl of Bute. He was also an admirer of the Marquess of Rothgar, who had been cultivating him for years.

Rothgar was no saint, but he was discreet, which Ash had never bothered to be. There'd been no hope of changing his reputation in a day, so the Trayce family were in the shadows, and the Mallorens basked close to the sun.

Now, at last, he had a new chance. Not to destroy, but to compete with the Mallorens in power, wealth, and prosperity. To gather the remnants of his family and build on that. To improve his land, to take his place in shaping the country's laws and systems.

But it required marriage and money. It required someone like Damaris Myddleton, whom he did not, could not—could never, he suspected—love.

"What I desire, my lord, is a husband. A true husband, a loving home, a safe, secure world into which to bring legitimate children."

Breath painful in his throat, Ash pushed that vision away. Duty must come before desire.

He couldn't face company. He returned to his room and found it pristine, all trace of love removed.

Chapter Forty-three

*B*oxing Day.

Genova opened her eyes and knew it must be late. She'd danced until the dancing stopped. Danced with every man in the house, she felt. Except Ash.

She'd not seen him again.

She'd kissed until the mistletoe boughs were stripped of power, and drunk to hold the numbness that let her dance and kiss. When she'd eventually staggered to her bed, she'd collapsed into sleep as soon as her head hit the pillow.

And here she was, awake to a miserable new day.

She felt smothered by too much sleep and the remnants of drink, but memory, alas, lived on. What a wonderful gift it would be to be able to scrub away painful memories as if scrubbing a spot off a wall.

Thalia was fast asleep and snoring. Genova ran her hands over her body, remembering. Despite the follies and dangers, their lovemaking could have been wonderful if she hadn't been so stupid. Now she had to face him again.

No sooner than she had to.

She climbed out of bed and went to summon Regeanne, but then remembered being told that at Rothgar Abbey, Boxing Day was the servants' holiday. As much as possible, people were to manage without.

Someone had lit the fire and left washing water by it to keep warm, so she used it, then dressed, choosing a simple, dark green gown. There must be breakfast laid out, but she was reluctant to emerge to face the world. To face Ash.

In any case, she wasn't hungry. Her eye caught the automated hearth. Fire on demand. Fire under control. What message had there been in that gift?

She sat by the window, looking out over the estate. She supposed Ash's estate at Cheynings must be similar. But then she remembered Lady Calliope saying that it was neglected because *that woman* spent nothing on it.

Doubtless Damaris Myddleton's money would create a deer park, topiary, and a knot garden. That lay below this window, beyond a small lawn edged with box.

A dog raced into the area as if pursuing prey. Then another. A moment later, she realized they were chasing a ball. One caught it and ran back, pursued by the other. They met a man. Two men. And two children.

Lord Rothgar and his brother Lord Bryght were laughing at something, their two elegant dogs frisking, begging for the ball to be thrown again. Persian gazelle hounds someone had told her. Lord Bryght hurled the ball over the hedge, and the dogs streaked off.

Little Master Malloren, bundled up in layers until he was almost round, toddled after, chirruping. An older boy—one of the guests, but she didn't know his name—went after, apparently to keep an eye on the little one.

The dogs ran back and one gave the ball to Rothgar. He carelessly dried it on his breeches, then called to the boy. The boy turned and, grinning, caught the ball. The dogs loped over to him, tails wagging. The boy hurled, but it only went as far as the hedge. One dog raced after it anyway. The other had a toddler around its neck.

Genova rose, even though she was too far away to do anything, but the dog lay down as if trained to it and obliged with a sort of gentle wrestling match until Lord Bryght rescued it by scooping up his son and tossing him into the air. Lord Rothgar produced another ball and joined with the older boy in amusing the indefatigable dogs.

Genova leaned against the windowsill, watching this family play, touched that it survived, even among the aristocracy.

Someone knocked on the door.

She opened it and found a maid there, curtsying. "Lady Arradale and Lady Bryght are breakfasting in Lady Walgrave's room, and invite you and Lady Thalia there, Miss Smith."

She supposed a lying-in meant some servants were needed.

Genova considered the invitation warily. Could the ladies have learned what she and Ash had done? What would be the result? An attempt to force the marriage? If true, better to deal with it swiftly, but there was no need to wake Thalia.

She took up her shawl and followed the maid.

She was ushered into a quite crowded room, since as well as the three ladies, a nursery maid sat by the cradle, and an older woman sat by the window. She was probably the midwife. Genova was welcomed with apparent delight and invited to the sofa where Portia and Lady Arradale sat. A table before them was spread with food, and carried pots of tea, coffee, and chocolate.

Lady Elf, blooming, was lying on a chaise.

Genova was braced to be quizzed about Ash, but chatter was general. Portia teased her on enjoying last night but seemed to have no suspicion of anything but dancing.

At a pause in the conversation, Genova said, "I saw Lord Rothgar and Lord Bryght out in the garden with the dogs and Master Francis."

"They all needed to work off Christmas fidgets," said Portia. "Especially Francis!"

"He's a charming child."

"Isn't he? May the next one be as perfect."

Something in her smile suggested that the next one might be on the way. Lady Elf announced that children were always different, giving her own family as example, and relating some hair-raising tales.

One involved the twins climbing out of a window and down the ivy on the north wall. For some reason, this made Portia blush. That story led to concern over Lady Elf's twin, who was in Nova Scotia, where matters were stirring unpleasantly due to some problems over taxation and the military.

Talk wandered between politics, society, and family, and Genova learned that Lord Rothgar had been here a number of times. He'd held the baby, even though it had been fussing.

A quiet excitement alerted her to the significance of that. Lady Arradale's eyes were bright, and the other ladies seemed as thrilled. Had Lord Rothgar finally proved to his own satisfaction that he could deal with a crying baby?

Had that problem been part of the reason for having this *accouchement* here? If so, it was an extraordinary gesture by his sister and brother-in-law.

The baby began a warbling complaint, and everyone's attention turned to him as he was brought, fussing, to his mother to feed. The guests stood to leave.

When Lady Arradale and Portia picked up a tray each, Genova remembered the lack of servants. It was extraordinary and could end up being amusing. Could these grand people fend for themselves? Then she wondered if the nursery staff was on holiday, too. She must go and see how Sheena was.

Outside the door, Genova and Portia were alone for a moment. "Are you still going to divorce yourself from Ashart?" Portia asked.

Genova prayed nothing showed on her face. "That is our arrangement." In fact, she would do it today. They didn't argue anymore, but surely she could find some pretext.

"But you deal extremely well. Everyone notes it."

"We merely act well, Portia."

With that, Genova escaped. She found the nurseries deserted apart from Sheena, Lawrence, and the baby.

Lawrence Carr started nervously. "I have permission to be here, ma'am!"

Someone had found him sturdier clothes, and he'd had either a bath or a good wash. This was a kind house, but he'd be more comfortable elsewhere. What was she to do with them, and why were they here? Were they hiding from the servants' holiday because they felt out of place?

"Would you be welcome down at the servants' feast, Lawrence?"

"We were asked, ma'am, but Sheena's shy. Then there's the baby. There's no one else to look after him."

Charlie was awake but happy. "Has he been fed?"

"He has, ma'am. Not long ago."

Genova went over. "Give him to me, then, and go off and enjoy yourselves."

"I don't know, ma'am. . . ." But he turned and spoke to Sheena, whose eyes lit with uncertain hope.

Genova smiled at her and took the baby. "Off with you. If he's any trouble, I promise to find you."

Lawrence translated, clearly urging. Sheena whipped off her mobcap and apron, and hand in hand they hurried away.

"And may they enjoy themselves," Genova said to the baby as she carried him downstairs. "Now you're to behave yourself, Charlie. It's true that perhaps Lord Rothgar won't be hurt by your wailing, but it's never pleasant, so be good."

To amuse him, she brushed by the tinkling bells all the way down the staircase, then she wondered where to go. She wanted to avoid Ash, but there was no point in that, either. He couldn't be avoided entirely unless she ran away.

Sounds of childish laughter drew her to the Tapestry Room, and she found it had become a temporary nursery. A gaggle of children was playing under the eyes of various women, some of them looking more comfortable with the situation than others. She noted that the older guests had taken themselves elsewhere, and it was not surprising. Mayhem threatened.

She retreated. It didn't seem suitable for a tiny infant. She almost collided with Ash.

They stepped back from each other as if pushed by a spring, and an awkward silence settled. She'd throw the grand disengagement fight now if she didn't have a baby in her arms.

"I'm looking after Charlie," she said, managing a smile, "so Sheena and Lawrence can enjoy themselves with the servants."

"I see." He looked at the baby. "Strange, but though I never thought him mine, I feel an interest. I thought of asking the young man if he wanted employment. He seems loyal and enterprising."

It wasn't hard to smile at him then. "That's a kind thought. They might want to return to Ireland, though."

"True. I should be able to arrange something for them there, I suppose. I have to make up for my many sins in some way."

He looked as if he was seeking words. She couldn't bear more apologies.

She stepped aside. "I'm blocking your way, but it's mayhem in there."

"So I gather. Genni . . ."

There was a sudden pounding on the door.

"Good Lord," he said, turning. "Are we invaded?"

"No servants, remember." They were alone in the hall, so Genova thrust the baby at him. "Here. I'll open it."

She was halfway there when Lord Rothgar overtook her. "Permit me."

He swung open the door to reveal a man in a heavy caped cloak, who instantly stepped aside to reveal a short woman swathed in a blue, fur-lined cloak.

"Grandmother," said Rothgar, sounding genuinely at a loss. "What a delightful surprise."

"Out of my way!" she snapped. She marched forward and the marquess obeyed.

"Where is my grandson?" The dowager marchio-ness stopped dead. "By gemini, Ashart, what folly have you sunk to now?"

Genova hurried over and grabbed the baby. "It's not his—it's mine!"

She realized that didn't sound right, but she didn't want to be the cause of more trouble. She had the distinct impression that if the Dowager Marchioness of Ashart had a cannon, she'd be firing it.

The old lady didn't, however, look like Loki. She was short and round, and soft white curls bubbled out from a lace-frilled cap topped by a mannish but ele-gant three-cornered hat. The cap was tied beneath her double chin with bright blue ribbons.

Her eyes were formidable enough, however, when she glared at Ash. "What are you *doing* here? You'll drive me to my grave!"

People were coming out of rooms to see what was going on. Genova wanted to gag the impossible old woman.

Ash walked toward her, seemingly at ease. "Cele-brating, Grandy." He bent to kiss her cheek. "Merry Christmas."

She pushed him away. "Fiddle-faddle. Come. We are leaving."

"Is that the royal *we*?"

The dowager stared at him, and Genova was sur-prised not to see steam.

"Why not stay?" Ash coaxed. "There are things to talk of."

He was going to try to change her mind here, in front of a houseful of Mallorens? Genova had to fight a need to protest.

Lady Ashart felt no such restraint. "I wouldn't stay in this house if it were the last one in England!"

"Oh, stop your foolery," said a gruff voice. Lady Calliope was borne down the stairs by her servants, crowned by her monstrous red wig. It was a magnifi-cent entrance.

"You're here, Sophia, and your servants are in time

for a rollicking good party belowstairs, which they doubtless deserve if you've dragged them over three counties at Christmas."

"That's true," said Thalia, appearing with a fan of cards in her hand. "What a shame to run away! A shame all around, for as Genova said, if anyone was ever at fault, they're all dead now."

"You always were a twit. And who the devil's Genova?"

"My promised bride," said Ash, taking Genova's free hand in a way that showed the diamond ring.

If she'd not been burdened with a baby, she might have knocked him over with a buffet. As well that she didn't. There was altogether too much firing already.

"What?" the dowager exclaimed and Genova understood why brave men quailed before her. "I heard the Myddleton chit was here." The dowager's eyes swept the room. "Where is she?"

"Here." Damaris Myddleton walked forward and curtsied to the old lady. "I'm glad you've arrived, Lady Ashart. I haven't known what to do." She turned to face Ash and Genova, with a steady gleam of victory in her eyes. "As you know, my lady, Ashart is already promised to me."

Chapter Forty-four

S ilence fell except for the faint laughter and calls of children.

For a moment Genova believed it, but then she knew the claim was impossible. "You must be mistaken, Miss Myddleton."

"Of course she is," Ash snapped.

Damaris Myddleton laughed, cheeks fiery. "How could I be mistaken about that?" She swung to the dowager. "Is it not true?"

It seemed as if a hall full of avid listeners held their breath.

"Yes," the dowager said.

Genova saw that Ash was frozen. He didn't want to prove his grandmother a barefaced liar.

There was one way out of this disastrous moment. Genova saw Lady Arradale nearby and passed the baby to her. Then she turned on Ash.

"You rancid fish!"

He blinked at her.

"Scum on the sewer of life!"

"Genni . . . ?"

She'd already noted the open door to the breakfast room, and now she ran for it. Clearly breakfast had been provided from yesterday's food along with preserved fruits and such. There was a bit of everything.

"Genni, for God's sake—"

He was close behind. She picked up a bowl of stewed plums, turned, and hurled the contents full at him. "You scurvy blackguard! I never want to see you again!"

He swept plums off his face. "Genova—"

She scooped out soft butter and threw. "Canker!" Cream. "Dunghill cock!" A jug of ale. "Strutting capon!"

"Capon!" he roared and threw himself at her so they tumbled squishily to the floor in the doorway.

She wriggled free because of a lucky elbow to the nose and pulled off the ring. As he scrambled up, she hurled it at him. "Gilded popinjay. Take back your vile diamond!"

They certainly had a fine audience, and despite a broken heart, Genova was enjoying herself.

She ran into the hall and saw an almost empty dish of sugarplums. She tossed the contents, frosting him with sugar. Then she grabbed a basket of walnuts and pelted him with them, one after another as he kept coming after her, undeterred.

When she ran out of nuts she looked for more missiles and realized she'd made a tactical error. He had her trapped near the fire and the *presepe*. When he lunged and grabbed her, she couldn't escape.

She tried to wrench free back in the direction of food, but he cinched her to him unbreakably, her back to him. "Damn you, woman, I love you! Only you!"

"To hell with that!"

"To hell together, then." Close to her ear, he hissed, "Break up over Damaris, dammit, and I'll have to marry her!"

That fueled true fury. Genova bent forward, then swung back hard, connecting with his jaw. He cursed and his grip loosened. She ripped free and ran for the food. She turned back swinging a large ham bone.

He went down on one knee, stained, messy, and gorgeous, holding out the diamond ring. "Sweet Genni, forgiving Genni, redoubtable Genni. Marry me? Don't hold my stupid words against me. It's not really my fault if you turn me into a gibbering idiot."

It was like running aground on hidden rocks. Distantly, Genova heard the dowager cry, *"Ashart!"* and Miss Myddleton shouting something.

Genova's attention was all on him. "What?"

"I love you, Genni, I adore you, and I want to marry you. I need to marry you. You're my sanity, my anchor, my balance on the edge. I was trying to find the right words earlier when my grandmother arrived."

Genova looked around at the shocked but entertained guests.

Damaris Myddleton, seething, was locked in Mr. Fitzroger's arms, presumably to stop her joining the fray. The Dowager Lady Ashart stood stock-still, glaring as if she wished she were the Gorgon and could turn Genova to stone.

It was also as if she was daring Genova to say yes.

Genova turned back to Ash, happiness bursting out in a laugh of delight. "Yes, Ash, beloved, I'll marry you. But please, not that ring!"

"No!" cried Miss Myddleton. "He's *mine*!"

Genova didn't take her eyes off Ash's brilliant, joyful face. He rose, pocketing the ring. "You see, you're my wisdom, too. But," he said, taking her into his arms, "I am *not* a capon."

She smothered laughter in his sugary shoulder. "I know that." She wove her arms around his neck, and they kissed slowly, gently, a sweet promise of a lifetime of heady delights.

But then a voice spoke, mildly but firmly. "Ashart."

With a wry expression, Ash turned to his grandmother. Perhaps governed by tact, their audience was dispersing, chattering. Genova couldn't see Damaris Myddleton. She felt rather sorry for her rival, for Damaris had not only lost, but mortified herself before everyone.

Only Rothgar remained.

Ash kept Genova's hand in his as they walked over to the apparently calm old woman. Her eyes were not calm at all, however, unless ice is calm.

"A word with you, Ashart. Rothgar, provide us with a room."

"Follow me, Grandmother."

Genova saw the old lady's face pinch as if she'd like to disavow the relationship, but she turned and marched after him. Genova and Ash followed.

This would not be pleasant. Lady Ashart intended to fight. Genova would give as good as she got. She would not let the old tyrant cause Ash any more pain.

Rothgar opened the door to a room Genova hadn't previously seen. It was of modest size, and gloomy for lack of windows, though one wall hung with heavy curtains.

"This is the Garden Room," Rothgar said. "The curtains conceal doors leading to a conservatory. Pleasant in summer, chilly in winter, even with the fire."

He touched a taper to the fire and lit candles, making the room brighter, though nothing could brighten the atmosphere.

He left and the dowager sat like a queen on a throne, still in her hat and rich, blue cloak. "Only you, Ashart, could have three women fighting over you."

"Three?"

"Lady Booth Carew. You denied ruining her, too."

"I did not get her with child, Grandy. The proof of that is on the premises, if you doubt my word."

The dowager's eyes narrowed, but she didn't challenge him. "You won't get an admission of guilt from her. She's gone abroad."

"What?"

"She's married an Irishman called Lemoyne who has business in the West Indies, and gone there with him. I heard the story from Lady Dreyport in London en route here."

Ash and Genova shared a look. The final piece. Somewhere late in her venture, Molly Carew had met a rich man who would marry her and even take her away from the scandal she'd brought on herself. But she'd needed to get rid of the baby, and had done it as a final, spiteful slash without a thought to Sheena and her child.

Genova hoped Molly Carew got what she deserved in life.

"Which leaves you," the dowager said, as if Genova wasn't present, "free to marry Miss Myddleton. I see that you care for another, but it will not do. I gather she has nothing."

"She has herself."

"Feeble nonsense, and Miss Myddleton has a prior claim."

"If you made promises on my behalf, you had no authority to do so. I intend to marry Genova."

He spoke calmly, but Genova felt the tension in him. The dowager stiffened. "Against my wishes?"

"If necessary, yes."

It was as if all stood still. Genova was astonished to hear a clock daring to tick.

"Then I will leave your house and never speak to you again."

Genova felt Ash's hand clench on hers, but nothing in his voice betrayed him when he said, "That is neither my wish nor Genova's, Grandy, but we cannot stop you."

The old mouth tightened. Then tears glistened.

Genova went to her knees beside the dowager. "Oh, my lady, don't. Ash doesn't need to marry money. He can put food on the table and coals in the hearth. We can build. Together we can build fortune and family."

"With *what*?" the dowager spat. "You can hardly be a credit to him at court!"

"There is more to the world than court!"

Ash raised Genova, perhaps moving her out of range. "Grandy, Genova's right. I intend to build up the estates in many ways. There are fortunes to be made through trade."

"*Trade!*" It was a snarl of outrage.

"Even the Duke of Bridgewater is repairing his fortunes with canals to ship his coal. Rothgar has given me advice, and Bryght Malloren—"

The old woman surged to her feet. "*What?* Never! Do you want to drive me into my grave?"

Genova thought it was a dangerous possibility and welcomed a knock on the door. When had Ash sought

this advice from Rothgar? It had to have been this
morning, and she realized, happiness blooming from
bud to perfect flower, it had been part of his decision
to marry her, long before things exploded.

Mr. Fitzroger came in, carefully expressionless, though
he surprised Genova by winking at her. He had Lady
Augusta's journal, and he gave it to Ash, then left.

Ash coaxed his grandmother back into her chair
and put the book on her lap. "That's Aunt Augusta's
journal, written during her marriage. I've read it. It
leaves no doubt in my mind that whatever drove her
to murder, it wasn't the Mallorens."

"Forgery!" she snapped, but she gripped the book
written by her youngest child.

"Book, writing, and style match the earlier journals
at Cheynings."

"And it paints a picture of an idyllic marriage?"
The curl of the dowager's lip showed that she knew
better.

"It paints a picture of a girl too young to be married, too young to be a mother. Perhaps in time she
would have been ready, but she wasn't when she
wrote that."

"You're speaking of a person you never knew. She
was sweet, innocent, unspoiled."

Ash didn't contradict her.

"It was the perfect match!" the dowager protested.
"He was handsome and good-humored, and would be
a marquess. She wanted it."

Again Ash didn't speak, and Genova gripped her
hands to force her own silence. She recognized that
the dowager would listen to no one but might come
to express the truth herself.

"Are you saying I was wrong to arrange it?" the
old woman demanded, lines seeming deeper in her
face. "How could I have known how it would be? I
married at seventeen . . ."

"Perhaps you couldn't have known," Ash said gently, "but she did write pleas for help."

So he'd read the letters.

"Megrims and moods. The next letter, she'd be like a lark."

"Perhaps you read into her words what you wanted to."

The dowager's jaw set and she glared at him. "It is all my fault, then? Everyone else is a saint?"

He went down on one knee and took a clenched hand. "No one was a saint, but no one was a devil, either. Cry peace, my dear, and as Genova says, let us build."

My dear. Only the worst families have no happy memories, and this was not the worst family. There must have been many happy times.

"You expect me to turn my gown and dig potatoes?" the dowager grumbled.

"An unlikely picture," he said, laughter in his voice, "though you are equal to it. As I said, I have the offer of help and advice from the Mallorens, and I intend to take it. I intend to claim the rights of kinship."

Genova winced at the ruthlessness of that, and the dowager's nostrils flared. One hand formed a claw on the arm of her chair.

Perhaps she mellowed, or perhaps she recognized a will even stronger than her own, but she snapped, "I'm old! I've rattled through the night in our second-best carriage. I want hot tea and a warm bed!"

Ash looked up. "Genova?"

Grateful for escape, Genova left the room, wondering how a suitable room could be found in this full house, and what would happen next. She didn't believe that the dowager would give up the fight so easily, and there were true grievances on the other side. The old woman had done her best to hurt the Mallorens.

Genova found Rothgar and Lady Arradale in the hall.

Hovering, one might even say.

"It's going to be all right, I think," Genova said, rather breathlessly. Reaction and bliss were taking their toll. She realized that she was also damp, sticky, and smelling of spiced plums.

She brushed at her bodice, but then gave up. "She

wants tea and a bed. The dowager, I mean. I think she intends to stay!"

Instead of looking shocked, they both smiled. The old lady was Lord Rothgar's grandmother, but all the same, he and Lady Arradale showed noble forgiveness.

"She can have my room," Lady Arradale said. "I'll suffer in the cause and sleep with my husband."

The look she shared with Lord Rothgar before hurrying away indicated that one or the other bed was often empty anyway.

Genova blew out a breath and looked around. "I'm sorry. We made rather a mess, and it's the servants' holiday."

"If we were saints, we'd clean it up. As it is, I intend to leave it until tomorrow."

Genova suspected that plums might damage the wood if left that long, and resolved to deal with it. She wouldn't bother him with it, however. It wasn't his mess.

"What happened to Miss Myddleton?" she asked.

"After Fitzroger prevented her from trying to tear you from Ashart's arms? She fell into a fit, and is now lying down with a vinegar cloth on her head, recovering from a momentary dementia brought on by greensickness."

"That won't work, will it? So many heard her."

"All Mallorens. They will be discreet."

"I feel a little sorry for her. I think the dowager did tell her she was to be his bride."

"I'm sure of it."

"I'm surprised Miss Myddleton doesn't want to flee the house."

"She did. I persuaded her otherwise."

She frowned at him. "Is that kind?"

"It's necessary. When she appears composed, and accepts your betrothal, people will adjust their memory. However, Uncle Henry and Aunt Jane can't be pleasant guardians. It's not surprising if Miss Myddleton is desperate to marry. Matters must be better arranged."

She gave him a look. "Ensuring that the world turns smoothly, my lord?"

He smiled. "It's a fatal obsession, Miss Smith. You are warned. Which reminds me, I must go among my guests and make sure the gossip is already growing in the right direction."

Genova watched him go upstairs, presumably to the drawing room, then turned her mind to cleaning. The nursery and schoolroom were deserted, and they would have the necessaries. She hurried up there and returned victorious with a bucket and cloths, having filled the bucket with her own used washing water.

Ingenuity could solve most problems.

She had to duck out of the way before descending the last stairs, however, because Ash was escorting his grandmother up them.

The dowager looked fierce and unhappy, but even so, her love for Ash was obvious, and Genova loved him even more for his kindness to the old dragon.

Once they'd passed, she hurried down and cleaned up the mess she'd created, grinning at the memories. Without the happy result, the fight would still be a memory she'd cherish. How could she have known how much fun it would be? How could she find an excuse to do it again?

She turned with the bucket to see Ash staring at her. "What are you doing?"

"Cleaning up the mess we made."

"There are servants. . . . No, not in this madhouse, of course. But really, Genni!"

She put down her bucket, eying him. "Am I not suited to be a marchioness, then?"

He came toward her. "You won't trap me that way."

She danced backward. "I was hoping for another fight."

"You like cleaning?"

"I don't mind. I'm not a fine lady, after all."

"You're a fine enough lady for me."

"You're mad."

"It's this house. It drives Trayces insane."

"No, in this case, it restores sanity." She let him catch her. "I adore you, Ash."

As their lips touched, they heard, "Oh, Ashart! Genova, dear!"

With a rueful look, they turned to see Lady Thalia waving from the balcony. Hand in hand they went up to her.

"I just wanted to be sure you hadn't hurt yourself too badly, dear," she said to Ash.

"In falling? No, and Genova's fine, too."

"Oh, no, not that, though it was most entertaining. I mean last night."

He shared a puzzled look with Genova, then looked back at his great-aunt. "You must be confused, Thalia. No one has been hurt. Don't worry."

She crinkled her brow at him. "But Regeanne told me that there was blood on the sheets you sent to the laundry. Was it poor Mr. Fitzroger? I must go and see. Such a charming young man!"

She turned and trotted off, long ribbons on her lacy cap fluttering behind her.

Genova stood frozen, not sure what would happen now. Why hadn't she realized that even with so little pain there might be some blood?

"Genni?"

She turned to him because she must. This shouldn't damage anything, but she felt it might. He was frowning.

"How could I not have known you were a virgin?"

"I gather some women . . ."

He shook his head. "I mean your nature, your honor. I'm such a fool. And I tried to persuade you to be my mistress!"

She grabbed his hands and squeezed them. "Don't buy a hair shirt yet. Barbary pirates, my bold manner, my language, my kisses. I went to your bed never expecting marriage, Ash. I will be hurt if you begin to suggest that I would have been a lesser woman if I had not been a virgin."

"You're tying me in knots again. And Thalia spilled that little bit of information deliberately. Women!"

Genova laughed, bringing his hands to her lips to kiss them. "We're a terrible challenge, aren't we? I think she believes in honesty as much as we do. She was right. Don't you agree it's better to have this straight?"

"Yes. It doesn't change how I love you, but I'd have behaved differently. . . . It didn't hurt?"

"Only a twinge that I scarcely noticed." But she glanced around, knowing her cheeks were red. "We can't talk about things like this here!"

Smile turned to grin. "You're bashful."

"I am not. I'm *discreet*."

He turned her hand and kissed her palm. "Very well, I'll be discreet, too. For now. Come back down with me. I have something to show you."

She let him draw her down the stairs, accompanied by tinkling bells, and across to the *presepe*. There, he took something out of his pocket. His handkerchief. No, something wrapped in his handkerchief. He gave it to her.

"A ring?" she asked. "Do you carry around a selection of ladies' rings?"

"No, you'll have to wait until I can have the perfect one made for you."

Puzzled, she unwrapped the handkerchief to find, not a ring, but a tiny dove, carved out of pale wood. A dove of peace, wings spread.

"You missed a new figure for the *presepe* on your birthday," he said, "so I rose early and begged the house carpenter to whittle this for me. He'll paint it white. . . ."

She looked up at him, tears blurring her vision. "You are the most wonderful man." She fixed the dove on the peak of the stable roof, then turned back to go into his arms.

"No," he said. "But with you by my side, I can try."

Lady Thalia watched from the landing. "There, see," she said to her open locket. "Did I not say it would be so? Love will have its way, dearest. It only needs a little help."

Author's Note

I hope you have enjoyed this return to the Malloren world. If you are new to it, I hope you are now eager to pick up the five previous books and catch up on the adventures of Elf, Portia, and, of course, Rothgar.

The titles of the previous Malloren books are

My Lady Notorious (Cyn and Chastity)
Tempting Fortune (Bryght and Portia)
Something Wicked (Elf and Fort)
Secrets of the Night (Brand and Rosa)
Devilish (Bey and Diana)

Secrets of the Night is out of print, but it will be reissued in March 2004. All the others are available. As with all in-print books, if your bookstore doesn't have a copy, the shop can order it for you at no extra cost. You can also buy the books on-line.

The theme of family runs strongly through the Malloren books, so it's no surprise that it is important in *Winter Fire*, too. I hadn't really thought much about Rothgar's mother's family, since he had little to do with them, but when I looked at the scraps of information I'd included in other books, the Trayces were clearly a troubled lot. Thus, Ash took form, an inheritor of all this, struggling to create a life for himself and his family under Rothgar's shadow.

The emphasis on court may be a bit uncomfortable for modern readers, but we still have the equivalents in today's world, especially at the highest levels, where "dressing for success" and not offending those in power can be crucial. In the 1760s, the Court of St. James—the royal court—was the heart of power and influence. In the next forty years this would change, in part because of the illness of George III—the madness of King George—but also because the world was about to change. We are on the eve of two great revolutions, the American and the French. Remember that little problem of the army and taxation that worries Elf because Cyn is in Canada?

Power is going to shift to Parliament, and to coalitions of great families. I'm sure the Trayce/Malloren/Ware one will play its part.

Readers ask if I will write books about the next generation. The answer is, probably not. I don't like to travel with my characters into old age and death. (Of course they do all live productive lives into old age before death!)

However, I do plan to expand the world of the Mallorens and write other novels in which they'll play a part. The next one will be about Damaris Myddleton and Octavius Fitzroger, who has his own special reasons for becoming friends with Ash. You can expect that book sometime late in 2004.

New and reissued books of mine have been flowing over the past few years, but I normally write a book about every nine months, so that's how often you can expect them from now. I know it seems a long time to wait—I feel the same about my favorite authors!—but to paraphrase what they say in restaurants, good books take time. To know when to expect my books on the shelves, please ask to be on one of my mailing lists. That information is at the end.

My other recent books have been set in the Regency period—1811–20—and center on a group of young men who met at Harrow School. They called themselves the Company of Rogues. There are already novels about some of the Rogues, and also books that spin off to deal with friends and other contacts. That series runs as follows.

An Arranged Marriage, An Unwilling Bride, Christmas Angel, Forbidden, Dangerous Joy, The Dragon's Bride, The Devil's Heiress, Hazard, St. Raven.

Fans of the Rogues want to know if they'll all have stories in the end, and the answer is yes. I get many letters asking when there'll be a book about Lord Darius Debenham. I can't say for sure, but there will be one. He needs a bit of time to recover from his adventures. I won't say any more so as to avoid a "spoiler." I think (no promises) that the next book will take Stephen to the altar.

Forbidden will be reissued in December 2003, so keep an eye out for that if you need a copy. Also, for something different, I have a science fiction romance novella in a collection called *Irresistible Forces,* which will be out in February 2004. This is SF, and you will probably find it in the SF section of the bookstore, but I hope many will cross-file it with romance, because the stories do all have a strong love story. You'll know that when I tell you that one of the other authors is Mary Jo Putney.

I enjoy hearing from readers. You can contact me by e-mail at jo@jobev.com, or by mail through my agent. Write to me c/o Margaret Ruley, 318 East Fifty-first Street, New York, NY 10022. Please include an SASE if you would like a reply. You can also ask to be on my e-mail list for my monthly newsletter.

My Web page, www.jobev.com, provides a booklist and background information about my novels. Please visit and explore.

All best wishes,
Jo

Something Wicked

Disguised as the mysterious beauty Lisette, Lady El-fred Malloren anticipates only fun and flirtation at the Vauxhall Gardens Masquerade. Instead, the dark walkways lead to an encounter with treason, a brush with death, and a night of riotous passion with her family's most dangerous enemy—the elusive Fortitude Ware, Earl of Walgrave. His control is indisputable, his power unquestionable, and his attraction undeniable. And after just one night, Elf knows she will never forget the man she should not love. . . .

"A fast-paced adventure with strong, vividly portrayed characters . . . wickedly, wonderfully sensual and gloriously romantic."   —Mary Balogh

"*Something Wicked* will delight."
                          —*Lake Worth Herald* (FL)

Secrets of the Night

Rosamunde Overton is forced into a daring deceit when her elderly husband's inability to sire an heir threatens everyone she cares for. Fleeing a scandalous masquerade, she rescues a handsome, injured gentleman, finding the answer to her prayers—but instead of a nobody, she has snared a member of the powerful Malloren family. Intrigued, Lord Brand Malloren follows the lead of the lovely masked lady, but neither he nor Rosa is prepared for impossible, disastrous love.

"Jo Beverley is up to her usual magic. . . . She sprinkles a bit of intrigue, a dash of passion, and a dollop of lust, a pinch of poison, and a woman's need to protect all those she loves."   —*Affaire de Coeur*

"Incredibly sensual . . . sexy and funny. . . . These characters [are] wonderfully real."
—All About Romance

Devilish

Two of the strongest wills in England clash when Lord
Rothgar is commanded by the king to escort fiercely
independent Diana Westmount, the Countess of Arradale, to London. Though Rothgar, tortured by a tragic
secret, has become a master of resisting temptation,
Diana proves a challenge to his steely resolve. When
his icy self-control melts in a moment of peril—and a
night of passion—he must find the strength to surrender his heart to another. . . .

"Beverley beautifully captures the flavor of Georgian
England. . . . Her fast-paced, violent, and exquisitely
sensual story is one that readers won't soon forget."
—*Library Journal*

"Jo [Beverley] has truly brought to life a fascinating,
glittering, and sometimes dangerous world."
—Mary Jo Putney

RITA Award Winner

A Most Unsuitable Man

Damaris Myddleton never expected to inherit a vast fortune, but she's ready to use it to buy the most eligible title in England. When disappointed by a marquess, she simply sets her sights higher—on a duke. But then there's plain Mr. Fitzroger, the dashing but penniless adventurer who first saves her from social disaster and then saves her life. Entangled in mystery, danger, and forbidden intimacy, Damaris fights to avoid surrendering her freedom and her heart to a most unsuitable man. . . .

"Her strong characters and finely honed dialogue, combined with a captivating love story, are a pleasure to read."   —*Romantic Times* (top pick)

"Once again readers are treated to a delightful, intricately plotted, and sexy romp set in the slightly bawdy Georgian world of Beverley's beloved Malloren Chronicles."   —*Library Journal*

CLASSIC WINTER ROMANCE
TO READ BY THE FIRE